A Texas Soldier's Family

CATHY GILLEN THACKER

MILLS &
BOON

First Published in Great Britain 2016
By Mills & Boon, an imprint of HarperCollins*Publishers*
1 London Bridge Street, London, SE1 9GF

Large Print edition 2016

© 2016 Cathy Gillen Thacker

ISBN: 978-0-263-06613-5

Our policy is to use papers that are natural, renewable and recyclable products and made from wood grown in sustainable forests. The logging and manufacturing processes conform to the legal environmental regulations of the country of origin.

Printed and bound in Great Britain
by CPI Antony Rowe, Chippenham, Wiltshire

Cathy Gillen Thacker is married and a mother of three. She and her husband spent eighteen years in Texas and now reside in North Carolina. Her mysteries, romantic comedies and heartwarming family stories have made numerous appearances on bestseller lists, but her best reward, she says, is knowing one of her books made someone's day a little brighter. A popular Mills & Boon author for many years, she loves telling passionate stories with happy endings and thinks nothing beats a good romance and a hot cup of tea! You can visit Cathy's website, cathygillenthacker.com, for more information on her upcoming and previously published books, recipes and a list of her favorite things.

Chapter One

"Welcome aboard!" The flight attendant smiled. "Going home to Texas…?"

"Not voluntarily," Garrett Lockhart muttered under his breath as he made his way through the aircraft to his seat in the fourth row.

It wasn't that he didn't *appreciate* spending time with his family, he acknowledged, stowing his bag in the bulkhead and stuffing his six-foot-five-inch body into the first-class seat next to the window. He did.

It's just that he didn't want them weighing

in on what his next step should be. Or what he should do with his inheritance. The decision was hard enough. Should he sell out or stay and build a life in Laramie, as his late father had wanted?

Reenlist and take the considerable promotion being offered?

Or take a civilian post that would allow him to pursue his dreams?

He had twenty-nine days to decide.

And an unspecified but pressing family crisis to handle in the meantime.

And an expensive-looking blonde in a white power suit who'd been sizing him up from a distance, ever since he arrived at the gate…

He'd noticed her, too. Hard not to with that delicately gorgeous face, a mane of long, silky hair brushing against her shoulders, and a smoking-hot body that just wouldn't quit.

Two years ago…before Leanne…he might have taken her up on her invitation…

But his failed engagement had taught him too

well. He wasn't interested in any woman hell-bent on climbing her way to the top.

He wanted a partner who understood what was important in life. Not a woman who couldn't stop doing business even long enough to board a plane. She'd been talking on her cell phone nonstop and was still on it as she stepped into the cabin. With a thousand-watt smile aimed his way, oblivious to the three backpack-clad college boys queued up like dominoes behind her, she continued on down the aisle, checking her ticket for her seat assignment as she walked.

Phone to her ear, one hand trying to retract the telescoping handle of her suitcase while still managing the equally roomy carryall over her shoulder, she said, "…have to go…yes, yes. I'll call you as soon as I land in Dallas. Not to worry." She laughed softly, charmingly, while shooting him another glance and lifting her suitcase with one hand into the overhead compartment. "I always do…"

Annoyed, he turned his attention to the tarmac and was watching bags being loaded into the cargo hold when, in the aisle behind him, commotion suddenly erupted.

"If you-all will just *wait* until I can—*ouch!*" He heard the pretty blonde stumble toward him, yelping as her expensive leather carryall tumbled off her shoulder and crashed onto his lap. Her elbow landed hard against his skull, just above his ear, while a pair of sumptuous breasts burrowed into his face. Only the quick defensive movement of his right arm kept the lady exec's head from smashing into the wall above the airplane window.

However, nothing could be done to stop the off-kilter weight of her from sprawling inelegantly across his thighs, while the trio of impatient college kids responsible for her abrupt exit from the aisle continued unapologetically toward the rear of the plane.

She lifted her head, regarding him with a stunned expression as their eyes met. Heat swept her pretty face. He inhaled a whiff of vanilla and—lavender, maybe? All he knew for sure, he thought, as he heard her moan softly in dismay and felt his own body harden in response, was that everything about this woman was incredibly sexy.

Too sexy...

Too tall...

Too everything...

"Ma'am?" he rasped, trying not to think what it would be like to have this sweet-smelling bundle of femininity beneath him in bed. Never mind just how long it had been...

With effort, he called on every ounce of military reserve he had, sucked in a breath and looked straight into her wide, emerald-green eyes. "Are you all right?"

THIS, HOPE WINSLOW thought with an embarrassed grimace, was not how her day was supposed to go. Seven months out of the workplace might have left her a *little* rusty. But completely without social skills or enough balance to stay on her feet no matter how hard she'd been shoved?

Furthermore, it wasn't as if she had *wanted* to take that last call from the client. She'd had no choice. She needed the income and acclaim this job was going to bring in, and like it or not, high-paying clients required high-level hand-holding. Plus, she had a soft spot in her heart for this current one…and that made any of Lucille's requests difficult to resist.

But her quarry—the guy she had accidentally fallen on—would likely not understand any of that.

Resolved to retain whatever small amount of dignity she had left, Hope forced another small—apologetic—smile, inhaled deeply, then put her left hand down on the armrest beneath the window and shoved herself upright. Only it wasn't an armrest, she swiftly found out. There wasn't one there. It was the rock-hard denim-clad upper thigh of the man who'd caught her in his arms.

Mortified, she plucked her fingers away before they encountered anything else untoward. Then she promptly lost her balance, fell again and had the point of her elbow land where her hand had been.

Her gallant seatmate let out an *oomph* and looked alarmed. With good reason, Hope thought.

Another inch to the left and…!

"Let me help you," he drawled, his voice a smooth Texas-accented rumble. With one hand hooked around her waist and the other around her shoulders, he lifted her quickly and skillfully to her feet, then turned and lowered her so her bottom landed squarely in her own seat. That done, he handed her the leather carryall she'd inadvertently assaulted him with.

Hope knew she should say something. If only to make her later job easier.

And she would have, if the sea-blue eyes she'd been staring into hadn't been so mesmerizing.

She liked his hair, too. So dark and thick and… touchable…

The pictures she had seen of him and his siblings hadn't done him justice. Or indicated just how big and broad shouldered he was. Enough to make her own five-eleven frame feel dainty…

And heaven knew *that* didn't happen every day. Even in Texas.

"Ma'am?" he prodded again, less patiently.

Clearly he was expecting some response to ease the unabashed sexual tension that had sprung up between them, so she tore her eyes from the way his black knit polo shirt molded the sinewy contours of his chest and taut abs, and said the first thing that came into her mind. "Thank you for your assistance just now. And for your service. To our country, I mean."

His dark brow furrowed. His lips—so firm and sensual—thinned. Shoulders flexing, he studied her with breathtaking intent, then asked, "How'd you know I was in the military?"

IT WAS A simple question, Garrett thought.

One that shouldn't have required any dissembling.

But dissembling was precisely what his seatmate appeared to be doing as she discreetly tugged the skirt of her elegant, white business suit lower on her shapely thighs, then leaned forward to place her bag beneath the seat in front of her, as per preflight requirements.

"Um…your hair," she said finally.

Oh, yeah. Military cut. Made sense.

"Well, that and the duffel in the overhead." She glanced at the passengers seated across the aisle, a young mother and a child with a *Dora the Explorer* backpack. The rest of the luggage stored above them was pink. Whereas his, he knew, was army green.

Point made, she sat back and drew the safety restraint across her lap, once again drawing his attention where it definitely should not be. "So, how long have you been in the military?" she asked pleasantly.

He watched as she fit the metal buckle into the clasp, drew it taut. Was there any part of her not delectable? he wondered. Any inch of her he did not want? "Eight years." And why was it suddenly so hard to get the words out?

She wet her lips. Suddenly sounding a little hoarse, too, she inquired, "And what do you do?"

"I'm a physician."

She pursed her lips in a way that had him wondering what it would be like to kiss her. "Which must make you a…?"

Not just kiss her. Make love to her. Hot, wild, passionate love, he thought, drinking in the soft, womanly scent of her. "Captain," he said.

She extended a hand. It was as velvety soft as it looked, her grip warm and firm. "Well, it's nice to meet you, Captain…?"

He let her go reluctantly, the awareness he'd felt when she'd landed in his lap returning, full force. "Lockhart. Garrett Lockhart."

Her expression turned even more welcoming. She studied him intently. "I'm Hope Winslow."

Okay, so maybe his first impression of her hadn't been on point. Even if she wasn't his type, there were worse ways to pass the time than sitting next to a charming, gorgeous woman. And she *was* gorgeous, Garrett reflected, feeling a little unsettled and a lot attracted as the plane backed away from the gate and the flight attendants went through the safety instructions.

Tall enough to fit nicely against him. With legs that were made for high heels and curves that just wouldn't quit pushing against the taut fabric of her sleek summer suit. Honey-blond hair as straight and silky as spun gold brushed her shoulders and long bangs fell to frame her oval face. Her features were elegant, her bow-shaped lips soft, pink and full, her emerald eyes radiating wit and keen intelligence.

He doubted there was anything she set her mind to that she didn't get. Her ringless left hand said she was single.

It was too bad he wasn't in the market for a high-maintenance, high-powered career woman.

"So what do you do for a living?" he asked, after the flight attendant had come by to deliver bowls of warmed nuts and take their drink orders. Milk for her, coffee for him.

She picked out an almond. Then a pecan. "I'm in scandal management."

Okay, he could see that.

She seemed like the type who could take a highly emotional, probably volatile situation and boil it down to something manageable. "I recently started my own firm." She reached into a pocket of her carryall and plucked out a business card. *Winslow Strategies. Crisis Management by the Very Best.* It had her name featured prominently, printed in the same memorable green as her eyes, and a Dallas address.

He started to hand it back. She gestured for him to keep it, so he slipped it into the pocket of his shirt. "Business good?"

She gestured affably, looking reluctant to be too specific. "There's always someone in trouble."

I'll bet. "But to have to hire someone to get yourself out of it?" He couldn't keep the contempt from his voice.

"People hire lawyers all the time when they find themselves in a tight spot."

Imagining that line worked on a lot of very wealthy people, he sipped his coffee. "Not the same thing."

She turned slightly toward him, tilting her head. "It sort of is," she said, her voice a little too tight. "Words can hurt. Or mislead. Or falsely indict. So can actions." She paused to sip her milk and let her words sink in, then set her glass down on the tray. "It's important when in the midst of a potentially life-altering, and especially life-damaging event, to have someone on your side who isn't emotionally involved, calling the shots and orchestrating everything behind the scenes."

Her exceptional calmness rankled; he couldn't say why. "Creating a publicly acceptable narrative," he reiterated.

She lifted a delicate hand, gesturing amiably. "I prefer to think of it as a compelling explanation that will allow others to empathize with you. And, if not exactly approve of or condone, at least understand."

"And therefore let your client off the hook," he said grimly, reflecting on another time. Another situation. And another woman whose actions he resented to this day. "Whether they deserve to be spared any accountability for what they've done or not."

Taken aback, Hope Winslow squinted at him. "Are you speaking personally?"

Hell, yes, it had been personal! Being cheated on and then backed into a corner always was. Not that he regretted protecting the innocent bystanders in the situation. They'd done nothing to deserve having their names dragged through the mud.

"I'm guessing that's a yes," she said.

The silence stretched between them, awkward now. She continued to look him up and down, asking finally, "Are you always this black and white in your thinking, Captain Lockhart?"

His turn to shrug. He finished what was left of his coffee. "About some things, yeah." He set the cup down with a thud. The flight attendant appeared with a refill.

When they were alone again, Hope continued curiously, "Is that why you chose the military as a career?"

It was part of it. The rest was more personal. "Both my grandfathers served our country." His dad had passed on the opportunity. He and one of his four siblings had not.

"And...?" she prodded.

He exhaled, not above admitting that honor was everything to him. "There's not a lot of room for error—or gray areas—in the military. It's either right or it's wrong." *Simple. Basic. Necessary.* Unlike the way he'd grown up.

She stared at him. "And you think what I do is wrong."

"I wouldn't have put it that way," Garrett said.

A delicate pale brow arched. "But you think it, don't you?"

Wishing she hadn't put him on the spot, he returned her sharp, assessing gaze. "You're right. I do."

"Well, that's too bad, Captain." Hope Winslow took a deep breath that lifted her opulent breasts. "Because your mother, Lucille Lockhart, has hired me to represent your entire family, as well as the Lockhart Foundation."

He took a moment to let the blonde's announcement sink in. Feeling as if he had just taken a sucker punch to the gut, he grumbled, "So the way you kept checking me out before we boarded, the fact that we're both seated in first class on this flight, side by side, was no accident."

"Lucille said you'd be difficult. I needed to

talk with you before we landed and I wanted to get started early. And to that end…"

She finished her milk, put her tray away, retrieved her carryall from beneath the seat and took out a computer tablet. She brought up a screen titled Talking Points for Lockhart Foundation Crisis and set it in front of him. "I want you to memorize these."

One hand on the cup, lest it spill, he stared at her. "You have got to be kidding me."

The hell of it was, she wasn't. "There's a press conference later today," she informed him crisply, suddenly all business. "We need you to be ready."

This was like a replay of his past, only in a more formal venue. He hadn't played those games then, and he certainly wasn't getting sucked into them now. "No."

Hope leaned closer, her green eyes narrowing. "You have to be there." Her tone said the request was nonnegotiable.

His mood had been grim when he got on the

plane. It was fire and brimstone now. No wonder his mother hadn't wanted to be specific when she'd sent out that vague but somewhat hysterical SOS and let him know he was needed in Dallas ASAP.

He worked his jaw back and forth. "Why? I don't have anything to do with the family charity."

"You're on the board of directors."

Which basically did nothing but meet a couple times a year and green light—by voice vote—everything the CEO and CFO requested. "So are my mother and all my siblings."

"All of whom have been asked to participate and follow the plan." Hope paused, even more purposefully. "Your mother needs you to stand beside her."

Garrett imagined that was so. Lucille had been vulnerable since his dad's death. Knowing how much his parents had loved each other, that they'd been together for over forty years, he imagined the loss his mom felt was even more palpable than his own.

But there were limits as to what he would do. In this situation or any other. "And I will," he promised tautly. "Just not like a puppet on a string. And certainly not in any scripted way in front of any microphones."

ONE LOOK AT the dark expression on Garrett's face told Hope there was no convincing him otherwise. Not while they were on the plane, anyway.

So she remained quiet during the descent. Thinking.

Strategizing.

By the time the aircraft landed in Dallas, she knew what she had to do.

She waited for him to catch up after they'd left the Jetway and walked out into the terminal, dragging her overnight bag behind her. "Your mother is sending a limo for us."

He slung his duffel over one brawny shoulder. "Thanks. I'll find my own way home." He turned in the direction of the rental cars.

Hope rushed to catch up, her long strides no match for his. "She's expecting us at the foundation office downtown."

"Okay."

Desperate to keep Garrett Lockhart from getting away from her entirely, she caught his arm, steering him off to the side, out of the way of other travelers. "Okay, you'll be there?" she asked, as amazed at the strength and heat in the powerful biceps as by the building awareness inside of her. She had to curtail this desire. She could not risk another romantic interlude like the last. Could not!

One second she'd been holding on to him. Now he had dropped his duffel and was holding on to her. Hands curved lightly around her upper arms, oblivious to the curious stares of onlookers, he backed her up against a pillar, his tall, powerful physique caging hers. The muscles in his jaw bunched. "Get this through that pretty little head of yours. You are not in charge of me."

Like heck she wasn't! This was her job, gosh darn it. Refusing to be intimidated by this handsome bear of a man she lifted her chin. Valiantly tried again. "This crisis…"

He stared her down. "What crisis?"

He had a right to know what they were dealing with, but best they not delve into the exact details here, with people passing by right and left. She swallowed in the face of all that raw testosterone, the feel of his hands cupping her shoulders, the wish that… Never mind what she wished! "I'd prefer…"

He didn't wait to hear the rest. Pivoting, he picked up his olive-green duffel, slung it back over his shoulder and headed for the doors out of Terminal B.

She raced after him, her trim skirt and high heels no match for his long, masterful strides. She would have lost him entirely had it not been for the contingent waiting on the other side.

No sooner had he cleared the glass doors than a group with press badges rushed toward him, trailing his sixty-eight-year-old mother.

As usual, the willowy brunette socialite was garbed in a sophisticated sheath and cardigan, her trademark pearls around her neck. Despite the many conversations they'd had this morning, Lucille Lockhart also looked more frazzled than she had the last time Hope had seen her. Not a good sign.

"Garrett, darling!" Lucille cried, rushing forward to envelope her much taller son in a fierce familial hug, the kind returning military always got from their loved ones.

Just that quickly, microphones were shoved into his face. "Captain Garrett! What do you think about the broken promises to area non-profits?" a brash redhead demanded while cameras whirred and lightbulbs went off.

"Were you in on the decision not to pay them what was promised?" another reporter shouted.

"Does your family want the beneficiary charities to fail in their missions? Or did they take the money from the foundation, slated for the area nonprofits, and use it for personal gain?"

Lucille clung to Garrett all the harder, her face buried in his chest. With a big, protective arm laced around his mother's shoulders, Garrett blinked at the flashbulbs going off and held back the approaching hoard with one hand.

"Don't answer," Hope commanded.

LIKE HE HAD an effing clue what to say. He had no idea what in tarnation the press was referring to.

Out of the corner of his eye, Garrett saw another woman approaching. She was pushing a convertible stroller with a hooded car seat snapped into the top. Dimly aware this was no place for an infant, Garrett turned back to the crowd. His mother looked up at him. "Listen to Hope," Lucille Lockhart hissed.

Like hell he would.

More likely than not, it was Hope Winslow's

"management" of the crisis that was turning it into even more of a media circus. Certainly, she'd whipped his mother into a frenzy with her dramatics.

"Of course we didn't take money out of the foundation for our own personal use," he said flatly, watching as Hope signaled vigorously to an airport security guard for help. "Nor do we want to see any area charities fail." That was ridiculous. Especially when his family was set to give away *millions* to those in need.

"But it appears money did not end up in the right hands," another chimed in. "At least not this past year."

"Say the foundation is looking into it," Hope whispered, just loud enough for him to hear.

Ignoring her, he turned back to the reporters and reiterated even more firmly, "No one in my family is a thief."

"So they are just what, then? Irresponsible?" another TV reporter shouted. "Heartless?"

An even more asinine charge. Garrett lifted

a staying hand. "That's all I have to say on the matter."

More flashbulbs went off. A contingent of airport security stepped in. They surrounded the reporters, while on the fringes the young woman with the baby resumed her resolute approach. As she neared, Garrett could see it looked as though the young woman had been crying. "Hope! Thank heavens we found you!" the young lady said in a British accent.

Now what? Garrett wondered, exhaling angrily. Was this seemingly heartfelt diversion yet another part of the scandal manager's master plan? Bracing for the answer, he swung back to Hope, eyes narrowing with suspicion. "Who's this?"

Abruptly, Hope looked as tense and on guard as he felt. "Mary Whiting, my nanny," she said.

Chapter Two

Nanny? Hope Winslow had a *nanny*, Garrett thought in shock. And a *baby*?

"Mary? What's going on?" Hope asked in alarm. She dashed around to look inside the covered car seat on top of the combination stroller/ buggy. Not surprisingly, Garrett's mother—who longed for grandchildren of her very own—was right by Hope's side.

All Garrett could see from where he stood was the bottom half of a pair of baby blue coveralls, two kicking bootie-clad feet and one tiny hand trying to catch a foot.

Hope's smile was enough to light up the entire world. She bent down to kiss the little hand. Garrett thought, but couldn't be sure, that he heard a happy gurgle in return.

Apparently, all was well. With the infant, anyway, he acknowledged, as his mom stepped back to his side.

Hope put her arm around the young woman. "Has something happened?"

The nanny burst into tears. "It's my mum! She collapsed this morning. They say it's her heart. I've got to go back to England."

Ignoring the inconvenience for her and her child, Hope asked briskly, "Do you have a flight?"

Mary pulled a boarding pass out of her bag. "It leaves in an hour and a half."

Hope sobered. "Then you better get going, if you want to be sure and get through international flight security."

Mary handed over the diaper bag she had looped over one shoulder. "Max's just been fed and burped, and I changed his nappy. Unfortunately, I don't know how long I'll be gone."

Hope nodded. "Take all the time you need…"

"Thank you for understanding!" Mary hugged Hope, gave the cooing baby in the carriage an affectionate pat, then rushed off to catch her flight.

Meanwhile, the reporters were still trying to talk their way past the security guards. Eyeing them, Hope said, "We better get out of here."

Garrett's mom pointed toward the last section of glass doors off the baggage claim. "There's my driver now."

GARRETT HELD THE door while Hope and his mother charged into the Dallas afternoon heat.

His mom entered the limo first and slid across the seat. Hope disengaged the car seat from the stroller and gently set it inside. She followed, more concerned with getting her baby settled and secured than the flash of leg she showed as her skirt rode up her thighs.

Ignoring the immediate hardening of his body, Garrett got in after them. Trying not to let what he had just seen in any way mitigate his initial impression of Hope, he sprawled across the middle of the opposite seat while the two women doted on the baby secured safely between them. "You are such a darling!" Lucille cooed to the baby facing her. "And so alert!" His mother beamed as the infant kicked a blue bootie-clad foot and waved a plump little hand. "How old is he?"

"Twelve weeks on Wednesday," Hope announced proudly.

Which meant she was just coming off maternity leave. Suddenly curious, although he had never actually considered himself a baby person, Garrett asked, "Does the baby have a name?"

Hope's chin lifted. The warmth faded from her eyes. "Max."

Garrett waited for the rest. "Max or Maxwell…?"

Her gaze grew even more wary. "Just Max."

She still hadn't said her son's last name. Nor did she seem about to do so, which made him wonder why.

His mother gave him the kind of look that ordered him to stop fishing around for Hope Winslow's marital status.

Was that what he had been doing? *Maybe.* But who could blame him? He was going to have to know a lot more about Hope Winslow, before he could trust her to handle this crisis for his family.

Satisfied her baby was set for now, Hope turned her glance away from his, pulled her phone out of her bag and quickly checked her messages. "Everything is set up for the press conference," she told his mom.

Not liking the way she seemed ready to cut him out, Garrett asked, "If there's going to be a press conference, why were there reporters at the baggage claim?"

Lucille sighed. "There probably wouldn't have been if I hadn't decided to come and greet you, last minute. The press followed me to the airport."

Hope glanced his way, sunlight streaming in through the window and shimmering in her gilded hair. "They were probably hoping you would be in uniform. Or that you'd say something unfortunate like 'I am not a crook.' Which—by the way—did not even work for Richard Nixon."

He mimicked her droll expression. "You're seriously comparing me to a disgraced politician?"

Hope shrugged in mock innocence.

Lucille looked from Garrett to Hope and back again.

"This is no time to be flirting."

"We're not!" Hope and Garrett said in unison.

Lucille lifted a dissenting brow. "Exactly what I said before I started dating your father."

Garrett felt a flash of grief.

His mom was able to talk freely about his dad, recalling everything about their life together with affection. Not him. Some two and a half years after his dad's passing, thoughts of his late father still left him choked up. Maybe because so much had been left unresolved between them.

Would finally dealing with his inheritance give him the closure he needed?

Hope gave him a long, steady look laced with compassion, then dropped her head and rummaged through her bag. "Let's concentrate on the press conference." She produced the talking points again.

Garrett had been forced into sugarcoating the truth once. He wasn't doing it again. Refusing so much as a cursory glance, he handed Hope her computer tablet back. "Why are you so intent on cleverly orchestrating every word?"

She checked the near constant alerts on her phone as the limo stopped in front of the downtown Dallas high-rise that housed the foundation and numerous elite businesses. With a beleaguered sigh, she predicted, "You'll see."

And he did, as soon as he walked into the elegant ninth floor suite that housed the Lockhart Foundation. A reception area, with a desk and comfortable seating, opened up onto a marble-floored hall that led to four other offices and a boardroom where, he soon discovered, three of his other siblings were waiting.

A collection of laptop computers was spread out on the table. Running on them were clips from every local news station, showing his arrival at the airport, looking grim while declaring his family innocent of all charges, and menacing when his mother turned away from the press and buried her head in his shirt. They even had shots of Max's nanny bursting into tears while approaching Hope, though they didn't say what that was all about.

The longest and most dramatically edited rendition ended with Hope ushering his mother into the limo while looking like a force to be reckoned with. Footage of her baby had been cut. Garrett was happy about that, at least. Her child had no place in this unfolding drama. But there was a shot of him climbing in after the women, just before the door closed, that had him glowering.

The reporter turned back to the camera. "Renowned scandal manager, Hope Winslow, best known for her handling of the crisis involving the American ambassador's son in Great Britain last year, has been retained by the Lockhart family to manage the situation. Which can only mean they are expecting more fireworks to ensue. So stay tuned…"

Looking as stubborn and ornery as the bulls he raised—despite a suit and tie—Garrett's brother, Chance, slapped him on the back and quipped, "Nice job handling the press."

Wyatt also stood, no trace of the horse rancher

evident in his sophisticated attire, and gave him a brief hug. Then, grinning wickedly, he agreed, "Articulate, as usual, brother."

His only sister, Sage, in a pretty tailored dress and heels that was very different from her usual cowgirl/chef garb, embraced him warmly. "I don't blame you," she consoled him. "You were caught completely off guard."

Garrett hugged Sage, who'd seemed a little lonesome lately when they talked, and glanced around. Only one Lockhart was missing from their immediate family. His Special Forces brother.

"Zane's out with his unit," Sage informed him.

Which meant no one knew where he was or when he would return.

"In the meantime, we need you to put this on." Hope handed him a garment bag. Inside was a suit and tie, reminiscent of his prep school days.

Thanking heaven they hadn't expected him to

wear his army uniform for this sideshow, Garrett rezipped the bag.

"And please…" She took him aside, a delicate hand curving around his arm, and looked him in the eye. "This time, when we assemble before the press, stick to the plan. Say nothing. Just stand in the background, along with the rest of your siblings, and look extremely supportive of your mother."

That, Garrett figured, he could do. At least for now.

When he emerged from the men's room, still tying his tie, there was a team there, doing hair and makeup.

"Don't even think about it," he growled when they tried to put powder on him. His brothers were equally resistant.

Hope stood nearby, her baby in her arms, sizing him up.

He wondered if she was that observant when she made love. And why the notion that she might be was so sexy.

But there was no more time to think about it, because Hope was giving his mother one last pep talk, and then it was show time. After handing her baby off to Sharla, his mother's executive assistant, Hope and the family took the elevator down to another floor and filed into the meeting room reserved for the occasion, where two dozen members of the press were already assembled.

His mother stepped up to the microphone. "Thank you all for coming. Like you, we have been shocked and alarmed to hear allegations that not all of the funds from the Lockhart Foundation have been sent as promised to the local organizations we assist. We haven't yet been able to verify what has actually happened but we are looking into the matter."

"You seem skeptical that any payments were missed," a reporter looking for a more salacious story observed.

From the front row, where she was seated,

Garrett could see Hope shaking her head, word-lessly warning his mother not to answer.

But Lucille could not remain silent when her integrity was in question. "I admit I don't see how it could have happened, when I signed all those checks myself."

At that, it was all Garrett could do not to groan. His mother had just announced she was personally liable for whatever had happened.

"And yet there are now—at last count," the chief investigative reporter from the *Dallas Sun News* said, "*sixteen* charities claiming they've been shorted. It's pretty suspicious that all those groups would be claiming the same thing, don't you think?"

Sixteen, Garrett thought, stunned. Just a few hours ago, when Hope had shown him the talk-ing points on her tablet, it had been *three*.

Hope got up gracefully to her feet and moved across the row to the aisle.

"Why isn't the Lockhart Foundation's chief

financial officer, Paul Smythe, answering any of our questions?" another correspondent asked.

"He's out of town on a personal matter," Lucille said calmly. "When he returns, we'll get to the bottom of this."

"And if you don't?" another journalist pressed, as Hope glided onto the stage. "Are you prepared to fire Mr. Smythe and/or anyone else involved in what increasingly looks like a severe misappropriation—if not downright embezzlement—of funds?"

His mom faltered.

Hope took the microphone. "Now, Tom, you know as well as I do that's premature, given that nothing has been confirmed yet..."

With grudging admiration, Garrett watched Hope field a few more questions and then pleasantly end the conference with the promise of another update just as soon as they had information to share.

"So what's next?" he asked when the family had reassembled in the foundation quarters.

Hope lifted Max into her arms, cuddling him close, then looked at Lucille. "We move on to Step 2 of our scandal-management plan."

"DID YOU VOLUNTEER to drive us out to Laramie County? Or were you drafted?" Hope demanded two hours later, when Garrett Lockhart landed on the doorstep of her comfortable suburban Dallas home.

She already knew he wasn't gung ho about the plan to have his mother stay at the Circle H, the family's ranch in rural west Texas, to get her out of the limelight until they could figure out what was going on with the foundation.

Garrett shrugged. Clad in a blue shirt, jeans and boots, with the hint of an evening beard rimming his jaw, he looked sexy and totally at ease. "Does it matter?"

Yes, oddly enough, it did matter whether he was helping because he wanted to or because he had been forced to do so. "Just curious."

He flashed a half smile. "Combination of the two."

It was like pulling mud out of a pit. "Care to explain?" Hope directed him and his duffel bag to the driveway, where a ton of gear sat, ready to be loaded into the back of her sporty red SUV.

He fit his bag into the left side, where she pointed. "Given how we feel about each other, a three-plus hour journey locked in the same vehicle is bound to be a little awkward."

No kidding. Hope set a pack-n-play on top of his bag. "Then why bother?"

He lifted her suitcase and set it next to his. "I don't have a vehicle of my own to drive right now, and I won't until I get to Laramie County and can borrow a pickup from one of my brothers. Going with you will save me the hassle of renting a car here."

"You could have ridden with your mother and her chauffeur."

Arms folded in front of him, he lounged to one side. "Not going to happen."

She slid him a glance, wishing he didn't look so big and strong and immovable. "Why not?"

His gaze roved her knee-length khaki shorts and red notch-collared blouse before returning to her face. "Because I don't want to spend the entire journey dodging questions I don't want to answer."

His lazy quip brought heat to her cheeks. "Hint, hint?"

"If the shoe fits…"

Boy, he was maddening.

Worse, she didn't know why she was letting him get under her skin. She dealt with difficult people all the time.

Maybe they weren't six feet five inches tall and handsome as all get-out, and military-grade sexy, but…still…

Aware he was watching her, gauging her reactions as carefully as she was checking out his, she lifted her chin. "What were the other reasons?"

This time he grinned. Big time. "It'll save me from leading the search party later."

Knowing a thinly veiled insult when she heard one, Hope scowled. "*What* search party?"

"The one that's sent out to find you and your baby in the wilds of Laramie County when you get lost after dark."

Hope inhaled deeply. Breathed out slowly. Gave him one of her trademark *watch it* looks. "I think I can read a map, *Captain*."

"No doubt, sweetheart," he said in a droll tone. "But unless you can telepathically figure out which road is which when you come to an unmarked intersection in the Middle of Nowhere, West Texas…you might want to rethink that."

Being lost with a baby who needed to be fed and diapered every few hours was not her ideal scenario, either. "Fine." She gave him a warning glance. "But you're driving so I can work."

He took the keys. "Wouldn't have it any other way. My only question is—" Garrett eyed the pile of luggage and baby gear still sitting in her driveway "—can you and/or your *significant other* load the car?"

There he went with the questions about her private life again. Although, why it would matter to him she had no idea. But to save both of them a great big headache, she figured she might as well be blunt.

"First of all, there is no significant other," she retorted, and thought—but couldn't be sure—that she saw a flash of something in his blue eyes as she continued expertly packing the cargo compartment with the rest of her gear. "Second, it's not that much stuff." She went into the house and returned, toting a sound-asleep Max—who was already belted into his safety seat—to the roomy SUV. Garrett watched her lock Max's carrier into its base in the center of the rear seat.

"If you say so."

Clearly, he still had something on his mind. Hope straightened. "What is it?"

"I'm all for getting my mother out of the public eye. But are you sure this is going to work? Property records are public. The press could still figure out where she's gone."

Hope appreciated his concern for his family's welfare. "They could."

"But…?"

"It's unlikely a Dallas news crew will travel three hours out to Laramie, and then back, just to hear a *no comment* from someone other than your mother. When they could easily interview someone from a nonprofit right here in the metroplex who has a lot to say about how they and the people they serve have been wronged."

"You're the scandal manager." Garrett settled behind the wheel, his large, muscular frame filling up the interior of her car. Frowning, he fit the key into the ignition. "But can't you pressure the news organizations to present *both* sides of the story?"

"Yes, and for the record, I already have." Hope climbed into the passenger seat and closed the garage via remote. "But the Dallas papers and TV stations can still keep the story going—and ostensibly show your side, too—although not necessarily in a positive light."

His brow furrowed at her careful tone. "How, if my mother isn't available for any more interviews?"

Nor was anyone else in the family, Hope knew, since his only sister, Sage, was already en route back to Seattle, to handle a catering gig the next day. Chance and Wyatt were headed back to their West Texas ranches, to care for their herds. And Garrett had certainly made it clear he didn't intend to cooperate with the press. She exhaled. "The media can show old news footage of your mother and father when they announced the formation of the Lockhart Foundation."

Garrett's shoulders tensed. "That was a black-tie gala."

"Right. And would likely be salaciously depicted, at least by some outlets, as the Haves versus the Have Nots."

Garrett slid a pair of sunglasses on over his eyes. "So, in other words, we're damned if we stay and have reporters chasing after us with every new accusation. And damned if we leave town and avoid their inquiries, too."

"Not for long, if I do my job, which I certainly plan to do."

To Hope's relief, for the first time since they'd met, he seemed willing to let her take charge of the volatile situation. At least temporarily. So, while Garrett drove, she worked on her laptop computer and her infant son slept.

It was only when they entered rural Laramie County, near dusk, that the trip took an eventful turn.

"Do you see that?" Hope pointed to a disabled pickup truck ahead. The hood was up on the battered vehicle. A young couple stood beside the smoking engine, apparently as unhappy with each other as they were with their transportation.

Worse, the young man—with a muscular upper body and military haircut—was on crutches, his left leg obscured by pressure bandages and a complicated brace.

Garrett drove up beside them. "Need a helping hand?"

"I'm Darcy Dunlop," the young woman said, her thin face lighting up with relief. "And yes!"

"We've got it." Her grim-faced companion shook his head.

"Tank!" Darcy said, wringing her hands in distress.

"We'll just wait for the tow truck."

"But the mechanic said we didn't have to be here! As long as we leave the truck unlocked, he can take it back to the garage in town on his own."

Tank's jaw set, even more stubbornly.

Garrett stuck out his hand, introducing himself. "Army Medical Corps…"

The other man's expression relaxed slightly.

"Infantry. Until this." He pointed to his injured leg. "Not sure what I'm going to do next..."

They talked a little about the fellow soldier who had saved Tank's life, and the IED fragments that had made a mess of his limb. How his parents—who lived locally—had taken them in during the year it was going to take to recover and get his strength back.

"That's rough," Garrett said in commiseration.

Darcy's lower lip trembled. "What's worse is how far we have to go so Tank can get treatment. We either drive back and forth to the closest military hospital—which is a couple hours from here—or Tank gets his care in Laramie. And the rehab there, well, I mean everybody's nice, but they have no experience with what's happened to Tank."

Garrett understood—as did Hope—that there were some things only fellow soldiers, who had served in a war zone, could comprehend. The camaraderie was as essential to healing as medical care. Garrett gave Tank a look of respect. "How about we give you a lift home."

Darcy gave her husband a pleading look.

Shoulders slumping in relief, the former soldier consented. "Thanks."

Knowing Tank would have more room for his leg brace in the front, Hope climbed in back to sit with Max, who was beginning to wake up. Darcy took the other side. The two women chatted while Tank gave directions to his parents' home, a few miles north.

When they arrived, Garrett scribbled a number on the back of a business card and handed it to the other man. "I'll be around for the next few days, taking care of some family business, so if you need anything..."

Tank shook his hand. "Appreciate it."

Hope could see the meeting had affected Garrett. It had affected her, too.

"I don't understand how the military can boot someone out, just because they got injured," she fumed, as they drove away.

Garrett paused to study the unmarked intersection of country roads. No street names were showing up on her GPS screen, Hope noted. Which meant she might, indeed, have gotten lost trying to find her way to the ranch.

"It was probably his choice to get a medical discharge rather than stay in," Garrett pointed out, pausing to glance at a set of directions he had in his pocket, before turning south again.

"Why would Tank do that when he clearly loved being part of the armed service?"

"Because doing so would have meant taking a desk job, once he had recuperated, and my guess is Tank didn't see himself being happy that way. He probably wanted to be with his buddies—who were all still in Infantry—or out of the service completely," he said, as they reached the entrance to the Circle H Ranch.

Hope wasn't sure what she had expected, since Lucille had promised they would all be quite comfortable there, and have as much privacy as they needed. Maybe something as luxurious as

Lucille's Dallas mansion. But the turnoff was marked by a mailbox, and a wrought-iron sign that had definitely seen better days. The gravel lane leading up to the ranch house was bordered by a fence that was falling down in places. The barn and stables looked just as dilapidated.

Garrett cut the engine.

Handsome face taut with concern, he got out and opened the door for her. "Mom and her driver were supposed to be here ahead of us."

Obviously, that had not happened. Max, who'd been remarkably quiet and content, let out an impatient cry.

"I know, baby," Hope soothed, patting her son on the back. "You're hungry. Probably wet, too." She lifted him out of the car seat and moved to stand beside Garrett. "But we're going to take care of all that."

Garrett led her up onto the porch of the rambling two-story ranch house with the gabled roof. He unlocked the door and swung it open. Like him, Hope could only stare.

Chapter Three

The interior of the ranch house had not been updated in decades, was devoid of all furniture and was scrupulously clean. In deference to the closed window blinds, Garrett hit switches as he moved through the four wood-paneled downstairs rooms. Sighing, he noted, "Well, at least all the lights work."

"Does the air conditioning work?" she asked, their footsteps echoing on the scarred pine floors. It was much hotter inside the domicile than outside. And the outside was at least ninety degrees, even as the sun was setting.

"No clue." Garrett headed upstairs. There were only two bedrooms. One bath. No beds. Or even a chair for Hope to sit in while she nursed.

They headed back downstairs, Max still fussing. Worse, she could feel her breasts beginning to leak in response. "When was the last time you were here?" Glad she'd thought to put soft cotton nursing pads inside her bra, she opened up the diaper bag she'd slung over her arm and pulled out a blanket.

Garrett stepped out onto the back porch, where a porch swing looked out over the property. "Ah—never."

Deciding her son had waited long enough, Hope sat down on the swing and situated Max in her arms. Waving at Garrett to turn around, which he obediently did, she unbuttoned her blouse and unsnapped the front of her nursing bra. Max found her nipple and latched on hungrily. "I was under the impression this was family property." She shifted her son more comfortably in her arms and draped the blanket over him. As he fed, they both relaxed. "That your mother grew up on the Circle H."

"She did." Hands in his pockets, Garrett continued looking over the property, which was quite beautiful in a wild, untamed way. Overgrown shrubbery, dotted with blossoms, filled the air with a lush, floral scent.

He studied the sun disappearing slowly beneath the horizon in a streaky burst of yellow and red. "But she and my dad sold the place after my grandfather Henderson's death, when she was twenty-three. They used the proceeds to start Dad's hedge fund and stake their life in Dallas."

It was a move that had certainly paid off for Frank and Lucille Lockhart. They'd made millions. Hope turned her attention to the collection of buildings a distance away from the house. A couple of barns with adjacent corrals and a rambling one-story building with cedar siding and a tin roof. Maybe a bunkhouse? "When did the property come back into the family?"

Garrett reached down and plucked out a long weed sprouting through the bushes and tossed it aside. "My dad bought it for my mom as an anniversary gift the year he sold his company so he could retire. They were going to fix the ranch up as a retreat. He purchased property in Laramie County for all five of us kids, too. So we'd all have a tangible link to our parents' history here."

Hope shifted Max to her other breast, glad they had the light from the interior of the house illuminating the porch with a soft yellow glow now that it was beginning to get dark. It was just enough to allow her to see what she was doing and yet afford her some privacy, too.

"I gather your dad also grew up in West Texas?"

Garrett nodded, his handsome profile brooding yet calm as he surveyed the sagebrush, live oak trees and cedars dotting the landscape. "On the Wind River Ranch, here in Laramie County. My parents bought that back, too. My brother Wyatt started a horse farm there."

Max nursed quickly—a sign of just how hungry he'd been. When he was done, Hope shifted her sated son upright so he could burp, and used her other hand to refasten her nursing bra. "So you all have ranches then."

"No." Garrett paced the length of the porch, both hands shoved in the back pockets of his jeans. The action drew her attention to his masculine shoulders and spectacularly muscled flanks. Without warning, she recalled the feel of his rock-hard leg beneath her palm, the heat radiating from the apex of his thighs. Wondered what it would be like to be held against all that sheer male power and strength.

Then she pushed the disturbing notion away.

Oblivious to the lusty direction of her thoughts, he paced a little farther away. "My dad gifted me a house and a medical office building in town." He chuckled when Max let out a surprisingly loud belch.

"It's okay. I'm done," Hope said.

Garrett turned to face her. Noting she had rebuttoned her blouse, he ambled toward her once again. "Sage received a small café in the historic downtown section of Laramie and the apartment above it."

Hope spread the blanket out on the seat of the swing and laid Max down so she could change his diaper. "So you'd all eventually settle here?"

He moved even closer, gazing fondly down at her sleepy baby. The tenderness in his gaze was a surprise.

"That was their plan," he admitted in a voice so gentle it made her mouth go dry.

She drew in a breath for calm. Which, to her consternation, did not help.

She still was wa-a-a-a-y too aware of him. Still far too curious about the man who was proving to be such an enigma—all Texas military gentleman one moment, all tough, edgy alpha male the next. Telling herself to dial it down a notch, Hope cocked her head. "What's your plan?" she asked bluntly.

His gaze dipped to her lips, lingered. "To sell both properties and move on."

"Your mom said your tour of duty was about up."

"Twenty-nine days. I saved my time off for the end, so I'm on R & R through the rest of it."

"And then…?"

"I either reenlist and become a staff physician at Walter Reed in Washington, DC…"

She could see him doing that. And probably loving it. "Or…?"

"Head up a residency program at a hospital in Seattle."

"Where your sister Sage is living."

He nodded.

She could imagine him teaching, too. Having all the young female residents fall hopelessly in love with him. "Do you know what you're going to do?"

"Still thinking about it."

"But in either case you won't be returning to Texas." As his mother wanted.

His sharp, assessing gaze met hers. "No."

"Not tied to the Lone Star State in any way?" Despite the fact he and his siblings had apparently all grown up in Texas.

He raised his brows. "Are you?"

Hope nodded, her heart tightening a little in her chest. "I've worked in enough places to realize Texas is my home. And where I want Max to grow up."

Feeling oddly disappointed that it was a sentiment they obviously did not share, and at the same time determined to end the unexpected intimacy that had fallen between them, she finished diapering her son, then lifted Max into her arms. "Where are we going to bunk down tonight?" she asked, shooting Garrett an all-business look. "I assume your mom had some definitive plan when she suggested we come out here. Maybe a hotel in town, assuming there is one?"

Garrett reached for his cell phone. "I'll give my mother a call, see if I can find out what her ETA is."

Hope headed to the SUV to get Max settled in his infant seat, so they would be ready to lock up the house and go wherever they were headed next as soon as he got off the phone. To her relief, her little boy, exhausted from the chaotic activity of the day, was already fast asleep when Garrett came out of the house, informing her, "We've been directed to the bunkhouse."

Why did she suddenly have the feeling that was not a good thing? Hope stood, her hands propped on her hips. "When will everyone else be here?"

His expression as matter-of-fact as his low tone, he answered, "Noon tomorrow."

HOPE BLINKED. SHE could not have heard right! "Noon *tomorrow*?"

"My mother decided to stay in Dallas and handle some things there first."

"Unlike me, you don't seem all that surprised."

He narrowed his eyes. "What are you accusing me of?"

She flushed. "Nothing." She just knew that being alone with this sexy, virile man was not a good idea. "But," she continued hastily, "under the circumstances, I think it would be better if Max and I went into town and stayed in a hotel."

He choked off a laugh. "What? You're worried I'm going to put the moves on you?"

Actually, she was worried *she* was going to lose all common sense and put the moves on him. But not about to reveal that, she crossed her arms in front of her and quipped wryly, "Dream on, Alpha Man."

His eyes crinkled mischievously at the corners. *"Alpha Man?"*

Had she really *said* that? She must be punchier than she'd thought. Which was par for the course, considering she'd been lured back to work three months before she had planned and then, compounding matters, having to get up at the crack of dawn to take the six o'clock flight from Dallas to DC in order to be seated next to him on the return trip. Aware he was still waiting for an explanation, she lifted a hand. "It was an insult. A friendly one." Hope bit down on an oath. She was just making it worse.

He laughed, his husky baritone like music to her ears, as he continued giving her a long, sexy once-over. "Sounded more like a compliment to me."

He was twisting everything around, embarrassing her and putting her off her game. Indignant, she huffed, "Of course you would think that."

He held his ground, arms folded in front of him, biceps bunched. Again, that long steady appraisal. "Because I'm alpha?"

He definitely was *not* a beta.

She threaded her hands through her hair, wishing she'd thought to put it in a tight, spinsterish bun before he'd picked her up. "Can we end this repartee?"

His mother was right. They had been flirting. They were flirting now. Heaven help them both.

He leaned in and gathered her into his arms. "With pleasure."

The feel of him against her, chest to chest, thigh to thigh, sucked all the remaining air from her lungs.

"What are you doing?" she gasped, wishing he didn't feel so very, very good.

Wishing he hadn't just reminded her of all that had been missing from her life.

He threaded his hand through her hair, let it settle tenderly on the nape of her neck. "What any alpha male would do in this situation." Grinning, he bent his head toward hers.

Hope tingled all over. Lower still, there was a kindling warmth. Cursing the forbidden excitement welling within her, she whispered, "Garrett...for pity's sake...you can't...*I can't...*!"

He laughed again, even more wickedly. His

lips hovered above hers, so close their breaths were meeting as sensually and irrevocably as the rest of them.

"Kiss you and see if you kiss me back?" he taunted softly, stroking the pad of his thumb along the curve of her lips—top, then bottom. "Oh, yes, Hope Winslow, I sure as hell can."

Not only can, Hope thought, as an avalanche of excitement roared through her. Did.

His lips fit over hers, coaxingly at first, then with more and more insistence. She told herself to resist. Tried to resist. But her treacherous body refused to listen to her heart, which had been wounded, and her mind, which absolutely knew better.

She had been alone for so long.

Had needed to be touched, held, for months now.

She hadn't expected to be cherished as if she were the most wonderful woman on Earth. But that was exactly what he was doing, as he stroked his hand through her hair and, with his other palm flattened against her spine, guided her closer until her breasts were pressed against the unyielding hardness of his chest. Lower still, she felt the heat in his thighs and the building desire. And knew her life had just begun to get hopelessly complicated…

GARRETT HADN'T COME out to the ranch thinking they would be alone for one single second. Hadn't figured he would ever act on the need that had consumed him since the second her bottom landed square on his lap, the softness of her breasts pushing into his face.

Oh, he'd known he wanted her from the instant he had seen her checking him out in the DC airport. She was just so gorgeous, so haughty and unreachable in that all-business way of hers.

Seeing she had an infant whom she cared deeply for, knowing she was irrevocably wedded to life in Texas while he was not, had added yet another reason he should keep his hands off.

He might have managed it, too, if she hadn't been working so hard to curtail the attraction she so obviously felt.

Because Hope was right about one thing. Her denial had brought out the alpha male in him. Made him want to pursue her like she had never been pursued before.

That pursuit, in turn, had kindled his own raging desire. And then she had kissed him back, her tongue entwined with his in a way that could bring him to his knees and one day, hopefully, land them both in bed.

Luckily for the two of them she came to her senses and pushed him away. Breathing raggedly, she stepped back, a gut-wrenching turmoil in her low tone he hadn't expected. "I can't do this."

Pressing her hand to her kiss-swollen lips, she shook her head. "I can't lose everything because of one reckless moment. *Not again.*"

SILENCE FELL BETWEEN THEM, as awful and wrenching as her voice. Mortified, Hope yanked open her car door and climbed behind the wheel.

Garrett walked to the passenger side and pulled himself in beside her. "When did that happen?"

Hope concentrated on starting the engine. Driving, the normalcy of it, would help. She looked behind her, then backed up until she reached the gravel road that led to the barns. "I shouldn't have said that."

"And I shouldn't have kissed you," Garrett admitted gruffly, his big body filling up the passenger compartment the way no one else ever had. "But now that I did, and you kissed me back..."

He shrugged like a soldier on leave.

As if the fact that he had just returned from a war zone entitled him to something. Namely, a woman willing to have a fling.

She had found out the hard way, however,

through her ill-advised liaison with Max's daddy, that woman was not her.

"That shouldn't have happened, either," she said stiffly, as the SUV wound past the damaged wooden fence to the lone building a distance away from everything.

She didn't have to guess what it was.

A sign next to the door of the cedar-sided, tin-roofed building said Circle H Ranch Bunkhouse.

A bright red welcome mat stood in front of the heavy wooden door. Pots of flowers, a couple of small tables and some rough-hewn Adirondack chairs decorated the front porch. Lamps, emitting a soft yellow glow on either side of the entry had been turned on.

If the inviting exterior was any indication of the inside of the domicile, then Lucille had been right, they would be comfortable here.

Hope cut the engine and got out of the car. Quietly, she opened the rear passenger door, unfastened Max's safety seat from the base of the restraint and lifted him out. To her relief, her sweet little boy slept blissfully on.

Garrett grabbed the diaper bag and went on ahead, to find the key that had been left beneath the mat. "Is all this because you're working for my mother?" He reached inside and switched the interior lights on.

"Believe it or not—" Hope squared her shoulders as she passed "—working for your mother doesn't include making out with you."

GARRETT WAS PRETTY sure Hope hadn't meant to say that. Any more than she'd meant to do anything she had the last fifteen minutes or so. Nevertheless, he was pleased to see her letting down her guard. He wanted to get to know the real Hope Winslow, not the sophisticated facade she showed the world.

He watched as she set the carrier holding her sleeping infant down. "I won't interfere with that. Well, no more than I would have, anyway."

She smiled at him as if they hadn't just brought

each other's bodies roaring back to life. "Good to know, Captain."

Together, they took a quick tour of the newly renovated bunkhouse.

The central part of the structure included an open-concept kitchen with a breakfast bar that looked out onto the great room, complete with a TV and U-shaped sofa and a large plank table with a dozen chairs plus an arm chair on each end. On each side of it was a hallway that led to three bedrooms. All six bedrooms were outfitted identically, with a queen-sized bed, desk, dresser and private bath. His mom had been right, Garrett noted. They all could be very comfortable here.

Except for the awareness simmering between Hope and him...

"I don't understand why you think it would matter if we did become...closer. I'm not the one employing you—my mother is."

Hope sighed, apparently appreciating his use

of the least offensive word he could think of. "It would still look bad."

"And that concerns you, how things look?"

"Yes." Stepping closer, she slid him a surprised glance. "Doesn't it concern you?"

He exhaled his exasperation. "Not really. Something is either right or it's wrong. What we just experienced felt very right."

Hope turned away as if they hadn't just shared an embrace that had rocked his world. "It doesn't matter," she said, as if to a four-year-old. "Scandal management is all about appearances."

Ah, *appearances*. The bane of his youth.

He moved close enough to see the frustration glimmering in her eyes.

Her elegant features tinged an emotional pink, she said, "I just started my own firm. Your mother's scandal is the first crisis I'm handling, solo. It has to go well."

Of course business came first with her.

"Or?"

She sighed, completely vulnerable now as she met his gaze, seeming on the verge of tears. "Or my reputation really will be ruined."

That was almost as hard to believe as the way he was suddenly feeling about her, as if she might just be worth sticking around for. He moved closer yet. Seeing it *was* a tear trembling just beneath her lower lash, he lifted a thumb, gently brushed it away. "Over one job?" And one very long, satisfying kiss that had led him to want so much more?

She swallowed, stepped back. The tenderness he felt for her doubled.

"I made a mistake when I was working for my previous employer."

He couldn't imagine it being as calamitous as she was making it out to be. It was all he could do not to take her back in his arms. "What happened?"

For a second he thought she wouldn't answer, then she apparently thought better of it—maybe because she knew in this day and age almost anything could be researched on the internet.

Hope turned and walked back out to her SUV. She lifted out the pack-n-play, handed it off to him, then pulled out a box of diapers and a bag of baby necessities. "I got involved with a British journalist reporting on a scandal involving the American ambassador's son. Nothing happened between us during the crisis. But there was a flirtation that later turned into a love affair."

He grabbed her suitcase and headed up the steps alongside her. No wonder she'd reacted the way she had when his mother accused them of flirting. "I'm guessing it ended badly?"

Hope set her things down in the bedroom farthest from the living area. She opened up the pack-n-play, erecting it quickly. "I wanted marriage and a family. Lyle didn't. So we broke up. A few weeks later, he was killed in a motorcycle accident while on vacation with another woman. A couple of weeks after that, I discovered I was pregnant with Max."

Although he felt bad for all she'd been through, he realized he liked her better like this, showing her more vulnerable side.

"Sounds rough. But you were happy about the pregnancy?"

Hope smiled softly, glowing a little at the memory. "I was over the moon."

He could see that. And it was easy to understand why. She had a great kid.

Hope stroked a hand through her honey-gold hair. "My bosses, however, were not anywhere near as ecstatic."

Hope went back to put a soft cotton sheet over the crib mattress. She bent over, tucking in the elastic edges, while he stood by, watching, knowing she had no idea just how beautiful she was, never mind what she could do to a man, just by being, breathing...

She straightened, her green eyes serious, as she looked up at him. "My superiors worried, even though I had already arranged for a nanny from a topflight agency to assist me, that a baby would interfere with my ability to manage crises."

Her teeth raked her plump lower lip, reminding him just how passionately she kissed. "Plus, they were upset about the rumors started by some of my rivals that hinted I'd leaked confidential information to Lyle Loddington, prior to our affair. It wasn't true. I never disclosed even a smidgen of confidential information about anything to him. But you know how people think, where there's love, there is pillow talk..."

Pillow talk with her would have to be amazing. Not to mention everything that came before it.

With effort, he forced his mind back to the conversation. "So your employer fired you?"

"I was asked to resign."

It was easy to see that still stung. He got angry on her behalf. "You could have fought it."

He followed her back outside to the rear of her SUV. Together, they carried what was left of their luggage inside. "Yes," she agreed, "but if I had I would have done even more damage to my reputation in the process." He shut the door quietly behind them. "So I decided to use what I had learned and start my own firm—which would allow me to control the timing and length of my maternity leave—and go back to work when Max was six months old."

"Which would have been three months from now."

"Right. And I'm happy with that decision, even though I was persuaded to return to work a little earlier than I had planned. I *like* the way my life is shaping up, Garrett."

Able to see she didn't want to do anything to jeopardize that, he took her hand. "I'm sorry you had such a tough time." Crazy as it sounded, he wished he had been there to support and protect her. To help her though whatever upheaval she'd had to face. It's not something anyone should have to go through alone.

Her expression grew stony with resolve. "It was my fault. I was reckless. But I'm not going to be reckless again."

Chapter Four

"You're not planning to go back to work now, are you?" Garrett asked, a short while later. He opened up the fridge that had been stocked by the bunkhouse caretaker in advance of their arrival, brought out a big stack of deli meats and cheeses and laid them out on the concrete kitchen countertop, next to an assortment of bakery goods.

Hope set her laptop and phone down on the breakfast bar just long enough to grab a small bunch of green grapes and pour herself a tall glass of milk.

"No choice." Ignoring his look of concern, she settled on a tall stool opposite him. Ten thirty at night or not, she had business to conduct. And she needed to do it while her son was sound asleep. "I have to check the message boards for the news outlets reporting on the scandal, to see how the news thus far is being received."

Garrett spread both sides of a multigrain roll with spicy brown mustard, then layered on lettuce, tomato, ham, turkey and cheddar cheese. "There's nothing you can do about the way people think."

"Au contraire, Captain Lockhart."

He grinned.

Too late, she realized that flip remark had been a mistake.

He thought she was flirting with him again. And she definitely. Was. Not.

Hope turned her attention back to the task at hand. Her mood flatlined.

"That bad?"

Hope grimaced. "Worse than I expected and I expected it to be…bad."

"Hit me with the highlights," he said, twisting the cap off a beer.

Clearing her throat, she read, "'Those Lockharts should all be put in jail—'"

"We have not done anything illegal."

But someone might have, Hope knew. "'The whole foundation should be shut down…'" she continued.

Flicking a glance her way, Garrett crossed his arms over his chest. Fresh out of the shower, in a pair of gray running shorts and T-shirt stamped Army, he looked relaxed. And sexy as hell. "An overreaction."

Hitching in a quavering breath, Hope turned back to the article and recited, "'Why do the rich always feel the need to steal from the poor?'"

A ghost of a smile crossed his mouth. "I'm detecting a theme."

"This is serious."

Ever alert, he shrugged. "It's just people spouting off on the internet."

"Someone in the family needs to respond."

He ripped open a bag of chips and offered it to her. "And I'm the logical choice?"

She waved them off and ate a grape instead. "You *are* the eldest son, the patriarch, since your father passed."

He carried his plate around the counter and set it in front of a stool. "And I will make a public statement." He dropped down beside her, swiveled so he was facing her. "Once we have all the facts."

Their knees were almost touching but it would have been a sign of weakness on her part to move back. "You know why some politicians or businesses in trouble survive and others don't?"

His eyes on her, he took another sip of beer.

"Because they know every time an allegation is made, no matter how outlandish, a response must be given."

"Nothing makes a person look guiltier than constantly proclaiming they aren't."

"So I take it that's a no?"

"That's a no," he said, and devoured his sandwich.

With a sigh, she went back to her computer, logged on to the message boards for the news story with the most harmful coverage, and began to type.

Finished, he edged closer. "What are you doing?"

"Responding."

He stood behind her, so he could look over her shoulder. "Under your own name?"

Oh, my, he smelled good. Like soap and shampoo and man. "Under a fictitious screen name I set up. One of many."

"Isn't that…?"

She cut him off before he could say dishonest. "The way things are done today, and yes, it is."

He watched her fingers fly across the keyboard, then read aloud, "'What ever happened to being innocent until proven guilty? The Lockhart family has magnanimously supported over one hundred metroplex charities over the last thirty-five years. I say give them a chance to find out what has happened, before we all pass judgment."'"

Garrett returned to his stool. "Nice."

Seconds later, another Internet post appeared.

Hope shifted her laptop screen, so he could see. He read again, "'I agree with #1HotDallas-Mama. We *should* wait and see…'"

Several more posts appeared. Two out of three were positive.

Resisting the urge to do a touchdown dance, Hope turned to Garrett. "See?"

He polished off his chips, one at a time. "So that worked. Until someone puts up another negative rant, then other message-boarders are apt to agree with *their* posts."

Hope sighed her exasperation. "The point is to get another view out there. Repeatedly, if necessary, until the facts come in, and we can respond accordingly."

"Another press conference?"

"Or interview and statement."

She was not surprised to find he wasn't looking forward to any of it.

Telling herself that it didn't matter what Garrett Lockhart thought of her methods or her job, she carried her dishes to the sink. Turned, only to find Garrett was right beside her, doing the same thing. She looked up. He looked down. She had the strong sensation he was tempted to kiss her again. And she might have let him, had Max not let out a fierce cry. Thank heaven, Hope thought, pivoting quickly to attend to her maternal duties, her son had more sense than she appeared to right now.

"WHERE DO YOU want all these files?" Garrett asked his mother when she arrived at the bunkhouse late the following morning, Paul Smythe's daughter, Adelaide Smythe, in tow. A certified public accountant and forensic auditor, as well as an old family friend, the young woman had agreed to help them sort through the records and try to piece together what had happened.

Appearing tired but determined, Lucille pointed to the big plank table in the main room. "Just put them all there, thanks," she said.

Garrett set the boxes down, then returned to Adelaide's minivan to bring in the rest.

"When are you due?" Hope asked the visibly pregnant Adelaide.

"Four and a half months. I know—" Adelaide ran a hand over her rounded belly "—it looks like I'm a little further along, but it's because I'm having twins."

"Who's the lucky daddy?" Garrett asked, wondering how his brother Wyatt was going to take the news. The two had dated seriously in high school, but been extraordinarily contentious toward each other ever since they broke up at the end of their senior year. Why, exactly, no one knew. Just that there was still a lot of emotion simmering there.

"Donor number 19867." A beaming Adelaide explained, "I conceived the new-fashioned way."

Garrett wasn't surprised Adelaide had opted for pregnancy via sperm bank; she always had been very independent.

Hope sorted the multihued folders according to the names on the files. "Speaking of fathers...any luck getting ahold of your dad?"

Adelaide set up two laptop computers and a portable printer. "We're still trying, but he's apparently *not* on his annual fly fishing and camping trip in the wilds of Montana with the guys."

"Then where is he?" Garrett asked with a frown.

Adelaide glanced at Lucille, who seemed both understanding and sympathetic. Reluctantly, she admitted, "He's probably on vacation with this lady exec he's been secretly dating."

Hope tilted her head, her long, honey-hued hair falling over her shoulders. "Why secretly?"

Garrett itched to drag his hands through her lustrous mane, draw her close...

Adelaide sighed loudly. "Because I didn't like Mirabelle the first time I met her. I thought she was a gold digger, and I made the mistake of telling my dad that." She grimaced, recollecting. "Anyway, the whole thing got so ugly, we agreed not to talk about it ever again. So if my dad is on vacation with Mirabelle, as Lucille and I both suspect, he's probably not looking at his phone much at all."

Garrett could understand that. There were times when he wanted to get away from it all and enjoy the company of a woman, too. Like now...

"But he can never be disconnected from the world for too long, so we expect to hear from him soon." Adelaide plugged in power cords.

"Any idea what happened regarding the missing or misappropriated funds yet?" Garrett asked.

Again, Adelaide shook her head. "All we've managed to do thus far is gather all the records in one place. Which isn't as easy as it sounds, because there were some at the foundation office, some at Lucille's, some at Dad's house." She surveyed the stacks upon stacks of files. "We'll put it all together, but the actual audit is going to take a while."

"How long?" Hope asked.

"A couple of days."

She looked unhappy about that. "What can we do to help speed things along?"

His mother consulted the lengthy handwritten to-do list in her leather notebook. "You and Garrett could go into town. Talk with the director of the nonprofit the foundation is funding there." Lucille wrote out the information, handed it over. "If the foundation has indeed let down Bess Monroe and the wounded warriors she is trying to help, it's going to take both of you to fix things."

"THIS CAN'T BE RIGHT." Hope paused in front of the door to Monroe's Western Wear clothing store, Lucille's notes in hand. Yet the street address matched, as did the last names.

Garrett, who had decided to carry Max in lieu of getting the stroller out of the SUV, said, "Let's go in and see."

A young man behind the counter approached. "Can I help you?" he asked.

Briefly, they explained the problem. "I'm Nick Monroe. Bess's brother," the genial dark-haired man explained. "Bess is using our family store as the nonprofit's address because she doesn't yet have the funds for a facility."

"We'd like to talk to her."

"She's just about to get off shift at the hospital where she works." Nick Monroe paused. "Although I'm not sure how happy she is going to be to see you-all. She's not too happy with the Lockhart Foundation these days."

An understatement, as it turned out.

Although her shift had officially ended by the time they arrived at the rehab department, Bess Monroe was still deep in conversation with a little girl in a back brace and the girl's mother. The rest of the well-equipped physical therapy clinic was filled with all ages and injuries, including a couple of people who appeared to be former military.

Learning they were there to see her, Bess Monroe wrapped up her conversation and came toward them. She smiled tenderly at Max, who was wide awake, leaning happily against Garrett's wide chest, then turned back to Garrett and Hope with a frown. Directing them to an office with her name on the door, Bess shut the door behind them. Still holding Max, Garrett handled the introductions.

The registered nurse moved to the other side of her desk, but remained standing. "I told myself that if and when anyone from the Lockhart Foundation ever contacted me again, I would be cordial to them. No use burning any bridges when there is such desperate need, right? But..."

"I'm guessing your charity did not receive all of their funds, either," Hope prodded gently.

"Try any!" Bess exploded.

"None?" Garrett looked shocked.

Hope intervened. "The family really is trying to understand what's happened here, so they can make amends. It would be really helpful to us if you could share your experience."

Bess sat down and waited for them to take seats, too. "About a year ago, I drove to Dallas to meet with Lucille Lockhart at the foundation office. I explained the problem local veterans and their families were having, trying to get the support they needed, once they left active duty."

"Tank and Darcy Dunlop explained this to us."

Lucille nodded. "They're a great couple, and a perfect example. Although there are all kinds of problems that our nonprofit, West Texas Warrior Assistance, hopes to address."

"Like…?" Hope said, glad her hands were free so she could type notes into her phone.

"You want my wish list?"

Garrett nodded, holding a gurgling Max close.

"Temporary housing, close to the hospital. Support groups for warriors and every member of their family. Job counseling and placement. A separate rehab for those recovering from injuries incurred in battle, so they can still feel part of a team effort and urge each other on." Bess pulled a file out of her desk and handed it over. "A medical director familiar with combat injuries to coordinate care for the warriors and run the place. I could go on. And, in fact, I have. It's all in the pitch I gave your mother."

Trying not to notice how cute Max looked, snuggled against Garrett's strong shoulder, Hope prompted, "So when you initially met with Lucille…?"

"She was really enthusiastic about our mission and she agreed to help us, with a one-time donation of a half a million dollars, to be paid out in monthly installments over the course of a year. All I had to do was formally demonstrate the need and present a business plan, which I did, and a letter of intent to donate would be forthcoming. Along with the first check to get us started."

Bess reached into her desk. "Here's the letter I received from the foundation, but there was no check with it. And, as you can see, the amount promised to us in writing was five thousand dollars, instead of five hundred thousand."

Hope expected Garrett to hand Max over to her. Instead, he shifted her son to one arm, held the document with the other. When he had finished perusing it, he provided it to Hope.

She, too, noted all was in order, then gave the letter back to Beth for safekeeping. "I assume you called the foundation to tell them of the error?"

Bess's expression was grim. "I was told by your mother's assistant, Sharla, that I would have to speak to Paul Smythe, the CFO about that. I did and he apologized profusely for the mistake, and promised that he would investigate and I would have a new letter of intent to donate and a check within the next few weeks."

Hope shared Garrett's obvious concern.

Bess threw up her hands in frustration. "I did not receive either one, and my subsequent calls went unreturned."

Noting Max appeared to be reaching for Hope, Garrett finally handed her son over. "When was the last time you contacted the foundation?" he asked in a low, rough tone that sent shivers of awareness sliding down Hope's spine.

"Several months ago. Anyway." Bess stood, signaling their time had come to an end. "If you're worried I'm going to complain to the media, you needn't. I don't want what we're trying to do here to be any part of the bad publicity. I just want what was promised to us. That's all."

"WHY DIDN'T YOU reassure her you'd make things right?" Hope asked Garrett when they had left the hospital. She settled Max in his safety seat, then climbed into the passenger seat, once again letting Garrett drive since he knew the area better.

His broad shoulders flexed. He draped an arm along the back of the seat as he reversed the SUV out of the parking space. He paused to look her in the eye before shifting into drive. "Bess Monroe has suffered enough empty promises, don't you think?"

"You're on the board of directors, along with the rest of your family." Which meant he had sway.

"If someone has been stealing money from the foundation, there's no telling how much is actually left."

A breath-stealing notion. That the fifty-million-dollar Lockhart Foundation could be bankrupt was one she hadn't allowed herself to consider, until now. "So, what are you going to do?"

Garrett put the SUV in drive and turned out onto the street. "Wait for the results of the audit, look at everything, figure out where we stand. Then we'll make decisions on a priority basis."

"Kind of like a financial triage."

He nodded. "As far as right now…I need to drop by the real estate agency in town that is going to list my properties. The broker said it shouldn't take more than a couple of minutes to sign the papers." He gave her a second look. "If it's okay with you and Max. He's been a trouper so far."

"That he has. As opposed to last night…"

"I gather he doesn't normally wake up four times during a single night?"

So Garrett had noticed. "To nurse? No, he doesn't. But he was hungrier than usual last night."

In fact, they'd both been a little wound up.

Garrett shook his head fondly. "All that travelling."

"And being out on the ranch." She lifted a hand. "I'm kidding. He's a little young for any cowboy activity."

"I don't know." Garrett rubbed his jaw. "I could see him up on a horse someday."

So could she, oddly enough.

Garrett and herself, too.

Which was why she needed to put some barriers between them. Pronto.

"YOU'RE SURE YOU don't want to come in with me?" Garrett asked, parking in front of the realtor's office.

"Actually, I'd like to stay out here and change Max's diaper."

He nodded. "I'll make it quick."

And he did. By the time she had finished, he was returning, folder full of papers in hand, a frown on his face.

She knew how it felt to face one difficulty after another. Despite her earlier resolve, her heart went out to him. "Problem?" she asked lightly, putting Max back into his car seat.

He climbed behind the wheel. "My tenants moved out a week ago and left the house in a mess, which wasn't a surprise, since they stiffed me on the final month's rent." He drew in an exasperated breath. "And there's a leak in the office building, which could mean substantial repairs before it can be put on the market."

Hope figured she owed him a favor, given how much help he had given her with Max. "You want to run by and quickly look in on both properties before we go back to the ranch?"

He exhaled in relief. "The office building first."

It was several blocks from the hospital, toward the edge of Laramie. Built of the terra-cotta brick popular many years past, it was three stories high and rectangular in shape. Inside, there were obvious leaks on the ceiling and one of the three elevators bore an Out of Order sign. All but two of the tenants had left, and they had signs up announcing their upcoming moves to other spaces.

Garrett grimaced. Hope could understand why. This was not going to be easy to sell, unless he wanted to severely undervalue it. She resisted the urge to reach out and squeeze his hand. "I'm guessing you had no idea it was this bad?"

Despite the tense circumstances, Garrett still managed to grin down at Max, who was trying to grab on to his shirt. "Let's put it this way. My dad always said the best deals were the opportunities no one else recognized or properly valued. And he was all about getting the best deal."

"Sounds like a hedge fund manager."

Garrett moved close enough to let Max latch on to his pinkie finger. He beamed proudly when Max met his goal.

Lucille's eldest son might not know it, Hope thought, a ribbon of warmth curling through her, but he had real daddy potential.

Oblivious to her admiring thoughts, Garrett continued, "My dad felt the same way about his personal life. He and my mom never bought a home they didn't plan on fixing up until it doubled in value."

Max rocked his tiny body toward their companion, as if signaling he wanted to be picked up. Garrett took her son in his arms. Watching, Hope's heart melted a little more.

Garrett shifted his palm a little higher, carefully supporting Max's back, shoulders and head. "My dad also felt people never really appreciated something unless they had to work for it."

"So the properties you and your siblings inherited...?" Hope asked, inhaling Garrett's brisk masculine scent as they walked through the building.

"All had good long-term value. And a heck of a lot of work to be done." He handed Max back to Hope, then paused to hold the door open.

"I'm guessing the house you were gifted is in the same shape as this office building."

"Let's put it this way. Just now, the listing agent said it had great potential."

"Code for fixer-upper?"

"Probably."

The heat of his smile made her tingle. "You haven't been there, either," she guessed.

Garrett fell into step beside them as they made their way to the parking area. "I've seen pictures. But at the time I inherited it, it was rented and I was stationed overseas, so…no. I haven't seen it." He touched her son's cheek. "Think the little guy can handle one more excursion?"

The question was, could *she* handle it? Already she felt a lot closer to Garrett. Not good when she was supposed to be keeping her distance. As their eyes met and held, Hope felt a shimmer of tension between them. Man– woman tension.

"We'd both love to see the second part of your inheritance," she murmured.

Located a half block away, the house was a large white Victorian with a wraparound porch. Inside it was, indeed, a mess. Trash in every room. Dust and cobwebs in every corner. Bathrooms that pretty much defied description. And yet…

Hope studied the original woodwork, high ceilings and a plethora of windows in the century-old home. The house had multiple fire-places. Gorgeous wood floors just begging to be refinished. A backyard made for entertaining.

Garrett turned to her, a peculiar look on his handsome face. "Like it…?"

Love it. Adore it. Hope shrugged, for all their sakes, pretending she wasn't head over heels in love with this property. Wasn't imagining herself and Max living in a place just like it someday. With a man just as kind and sexy and good-hearted, just as fundamentally decent as Garrett.

Realizing she was getting *way* ahead of her-self, Hope forced her errant thoughts aside as they moved through the downstairs. It was post-pregnancy hormones. That was all.

She cleared her throat. "If you were to get a good cleaning crew in here…"

He stepped closer and her heart kicked into gear. "Or do it myself."

His pronouncement stopped her in her tracks.

She did a double take. "*You'd* tackle this?" What was he, some sort of superhero Alpha Man?

The tiniest smile played around the corners of his chiseled lips. His gaze locked with hers. "I've tackled a lot of things in some of the places I've lived. I don't mind."

Something else to admire about him, Hope noted dreamily. The fact that he'd been born rich but could easily be comfortable in less luxurious circumstances.

She pushed the burgeoning attraction away. She had to focus.

Had to remember he was the son of a client, nothing more. And speaking of the work she was supposed to be doing at this very second, she asked, "Are you going to have time to do that?"

"I've got another twenty-seven-and-a-half days of leave left. So, yeah, I can and will do what is needed to get both properties on the market before I leave Texas."

And when that happened, when the crisis was

over, her job finished, Garrett off to a job in either Seattle or DC, they'd likely never see each other again.

Nor would she have a reason to come back to the Circle H Ranch or Laramie County.

She had to remember that.

Stop fantasizing about what would never be.

She turned back to find Garrett studying her. "Problem?" he asked softly.

Not if I keep the proper perspective. Hope shook her head. "I'm just anxious to get back to the ranch. See how your mother and Adelaide are faring."

Chapter Five

Garrett walked into the Circle H bunkhouse, a wide-awake and slightly cranky Max snuggled in his big, strong arms. He took a moment to survey the scene. "Mom, you look like hell. You, too, Adelaide."

"Garrett!" Hope reprimanded him. She'd heard he was blunt, but wow! Although, she admitted reluctantly to herself, he was right.

In the three hours since she and Garrett had been gone, the long plank table had exploded with disorganized stacks of paperwork and multicolored file folders. Both women looked pale and completely overwhelmed. With his mother in her late sixties, and Adelaide's pregnancy, he was right to be concerned.

"When's the last time you-all ate?" he asked, reluctantly handing Max over to Hope.

The baby immediately began to fuss.

"I don't know." Adelaide and Lucille exchanged baffled looks. "Brunch, I guess, on the drive here."

"It's early, but you've got to have some dinner," Garrett decreed. "So we can either get back in the car and drive to town..."

All three women groaned at the thought of a twenty minute ride to Laramie and back. Never mind the time it might take to get seated, order and be served their meal. It would easily eat up a couple of hours.

Garrett headed for the kitchen. "Then I'm cooking."

If he cooked as well as he put together a sandwich, they were in luck. Eager to help, Hope said, "I need to feed Max and put him down. Then I'll give you a hand."

Garrett opened the fridge. "Take your time," he said over his shoulder. "I got this."

And he did, she found out some forty minutes later, when she emerged from the guest room where her son was fast asleep.

One end of the table had been cleared to allow for seats for four. Adelaide and Lucille had stopped working and were carrying table settings and the rest of the meal to the table.

Garrett was coming in through the mud-room door, a platter of burgers and roasted corn in hand. "I didn't know there was a grill out back," she said.

"A patio, glider and some outdoor rocking chairs, too," Lucille informed her. "I'm surprised you didn't notice that when you got here."

She might have, had it not been so late and she so enamored of her host's handsome son. If she hadn't taken time out to kiss him…

Guilt flooding through her, Hope shrugged.

Garrett's eyes crinkled at the corners, as if he, too, were recalling their steamy embrace and coveting another.

Wary of revealing herself, Hope quickly glanced away. Garrett gestured for everyone to have a seat. As they ate, he brought his mother up to date on their meeting with Bess Monroe.

"Sadly, her story matches the records I have," Lucille admitted unhappily.

"And those of many others," Adelaide concurred with a worried frown. "Although we've yet to go through everything."

"What have you learned for sure?" Hope asked, wondering if there were any concrete facts she could work with to build a compelling narrative.

Hesitating, Adelaide looked over at Lucille, who nodded at her to continue. "A year ago, the foundation had fifty million in assets. Today, the foundation has only twenty-five million."

"Which is as it should be," Lucille said, "since

we decided to give out twenty-five million in aid last year."

"So, where did the twenty-five million dollars go, if not all of it went to the earmarked charities?"

"We're still working on that."

"Meaning you think there is fraud involved." Garrett helped himself to a tangy vinegar-based coleslaw he'd found in the fridge.

"Certainly something untoward has gone on," the forensic accountant finally said.

"What, though, we don't yet know," Lucille said, cutting into a slice of watermelon. "The important thing is not to jump to any conclusions until we can show everything we have gathered to Paul."

The foundation CFO really needed to be there. *Now.* "When is he returning to Dallas?" Hope asked.

Adelaide exhaled. "My dad told me before he left he would be back home on Saturday afternoon, at two o'clock."

Or in roughly forty hours, Hope calculated, savoring the flavor of char-grilled beef and melted cheddar cheese nestled in a fresh brioche bun.

"We're planning to meet him at his home and bring him back to the ranch." Lucille looked pointedly at her son, clearly wanting a change of subject. "In the meantime, Sage called while you were out to check on things here and deliver her news."

"Something good, I gather?" Garrett added another burger to his plate.

Lucille beamed. "She's decided to move back to Texas as soon as she can arrange everything."

"Where in Texas?" Garrett asked.

"Here in Laramie, to her inheritance."

Garrett put down his fork. "Meaning…?"

"If the only reason you're considering moving to Seattle is to be close to your sister—don't."

Garrett sipped his iced tea. "Point taken, Mom."

An uncomfortable silence fell.

Hope wasn't sure what was going on. Was this Lucille lobbying for her son to move back to Texas? She'd told Hope she missed her children terribly. Wanted them all close to her again.

Enough to create a faux crisis with the foundation?

No, Hope immediately dismissed the notion. Whatever was going on here was real. And devastating. She had only to look at the shadows beneath Lucille's eyes to know that.

Garrett turned their conversation back to his little sister. "Does that mean Sage's finally given up on TW?"

Maybe it was the intimate setting, or the fact that Lucille had allowed Hope into her family's inner sanctum, at least long enough so that Hope could do her job, which compelled her to come right out and ask, "Who is TW?"

Adelaide sighed. "Terrence Whittier. This systems architect Sage has been following around for what…? Seven years now?"

Lucille nodded, clearly dismayed.

Garrett looked equally grim. "TW's made all sorts of promises to her, but kept none of them."

Lucille turned to her son. "I've taken a page from your book, in this instance, and said it as bluntly as I can. Time is running out if Sage wants to meet someone else, get married and have a family."

Adelaide lifted a staying hand. "TW and Sage did break up two years ago, Lucille."

"But Sage didn't leave Seattle." Lucille fretted.

Garrett defended his sister. "She had just started her cowgirl chef business up there, Mom. It was going great."

Hope could understand not wanting to leave that.

Lucille worried the strand of pearls around her neck. "I have a feeling TW came back in her life last winter—at least briefly."

Garrett assumed his usual poker face. "Did she tell you that?"

"No." Lucille looked at her eldest son steadily. "She didn't have to tell me. I'm a mother. I just know these things."

"IS THAT THE way it is?" Garrett asked Hope later, when they were alone once again. His mother and Adelaide had gone to bed, vowing to get up early and pick up where they had left off.

He followed her into the mud room, where the washer and dryer were located. Hope wished she could say she was immune to his charm; she wasn't. There was just something really satisfying about spending time with him, even when they were doing really mundane things like errands, or dishes or, best of all, baby care. "Do mothers just instinctively know things about their kids?" he continued.

Hope sorted baby clothes and blankets into whites and pastel blues and dropped the latter into the tub. Eager to get the spit-up laundered out of all their garments, she added her own similarly hued shirts and pajamas. "Sort of. At least, I do."

She turned toward him. Inhaling his brisk masculine scent and the mint on his breath, it was all she could do not to think about kissing him again. "I read up a lot on infants and the ways they communicate before Max was born. For instance, when he's hungry, he makes a *meh* sound. It's supposed to be *neh*, but I think he's combining that with Mommy, and it comes out *meh*."

Garrett grinned at her maternal bragging, as she meant him to.

Proudly, Hope continued, "When Max is sleepy he yawns. And when he has air in the tummy he wants to get out, he makes an *eh* or *earh* sound."

Garrett rummaged around the cabinet until he produced a bottle of extra-gentle laundry detergent. "When he needs a diaper change?"

The backs of their fingers brushed as he gave the detergent to her. Ignoring the resultant tingle, Hope concentrated on measuring the clear liquid into the cap, then pouring it into the dispenser. "He kicks his legs a lot and says *huh* repeatedly."

Garrett shifted, his big body exuding warmth in the small space. "Does he get mad at you?"

"Sometimes." Hope set the dials, switched on the washer, then left the room before being with him in the small space revved up her latent desire and them falling into each other's arms again. "Like when we're driving somewhere and I can't stop until we get there. Although," she added, continuing into the kitchen to help herself to one last glass of milk before bed, "if Max has to wait more than five minutes for me to be able to stop and get him out of his car seat, the motion of the vehicle usually lulls him to sleep."

Garrett surprised her by pouring himself a glass of milk, too. "So, even when you do have to drive a little longer than Max would like, it's not so bad." He stepped into the pantry, emerging with a bag of gourmet butter cookies.

Hope accepted one. "For either of us." Keeping her voice low, so as not to wake anyone, she stepped out onto the front porch of the bunk-house. There, she could hear Max if he cried.

The night was warm and breezy, the velvety black Texas sky was sprinkled with stars surrounding a brilliant yellow quarter moon.

Leaning against a porch post, she looked over at Garrett, who seemed to be enjoying the late summer evening on the ranch as much as she was.

His gaze roved the messy confines of the knot on the top of her head. "Have you heard from your nanny?"

Aware she hadn't done a very good job of putting her hair up in an elastic band before she'd nursed Max the last time, Hope set her glass on the rail. Determined to appear at least a little more professional, and less Mommy On Vacation, she reached up and shook her hair out, combing it with her fingers as best she could.

"Mary Whiting? Yes. She emailed me this

afternoon. Her mom's heart surgery was successful,"

Which was really great—for Mary and her family.

"But it's going to be at least a six- to eight-week recuperation. And Mary is going to stay with her family to help out."

Which was really bad—for her and Max.

"Can you get another nanny?"

"The agency is already sending me candidate profiles for an interim replacement."

He came near enough she could feel his body heat. "But...?"

Ignoring the melting sensation in her tummy, Hope lifted a shoulder. "Mary's going to be hard to replace, even temporarily. She was perfect with Max. He hasn't bonded with anyone so readily except yo—uh...er..."

Oh, darn, had she really almost said that?

Apparently, judging by the supreme masculine satisfaction emanating from him, she had.

DELIGHTEDLY TRACKING THE flush that started in her chest and crept up to her face, Garrett palmed the center of his chest. "Me?"

She thought about trying to deny it but realized that was pointless. "Surely you noticed how much Max loves it when you hold him…"

Garrett shrugged. "I love holding him, too."

That said, he gazed at her lips. Her breath caught as he took her glass. Set it aside. Bent his head.

The next thing Hope knew she was all the way against him. His arms were wrapped around her. Their mouths were fused.

If anything, this kiss was sweeter than the first they had shared.

Shorter, too.

He drew back. Enough light poured out from the interior of the house that she could see the desire glimmering in his eyes.

She had sure as heck *felt* it in his kiss.

Her chest rose and fell as she tried to find the will to admonish him, but the words just wouldn't come. So she did the only thing she could. She picked up her glass and disappeared into the house and then her bedroom, shutting the door firmly behind her.

Garrett knew he was pushing the boundaries Hope had set. But with only a few days to convince her they had something worth pursuing, he had kissed her, anyway.

Felt her respond.

And knew all he had to do was continue getting to know her—and her adorable little son—and let the rest of the situation play out. Go from there.

In the meantime, they all needed sleep, so he headed to bed.

He was awakened at one thirty in the morning, when Max cried.

"Meh…meh…meh…"

Which meant, Garrett knew now, Max was hungry.

The house fell silent once again.

Which meant Hope was nursing.

Two hours later, Max woke again, demanding to be fed. Eventually the house grew quiet.

At five thirty, Max woke for the third time in six hours. "Meh…meh…meh…" And this time, he wouldn't stop.

Garrett lay in bed, wondering if he should offer to help, or stay put and let Hope deal with it as expertly as she usually did.

The sound of the front door opening and a crying Max being carried outside had him vaulting out of bed.

He joined Hope and the baby in the yard.

She was standing with her hand on the car door, tears streaming down her face. And still an apparently hungry—and healthy—Max cried. "Meh, meh, meh."

"What's going on?" Garrett asked, gathering the infant into his arms.

Hope was still in her menswear-style pajamas, which were buttoned crookedly up the front, her hair a tousled mess. She had her keys but no purse.

And the tears continued to spill from her eyes. "Max wants to nurse again," she sobbed softly, "and my breasts are dry!"

He could see where that was a problem, a big one, for both mother and child. Resisting the urge to take Hope in his arms, along with Max, and hold them both close, he asked, "So what's the plan?" Obviously, she had one.

Hope let out a shuddering breath and ran both her hands through her hair. Her chest rose and fell with each agitated breath. "To drive him back and forth on the ranch until he falls asleep again. Or I make more milk." She gestured helplessly. "Whichever comes first."

The physician in him rose to the challenge. He met and held her eyes. "I have a better plan. Why don't you go inside and get dressed?"

Chapter Six

Ten minutes later, a fully dressed Hope climbed into the back of the SUV next to her intermittently wailing son. Garrett slipped his phone into the pocket of his shirt and settled behind the wheel. From the doorway, Lucille and Adelaide, who had been awakened by all the ruckus, waved.

Embarrassed that she was turning out to be so inept a mother, at a time when she most needed to be at her best, Hope drew a deep breath.

She knew she shouldn't need a man in her

life. And she didn't. But it was sure nice to have Garrett here right now. Even better that he was a doctor.

"You're sure we should take Max to the emergency room?" she asked, as he started the drive to town. She couldn't help but worry that she was overreacting, as she had a tendency to do when it came to her twelve-week-old son.

Yet Max's continued distress, his persistent crying, his absolute refusal to take his pacifier was real. As was the lack of milk in her breasts, the soreness of her tender nipples. Although none of that was a surprise, given how often he had been nursing in the last thirty-six hours.

Garrett nodded confidently.

He had taken the time to brush his teeth and splash some water on his face, as had she. He hadn't shaved, and the rim of beard on his face gave him a ruggedly handsome look.

"Lacey McCabe is the best pediatrician in the area. She agreed to meet us there, before her rounds. Make sure there's nothing wrong."

"But you're a physician. Can't you tell?" *Put my mind at ease right now!*

He cast her a brief, consoling look in the rear-view mirror. "I'm an internist who specializes in traumatic injuries—and recovery—in soldiers. Max needs a pediatrician, and although it might be able to be handled over the phone, Lacey and I both agreed it would be better if he was seen."

Hope couldn't argue with that.

Plus, she appreciated Garrett's protectiveness toward her son, which mirrored her own.

"Besides," he continued in a raspy growl. Finding the aviator sunglasses he'd hooked in the opening of his shirt, he slipped them on, obscuring his gorgeous blue eyes from view. "I'm emotionally involved."

Just that suddenly, something came and went in the air between them. The slightest spark of hope of all-out romance.

Hope gave Max's pacifier yet another try.

To her relief, this time her son accepted it and began to suckle, his little lips working furiously.

Needing to understand exactly what Garrett meant by "emotionally involved," and appreciating the blissful silence that fell in the interior of her SUV, Hope asked, "You mean with Max?"

Garrett's hands tightened on the steering wheel. His voice dropped another notch. "With both of you." Oblivious to the leaping of her heart, he kept his attention on the road. "A smart doctor never treats those he is close to— it's too easy to let your feelings get in the way and overlook something you don't want to see."

Like what? Hope wondered, feeling the weight of his concern.

"Then this could be serious?" she probed nervously, as Max abruptly spit out his pacifier and continued his *meh meh meh*…albeit a little more softly and a lot more hoarsely.

She saw Garrett's lips tighten in the rearview mirror, but when he spoke it was with a physician's calm. "Yes, but there's a much higher chance it's not. Still, with a child this young, it's just best not to take any chances."

Hope nodded and turned her attention back to her son, doing everything she could think to soothe him, but nothing worked. Not the touch of her hands, the motion of the vehicle or her voice. Not even the relaxing music when Garrett turned on the stereo. Max fussed the entire way, his hoarse cries breaking her heart—to the point that she was wiping away tears herself.

Finally, they pulled into the emergency entrance of the Laramie Community Hospital and parked in a slot designated for ER patients. Her breasts aching—and empty—Hope struggled to pull it together. She was not going to let Max down even more. She was *not* going to cry.

"We'll get this taken care of in no time. Just hang in there," Garrett said, his voice a tender caress.

He leaped out to assist.

Unfortunately, by the time Hope got Max out

of his car seat he was in full temper, arching his back and wailing at the top of his lungs. Hoping Garrett could calm him, Hope handed her son over, then emerged from the car herself.

To her chagrin, Max didn't appear to want either of them to hold him. So Hope settled him back in her arms. Worse, his wails sounded all the louder in the early morning quiet of the emergency room.

Luckily, they had staff waiting for them.

To her surprise, the nurse approaching them looked familiar, except her hair was different. Longer.

"I'm Bess Monroe's twin, Bridgett Monroe," the woman said, apparently used to the confusion. She grabbed a clipboard and pen as they passed the admitting desk. "We're both nurses here. I usually work in the hospital nursery, but Dr. McCabe asked me to come down for this. So…" Bridgett smiled, assessing their trio. "You're Hope Winslow and this indignant little fella is Max?"

"Right."

Bridgett turned to their gallant escort. "And you're the Dr. Garrett Lockhart I spoke with on the phone?"

Garrett nodded his greeting, abruptly looking all confident, capable military physician. "Affirmative."

"Nice to meet you, Doc. Did you want to come back to the exam area or stake out a place in the waiting room?"

It took Hope no time at all to decide the answer to that. "I'd like him with us." She paused, wondering belatedly if she had overstepped, and searched his eyes. "Is that okay?"

Looking as though there was no place else he would rather be, Garrett volunteered, "I can hold him while you fill out the paperwork."

Together they went into the exam room. While Hope answered the questions on the hospital intake forms, Garrett propped Max up on his shoulder and walked him back and forth, whispering soft, soothing words in his ear all the while.

Max rested his head on Garrett's big shoulder, his fussing finally beginning to lessen. Seconds later, Dr. Lacey McCabe walked in. The petite, silvery blond pediatrician introduced herself, then asked Garrett to put Max on the exam table. Bridgett stepped in to help undress the infant and assisted with the physical exam. When she had finished, Lacey swaddled Max in an ER blanket and handed him to Hope for comforting. Stethoscope still wrapped around her neck, Lacey pulled up a stool and indicated for them to get comfortable, too. "Tell me what's going on."

Hope settled on the gurney, Max in her arms. Garrett stood close beside her while she brought the pediatrician up to date.

Lacey listened while the nurse typed into a computer tablet. "And up to now you've been feeding on demand?"

"Yes." Hope was glad Max had quieted, at

least temporarily, now that he was back in her arms, his pacifier in his mouth.

"And that's worked well for you?" Dr. McCabe continued. "His weight gain has been on track?"

About that, Hope could brag. "It's been perfect."

"But otherwise, you've been able to keep up your milk supply?"

Hope felt a surge of regret. "Until I went back to work earlier this week."

"How has that been going?" the doctor asked empathetically.

Not nearly as great as I'd like it to be.

Garrett reached over and squeezed her shoulder. Appreciating his support, Hope leaned into his touch while she answered the pediatrician's questions. "It's complicated," she said finally.

Understanding shone in Lacey's gaze. "Stressful?"

"Um, yes…and no. It just sort of depends on what is going on, like in all jobs."

"But the last few days in particular…?" Dr. McCabe prodded.

The heat of embarrassment welled in Hope's chest. "Have been pretty stressful," she admitted reluctantly. "What with Max's nanny getting called away on a family emergency, just when we needed her most." If it hadn't been for Garrett during the last couple of days, she honestly didn't know how they would have coped.

Lacey nodded. "Okay. Well, there's a good reason why you and Max are out of sync. And, just so you know, it happens to all new moms when they make the transition from maternity leave to work. It does get better."

"Thank heaven." Hope sighed, suddenly feeling on the verge of tears again. "Because I'm not sure I could take it if Max continued to want to nurse every two hours instead of every three or four!"

"Unfortunately, that may not happen for a while," Lacey warned her. "Max is in a growth spurt. And like all healthy males, he wants what he wants when he wants it."

Everyone in the room chuckled at the pediatrician's joke, including Garrett.

Hope met his eyes.

He shook his head, grinning.

A new spiral of warmth slid through her.

Humor, she realized, could do a lot to get them through. Well, that and a little romance...

"So, there are two options," Dr. McCabe continued, bringing Hope back to the problem at hand. "One, is to tough it out and let your innate maternal response to your baby's distress push your body into producing more milk. That usually takes a few days. The other is to keep nursing at a rate you feel comfortable with and supplement with formula to give your body a little break," Lacey continued with a nonjudgmental practicality and compassion Hope really appreciated. "Which is what I did when my six daughters were young. I found combination feeding was the best of both worlds for me."

Lacey paused to let Hope consider.

"But it's really up to you, Hope. Both options are perfectly fine. It just depends on what you, as Max's mother, want to do."

That was easy, Hope thought in relief. "I'd like to try the combination."

Lacey McCabe stood. "Okay, then how about we set you up with a day's supply of formula until you can get to the pharmacy or grocery on your own. And in the meantime, Hope?" The pediatrician paused at the exam room door. "Be sure you drink enough fluids, take in enough calories and get plenty of rest. You need to take care of yourself, too."

"I second that," Garrett said, as soon as the nurse and doctor had exited. He stroked Max's head, paused to look deeply into Hope's eyes, demonstrating once again what a good father—and husband—he would make someday.

A thread of wistfulness swept through her.

"And to that end," he added gruffly, as her

gratitude grew by leaps and bounds, "I'll do whatever I can to assist you both."

SHORT MINUTES LATER, Hope watched Max finish the bottle in no time flat.

"And here I thought he might not like the taste of formula," she murmured, turning her son upright to give him one last burp.

Garrett, who had been texting his mom to let her know that Max was okay, put his cell phone back in his pocket. He shook his head fondly at both of them. "You know how it is when you're really hungry..."

She warmed at his lazy once-over. However, just because he was being exceptionally kind and considerate did not mean he was auditioning to be the man in her life. "Good point." Flushing slightly, she put Max down and, while changing his diaper, drew a stabilizing breath and worked to keep up the witty repartee. "When you're famished, anything tastes good." And some things, like Garrett's kiss, were amazingly good…

She had to stop thinking this way.

Letting her fatigue, and her current need to lean on someone's strong shoulder, make more of their temporary friendship than there was.

Garrett picked up the diaper bag and her purse. Some men would have looked ridiculous carrying both. The contrast only made him look more impossibly masculine. Sea-blue eyes twinkling, he held the door for her and Max. "Well, there are some things I don't think I'd like, regardless."

Hope wondered how much she had really put him out the last few days. Garrett acted as if charging to her rescue—continually—was nothing. She knew better. He had important decisions to make. And only so much military leave. There were also family and friends he probably wanted to spend more time with. Yet he'd remained with her and Max, even though his brother Chance had dropped a Bull Haven Ranch pickup off for him the previous morning.

"In fact, there are some things I downright loathe." He chuckled.

Hope fell into step beside him. "Like...?"

He escorted her outside. The air was warm and scented with flowers, the sky a clear light blue overhead.

"Pickled beets. Can't stand 'em."

Hope couldn't help but laugh. "Me, either," she murmured, as a yawning Max drowsily watched them both.

Garrett shortened his steps as they wound their way through the parked vehicles in the emergency services lot. When they reached the car, he leaned in to help Hope get a now-asleep Max into his safety seat.

"Well, what do you know?" Garrett observed with a tenderness that nearly stopped Hope's breath. "He's fast asleep."

Hope luxuriated in the shared emotion. It was

at times like this that she missed having a daddy for Max, and a husband for herself, the most.

"No wonder." Deliberately, she returned her attention to her son. He looked as precious as could be, his long blond lashes resting against his cheeks, his bow-shaped lips working soundlessly. "He wore himself out…"

Whereas she—and Garrett—both seemed to be running on adrenaline.

Because it would be easier to talk quietly if she were seated beside Garrett, Hope climbed into the front seat of her SUV. Once again aware of how cozy and domestic this all felt, she asked, "What did your mom have to say when you texted?"

He squared his jaw and kept his eyes on the road. "She and Adelaide are glad Max is okay."

Uh-huh. And what else? Feminine instinct told her that he was deliberately holding something back. "And…?"

He hit the signal and turned left, which was,

if memory served, not the way out of town toward the Circle H.

"They need more information from the bank if they're going to figure out where all the money went. The only way to quickly take a look at the cancelled checks, and discover where they were being deposited, is to go to the foundation's bank in person. So they're driving back this morning. They left as soon as they knew Max was okay."

Or in other words, twenty minutes ago.

Hope settled back in her seat, not sure how she felt about that. She turned to study Garrett's handsome profile. "When will they return?"

"Tomorrow, at the earliest. Depends on how quickly they're able to get all the data."

Aware she hadn't checked any of her work messages since close of business the previous day—a definite mistake when in the midst of any scandal—Hope pulled out her cell phone. In work mode once again, she bit her lip. "I wonder if we should go back to Dallas, too."

"I texted that option while you were feeding Max, back at the hospital. Mom said she would prefer we sit tight. She will call us as soon as they discover anything. But right now her plan is to return to the ranch with Adelaide, and Paul, as soon as possible. And go from there."

Nodding, Hope scanned the Dallas news headlines on the internet.

Garrett slanted her a glance. "Anything?"

"Six more charities have come forward to say they were stiffed by the foundation. But it's only a mention." Hope sighed her relief that the ugly gossip was dying down. "Not the lead story."

"Is that good?"

"It means public interest is waning—for now. It'll crank back up again as soon as we learn whether the foundation is at fault or not and people begin to react to that."

Sighing, she put her phone back in her purse.

"You need to eat something." Garrett detoured into a drive-through restaurant famous for its breakfast tacos.

He ordered two for her, three for himself, a couple of hash brown potato patties, coffee and milk.

He handed her the bag, then headed back out on the road.

They ate in the car, knowing that if they stopped for long Max would likely wake. Happily, Max slept for the rest of the ride back to the ranch.

Together they eased him out of the car, into the bunkhouse and into his bed. Realizing how lucky they were that Garrett had been there to help them, and Max's health crisis had been so easily resolved, Hope stood a moment, just drinking in the sight of her baby boy, memorizing everything about him. With his cheeks full of healthy color, one tiny fist tucked under his chin as he slept, he looked so sweet and peaceful. Emotion clogged her throat.

She turned away and walked out of the room.

Garrett followed her, his steps as silent and languid as his mood.

Suddenly feeling unutterably fragile, Hope kept her back to him and said what she should have a lot earlier, "I owe you a lot for this morning. In fact, for the entire past few days..."

She wouldn't have been able to get any work done without him. Max was certainly better off, too, with Garrett there.

He put a light hand on her shoulder. "Glad to help," he told her huskily, turning her around.

The next thing she knew, instinct was taking over. She was all the way against him, wrapped in his strong, steady warmth. His head slanted, dipped. And then there was no stopping it. Everything she felt, everything she wanted, was right there, in that moment, in his arms.

GARRETT HAD PROMISED himself he wouldn't kiss Hope again or let things get out of hand. At least, not until the foundation scandal was over and he could pursue her the way he wanted to pursue her—with no holds barred.

But the moment she turned her vulnerable

green eyes to his and launched herself against him, all previous resolutions were off. She made a sexy little sound in the back of her throat as her mouth softened under his, opening to allow him deeper access.

"What are you doing to me?" she whispered. "What are we doing to each other...?" And then her hands were coming up to cup his head. She was standing on tiptoe, pressing her body against him, tangling her tongue with his.

Had she not surrendered so completely to the pressure of his mouth against hers, maybe it would have been a lot easier to do the gallant thing and walk away. Before things heated up even more.

But she didn't pull away. Nor did he.

He felt the need pouring out of her, matching his own. Felt the barriers around her heart lower, just a little bit. Because Hope was right about one thing—whatever he was doing to her, she was doing it to him, too.

Succumbing to the moment, he pulled her in

a little closer, a little tighter, enjoying the heady rush of their adrenaline-fueled tryst, and she was right there with him, surrendering, even as she demanded more.

He had an idea she'd regret this.

But for now, she was all about the moment.

And he knew this wasn't an experience likely to come again. At least, not any time soon. So he went with it, lifting her so her legs wrapped around his waist and carrying her, still kissing, all the way to his bed.

They tumbled down onto it. She shoved him to his back and sprawled on top of him.

He groaned softly, thinking that he deserved a swift kick in the rear for doing this. There wasn't a smidgen of commitment between them and Hope wasn't anywhere near a one-night-stand woman.

Still struggling with his conscience, Garrett lifted his head long enough to rasp, "I feel like I'm taking advantage."

"Don't," she whispered back, kissing his jaw,

his cheek, his lips with wild abandon. "I'm a grown woman. I know exactly what I'm doing."

Did she?

He wondered. Yet, when she spread her hands across his chest and shoulders, caressing, molding, exploring, he couldn't help but haul her even closer and kiss her again.

"And I'm pretty sure..." she murmured, letting her quest drift lower to the proof of his desire "...the one taking advantage here..." she sighed with obvious delight as his body went hard and he swore, low and rough "...would be me."

His hands tightened on her, squeezed. She smelled so good, tasted so good, felt so good. "You're certain this is what you want?" he gritted out.

She looked him in the eye, confirming lustily, "What I need."

Well, what do you know? You're what I need right now, too. "Okay, then," he said with a reckless grin that matched her own. "Permission granted."

Emerald eyes sparkling, she unbuttoned his shirt, spread the edges wide. Admired, even as she kissed his shoulders and chest. Sensually explored her way down the goody trail to the clasp of his belt. Kissed her way back up even more slowly and decadently.

"Not to worry." She paused to make a thorough tour of his mouth. "We'll apologize and forgive each other later," she promised, her honey-blond hair sliding across his skin.

No, he thought, we won't.

He wasn't surprised she had already anticipated her next move, though.

This was the Hope he'd first met. Dynamic. Determined to be in charge. Following a plan and focused on a goal. Which, at the moment, was making love with him while irrefutably dismissing the possibility of anything more.

Figuring they could sort all that out later, after they'd rocked each other's worlds, he ran a hand up the inside of her thigh. She shot to her knees, her smooth, velvety skin quivering and warming beneath his palm. Lips parted, breath erratic, she rose above him and splayed her hands across his chest, seeming to dare him to make her want him even half as much as he already yearned for her.

Little did she know how up to the task he was. Libido roaring, he shifted her so she was beneath him. He unwrapped her with delight— first her shorts and panties, then her blouse and bra.

She was even more beautiful than he had imagined. With soft, full breasts, a slender waist, rounded tummy and sleek, gorgeous thighs.

Clearly appreciating his admiration, nipples tightening into hard buds of arousal, she unfastened his belt. "Let's see what you've got, Captain."

"Yes, ma'am." He rose long enough to strip down, too.

Her eyes moved over him, in sweet, solemn awe that sent his pulse roaring even more.

"That," he told her, moving back over top of her, pressing the hard ridge of his erection against her welcoming softness, "is what you do to me."

She drew in a halting breath, said, "Then let's see what *you* can do to *me*."

Chapter Seven

It was a challenge, Hope soon realized, Garrett was completely up for. He caught her against him, so they were flush against each other, tunneled his hands through her hair and fitted his mouth to hers, giving her a long, thorough kiss designed to shatter her resolve. Until she was no longer able or willing to put any limits whatsoever on their lovemaking.

Excitement flooded through her. She sank into him, luxuriating in the hard length of him and the overwhelming provocativeness of his kiss.

"Oh, my…" she whispered long minutes later, when he finally lifted his head. When had simply making out—naked—been this incredible? When had any man been this sexy and tender and kind? Or left her feeling so completely wanton and desirable?

"My feelings exactly," Garrett rasped. Gazing into her eyes, he cupped the side of her face with his large hand. Kissed her again—hotly, possessively—then slid down her body, stopping to caress and kiss every inch along the way—the curves of her breasts, the sensitive tips, the dip of her waist, the belly still rounded from childbirth. Lower still, to the nest of soft curls and the blossoming dampness within.

The pressure of his mouth, coupled with the questing caress of his fingertips, sent her arching up off the bed. The rough wild rasp of his tongue, coupled with his gentle suckling, catapulted her all the way over the edge. Her cry

of ecstasy had him chuckling in masculine satisfaction. His heart pounding in tandem to her
own, he moved up her body. Found the condom
in his wallet, and swiftly rolled it on.

Ready to see to his own needs, he eased between her thighs, taking her in one smooth,
deep stroke. The rhythmic pressure of his body
and his mouth took her to new heights, making
her burn and tingle and *want* inside. She tee-
tered on the edge of something thrilling and
wonderful, yearning for more than she had
ever thought possible, as he transported her to
a place where she had never been. A place that
was not just sexy as all get-out, but safe and
warm and oh-so immensely satisfying, too.

It was just too bad, she thought dazedly, as
they slowly stopped shuddering and returned
to reality, it could never happen again.

GARRETT FELT THE change in Hope as soon
as their breathing returned to normal. Reluctantly he disengaged their bodies and shifted

his weight to the side, but did not let her go. Although this was what he had expected all along—a ready ticket to the exit—he could not say he welcomed it. He knew their situation was complicated. Complicated was more than okay when it led to results like this. He just had to convince her of that.

"Regrets?" He kissed her temple.

Still trembling, Hope closed her eyes and didn't answer, preventing him once again from getting lost in her emerald-green eyes.

Determined to ease her worries, he smoothed a hand through her silky mane. "If you're worried about a conflict of interest—don't be. I wouldn't have hired you. I still wouldn't hire you." He chuckled. "Or any scandal manager for that matter."

She met his gaze. Her eyes were filled with mischief. "That's good to know. I wouldn't have accepted a job working for you, either."

That he could believe. He bent to kiss the inside of her wrist. Her elbow. Shoulder. "Then?"

Hope rose and, sheet draped around her, perched wearily on the edge of the bed. She grabbed her clothes off the floor. Keeping her back to him, she slipped on her bra, fastened it in front. "When people see a resolution to a crisis, they feel exultant and relieved, reckless and needy."

He lay back on his side, watching as she slipped her arms into the sleeves of her blouse. Although the sheet obscured the lower half of her, he could well remember the lissome lines of her hips and thighs, the sweet spot in between.

He felt himself grow hard again.

"This has happened to you before, then?"

Her eyes drifted lower and she caught her breath. Discreetly eased her way into her panties. Stood. "No. I've never been involved with a client." She stepped into her shorts, apparently oblivious to the fact that he found it just as arousing to watch her get dressed as it had been to undress her, just minutes earlier.

She wound her hair into a knot at the base

of her neck and secured it there with one of the elastic bands she always seemed to have wrapped around her wrist whenever she was caring for Max.

Walking into his bathroom, she bent and splashed some cold water onto her face, pausing to dry her face and look into the mirror.

From his vantage point on the bed, he saw her stare at her flushed cheeks and passion-glazed eyes, as if seeing a stranger. Her breasts rose as she took a deep enervating breath. Then turned, all cool reserve once again, and walked back into the bedroom to join him.

She bent and tossed him his clothes. "I'm always orchestrating the end of a crisis. I'm not involved in it." She turned her back, wanting to continue this conversation. But clearly, he realized, not so long as he was hard and naked.

Reluctantly, he shucked on his boxers and jeans.

The erection he could do nothing about.

When she heard the rasp of his zipper, she

turned back to him. Face pale, she said, upset all over again, "But this morning, with Max suddenly in such distress—the fact we had to take him to the ER—made me realize all over again how much I love him and want to protect him." Her eyes grew misty, her voice turned hoarse. "The idea that there might come a time I might not be able to keep him safe and healthy, really rocked me to the core."

He nodded, understanding.

What would any of them do without Max?

Without any of the people they loved in their lives?

He'd felt the same jolt of fear and anxiety when his father had been diagnosed with a degenerative heart disease.

Yet loss, in every life, was inevitable.

Which was where faith came in. Faith and the people around you…

"Which is why you turned to me," he guessed, pulling on his shirt.

Hope wiped away her tears before they fell.

She squared her shoulders, and seemed to pull herself together, as she surveyed his chest. "Well, that and your hot bod," she teased.

He winked, following her easy lead. "Turned you on, did I?"

"I admit it. You're so different from the men I usually date. I was curious what it would be like to hit the sheets with you."

He came closer, aware he didn't like the mental image of her in any other guy's arms. "What kind of men do you usually go out with?" he asked gruffly, already wondering how to get rid of the competition.

She tapped her index finger on her chin. "Tactful."

Ha-ha. "You mean wusses?"

She shook her head. "Nonmilitary."

"So in other words, execs…"

"One reporter."

"Your basic white-collar types."

"Yes."

The kind of guy, he figured, she could probably dominate. The kind of guy that, in the end, would bore her silly. He tilted his head and flashed her a cocky grin. "You've been missing out."

For a moment, she seemed to agree. At least in bed. Which made him wonder. "So, now that your curiosity about my sexual prowess has been satisfied...?" He fished around for a little more information.

"I realize you are talented in many areas."

He laughed, as she'd meant him to.

The impishness in her gaze faded. She touched his wrist in a way that felt like goodbye. Slowly met his eyes. "Seriously. I'm sorry if I took advantage of you."

He shrugged and caught her hand with his. "I think it was mutual."

She disengaged their palms, stepped back, all professional scandal manager. "In any case, it won't happen again."

His gaze drifted over her lazily. "You really

don't think so?" Because if it were up to him, it would.

Her conflicted attitude faded as fast as it had appeared. She walked out into the kitchen, poured herself a glass of milk. "I get that we had fun here, Garrett. But I have a job to do. That has to take precedence."

He helped himself to a bottle of water, took a long thirsty drink, before promising, "I won't interfere with that."

He could see she didn't believe him. But she had stopped trying to run away. Garrett decided to try another tack. He leaned back against the counter. "Did you ever see *When Harry Met Sally*?"

Hope stopped in mid-sip. "One of the greatest romantic comedies of all time? Ah, yeah, about a million times when I was growing up." She lounged opposite him, a curious expression on her face.

"Well, so did Sage."

Understanding dawned. "Which meant you watched it a lot, too."

Way too many times. Or so he'd thought then. Later, he had realized what valuable information the movie contained about the differences between the sexes when it came to dating and relationships.

"You know those little vignettes that were woven throughout, about how couples met each other?" he continued.

"And fell in love?" Finishing her milk, she sighed in wistful appreciation. "They were all so funny and unique. And real."

And she deserved even more than that. "Well, this is our story, Hope." He took her glass, put it aside and drew her back into his arms. "And one day soon, maybe even today, you'll look back and see our initial hookup was even more original than any of those."

She splayed her hands across his chest. "You're sure that's all this is? A hookup?"

He rubbed the pad of his thumb across the

softness of her cheek. "Would it make you feel better if it were?"

She hesitated, but just for a millisecond. "Between work and Max, it's really all I have room for in my life right now."

He could understand that. What she didn't know was that she wouldn't be this busy—or conflicted—forever. He lowered his mouth to hers, fibbed, "Then that's what it is."

And before she could argue further, he made love to her again.

HOPE NEVER MEANT to fall asleep. She meant to get up out of the bed after they'd made sweet, wonderful love the second time. But the next thing she knew late afternoon sunlight was streaming in through the windows and she heard her son gurgling happily.

She glanced at her watch. Realizing it had been a good seven hours since she had fed Max last, she threw back the covers, wrapped a sheet around herself and headed for her bedroom.

The port-a-crib was empty.

The laughter, however, continued. This time with Garrett joining in.

Hope exchanged the sheet for her robe and followed the sound.

Garrett was slouched on the big U-shaped bunkhouse sofa, his back to her, Max held upright against his chest. Plump little arms out in front of him, as if he were doing push-ups, Max was staring up at Garrett, enthralled.

"See here's the thing about women," Garrett was telling Max. "You always got to treat 'em right. I know, I know," he replied, after another spurt of baby talk from Max, "you think you're too young to be thinking about all this, but trust me, there will come a day, and that's all you'll be thinking about…"

Max gurgled again, then let out an astonishingly loud burp.

Hope couldn't help it, she laughed, right along with Garrett.

He turned in surprise. "Did we wake you?"

"I think the bigger question is," she murmured, joining him on the sofa, "why didn't you get me?" She nodded at the empty bottle of formula on the coffee table. "I would have fed him."

"I know. I thought it might be better for you to get some sleep."

Garrett was probably right, given the fact that her breasts still only felt half full. It would be at least another hour, if not more, before she was ready to nurse her son again.

She kissed the tuft of blond hair on the top of Max's head. Though normally he reached for Hope, insisting that his mommy hold him, this time her son seemed remarkably content just where he was. "How long has he been up?"

Garrett grinned as Max continued to do vertical baby push-ups against his chest. "A couple of hours."

Hope did a double take.

Garrett slanted her a glance. "He hasn't seemed to want to go back to sleep."

She wouldn't either, if Garrett were holding her like that in his big, strong arms and turning on the charm.

Hope snuggled closer, wanting to join in the fun. "What have you two been doing?"

"Well, first he had a bottle of formula, then a clean diaper change, then we went out back and sat on the glider for a while. But it got kind of hot, so we came in to the air conditioning. And we lay on a blanket on the floor for a while, and he showed me all his toys and rattles. And then we sat in a chair...and then you came in..."

"Wow."

"I know," Garrett acknowledged solemnly. "Max and I have had a very busy afternoon."

She peered at him facetiously. "You sure you don't want a job filling in for a British nanny on an emergency basis?"

Rubbing a hand across his freshly shaven jaw, he pretended to consider it. Finally he asked, with a teasing leer, "Does it come with fringe benefits?"

Hope groaned facetiously. She slapped a hand across her heart as if the mere idea were an insult. "Captain Lockhart!"

"Uh-oh, buddy." Garrett winked at Max. "She's using my rank and surname. Guess we better rein in the loose talk."

No kidding, Hope thought. Otherwise he'd have her back in bed with him before she knew what had happened.

Garrett turned to her, his mood as lively as her son's.

Hope could see Garrett had already had a shower and dressed in clean clothes. Suddenly, she yearned for the same. "I hate to ask…"

He read her mind. "Take your time."

Hope tried not to wonder what would happen if Garrett continued being this good with Max, and this sexy and appealing, and ultraprotective. "You sure?"

"Yep. I could use the practice."

Once again caught unawares, Hope queried, "For…?"

Garrett shrugged happily. "When I have kids."

SEVERAL HOURS LATER, her shower completed—and vastly enjoyed—numerous media requests and inquiries regarding the scandal all answered and Max down for another nap, Hope joined Garrett in the kitchen, where he was already making dinner.

She watched him prick two russet potatoes with a fork, coat them with olive oil and sea salt and wrap them in foil. "Did you mean what you said about wanting a family?"

"It's why I haven't already accepted the job at Walter Reed in Bethesda."

She took a seat on the other side of the breakfast bar. "Because it means reenlisting."

He slid the potatoes into the oven to bake. "And reenlisting means my orders could change at any time. I'd be sent where they need me. As a single guy, with no responsibilities to anyone other than myself, I've been happy to comply. As a family man, I'd want more control."

Hope had never realized just how tantalizing it was to see a man in the kitchen—until now.

Or just how much she had come to enjoy just being with him. "Is that why you haven't married? Because you were on active-duty military?"

"Actually, I was going to get married a few years ago."

Something in her went very still.

It shouldn't have been a surprise. And yet it was. "What happened?"

Garrett poured olive oil and lime juice into a glass baking dish then chopped up fresh oregano, garlic and cilantro and added them, as well. A sprinkling of dried chili powder and cumin followed.

"I discovered there are two kinds of women who don't mind their mates being away for long periods of time." He paused to look her in the eye. "Those who are truly devoted to their men and understand the patriotic need to serve one's country. And those who want the respectability and stability of an official relationship, while still enjoying plenty of time and freedom to pursue other romantic interests."

Ouch.

The sting of betrayal came and went in his eyes.

Heart going out to him, she said, "I'm guessing your engagement fell into the latter category."

He added a slab of flank steak to the aromatic marinade in the glass dish. "You would guess right." He turned to wash his hands.

"Care to be more specific?"

His shoulders tensed. "My ex is Leanne Sharp."

"Chief of staff of Congressman Jared Thiessen?"

His eyes narrowed. "You know her?"

"I know of her." She was a gorgeous, ambitious Southern belle, from a very well-connected and wealthy Dallas family. Just imagining her with Garrett conjured up a stab of jealousy, which was, Hope knew, completely uncalled for. Whatever they had shared was a one-time thing.

"In my previous job I had a lot of dealings with politicians."

His mouth thinned. "Thiessen?"

"One of his colleagues—Len Miller—had a pretty messy divorce. We enlisted Thiessen, who's public reputation is stellar, to vouch for my client's trustworthiness."

Garrett's expression darkened. "I remember that. You-all spun Miller's infidelity as a domestic dispute, a symptom of the problems in the Miller marriage, instead of the problem."

Which had been true, as far as Hope could discern, anyway. "Len Miller still lost his next election, but I think that had more to do with his voting record, or lack thereof, than his infidelity."

Garrett chuckled grimly, shook his head.

Hope wanted to be let in on the joke. "What?"

His mouth tightening, Garrett turned to get a beer from the fridge. He twisted off the cap, took a swig. "I just find it ironic that you would use *Jared Thiessen* as a moral barometer and character reference."

"Why?" Hope got up to help herself to another glass of milk. Deciding to live dangerously, she stirred some chocolate syrup into it. "Jared's got a great reputation as a family man. Plus, he has won eight straight elections."

Garrett went still.

Hope waited.

Finally, eyes level, he said, "Congressman Jared Thiessen is the love of Leanne's life. She only got involved with me as cover for her affair with him."

Oh, my God. Hope shared his devastation. "How did you find out?"

Garrett began to slice zucchini and yellow squash. "Usual way. Stumbled on some racy texts on Leanne's phone when she asked me to look up our dinner reservations while she put on her makeup."

"That must have been unpleasant." Not to mention careless on his ex's part.

"You'd think that would have been rock bottom." He reached for a couple of carrots and sliced them on the diagonal, added them to the sauté pan.

"It wasn't?"

He turned the heat up beneath the veggies. "She asked me to lie about why we broke up."

"And did you?"

Garrett's face remained implacable. "I saw no reason to hurt his wife and kids. They were innocent and he was a public figure. Had it become known, it would have been all over the news, and the kids would have been devastated."

"So you kept quiet."

Garrett inhaled sharply. "Reluctantly, but yeah."

"Which is why you hate scandal management."

He pinned her with his hard blue gaze. "I hate any hiding of the truth."

HOPE UNDERSTOOD. HE'D BEEN caught in an impossible situation. Still was, in certain respects. His honor was one of the things she loved most about him. "I'm sorry you went through all that."

He snorted in derision. "Live and learn."

Needing to comfort him, she closed the distance between them. Started to reach for him. A knock sounded at the door.

Hope sighed.

He lifted a brow. "Expecting someone?"

"No. Although Lucille texted me earlier and said your brothers might drop by later."

"Doubtful," Garrett said. "At least for tonight. I heard from them, too. Wyatt has a mare in extended labor. Chance is in the midst of re-homing a couple of his prime bulls."

Hope put her hands on her hips. "Well, then."

"I know." Garrett grinned, his usual good humor returning as he strode for the bunkhouse entrance. "I just don't rate." He opened the door.

Darcy Dunlop stood on the other side, a covered dish in hand, a pinched look on her thin face. "Is this a bad time?"

"Not at all." Immediately compassionate, Garrett ushered her in.

Hope smiled. "Hi, Darcy."

"Hi."

"Tank okay?" Garrett asked.

"That's why I came over. To talk to you and give you this." She took the top off the most delicious-looking berry crisp Hope had ever seen. "As a thank-you for helping us out the other night."

"No problem." Garrett looked past her. "I see you got your pickup running again."

"Yeah," Darcy replied nervously. "Smitty's repair shop does a great job."

Garrett gestured for her to have a seat at the counter. "So, what's going on?"

"Tank has stopped going to his physical therapy sessions in town. He was hit or miss before, but this week he's refusing to go at all."

Garrett warned, "He's not going to regain full range of motion with that leg unless he does the work."

"I know," Darcy said sadly. "The physical therapists have all told him that."

"Then...?"

"I think he's starting to give up on thinking things are ever going to get better," Darcy admitted hoarsely. "Anyway, I was wondering, do you think you could come by and talk to him? You were able to make him see reason the other night..." Darcy broke off, tearing up. "If you could do it again..."

"Where is Tank now?" Garrett asked gently.

"Home. His parents went to visit family so we'd have the house to ourselves for a week or so. They thought it would help. But so far, it's just not." Her lower lip trembling, she slid off the stool and backed up. "But I can see I'm interrupting you-all's dinner plans. I should have called first."

If there was one thing Hope knew, it was a

person in distress. Crises like this called for immediate action. She looked at Garrett, letting
him know with a glance their evening together
could wait. He nodded in wordless agreement.
Putting a big arm around Darcy's thin shoulders, he said, "Why don't we go see Tank right
now."

"You're s-s-sure?"

Garrett nodded.

"Actually," Hope said, "it's a really good
time."

Thanks, Garrett mouthed.

He got out the keys for his pickup truck and
patted his cell phone. "Call me if you need anything."

She noted he did not promise when he'd be
back.

"Will do." She flashed another smile.

Garrett and Darcy left.

Hope finished sautéing the veggies, grilled
the marinated flank steak and removed the perfectly baked potatoes from the oven. Although

she would have liked to wait for Garrett to return to eat, the fact that she was nursing and still trying to get her milk supply back up dictated otherwise.

So she ate in silence.

Did the dishes.

Nursed Max when he woke up and gave him his evening bath.

Then nursed him a little more for good measure before putting him back to sleep.

And still no Garrett.

She had just finished brushing her teeth and getting ready for bed when she heard the bunkhouse door open and close. She walked out, clad in a pair of pink floral pajamas.

Garrett's dark hair was rumpled, as if he'd been running his hands through it. The faint shadow of an evening beard lined his jaw, circles of fatigue rimmed his eyes.

Resisting the urge to admit how much she had missed him and launch herself into his arms, she asked casually, "Everything okay?"

He sank down on the middle of the sofa, draped both arms across the back, and stretched his long, jeans-clad legs out in front of him. "I talked Tank into going back to PT."

Hope perched in the corner next to him. "Good for you. That will help."

He took her hand in his. Tingles sparked and spread outward, through not just her arm but her entire body.

He smiled. "Physical activity always does."

Feeling somehow unbearably restless, she disengaged their palms and stood. She strode into the kitchen, picked up a near-empty glass off the counter, drained it and set it in the dishwasher. "Did you eat?"

He studied her as she shut the dishwasher door with a snap. Slowly he got to his feet. "Darcy fixed something for both of us."

"Good."

He came closer. Moved around the counter to face her. "Sorry I missed dinner."

The cooking area suddenly seemed awfully

small. She crossed her arms in front of her and said seriously, "This was important." Helping people always was.

He nodded. The casual affection in his gaze deepened. He gave her lips a long, thorough once-over. "Not sure most women would understand that."

Oh, heavens, she wanted him to kiss her again. More than that, actually. Hope stepped back. One palm pressed to her head, the other to her waist, she preened like a 1940s pinup girl. "I thought I made it clear." For added emphasis, she tossed her hair, too. "I'm not most women."

Amusement tugged at the corners of his lips. "You might have, at that." He wrapped his brawny arms around her, nuzzled her temple. "Max okay?"

Excitement roared through her and her breath hitched. "He is."

His lips blazed a trail across her cheek. "That's good to hear."

"It is."

He found the sensitive spot behind her ear. Her knees went wobbly.

Hope stopped him, her hands splayed on his chest. The practical side of her knew this was a bad idea. This morning's activities had been reckless enough. She swallowed, determined to enforce at least some limits. "You know this is private."

He stepped back slightly, hands down. "Between the two of us? Of course."

"And only temporary."

Looking impossibly handsome and determined in the muted light of the bunkhouse kitchen, he asked, ever so softly, "Is it?"

Their eyes met, held for several long moments. Her heart pounded and her body pulsed with yearning. "You're headed off to Walter Reed..." Which was much too far away from Dallas.

He stepped forward and closed the distance between them, sending an even higher level of reckless excitement pumping through her veins. "Not necessarily," he said with a shrug. "And definitely not yet."

Chapter Eight

Garrett planted a hand on the counter on either side of Hope and leaned in close enough that she could see the passion gleaming in his eyes. "I realized something today," he told her soberly. "The soldiers most in need are the veterans who are no longer in the military. More has to be done for them."

She wished he didn't look so good, even in jeans, a black cotton polo and boots. She lounged back against the counter, trying not to feel his body heat. "There are existing organizations. Wounded Warriors, for one…"

His gaze roving her upturned face. "And they do a great job. No question. But they can't be everywhere." Lifting his hands, he moved away from her, opened up the fridge and pulled out a beer. "Right now, Laramie County has a growing population of former soldiers. Many aren't physically wounded. But all of them could benefit from more readily available services."

She watched him twist off the cap. Wished she could join him. She poured herself another glass of milk, instead. "Like support groups?"

He toasted her wordlessly. "And physical therapy, taken alongside other vets. Job training. Assistance making the transition into civilian life." He smiled at the intent way she was listening to his plans. "Bess Monroe is doing a great thing in starting West Texas Warrior Assistance. But the Lockhart Foundation really let her down." He shook his head in dissatisfaction. "I'm going to fix that."

She loved it when he was on a mission.

"Singlehandedly?"

Mischievously, he waggled his brow. "I have sway with the board of directors."

Unable to do anything but laugh, Hope quipped in return, "So I've heard." His family did seem to adore him.

She was beginning to adore him.

Especially when he looked at her as if she was the most beautiful, desirable woman on Earth.

He reached up to tuck a strand of hair behind her ear, gazing at her with the same smitten look she had seen other men give their wives in the maternity ward.

"Seriously, I'm going to make sure the dream becomes a reality for the people here in Laramie County, sooner rather than later."

She believed him. Just as she believed he was wildly attracted to her—for the time being. But she had to ask, "How?"

Another lift of his impossibly wide shoulders.

"That I haven't quite figured out yet, but I'm working on it."

For a moment, her optimism rose, while her ability to censor her questions failed—big time.

A veil dropped over his emotions. His lips curved ruefully, as if to say, *Let's not get ahead of ourselves.*

Which, really, was what she should have expected, Hope reminded herself. She had no more business weighing in on his career decisions than anyone else in his family.

This was something he had to decide for himself.

"I have a few weeks left, before I have to give the army an answer."

Which begged her next question. Did he know what it was going to be? The maddeningly implacable look on his face gave her no clue.

"So, at least temporarily, I can stay right here in Texas."

Temporarily being the operative word. Hope pushed aside her selfishness. "Well, that's good," she murmured, forcing a smile. "I'm sure your very philanthropic mother will be really proud of you." As would his whole family.

His sexy grin widened. He put his quarter-finished beer aside, lowered his head and scored his thumb across her bottom lip. "What about you? Are you proud of me?"

A thrill soared through her. Hope caught her breath.

He touched his lips lightly to hers in an angel-soft kiss. Paused long enough to undo the butterfly clip on the back of her head. "'Cause if I'm going to get a gold star for good behavior," he rasped, seductively combing his fingers through the tumbling strands of her hair, "I'd sure like to get it from you."

COMMON SENSE HAD told Hope they shouldn't be doing this again. At least, not while she was still working for his family foundation.

But for now, she thought, as they kissed their way to his bedroom once again, she couldn't think about anything but the closeness she felt whenever she was with him. What was one more moment in time, one more blissful, passion-filled night, except an interlude to be grateful for? And she *was* grateful for the feel of his strong arms around her as he disrobed her, and then himself, and stretched out alongside her on the bed.

Sliding one arm beneath her shoulders, he lifted her head to his. He kissed her temple, jaw, throat. "Have I told you how much I like it when you catch your breath and look at me like that?" He caressed his way down her body, then returned to her mouth and kissed her again, deeply and provocatively this time, the kiss a melding of heat and need. "As if you can't help but want me as much as I want you."

Hope felt treasured in that special man–woman way. To the point that, if she hadn't known better, she would have thought she had finally found the soul mate she had been searching for her entire life.

Maybe love wasn't involved here, but everything else that mattered was present. Which made her feel as if their coming together was a step toward something unconventional—and yet wonderful.

His lips closed over the tips of her breasts. Laved delicately. Sensation warred with the thrill of possession, as he kissed his way lower, across her ribs, her navel, hips. Lower still, he traced the insides of her thighs to the dampness within. His ministrations felt incredibly good, incredibly right. Hope closed her eyes, clung to him and surrendered all the more. The eroticism of his touch flowed over her in hot, exciting waves. Trembling from head to toe at the long, sensual strokes of his tongue and the soothing feel of his lips, she caught his head in her hands and tangled her fingers in his hair. Until, at last, her head fell back; her body shuddered with pleasure. Yearning spiraled deep inside her. And then she came apart in his hands.

He held her through the aftershocks.

"My turn," she teased.

Wanting to take the lead, she shifted positions, tracing the bunched muscles and hot satiny skin, learning the mysteries of him, just as he had come to know hers. Her hair brushed over his ripped abdomen and hard, muscular thighs. Inhaling the tantalizing masculine scent of him, she teased, tormented and pleased. Tasted the salt of his perspiration and the familiar sweetness of his skin. Aware she had never felt so alive, so safe and treasured and loved, she focused on one seductive plateau after another, until he could not help but groan.

Trembling, he reached for her. He shifted her upward, across his body, then over, onto her back.

The warmth and strength of his body engulfed her. She wound her arms around his neck and opened herself up to him, to the sensation of being taken. He lifted her with one hand and then they were one. All was lost in the blazing hot passion and the overwhelming need.

Adrenaline rushed. Pleasure spiraled. And in the sweet blissful satisfaction that followed, Hope realized that the notion that she might one day have an adoring husband, in addition to her amazing little boy, and a loving family of her own, was not so far-fetched, after all.

EARLY THE NEXT AFTERNOON, Garrett's only sister breezed through the bunkhouse door. Hope blinked in surprise. "Sage?" This was certainly unexpected!

Garrett came in to stand beside Hope, Max snuggled drowsily in his arms. He bussed the top of his little sister's head. "What are you doing here, little sis?"

Sage set her overnight bag down. "Mom asked me to fly in first thing and meet you all at the ranch. I wanted wheels of my own so I'd have maximum flexibility to come and go as needed, so I rented a car at the San Angelo airport."

"Mom's not here yet?" Chance walked in.

"Actually, she is." Wyatt joined them, with a

look over his shoulder at the limo stopping in front of the bunkhouse porch.

Both brothers turned back to Sage and Garrett. "What's going on?" Chance and Wyatt asked in unison.

"No clue," Garrett said.

That made two of them, Hope thought with a twinge of anxiety.

Lucille breezed in. Clad in her usual outfit— a silk-and-linen sheath and heels, trademark pearls around her neck, her hair and makeup expertly done—she managed to look both exceedingly well-groomed and as if she had the entire world sitting on her shoulders.

She was followed by Adelaide Smythe.

Wyatt froze at the sight of Adelaide right behind Lucille. His gaze dropped to Adelaide's rounded tummy and turned dark, then he looked away entirely.

That was weird, Hope thought, wondering what was going on between those two to cause such tension…

Inhaling, Lucille squared her shoulders. "Adelaide and I wanted to talk to you all at once." She paused to make eye contact with everyone in the room. "And we wanted to do it in person."

Which meant, Hope thought, the two women had figured out something…and she had a sinking feeling it had something to do with the annual fly-fishing trip Paul Smythe had secretly skipped this year. The trip he might have taken instead with Mirabelle Fanning.

"We need to have a board meeting," Lucille said, taking her place at the head of the long plank table. "So everyone get what you need to be comfortable, and then have a seat."

Five minutes later, Max was in his port-a-crib, snoozing away, and everyone was gathered around the table, coffee or sparkling water in front of them.

Lucille stood at the head of the table, practically buzzing with nerves. "There is no easy way to tell you this, so I'm just going to say it.

Twenty-five million dollars, or half of the foundation's funds, have been embezzled."

The matriarch waited for the reaction to subside.

"All the checks that were supposed to go to the nonprofit organizations we were supporting apparently had the 'pay to the order of' information changed, as soon as I signed them."

Another deathly silence fell.

"How is that possible?" Sage asked, upset.

Lucille turned to the forensic accountant.

Face pale, Adelaide explained grimly, "There's a very sophisticated Wite-Out that thieves use on checks that allows them to change whatever they want—the date, the amount, who the money is going to—and still keep the authentic signature of the account holder. On all of the checks from the foundation, only the beneficiary of the check was changed." She swallowed hard. "For instance, Metroplex Pet Rescue became Metroplex Pet Rescue Inc. Meals for Seniors became Meals for Seniors In Need.

Preschoolers Read! became Dallas Preschoolers Read! The amounts and dates all stayed exactly the same, which allowed the fraud to go undetected in the Lockhart Foundation ledgers for nearly a year."

"And your father never once caught on to this?" Wyatt asked skeptically.

Hope was surprised, too. From everything she'd heard, she had deduced that Paul Smythe was a very smart man.

Adelaide's voice cracked. "My father did the embezzling."

For a moment, everyone could only stare. Adelaide drew a deep breath, blinking back tears. "Believe me, I didn't want to believe it, either," she said hoarsely.

"Nor did I." Lucille opened up a file and passed around copies of the canceled checks, provided to them by the bank. "But there's no question as to what happened. Paul Smythe's signature is on the back of every single cashed check."

Adelaide nodded sadly. "Lucille and I visited all of the banks yesterday. The various financial institutions where the money was supposed to have been deposited. And wasn't. And the bank where my father used his position as CFO to open accounts in both the fake charities' and the Lockhart Foundation's names, so he could move the money around very easily."

Wyatt shrugged. "Well, if we know all that, can't we get the money back?"

Lucille shook her head.

"It's already been transferred out of the country," Adelaide explained unhappily. "He moved it to a bank in a country that has a no money-tracking agreement with the United States. And then he withdrew all the funds yesterday."

Another tense silence fell.

"Did he do this alone?" Chance said finally.

Adelaide grimaced. "Mirabelle Fanning was a VP at the bank where all the fraud occurred. She managed all the transactions and helped my father open all the bogus accounts. She took a long-planned early retirement last week. We assume they are together."

"Has your father contacted you?" Sage asked quietly, as sympathetic toward her old friend as she was distraught over what had just happened to their family charity.

"He texted me this morning. Said, 'I left the trail so no one else at the foundation would be blamed. Don't bother to look further for the money or me—you'll never find either.' I tried calling him, but his cell phone provider said the account was canceled right after that message was sent. I'm sure he took the battery out and destroyed the phone so there would be no tracking it, either."

"Have you reported all this to the police?" Chance asked.

"No," his mother retorted. "And I don't plan to until after I've personally made this right, visiting every charity in person and paying what is due to them."

"Are we going to have enough money to do

that?" Garrett asked, no doubt thinking about the local group that still needed so much help.

Adelaide consulted her computer. "For all but West Texas Warrior Assistance. There, the foundation is going to have to give them what was offered in writing, five thousand dollars, instead of the five hundred thousand that Lucille wanted to give them."

Garrett looked extremely unhappy about that. Hope felt the same. She also knew there was little else that could be done, at least for now.

"And then what?" Sage bit out.

Lucille paused. "I need to talk to Hope in private about that."

"ARE YOU DOING OKAY?" Hope asked Lucille, as the two set out for a walk. The afternoon was hot, but overcast. A stiff breeze blew across the rolling plains.

The older woman adjusted her wide-brimmed straw hat. "I'll be better when I've made my apology and compensation tour."

"Would you like me to go with you?"

"No. I need to handle this alone. Although both Adelaide and Sage have promised to be nearby throughout, for moral support. What I want from you is what we initially discussed."

"A strategic response to what has happened."

"I want to go public as soon as all the reparations are made and we talk to the police."

"There's a chance it could come out before then," Hope warned, but for the moment she let it go. Lucille had enough to do just getting through the humiliating next phase. "What's the chance the money will be recovered?"

"Given the extremely clever way Paul went about all this?" Lucille drew an aggrieved breath. "Next to none."

"I'm sorry about that," Hope said softly.

Lucille turned her attention to the unkempt family ranch land. Although the area next to the bunkhouse had been kept up, the rest of it had not. She sighed. "I should not have been so trusting, old family friend or not."

Hope comforted the older woman the best she could. "Once people know what has happened, and I'll make sure they do, your family will not just be forgiven, you'll all be revered for the upstanding members of society that you are."

"I trust you to be able to handle that."

"And I will," Hope promised.

Lucille turned to look at Hope and said, "It's your ability to convince Garrett to stay in Texas and go along with our contingency plan— should the worst happen and it becomes necessary—that really worries me."

The truth was, it worried Hope, too. When it came to preserving appearances, and/or doing something just because it would look good to outsiders, Garrett had not exactly proved cooperative thus far.

"Have you been able to speak to him yet?"

Guilt flowing through her, Hope shook her head.

Lucille studied her a long moment, which made Hope wonder what the woman sensed.

Something, clearly. "Any particular reason why not?" Lucille asked.

Because I was too busy leaning on his big, strong shoulders and making love with him, Hope thought. She drew a deep breath. "I just haven't found the right time to bring it up."

"Laying the groundwork?"

"Trying to develop a rapport."

Lucille considered that. "Makes sense."

Did it?

Up until now, Hope hadn't considered her attraction to Garrett would make it impossible for her to do her job well. But that was exactly what was happening.

Fortunately, she could fix that. "I'll find the right way to broach it with him, if and when the time comes," she reassured Lucille.

She was still hoping it wouldn't, because the Lockharts had been through enough.

"See that you do," Lucille said. "Because the future of the foundation and our family are depending on both of you."

AN HOUR LATER, Sage and Adelaide had departed for Dallas. Chance and Wyatt had also gone back to their ranches—but not before Garrett asked them for a favor that he hoped would be well received by Tank and his wife.

In the meantime, he needed to find out what was going on with Hope. She hadn't looked him in the eye since she had left the emergency board meeting and gone off to confer with Lucille in private. "What were you and my mother talking about for so long?" Garrett asked.

Hope carried her laptop over to the table and powered it on. "Plans to rehabilitate the foundation's reputation. How and when we're going to announce our findings. What comes next, once all previous commitments have been met."

He sat down opposite her at the table and kicked back in a captain's chair. "What does come next—especially if half the money is gone? Has my mom told you what her plans are?" She hadn't told any of them.

Hope paused. *A-ha*, Garrett thought. She did know something she was reluctant to share.

Finally she looked up from the computer screen. Her green eyes lasered into his. "There are too many variables right now to figure that out. What we do know is that anything could happen, and most of it will likely be extremely damaging, at least initially. Which is why I'm staying behind to put together a film that will introduce your mother to the public."

Hope wasn't easy to read when she was in work mode. "What do you mean? My mother's been a fixture on the Dallas social and philanthropic scenes for years."

Hope made a note on the pad next to her, then tucked the pen behind her ear. She leaned back in her chair. "But that's all they know about her, Garrett. What they see in news clips on TV or in the papers." She paused to let her words sink in. "They see photos of Lucille stepping out of a limousine, or pictures of her gorgeous mansion in Dallas. They don't know how the family charity came about, or why she and your father wanted to do this in the first place."

Hope shook her head in mute frustration.

"They don't know where your mother and father grew up, or how life was for them in the beginning. Or how generous and loving your mother is—deep down." She leaned forward urgently. "We need to shed light on that so people understand that none of this was deliberate, that Lucille's heart was, and still is, in the right place."

"So your primary goal remains...?"

She regarded him stoically. "To do what I was hired to do and save the foundation first."

Which meant what, exactly? Garrett wondered, growing alarmed. His family and his mother were second? All he knew for sure was that once again Hope wasn't quite meeting his eyes. Never a good sign. He stood, shoving the chair back so abruptly it scraped across the wood floor. He stood, legs braced apart, hands on the table in front of him. "Tell me you're not planning to throw my mother under the bus."

"The media and gossip sites have already done that." He opened his mouth to argue, but she lifted a staying hand. "However, at the end of the day, the only people who should bear the brunt of the blame for this are CFO Paul Smythe and banking VP Mirabelle Fanning. Before all that information is made public, though, we have a lot to do. Which is why," Hope persisted, all kick-butt scandal management expert once again, "I need the *complete* cooperation of you and your brothers for the next few days."

FOR GARRETT, THAT started with a trip to town to meet with Bess Monroe the following morning. To say the West Texas Warrior Assistance organizer had mixed feelings about receiving a check for only five thousand—instead of the agreed-upon five hundred thousand—dollars was an understatement. So Garrett did what he could to make the situation better, which in his view wasn't nearly enough. He stopped by the grocery store, got plenty of milk for Hope and enough food for a few more days, then headed back to the Circle H.

Hope had Max in her arms, her phone headset on. She was pacing back and forth on the porch, trying to keep Max entertained while she spoke.

"...That's right. It's not common knowledge... Because Lucille Lockhart doesn't want anyone to know. But I know how fair you are in your reporting, and I thought you should be aware... As we speak! Yes, the checks are going out... No. Lucille doesn't want to formally announce until every organization has been paid... Of course. I think a sit-down could be arranged here at the family ranch. Maybe the day after tomorrow?... Thanks. You, too."

Hope swung around to see him standing there. A guilty flush crossed her face.

He had only one thing to say to her.

"What's going on, Hope?"

Chapter Nine

Garrett set the groceries on the kitchen counter with a thud. He had shaved before going into town, and the tantalizing fragrance of his after-shave still clung to his jaw. His dark hair was tousled. He had on worn jeans and an untucked dark blue shirt that brought out the intense sea blue of his eyes. "I thought you weren't going to throw my mother to the wolves."

Determined not to put herself in an emotion-ally vulnerable position with him, especially when it came to the foundation work, she said, "I'm not."

He strode closer, clearly trying to intimidate her. "Then?"

She feigned immunity to his disapproval. "Lucille called while you were out. Half an hour ago, the foundation's attorney received a demand letter from a lawyer representing fifteen of the charities." Keeping her voice low, she shifted Max a little higher in her arms so he could look out over her shoulder. "They're threatening to sue."

Garrett's gaze darkened as the information sank in.

"Apparently, it's going to be an exclusive for KTWX on the eleven o'clock news. Which is why I called my contact at rival KMVU, and told her the promised payments had been going out all afternoon at the foundation offices, and would be completed by 5:00 p.m. tomorrow."

"And my mother approved this."

"I spoke with her at length, while you were in

town. She understands that we have to make it clear she was doing the right thing *before* she received the threatening demand letter. Otherwise it looks as if she only followed through because she was facing legal action. Which brings me to the next thing we need to discuss…the personal check you wrote to West Texas Warrior Assistance."

As she moved closer, Max reached out and put a tiny fist in the short sleeve of Garrett's shirt. Ignoring the tender look he threw her son, Hope swallowed through the dryness of her throat and prodded, "In addition to the five thousand dollar check you were to deliver from the foundation."

His expression quickly became veiled. He squinted. "How did you know about that?"

Easy. "Bess Monroe wrote your mother an email, thanking her and citing your generosity. Your mom was impressed, by the way."

So was she.

"Don't make a big deal out of it," he told her

gruffly. "And don't even think about putting what I did in any press release."

Luckily she hadn't thus far. Mostly because she had wanted to speak with him first and find out what had prompted him to be so generous, when she knew from Lucille that he and his siblings lived only on what they were each able to bring in, which in his case was his military salary. She watched as Max fisted his other hand in Garrett's shirt. "Why not?" Figuring she might as well let Max have what he wanted, she transferred her little boy to Garrett's waiting arms.

"Because it's not really charity if anyone knows about it." Despite the tension hovering between them, Garrett flashed a heart-melting grin at the baby cuddled against his chest. "It's grandstanding for attention."

Tenderness drifted through Hope at the sight of her son's blond head nestled against Garrett's chest. "My grandmother used to say that."

"It's true."

Hope began putting groceries away. "That sentiment must put you at odds with the new family business."

Garrett lounged against the counter. "I think what my father and mother wanted to do was great."

Spying an opening for the job Lucille wanted her to do, Hope said offhandedly, "Ever thought of joining the foundation? Maybe as the new CEO?"

His brows lowered like thunderclaps over his gorgeous blue eyes. "No."

"It could help." She stood on tiptoe to put the cereal on the appropriate pantry shelf.

She felt his glance rove her bare legs, the trim lines of her skirt, blouse. "Ask Adelaide."

Her body warmed everywhere his eyes had touched. Hitching in a breath, Hope worked to keep her mind on the problem at hand. "Can't. Optics."

His gaze locked on hers. "Sins of the father...?"

"Something like that," she answered, flushing self-consciously. "It's best, at least for now, that Adelaide stay well in the background of any story on this. The last thing she needs when pregnant with twins, and absorbing her father's betrayal, is to be hounded by the press."

"True."

"So, back to the sit-down your mother is going to do here the day after tomorrow. The bunkhouse is great. We can film in here, but we'll also be taking a tour of the land, and we can't have the ranch looking so unkempt overall."

"It's already been taken care of," he informed her. "Chance and Wyatt are bringing over their farm tractors first thing in the morning. Tank and a couple other rehabbing vets are going to mow all the grass and pastures. They need the work and we need it done."

Wow. He was really on the ball. "Does Bess Monroe know this, too?"

Garrett grimaced. "I didn't mention it. I'd appreciate it if you didn't make a big deal out of it, either. These guys have had their manhoods

wrecked by their injuries. They don't need anyone painting them as charity cases, because
they're not."

"Got it, Captain."

Looking relieved, he turned Max around so
his diapered bottom was resting on Garrett's
forearm, his back to Garrett's chest. His tiny
little hands curled around the wrist stabilizing
his middle.

Max blinked at Hope. Smiled.

She smiled back at her son.

"Are you done working for the evening?"

Hope shook her head. "As soon as I nurse
Max again and get him down for the evening,
I'm going to work on the practice Q&A for your
mom. She has to rehearse for the TV interview."

Garrett's gaze narrowed skeptically. But for
once he had no ready remark.

"It will be much easier for her if she feels prepared," Hope explained.

He quirked his brow. "And to do that…?"

"I'll write the questions Lucille's liable to be

asked and then print out the answers she needs to memorize."

"Sure you don't need to make up some cue cards for her, too?"

Here at last was the sardonic man she had met on the plane. "That will come later."

He did a double take. "I was kidding."

"I'm not." Deciding she had been ensnared in Garrett's keen blue gaze far too long, Hope turned away. His increasing discontent was not her problem when she had a job to do. "We're also going to make a short, interview-style video of our own to put up on YouTube and the foundation website. That way we'll be able to make sure that everything that needs to get said will get said, in exactly the way it should be."

"And here I thought the overly scripted part of my family's life was over," he muttered. He looked at her long and hard. Loathing the suggestion she was somehow creating a fake tableau, she stared right back.

He exhaled roughly. "Guess not."

Carefully he transferred Max to her, spun around and walked out the door.

AN HOUR LATER, Garrett met his brother Chance at the office building he owned. His younger brother elbowed him in the ribs. "I thought you'd be making time with Hope tonight."

Garrett flipped him off. "Funny."

Chance needled him with a long look. "Sure seemed to be something happening between the two of you earlier today."

There had been. Until Hope had gone back to manipulating events to ensure the outcome she was determined to have.

Then something in Garrett had gone cold.

The last thing he wanted was to spend more of his life worried about how everything appeared on the surface, rather than what should be going on deep inside. He'd had enough of that in his childhood and when he was engaged. He wasn't going down that road again. Not professionally. And definitely not personally.

Garrett unlocked the door and strolled inside. "Next thing I know you'll be saying we were communicating without words."

Chuckling, Chance joined him in the small, outdated lobby. "Weren't you?"

"Keep it up and I'll tell you where you can put your asinine observations." Garrett switched on the lights.

Chance laughed all the more. When Garrett declined to join in, his younger brother finally slipped into general contractor mode. "So, what were you thinking of doing here?"

Garrett was surprised to hear himself say, "Gutting it and renovating it instead of selling it, as is, for pennies on the dollar."

"Keep going." Although he made his living raising and investing in rodeo bulls, Chance still earned money on the side, the way he had before he'd gotten into ranching, by doing home repairs and remodeling work.

"I want to take the elevators out of the center of the building and move them over to one side.

Have two of them, instead of three. And make them look like the freight elevators you have in lofts, with a cage door on the front."

Chance made notes. "It could be done. What else?"

"I'd like the first floor to be completely open. On the second and third floors, I'd like to have four private offices and a larger meeting room."

Chance looked up. "I'm assuming you already have a tenant in mind."

Which was, Garrett knew, in some respects even crazier for someone who wanted to cut ties with his past in Texas. Being careful to keep a poker face, he nodded. "I know some people who might be interested, if the work was done in advance. So can you get me an estimate?"

"Sure thing. What are you going to do about the Victorian?"

Another dilemma. One he hadn't expected. Garrett said gruffly, "I have to clean it up before I can do anything with it."

Chance's gaze narrowed thoughtfully. "And then…?"

Garrett rubbed the tense muscles in his neck. "Still thinking."

"Might not hurt to keep it for a while. As a home base, for when you visit."

And remember how Hope's eyes had lit up in wonder and delight the first time she walked through it with him?

Tensing, Garrett said, "Or not."

"Have you had any offers on that?"

"Just a call from Molly Griffin, that local interior designer and general contractor. She offered to redo it for me, if I wanted to make a little money on it."

Chance groaned. He scrubbed a hand over his face. "Do us both a favor and don't listen to Molly Griffin."

"Do I detect a little emotion there, brother?" Now this was interesting…

Chance scowled. "Just take my advice."

"Why?"

Another grimace. "Because she's a social-climbing pain in the ass."

Ah. Garrett shook his head at Chance. "Well, so long as you like her, then..."

"I. Don't."

"Now who doth protest too much?"

This time, Chance flipped *him* off. Garrett laughed despite himself as the two brothers walked out together.

"By the way, that was a pretty nice thing you did for the West Texas Warrior Assistance program," Chance said, when they reached their pickup trucks.

Garrett bit down on a string of oaths. Was nothing private around here? "How did you hear about it?"

His baby brother grinned and slapped his shoulder amiably. "In Laramie County, good news travels fast."

THE LIGHTS WERE on in the Circle H bunkhouse when Garrett turned the borrowed pickup into the driveway around 11:00 p.m. The blinds were pulled.

Inside, Hope was clad in a pair of thigh-length white cotton shorts that showed off her long legs to perfection and a loose-fitting pink cotton camp shirt. The sleeves were rolled up past her elbows. Her feet were bare. A blue cotton burp cloth had been thrown over one shoulder and Max had both his fists resting on her shoulder. Wide awake, with milk bubbles on his lips, he was looking around. He smiled when he caught sight of Garrett and bobbed his sturdy little body up and down excitedly.

Hope turned, a welcoming smile on her face.

If she was still piqued from their slight tiff earlier, Garrett observed, she wasn't showing it as she patted her son's back, nuzzling his blond head.

To his surprise, he found his irritation with Hope gone, too. The time-out from each other had helped. So had the realization that in a temporary hookup, which was what Hope kept insisting this was, each individual's values didn't have to line up the way they would in a successful permanent arrangement. In a fling, all that mattered was for a couple to have fun hanging out together, and they did, and have an even better time in bed. Which was also where they really clicked.

Work never factored into it.

Nor did their long-term wants, needs and expectations.

So there was no reason they couldn't continue to enjoy each other's company in the short amount of time they had left at the ranch.

Hope glanced at Garrett, admitting ruefully, "I think Max expects rocking up and down like this will actually launch him where he wants to go."

It certainly appeared that way, Garrett thought with amusement as he crossed the room to their side.

Max pushed up harder.

Hope's smile widened. "Do you mind holding him for a second? I'm trying to warm his bottle for him."

"Sure."

No sooner had Garrett shifted Max onto his shoulder than a loud burst of air escaped. Hope wrinkled her nose at the odor of digesting milk.

"Or maybe not..." she said. "Given what he's about to do."

The smell emanating from the diaper area told the whole story. He slanted her a glance. "You think I'm afraid of a little poop?"

She propped her hands on her hips. Lifted her chin. "Aren't you?"

Garrett knew when he was being tested. "Nah. Best he get it out now. Otherwise, it will wake us all later."

Hope wrinkled her nose. "True."

He glanced at the work spread out over the plank table. It appeared she had been as busy as he had.

"Still writing the Q&A?"

As much as he was loath to admit it, he figured it was necessary. His mother always felt better when she had a script to follow.

"No," Hope said cheerfully. "I finished that a few hours ago." She chuckled as her son balled up his fists, turned red and worked on his task with a few healthy grunts.

"Ah, the joys of parenthood," he teased.

Hope groaned and shook her head. "You have no idea…"

He was beginning to get one, though.

Garrett watched as she tested the baby formula on her wrist, then, still finding it lacking, put the bottle back in the bowl of warm water.

She ambled closer. The increasing odor had them both wrinkling their noses.

"Sure?" she teased, holding out her hands, as if to take Max. "It's not too late to change your mind."

This was all part of having a kid in your life. To his surprise, he liked every moment, even this. He would really miss Max when he was gone.

Max's mommy, too.

If he were honest…

Which was why he should keep things nice and casual between them.

He gave a wry smile. What better way to keep the romance out of the situation than by dealing with a little stink? He stared at her, deadpan. "To show you what a trouper I am, I'll even change his diaper."

Hope's merry laughter filled the bunkhouse. "This I have to see."

She accompanied them to the makeshift changing area she had set up on the sofa. Garrett laid the infant down on the thick, waterproof pad. Keeping hold of Max, the way he'd seen Hope do, he sat down, too. The snaps that ran down both legs of Max's sleeper were easy to undo. Same with unhooking the sides of the diaper.

He peeled it back. Dared a peek. Couldn't help but groan right along with Hope.

It was so gross.

"You can still bail," Hope challenged him.

"Nope." Garrett lifted the little boy off the mess, folded the messy diaper in half, put it aside and set Max back down on the waterproof pad. "I'm doing it. Aren't I, Max?"

Garrett plucked the wipes out, one after another, carefully cleaning until Max's entire diaper area was as clean as a whistle. Which wasn't exactly easy, since Max kicked his legs and feet the entire time and tried to grab the soiled wipes with his little hands.

Hope hovered. "You've got a little spillover on the changing pad..."

"I've got it." Using more wipes, Garrett cleaned that, too. And then Max's little hands and feet, for good measure. Satisfied all was well, he slid a fresh diaper beneath the baby, fit it against him, just the way he had seen Hope do dozens of times in the past week, then fastened the tabs. The sleeper got snapped up, too, although that took a moment to figure out. "Now you can have him while I go wash my hands," Garrett declared proudly.

"Good job, *Dad*," Hope teased.

Dad?

Funny, he liked the sound of that, unexpected as it was to hear.

Her hand flew to her mouth. "I'm so sorry," she rushed on. "I don't know why I said that. I must be getting a little punchy."

Or you just have your defenses down.

He paused to let her change places with him. He shrugged off her mistake matter-of-factly, for both their sakes. "It's probably because I've been acting like one…"

"Or because Max doesn't really have one." Hastily, Hope gathered her now fragrant-smelling son into her arms. "So no one currently has that title, which is why it was okay to make a joke, because I wasn't taking anything away from anyone else."

He stared at her in surprise as her face flushed bright red. He had never imagined she could be so embarrassed. "You really don't have to spin this, Hope," he said gently. "I'm not offended."

Flattered, maybe. Crazy as that sounded. But not offended. Nope. Not offended in the least. Still ruminating on the reasons behind her Freudian slip, Garrett went to the kitchen sink and lathered up well.

Hope followed him. "Okay. Because I—" she tipped her head up to his, Max still gathered against her breasts "—I really do appreciate everything you've done for us the past few days. From buying groceries to taking us to the hospital, to holding Max and giving him a bottle and changing his diaper."

He had pretty much done it all.

Aware she looked as if she felt she and Max had imposed on him, Garrett waved off her guilt. "You've been helping my family. I'm helping yours. It's the way the world works."

"Or should," she said, a slight catch in her voice.

Another silence fell, more companionable this time.

Max looked at the bottle of milk. He gave a little lurch. "Meh...meh..."

Garrett took it out of the warm water, wiped the outside dry then tested it on Hope's wrist. "Perfect," she said.

He handed it to her and she settled on the sofa, Max in her arms, and began to feed him. But not before he'd gotten in a few more hungry cries.

Garrett settled beside them, observing softly, "It almost sounds like he's saying *Mom, Mom*, instead of *meh, meh.*"

"I know." Hope smiled tenderly, admitting, "I can't wait for the day when he really does call me that."

The question was, would he be around to witness it? "It won't be too long," Garrett predicted, leaning close enough to breathe in the baby powder scent of them both.

Hope sighed wistfully. "Actually, it will be

months from now, according to the developmental timeline."

Months.

Would he even recognize Max by then? He knew how much babies could change in appearance as they grew the first couple of years. The differences were even more significant when you weren't seeing the baby every day, the way he was now.

He forced himself not to think about that.

Or grow maudlin—as Hope looked about to do.

After all, no permanent decisions had been made.

Garrett tucked his little finger into the center of Max's fist, grinned when the baby gripped it tightly. As if he didn't want to let Garrett go any more than Garrett wanted to let Hope and Max go.

"Yeah, well," Garrett predicted gruffly, pushing the unwanted emotion away, "I think Max is so exceptional he'll be way ahead of that."

Hope beamed. "I do, too."

They exchanged grins.

In that moment, he saw the faint shadows beneath her eyes that even makeup couldn't hide. He thought about the fact that she still wasn't making enough milk and that the prescription for that was a healthy diet and lots of rest. The latter of which she definitely had not gotten today.

"You look a little tired," he told her, not sure if it was the lover in him or the physician doing the talking. "Want me to finish feeding Max while you get ready for bed?" So she and her baby boy could drift right off to sleep?

Hope mistook his suggestion. The color came back into her cheeks. "Oh, I'm not headed for the sack," she said firmly, squaring her slender shoulders. "At least, not anytime soon."

Chapter Ten

Well, that made two of them making stupid verbal slips tonight, Hope thought in chagrin.

Drawing a deep breath, she tried to pretend her mind hadn't immediately gone in the same direction as his the minute bedtime had been mentioned. When the racing of her pulse, the innate desire to make up for their little tiff earlier in the sexiest way possible, said otherwise.

Aware he was still assessing her intently, Hope forced a smile. "I have several more hours of work to do, minimum, before I call it a night.

But…" Being careful not to dislodge the bottle of formula from Max's mouth, she handed over her son. "If you want to feed Max for me, I really would appreciate it."

Garrett shifted the little boy against himself and settled on the sofa, one brawny arm resting on the cushioned end, Max snuggled against his chest. "No problem." His mood just as purposeful as her words had been, he continued giving her son the bottle.

Was he just doing this to make up for how short he'd been with her earlier? Maybe. He was a mature adult. He knew she was just doing her job. That she was who she was, just as he was who he was. They would never share the same view about how necessary appearances were in life. Never mind whether or not they should be manipulated to secure an outcome.

She'd never be as blunt as he was.

And he sure as heck was never going to be anywhere close to discreet.

It didn't mean they couldn't be friends, Hope

rationalized, doing her best to protect both their hearts.

And interim lovers...

All she and Garrett had to do was accept that whatever was going on with them was only temporary, and take it day by day, moment by moment.

That would certainly lessen the overall stress of the situation. And wasn't that what she was all about? Choosing the path of least conflict? For everyone?

OBLIVIOUS TO THE tumultuous nature of her thoughts, Garrett looked up at her as Max's feeding slowed down. Seeming no more anxious to revisit their earlier tiff than she was, he asked curiously, "What was Max drinking earlier? When I came in?"

When Max had still had frothy white bubbles on his lips. Once again, Hope had to work not to appear self-conscious. "Breast milk."

"Then, if he was just fed a few minutes ago…?"

"I didn't have enough."

His glance went to her breasts.

Her nipples immediately tingled, but not because she didn't have enough milk.

Funny, he hadn't noticed the loose fit of her blouse. But then, he'd been too busy looking deep into her eyes…as if trying to figure out what to do about the hopelessly intimate situation they'd let themselves get into.

Hope swallowed. "I could have put Max back to bed, but I knew he was still a little hungry, so if I had gone ahead and put him down he would be up again in two hours. On the other hand, if he gets as many calories as he needs now, even if takes a little longer to feed him since he's not as intensely interested as he was a little while ago before he had the edge taken off his hunger, he will probably sleep a good six hours."

"Six hours? Really?" Once again, Garrett looked as interested as any proud daddy.

But he wasn't Max's daddy.

And would never be.

She needed to keep reminding herself of that.

Hope moved away from the compelling sight of Max snuggling up to Garrett.

So Garrett was not just strong and protective, he was also laudably tender, too. So what? It didn't change anything between them. *Couldn't.* And if she let herself imagine otherwise, they'd both be in big, big trouble. "He slept that long last night," she reported, trying to distract herself by tidying up the kitchen, emptying out the plastic bowl and putting it in the rack to dry.

"But, again, that's what is on the developmental schedule." Hope paused to dry her hands. "I think the only reason Max wasn't doing it before this was because he was growing and wasn't getting quite enough nutrition from my breast milk alone to help him sleep through the night."

Garrett's eyes tracked her every movement as

she walked around the breakfast bar. "So you're okay with combination feeding now?"

Hope settled in front of her computer once again. "I'm beginning to see the beauty of it." She pulled her chair up. Elbows on the table, she rested her chin on her folded hands. "I also realized I don't have to be so hard on myself. As a mom, I don't have to do everything perfectly. I just have to try to do my best."

The upward curve of his masculine lips was as encouraging as the gleam in his eyes. "I'm glad."

Once again their glances meshed, held. Once again Hope wished she wasn't working for his mother and the foundation. That the two of them could put everything else aside and just be together like this.

But she *was* working for the Lockhart Foundation.

And she had a job to do if she was going to protect Lucille and the family's reputation the way she had promised. So, without another word, she turned her attention to the computer screen and went back to work.

GARRETT HAD BEEN wondering if a formal apology for their earlier disagreement was warranted.

She'd quietly indicated it wasn't.

Now, as she immersed herself fully in her work, he had to wonder if he'd read her mood correctly, after all. Frustration formed a knot in his gut.

How was it he had just ended up in the confusing morass of his youth? With everyone surreptitiously working to protect each other's feelings, appearances of civility reigning supreme and no one saying what they really meant or felt?

Suddenly, the idea of reenlisting in the military, where everything was short and to the point, seemed a lot more appealing than it had just twenty-four hours before, when he'd been wrapped in Hope's arms.

Maybe his earlier self-assessment was right. He just wasn't cut out for this.

With a decisive frown, Hope picked up her laptop and brought it over. She settled beside him, close enough so he could see the screen while still giving their tiny chaperone his bottle.

She picked up a throw pillow and wedged it between the two of them. So she could rest her elbow on it while she worked? Or to ensure they wouldn't physically touch?

He didn't know the answer to that.

However, he *did* know she still smelled like lavender baby powder and the vanilla-scented hand soap she favored.

They were both, he noted, very soothing fragrances.

Max, opening his eyes to grin up at his momma, seemed to think so, too.

Hope spared her son a sweet smile, causing Garrett's heart to lurch painfully in his chest, then went back to the task at hand, explaining, "I'm still trying to put together the backstory on

242 — A Texas Soldier's Family

the foundation. Not the abbreviated one that's on the Lockhart Foundation website, which tells us virtually nothing about your parents except that they are rich and want to do good."

"Wow. That's harsh." But true in a way he never would have expected an exceedingly tactful woman like Hope to come out and say.

"I know. It doesn't begin to cover how the foundation came about. And I need that."

"Why?"

She scooted as close as the pillow wall she had built would allow. "Because of this." She clicked the split-screen function. Eight different windows popped up. He read the titles of the stories out loud: "'Lockharts Try to Get Ahead of Potential Lawsuits.' 'Too Late to Do Good?' 'Boxed Into Giving, as Charities Revolt.'" He exhaled roughly, a muscle pulsing in his jaw. "Wow. I thought you said that leaking the information about what my mom is doing ahead of the eleven o'clock news would diminish the bad publicity."

"And it has." Hope clicked on another screen of multiple headline windows. "This is where we started."

He continued to read. "'Lockhart Foundation Stiffs Charities.' 'Lockhart Foundation Turns Its Back on Needy.' 'Nonprofits Tell the Ugly Truth about Lockhart Foundation Largesse.'"

Looking more accepting of the situation than he felt at that moment, Hope explained, "We went from all bad publicity to a press that is doubting whether your family and the foundation is bad or not. The next step is to take those doubts as an open window or door, and give the public another glimpse of who your parents really were when they started out and how their largesse all came to be."

"Makes sense." Noting Max had pushed the nipple all the way out of his mouth, Garrett set the bottle of formula aside and shifted Max upright, so the baby could look over his shoulder while working up a burp.

Hope tucked an errant strand of honey-hued

hair behind her ear. "So I've asked your siblings, and now I'm asking you as well, to tell me what you know about the family history. Sage sent me photos from her computer, of the ranch as it was when your mom and dad were growing up here in Laramie County."

Frank and Lucille stood in front of what then had been a sturdily built split-rail fence. The barn, painted red at the time, was behind them. Grazing cattle and horses could be seen in the distance. "They look so young." So…Western. Both were clad in worn jeans, plaid shirts, boots and straw hats.

Hope clicked on the keyboard. A new image appeared on the computer screen. "Here's another of them in their first home in Dallas. One of them standing in front of the Lockhart Asset Management office. Another of them with all five of you kids when you were in elementary school."

He nodded.

Their clothes were sophisticated, haircuts just as perfect. And yet...

"None of you look very happy in these pictures." Hope pointed out with a frown. "Which is why I asked Sage to find me some more photos of you-all having a good time."

Garrett reflected on that. Noting Max was starting his baby push-ups again, he slid his palm a little higher, to rest between the little fella's flexing shoulders. "I'm not sure there are any."

Hope's elegant brow furrowed. "That's what she said. Can you tell me why that is? So I don't accidentally open up a can of worms?"

"You want to know what it was really like when I was a kid?"

She nodded.

Garrett sighed heavily. "Dad was wrapped up in building up his hedge fund. He worked constantly—he was almost *never* home. My mom was always on the board of some charity or organizing some black-tie gala to help further the family's social connections." None of whom were apparently rallying around his mother now, he couldn't help but note. "All us kids were enrolled in private schools only the most elite of the elite could get into."

Garrett flicked a glance her way. "I always liked the academic challenge of school. Especially science and history." Which had led to his career in the military and medicine.

"Were you happy?" she asked quietly, her eyes lighting up with interest as she held his gaze.

Yes and no. "I wish there had been more of a connection between us," he admitted finally. "In the military, you work as a team. There was no teamwork in my family growing up."

"I see that now."

He wished she didn't look so beautiful in the late-night light of the bunkhouse, wished he still didn't want to make love to her quite so much. "We all became closer when my dad was diagnosed with his heart problems. We had time to reevaluate our lives before we had to say good-bye to him."

Max lurched and let out a loud burp.

Hope's proud grin matched his own.

A little amazed at how quickly he had become adept at feeding and caring for an infant, Garrett turned Max back around and settled him against his chest.

Enough with the questions about his childhood.

"What about you?" he asked Hope softly. "Your family? You've never said much about that."

He wanted to know all about her, too, he realized.

For a moment, he thought she wouldn't answer.

Head ducked down, so he couldn't see into her eyes, she watched him offer Max the bottle again. "I was an only child. My parents own an extended-stay hotel for the very wealthy."

"In Houston," he remembered.

"From an early age, I was expected to keep out of the way and, when I got older, to work as hard as possible to keep our well-heeled guests comfortable. Most of them were in some sort of personal crisis, due to relocation, home renovations that were lasting forever, nasty divorces, stuff like that."

"That doesn't sound...pleasant," he sympathized.

She shrugged. "I saw how people could 'spin' things, which in turn made their lives better, their crises a little less daunting."

"That's when you decided to go into public relations."

An accepting smile turned up the corners of her lovely lips. "It wasn't that hard of a leap to make. I already knew how to deal with highly emotional and volatile people, and not lose my own cool."

She was certainly good at handling the members of his family; they all adored her. In fact, they seemed willing to do anything for her. As would he. "Are you close to your parents now?"

Another short intake of breath. Hope fixed her stare on a painting on the wall. "I love them."

"That's not the same as being close."

Hope turned her glance to Max, who was drowsily sucking on the bottle. She reached over and tucked her little finger into his tiny fist.

The action had her forearm resting against Garrett's chest. He liked the feel of that. Even better was the fact that she didn't immediately pull away from the cozy physical contact.

"Do you and your parents not get along?" Garrett asked.

He could understand that, too.

There were times when he and his mother still irritated the heck out of each other. Usually because his mother was surreptitiously pushing him to do what she wanted him to do, not what was right for him, in his view.

Hope sighed. "My parents were always extremely critical." She shook her head, the pain in her eyes matching the pain in her voice. "There was simply no pleasing them." Her shoulders rose, then fell. "I disappointed them even more when I didn't join the family business."

"They must be proud of your success now."

"Yes." Seeing Max had, indeed, gone to sleep, she put her laptop on the coffee table, gathered her son into her arms and carried him into the bedroom.

When she returned, she settled on the sofa, removing the pillow she had previously put between them. Looking as weary as he expected her to be, at that time of night, she stretched both long, lissome legs out in front of her and propped her slipper-clad feet on the coffee table. Her head fell to rest against the back of the sofa. Noting how exhausted she seemed, how in need of comforting, he stretched an arm on the sofa behind her, and pulled her closer, into the curve of his body. Sighing blissfully, she rested her head on his shoulder, then she picked up the conversation as if no time had elapsed. "Yes, my parents are proud of my professional success," she said.

"But…?" he sensed there was more.

Her slender body tensing, Hope snuggled closer. His pulse took another leap at the effortless way their bodies aligned.

Hope sighed. "They didn't like the fact that I had a baby on my own. Or the fact that I got fired for being involved with a British reporter, after the scandal with the ambassador's son was resolved. They wish I'd move back to Houston, take a place nearby and raise Max there."

"I'm guessing that doesn't fit in with your plans?"

Her expression wistful, she admitted, "I do want him to have family. More than just me."

He could understand that. It was a lot to raise a child on your own. Still keeping her tucked in the curve of his body, he reached over and took her hand in his. Gratified, her fingers tightened in his. "But...?" he asked, just as softly, guessing there was a caveat.

She gazed down at their clasped hands, said fiercely, "I don't want him to ever grow up feeling like he is in the way, or somehow less than people who have more money, or feel criticized at every turn, like I did."

Garrett understood that. He wouldn't want that for either Hope or Max, either. "Okay, then," he said gruffly, bringing her closer still, wishing he had the power to make all their dreams come true.

"What *do* you want for you and for Max, ideally?"

WHAT DO I WANT? Hope thought, her emotions getting the better of her once again. *You in our life.* But aware it was way too soon to say something like that to Garrett, when thus far all they'd had was a tentative friendship and a fling that would likely end when he reenlisted and took the job in DC, she ducked her head and fibbed, "I don't know."

Garrett shifted her over onto his lap. Hand beneath her chin, he lifted her face to his so that she could not help but look into the mesmerizing depths of his eyes.

His smile was slow and sensual.

"How about this?" He lowered his head and kissed her in a way that was tender and provocative. Hope's lips tingled. Lower she felt a burning desire between her thighs. And still he seduced her with his lips and tongue, as if he were on a mission to fulfill her deepest wishes, to provide an intimacy that included everything but commitment and pure romantic love.

She drew back on a long, lust-filled sigh. Doing her best to contain her out-of-control emotions, she said, "I think you know the answer to that."

She did want to make love with him. Beyond that, she didn't know. But maybe she didn't have to think, she realized as he slid his hands to her waist and brought her flush against him.

Maybe she didn't have to be perfect.

As he had said, he hadn't hired her, so there was no conflict of interest between the two of them. All he wanted was to make love with her, and all she wanted and needed was to make love with him, too. This time, not as the result of some kind of crisis with Max. Or because they needed to discover if the first time was as good as they thought it had been. But because they were getting closer.

Pretending a great deal more detachment than she felt, she moved off his lap and said breathlessly, "Just to be clear." Because her legs felt wobbly, she settled on the sofa next to him once again. She turned toward him, so her bent knee nudged his rock-hard thigh. "You know this is still just a fling... That work still takes precedence?"

Was she speaking more to herself or to him? Who was she warning here? Garrett wondered.

His body thrumming with need, he drew her to her feet. He tangled one hand in the spill of Hope's hair. The other slid down her back, settled against her waist.

"I know we're headed into forbidden territory," he whispered roughly against her mouth.

And, as far as that went, it was fine with him. He didn't care what fibs Hope had to tell herself. As long as they came together like this, found more to life than either had been experiencing. His body igniting, he felt her melt against him.

"I know I want you." He kissed her again, until her breasts rubbed up against him, as did the rest of her from shoulder to knee. Needing more, he danced her backward to the wall, grinding his hips against hers until the hard ridge of his arousal pressed against the softness between her thighs. She trembled as they kissed. And shuddered even more as he divested her of her shorts and relieved her of her panties.

Her lips softened beneath his and she clung to him, her hands slipping beneath his shirt to caress his shoulders, back, spine. Able to feel how much she needed and wanted him, he opened her blouse and bra, slid between her thighs, pulled both her legs to his waist and set about exploring even more.

Joy pulsed through him. Her head fell back as, eyes closed, she gave herself over to his tender ministrations. And only when she was wet and ready did he step back long enough to drop his trousers and roll on a condom.

She leaned against the wall, their eyes locked, the air between them charged with excitement. She beckoned him close, running her hands over the hard muscles of his thighs, the curve of his buttocks, the small of his back, before coming back around to cup the weight of him in her hot, smooth palms. Stroking, learning, tempting. Fierce pulsing need swept through him as he pressed up against her, lifting her, positioning her as kiss followed kiss, caress followed caress. And still it wasn't enough, not nearly enough.

Needing to possess her the way he had never possessed any woman, Garrett wrapped her legs around his waist, and smoothly moved up, in, pushing his erection into her trembling wetness, until they fit together more snugly than he could ever have imagined.

She cried out and fisted her hands in his hair. "More..."

Arching against him, her hands slid down to his hips. Once there, she directed him to move with tantalizing slowness. Then faster, deeper. Filling and retreating. Finding meaning in every breath, every kiss, every sweet, hot caress. Until at last everything merged. Passion and need, tenderness and surrender. She met him wantonly, stroke for stroke. Satisfaction rushed through them, and there was no more fighting the free-falling ecstasy that warmed their hearts and filled their souls.

GARRETT THOUGHT THEY might call it a night and retreat to his bed, to sleep wrapped in each other's arms until Max woke, needing to be nursed again.

Instead, Hope disengaged herself from him almost immediately and slipped away. When she returned, she was wearing another pair of summery cotton pajamas. Her hair had been pulled back, her makeup washed off.

She was ready for bed, all right, but she couldn't have been more businesslike as she retrieved her laptop computer. "What was your favorite memory as a kid?"

Garrett strode off to his bedroom. He returned in his own nightwear, a pair of jersey running shorts and an army-issue T-shirt. "Tell me you're not still working."

She gave him a look. "You know I am."

She had warned him.

So why was he surprised?

Aware it was getting harder and harder not to spill his guts to her every time they were together, he went to the kitchen and plucked a crisp apple out of the fruit bowl. "Tell me you're not going to use any of this in your narrative."

She watched him take a bite of the sweet, delicious fruit. "Only if you give me permission."

Their eyes clashed. The closeness they'd felt when they were talking earlier and making love faded.

Garrett strolled closer, persisting, "I get to review everything that pertains to me and my family."

"Okay," she agreed from her place at the long plank table.

Garrett took a chair at the end, kitty-corner from her. "When I was a little kid, every once in a while my mom and dad would bring us out to visit my Grandpa Lockhart at his family ranch, the one where my brother Wyatt now lives."

Briefly, Hope consulted her notes. "The Wind River Ranch."

"Yes."

Her head lifted and her green eyes locked on his. "You did a lot of cowboy stuff?"

Exhaling sharply, he found himself wanting to be the stuff of her fantasies. "Yes and no." Summoned memories came flooding back. "Grandpa Lockhart was career military, so he spent more time showing my brothers and me how to defend ourselves and survive in the wild than how to wrangle a calf. But there was just something about being out in the countryside— small towns, in general. It was so different from Dallas."

"Sounds like you almost got emotionally attached to a part of the Lone Star State," she teased.

Garrett kicked back in his chair. "Maybe to all the military lore…it sure made me want to follow in my grandpa's footsteps. Anyway, Grandpa Lockhart died when I was ten, and my mom and dad sold the Wind River Ranch, the way they had sold my mom's family ranch, and put the money into expanding Dad's company. So we never came back until my dad got sick, when they told us they'd been out here, buying property in Laramie County, not just for themselves, but for all of us."

Hope typed a little more, then paused to look up at him. "It sounds nice."

He finished chewing another bite of apple. "I guess it was, as far as gestures go."

Hope rested her chin on her hand. "You think that's all it was? A gesture?"

He wasn't sure what she was getting at. "What else could it have been?"

"Chance and Wyatt live here now."

"Only because they had already been working as cowboys and always wanted to ranch. Zane and I…"

"Are military through and through?"

Two weeks ago, he would have said, yes, he was.

Now…

Now that he'd spent time with Hope, he wasn't sure what was true.

She went back to typing data into her computer, even more fiercely. Finally, she paused.

Narrowed her gaze. Surveyed him, head to toe. As aware as he that he still hadn't answered her. Mostly because he had no reply to give. Just yet.

"Does this mean you decided not to reenlist and take the slot at Walter Reed in Maryland?"

It means I don't know. And until I do...

He got up to throw his apple core in the trash, hesitating only long enough to wash his hands and get a drink of water before striding purposefully back to her side.

Decision made, he took her by the hand. Pulled her to her feet. "Enough questions."

Her breath caught audibly. "Garrett! What…?"

Figuring that the only way he could give either of them any peace at this moment was to make love to her, he wove his hands through her hair, lifted her lips to his. "It's late," he told her, kissing her until her knees went weak and she kissed him back just as passionately.

"There's only one thing we need to do now," he growled, breathing in the sweet, womanly scent of her and swinging her up into his arms. "And that's go to bed."

So they did.

Chapter Eleven

"Since when do you walk around with a baby strapped to your chest?" Chance asked Garrett the following morning.

Garrett adjusted the white sunhat on Max's head, making sure the infant was shielded from the harmful rays while still able to view all the activity. And there was a lot to see.

In the fields surrounding the ranch buildings, two large tractors were being operated by Tank and one of his rehabbing veteran friends. As the chest-high weeds disappeared, the smell of fresh-mown grass hung in the hot summer air.

"Since Hope only got about two hours of sleep last night," Garrett replied.

Some of which had been his fault. They had spent a couple of hours, total, making love.

The rest was all on her.

Chance asked sympathetically, "Max giving her a rough time?"

Garrett shook his head. "She was working on a revised written history of the formation of the Lockhart Foundation. Putting together some photos, making plans for the camera crew coming out today and tomorrow."

"They are everywhere, aren't they?" Wyatt said, joining them.

Garrett blew out a frustrated breath. "Not to mention constantly underfoot." Taking both video and still photos of the ranch entrance, the mown and unmown fields, and the barns, corrals and original ranch house.

"And what's with the 'staging' being done in

the bunkhouse?" Wyatt asked, not nearly as irritated as Chance to find interior designer/general contractor Molly Griffin there.

Garrett turned so Max could get a better view of the tractors. "Hope wanted some more Texana feel to the main room."

Chance chuckled. "Well, if that's the case, I could probably borrow some stuffed animal carcasses for the wall."

Garrett spared a glance at his younger brother. "I think you know what Hope probably would tell you to do with that suggestion."

Chance shrugged. "I know what *you* would tell me to do. Hope is a lot more polite."

So true.

"Although she can be direct," Chance said. He turned to Wyatt. "Did she ask you to bring over some horses?"

Wyatt nodded affably. "I said I'd give her one tomorrow morning, before the TV crew arrives."

"She wanted cattle from me but changed her

mind when I said all I had was bulls," Chance drawled.

The brothers all laughed.

"Has anyone heard? Is Mom coming back tonight?" Chance asked.

"Yes," Garrett said. "If all goes according to plan. She's been meeting with the charity CEOs in groups at the foundation office to speed up the delivery of the money. It appears once word got out on the news yesterday, everyone clamored for their money before it all ran out. So at least that part of wrapping up this whole mess will be done with."

Wyatt frowned. "What about the police?"

Garrett informed them, "Her attorneys are handling that for her. She'll eventually need to be interviewed by detectives, of course, but that can wait a few days."

Molly walked out of the bunkhouse. She attached flag holders to two of the front posts, then hung an American flag on one and the state flag of Texas on the other.

Garrett frowned.

So did his brothers.

Paying homage to their homeland was a very good thing. But as a means to an end...?

Temper rising, Garrett eased the baby carrier off his shoulders. He looked at Chance. "Mind walking this little fella around for me for a few minutes?"

Chance shrugged. "As long as he doesn't mind."

Because Chance was nearly the same size as Garrett, little adjustment was needed to the Baby Bjorn carrier. The sleepy Max frowned at the transfer, then paused, looking up at Chance.

Chance mugged comically and talked gibberish in a soft, soothing tone.

Max grinned.

Unable to resist, Garrett slapped his brother's shoulder. "Just so you know—it's only gas."

"Ha!" Chance crowed. "He likes me, don't you, Max?"

Chance and Wyatt walked over to the shade,

still doting on the baby. Garrett headed inside the bunkhouse. Hope was on her smartphone, video chatting with his sister Sage. "Thanks so much. I'll be sure you get all the groceries you need…Yes. Promise. See you tonight." Hope hung up. Immediately concerned, she asked, "Where's Max?"

"With Chance and Wyatt. He's fine." Garrett gestured to the window.

Hope peered out. Smiled. "For not being used to men, Max sure is adapting easily to this environment."

Too bad I'm not, Garrett thought sullenly.

Hope studied him. "What's wrong?"

WHAT WASN'T? GARRETT hissed out a breath, feeling as if he had been transported back to his youth. "For starters—" he gestured broadly "—all this."

Her emerald eyes widened. "You don't like the new vases filled with wildflowers?"

If only it were that simple. "I don't like false impressions."

She put her hands on her hips. "We're just sprucing things up a little bit, doing what Lucille would have done had she been here."

"You're making it look like something it's not. This isn't the true current state of the Circle H." Perpetrating another myth would only make the family reputation shakier. And while he couldn't have cared less what anyone said about him, this stuff did matter to his mother. Garrett strode closer, noting Hope looked exhausted, too. "Any good reporter could find a local resident to complain about the prior state of the ranch. Go on record as saying all this was only done for the TV interview."

Her chin lifted. "You'd prefer it be filmed looking rundown and unkempt, which is the shape most of the property is in?"

"Why film anything here at all? This is a zone of privacy, or it should be. Why not film in Dallas, at my mother's home there, or at the foundation offices where things could easily stay just as they are?"

Hope glared at him. "Because all of those places have negative connotations for the viewing public. They support the image of your mother that has been exaggerated and bandied about in the press. None of them show where she came from. Or how she and your father eventually discovered that money didn't bring them happiness, but giving to others, bringing their whole family back to their roots, did." Hope came closer. Another shimmer of tension floated between them. "It's a great story."

"Then why can't you just tell it openly and honestly instead of doing all this?" he asked her in frustration. "It's bad enough that you're writing advance questions and answers for my mom to rehearse with, and inviting a friendly journalist to cover the story." He shot her a disapproving look. "Which, by the way, I'm still not totally on board with. Remind me again why it's so important?"

Hope dug in all the more. "Because I think Lucille'll be more comfortable if she feels *prepared* rather than under siege." Clearing her throat, she added, "Of course, there is a way to make this easier on her…"

"Just issue a press statement and leave it at that?"

"No. One step better."

He waited.

"Your mom could step down as CEO."

Shock turned to anger that Hope could even suggest it. "Not. Going. To. Happen."

Her jaw took on the consistency of granite, too. "Have you spoken with Lucille about it—even in theory? Because I have to tell you, it's the best way to take the heat off her."

"No. And for the record, I don't want you or anyone else suggesting it to her, either."

For a moment, he thought she was going to argue the point. Cheeks pinkening, she stepped closer and, dropping her voice persuasively, tried another path. "Have *you* thought about taking a more active public role in managing the scandal?"

Garrett blinked at her in surprise. She was serious! He flexed his shoulders in an effort to make the increasingly unsettled feeling go away. "Such as...?"

"Heading up a task force?"

He couldn't help but laugh. "A little silly when the foundation only employs three—I guess now, two—people. My mother and her executive assistant, Sharla."

Hope lifted a delicate hand. "Again. It's all about optics."

He leaned over, until they were nose to nose. "And again. I'm not."

She stared up at him. Shook her head. Sighed. "Substance over style?"

The way she said it made it seem like a character flaw. "You betcha."

Hope paused again. She seemed to be wrestling with something. Finally, she sighed again, sifted both hands through her soft blond hair and said, "Look, I can see all this is bothering you."

You think?

"So why don't you take a break from it. Go off and find a way to relax, do something you like. I can interview your brothers this afternoon, get what we need for the revised family history from them."

R & R sounded tempting. Leaving her alone with his two very single brothers did not.

Although they had a rule about not going after the same woman, Chance and Wyatt did not know he'd staked a claim where Hope was concerned. Although they had sensed his interest, he couldn't tell them anything definitively because he had promised Hope he would keep their fling a secret between the two of them.

Although that, too, was a misnomer in his opinion.

"Well?" Hope prodded impatiently.

Garrett snorted. "Not sure you'll get anything

you can use from Chance or Wyatt." *Except maybe embarrassing stories about yours truly.*

"Mmmm." She considered for a long moment, then met his challenge with a level glance. "I bet I can." Her gaze softened. "Seriously, your mom and Sage will be back late this evening."

"Adelaide…?"

"Is staying in Dallas to help the police try and track down her father and Mirabelle Fanning."

That sounded like Adelaide. Responsible to the core. Which meant this scandal must be killing her, too.

"So you have plenty of time to take a time-out from all of this redecorating chaos, and enjoy what little R & R you have." She patted his arm. "In the meantime, have a little faith. And trust me to be able to put together a video perspective that does ring true."

"TRUST ME", HOPE had said.

Did he?

Personally, Garrett thought, the answer was

yes. When it came to anything one-on-one with him, he did trust her. But when it came to her doing her job, it was a different matter entirely.

There, he found it a lot rougher going.

Aware, however, that he couldn't do anything about that—he hadn't hired her, couldn't fire her—he decided to tackle something he could accomplish. Getting the Victorian cleared of all trash so it could be put on the market.

He worked through the rest of the morning and the entire afternoon without taking a break. The physical activity felt good. But not as good as seeing Hope walk through the door at dinner time, a pizza in one hand, a six-pack of flavored water in the other. She walked past him to the window seat overlooking the backyard and set both down. Hands on her hips, she turned around, first scanning the newly cleared-out downstairs, then him. Taking in the fact that he was shirtless, she smiled and quipped, "Too bad I'm not looking for studly actors to star in a soap commercial."

"Studly?"

She waved an airy hand. "I've been around horses all day."

"Plural?"

She sauntered closer. "Wyatt said since I declined all of Chance's bulls that he would bring me two horses, instead. They're really gorgeous, by the way. Your brothers put them in the corral between the bunkhouse and the barns."

Her hair shone like gold in the sunlight pouring through the windows. He itched to run his hands through it. "I thought the corral was in bad shape."

Shaking her head, she raked her plump lower lip with her teeth. "Chance brought some cowboys over and they fixed it. Put on a new coat of paint, too."

It was odd not to have their tiny chaperone. 'Cause right about now, he needed a chaperone to keep from following his base instincts. He put a twist tie on the trash bag he'd been filling. "Where's Max?"

"Bess Monroe came out to the ranch to film a pro-foundation bit for me, then offered to watch Max while I went off chasing you."

Was there anyone she couldn't charm into doing her bidding? "You could have called me on my cell. I would have watched him for you."

"I needed a break from all the action, too." She sat on the counter while he washed up as best he could with the hand soap and paper towels the renters had left behind. "Missed a spot." She pointed to his chin. He gave it a swipe. "Still missed." She pointed again.

"Third time's the charm." He gave it another try.

Eyes darkening, she smiled. "Or maybe not." She leaned over and did it for him.

He looked down at her. She looked up at him.

He had the feeling she wanted to make love with him as much as he wanted to make love with her.

But, once again, duty called.

She pushed off the counter and walked over to

retrieve the roll of paper towels, the pizza and the flavored water. There was no comfortable place to sit inside, so they took everything out to the back porch and settled on the steps that led down to the spacious yard. "I'm guessing you brought me dinner for a reason?" he asked dryly.

She handed him a slice of pepperoni pizza and a paper towel. "I did want to talk to you."

He uncapped a chilled beverage for them both. Taking a cue from her serious expression, he said, "I'm listening."

"I had a phone call from your mom a little while ago. She wants to shut down the foundation entirely. And make the announcement tomorrow afternoon."

Garrett enjoyed a bite of the hot, delicious pizza. "Makes sense, if all the money is gone."

"Does it?" Hope sighed. "We don't know for certain that law enforcement *won't* be able to recover the twenty-five million that was stolen. If they do…"

"In cases like this, it's always a long shot."

"But it happens, Garrett." She helped herself to a slice, too. "We shouldn't rule that possibility out."

Garrett arched a brow. "Nor should we push or guilt my mother into doing something she doesn't want to do anymore."

Hope pushed on in a surprisingly empathetic voice. "That's the thing. Lucille's not really in any position to make a decision like this right now. There's too much going on. Too many emotions. Too much shame and embarrassment."

She paused to look into his eyes. "Your mom hasn't had a chance to feel the accolades for what she has managed to do, for the last two years, the last week. There's still a lot she *could* do, even if she doesn't have anywhere near the financial resources."

Hope had a point. There was no reason to rush into or out of anything. Not the family's involvement with the foundation. Not his connection to Hope and Max, either.

"That's why you asked Bess Monroe to come and talk about West Texas Warrior Assistance, isn't it?"

"Yes, that's right," she said, nodding. "They need a lot more than what they have to meet their goals, but a little can still go a long way to get them started. It's going to be good publicity for WTWA. And, when your mother sees the video clip, I think it might give her a fresh perspective on the goals yet to be achieved."

"So she won't quit. And you won't have failed in your mission to save the foundation."

"Right."

"I still think it should be my mother's decision. I'll back up whatever she wants to happen."

Hope studied him as though he was a test she just had to pass. "Even if it's not what you want?" she asked finally.

Aware he'd been cut out of the loop in some

bizarre way, and Hope hadn't been, Garrett grimaced. "Even then."

BY THE TIME they'd finished eating, the last of Hope's dwindling supply of energy had seeped from her body. And it was only six thirty in the evening. How was she ever going to make it to Max's bedtime?

"You look tired," Garrett said, ruffling the hair on the top of her head.

She leveled him with a look. "Thanks."

He smiled at the sarcasm dripping from her voice. He wrapped his arm about her waist as he walked her to the curb, where her SUV sat parked behind his truck. "Why don't you let me drive you back to the ranch?"

Resisting the urge to curl up against him and take a good long nap, Hope fished the list and keys out of her bag. Now was not the time to lean on her military man. "Can't. I have to stop at the grocery store to get stuff for Sage to cook for the film crew and reporter tomorrow."

Garrett read over her shoulder. Swore at the lengthy and, in some cases, rather complicated ingredients.

Hope gestured aimlessly. "She's a chef."

"She's impossible."

Hope made a face. "I'll tell Sage you said so."

Garrett tweaked Hope's nose. "She already knows. I'll help you get the supplies. "

"I'd appreciate that. Bess said she could stay as late as nine o'clock, but I'm anxious to get home to Max."

By the time they hit the checkout line, Hope was yawning.

Garrett pushed the basket full of groceries out to her SUV.

He gave her another long, assessing look. She lifted a palm. "Not to worry. I may not be able to have coffee, but I can have a cup of ice chips. Chewing on those while I drive will keep me alert just as well."

With a frown, he headed for the Dairy Barn next door. "I'll get it for you."

Hope stifled another yawn. "You are a prince among princes," she called after him.

He turned and flashed her a sexy grin. The kind that said he'd accept payment for his kindness later.

With an amused shake of her head, she climbed behind the wheel, let her head fall forward onto the wheel and closed her eyes, just for a minute. It had been a mistake to spend time making love with Garrett the night before instead of using all available hours to sleep.

She could have gotten four hours of rest instead of just two. But she had wanted to be with him, so she had been. Besides, it wasn't as if she hadn't gotten by on even less sleep in times prior, when working in crisis mode.

It was only a few more days and then the scandal would be winding down. And then she'd be able to sleep as much as she wanted, she thought, as darkness descended around her.

Chapter Twelve

"Please stop asking me that. Everything is *fine*," Hope insisted agitatedly, for the third time, twenty minutes later.

Except clearly it wasn't, Garrett thought, as he drove them back to the ranch. "Are you angry because I woke you up?"

"Of course not." Resting her elbow on the SUV window, she shaded her eyes with her hand. "I couldn't just continue to sleep in a grocery store parking lot. Not when I have Max waiting and so much work to do."

He got that she was frustrated and embarrassed. But why unleash those emotions on him? Unless she somehow blamed him, too. For predicting she might doze off behind the steering wheel? For being there to protect her? For making love with her when she should have been bypassing their budding relationship and working, in her view?

And it *was* a relationship, even if she wouldn't yet admit it.

Still trying to coax a smile out of her, he teased. "Even if there had been a way to move you out of the driver's seat without rousing you, I'm not so sure it would have been good 'optics,' me lifting a quietly snoring woman out of one area of the car and stowing her in another."

Hope turned to him in sharply waning forbearance.

Irked to find them so completely out of sync, he surrendered. "Okay. Bad joke. You weren't snoring, loudly or otherwise. But..." Maybe it was better they get her emotions out in the open. Let whatever was bothering her surface, so they could deal with it. Together. He slanted her a deliberately provoking glance. "You do agree you were in no condition to drive?"

Hope shook another ice chip into her mouth. "You were right, okay?" she snapped finally. "I was too tired. I screwed up. And you win. Okay?"

No, it wasn't okay, he thought, as she continued staring out at the pastures dotted with cattle and horses, and the occasional goats or alpacas. And it hadn't been about winning. Or losing. Just safety. Pure and simple. That, and maybe his overwhelming need to take care of her. A need she now seemed to reject.

This, after accepting his assistance for days now, however and whenever she needed it. Garrett wondered if sleep would help. "You can close your eyes, if you want," he said softly.

She turned and gave him another long-suffering look that made him want to take her in his arms, hold her close and kiss her until her unprecedentedly grumpy mood passed. Her patience clearly at an end, she shook her head in silent remonstration. She sighed, pulled out her phone and punched in a number.

Maybe it was post-pregnancy hormones.

Knowing better than to suggest that, however, he paused at an unmarked intersection then turned onto the country road that led to the Circle H.

Listening, Hope smiled. "Hey, Lucille," she said with a sudden burst of cheerful energy. "We're almost there… Yes! As soon as I arrive. How's Max?" Hope listened some more, smiled again, then ended the call.

Maybe that was it.

Maybe she just missed her little boy.

To his knowledge, except for the first day they'd met, this was the first time she had been away from Max in a week. He could see where that would upset her.

After spending most of the day away, he missed the little tyke, too.

A minute later, he turned into the lane and drove up to the Circle H bunkhouse. His brothers had already left for their own ranches, to see to their herds. Inside, his mother, sister and Bess Monroe waited.

Hope said hello, then headed down the hallway. "Just let me peek in on Max…"

"He is such a sweet boy," Lucille said, her yearning for grandchildren of her own more evident than usual. Hope tiptoed back out. She went over to give Bess Monroe a hug. "I can't thank you enough."

Bess beamed. "My pleasure. Besides, I owe you for all those great ideas about how to get the WTWA message out there so we can ramp up the fund-raising."

"Let me know if I can do anything else." Hope encouraged, walking Bess out. The two women stood talking for a moment. Hope returned to the house while Bess drove away.

"You helped Bess, too?" Garrett asked. The last time he had seen Bess, she'd still been pretty frustrated with the whole situation. Now, thanks to whatever Hope had done, she seemed optimistic about the organization's fate.

Hope nodded. "It's a really good cause. I'm going to help them in any way I can."

"The foundation will, too," Lucille said.

Garrett glanced at his mother. "I thought you were closing the foundation, as of tomorrow."

Looking simultaneously bone weary and amazingly strong of will, Lucille waved off the suggestion. "Hope and Sage both helped me see that was simply a reaction to all that's occurred. Of course we're going to keep the foundation going," she said stubbornly.

All three women exchanged smiles.

Garrett suddenly felt as excluded as if he had wandered into a No Boys Allowed club.

Hope gestured toward the table. "Ready to see what we've done?" she asked Lucille.

His mother gave a little smile, even though

she was as pale with fatigue as Hope and Sage were.

This was ludicrous, Garrett fumed. It was nearly nine thirty. Everyone there had been going nonstop for days now. Hope and his mother, in particular, both had deep shadows under their eyes and looked like they were about to keel over. Someone had to save them from themselves.

"This can wait until tomorrow," Garrett said firmly. He pointed to Hope and his mom. "You two both need to go to bed."

Both women looked at him as if they had no idea who he was. And did not want to know.

"Tell me you did not just say that," Hope muttered.

As the head of the family and the man who cared deeply about all the women in the room, he stood his ground. "Sleep deprivation causes all sorts of serious health issues."

Sage was amused. And apparently amenable to reason. His mother and Hope were not.

He tried again. "If you won't listen to me as your son—" he stared down Lucille, who stood in solidarity with Hope "—or your..." He paused, looking at Hope. She lifted a brow, practically daring him to go on.

No way was he falling into that minefield of trying to put a label on what they had, when what they had was—at Hope's insistence— completely private. At least for now.

Once the scandal was resolved, he would see about that, too.

He shoved both his hands through his hair, aware he had never felt so aggravated. "Listen to me, ladies—*as a physician*, then. Left untreated, sleep deprivation can wreck havoc with every system in the body..."

Lucille interrupted, before he could go on in harrowing detail, "So can the stress and tension of important work left undone."

He blinked at his mother. Who was this woman who had been Go Along to Get Along his whole life?

Garrett turned back to Hope, who seemed to be the only person in the room Lucille was listening to at the moment. "Help me make her see reason," he gritted out.

To his surprise, Hope shook her head. Just as quietly defiant as his mother, she looked him in the eye. She retorted, "You're the one out of line here. So maybe it's you, Garrett, who needs to go bed."

PRIVATELY, HOPE KNEW Lucille was exhausted to her bones. She also knew the impossibly generous matriarch would spend another night, lying awake, worrying, if she did not see how much progress had been made remaking the foundation's image while she had been off making good on the financial promises of the Lockhart Foundation.

So, ignoring Garrett's fierce disapproval, she led Lucille and Sage over to the long plank table and sat down side by side with them in front of her laptop.

Hope pulled up the history of the ranch. The video montage and voice-over had been set to an orchestral arrangement of one of Lucille's favorite songs, "The House that Built Me."

Lucille put her hand over her heart, as the old black-and-white photos of the Circle H and of her childhood appeared on-screen. She caught her breath at the sight of the flags of Texas and the United States. Eyes glistening, she confessed emotionally, "When I got here tonight, and I saw the flags on the porch, the way they used to be when I was growing up, I was so happy I nearly burst into tears."

Hope smiled. There was no doubt from the photos she'd seen, and the stories she'd heard, that the Hendersons of Laramie County had been a very patriotic family. "I noticed them in the photos."

Lucille pointed to the bunkhouse, as it had been, years prior. "This photo was taken when my parents and I still lived here, instead of in the ranch house that was built later. Once we moved into that house, Dad hung our flags there." She shook her head. "It always meant so much to us. Dad being former military and all."

Out of the corner of her eye, Hope saw Garrett's look of chagrin, followed swiftly by apology. And on top of that, regret that he'd never noticed what she, as an outsider, had quickly seen.

Hope went through the rest of the video history, showing Lucille and Frank's humble beginnings, his business success, their rise in Dallas society and the start of the family's charitable foundation.

"We're going to use that to show how this all began."

"It's perfect, Hope. So much better than what has been in the press."

They still had work to be done.

"I'd still like to rehearse the Q&A, but if you're amenable, we can wait until tomorrow morning to do that," she said.

Lucille nodded. "You're right. We're all exhausted."

Abruptly, Max let out a cry signaling he was waking and needed to be fed. Hope smiled. "If you-all will excuse me…"

She stayed in her guest room to nurse. When she emerged forty-five minutes later to dispose of a soiled diaper, no one was up but Garrett. He followed her outside to the garbage cans. "I owe you an apology."

Hope stood for a moment, admiring the warm summer breeze and the deep black sky overhead. A full moon shone down upon them. "I misunderstood about the flags."

She pivoted to face him. "Obviously."

He continued soberly, "And I probably shouldn't tell you what to do."

She arched her brow. "You definitely should not tell me what to do," she reiterated as warmth spiraled inside her.

His expression gentled. "You worried me."

Hope sighed and met his eyes. "I worried myself," she admitted. "I've never done that, fallen asleep at the wheel."

He laid a comforting hand on her shoulder. "The car wasn't on."

"Still." She bit her lip. "If you hadn't gone to get ice…" The tears she'd been holding back clogged her throat. She drew another deep breath and tilted her face to his. "What would happen to Max if something happens to me?"

The next thing she knew, Garrett's arms were around her. He pulled her against his solid warmth.

"Nothing is going to happen to you," he told her gruffly.

With him there, beside her, she could believe it.

The problem was, he wasn't always going to be there to protect her, and/or Max. And when that day came…

More tears flowed down her face.

"It's okay," he soothed, holding her close. "I'm here."

And he stayed with her, until she caught her breath and and turned her face up to his. As grateful for his assistance as she was embarrassed over her own shortcomings.

Tenderness radiated in his gaze. "What else do you need?" he asked her softly.

Hope gulped, still too shaken up and too worn out to censor herself. "For you to hold me," she whispered, as a new wave of emotion swept over her.

"That, I can do," Garrett promised, wrapping his strong arms around her.

Holding her close.

Until she finally accepted his wordless urging and got into bed. He climbed in beside her, curling his big body around hers, protecting her as she drifted into a deep, much-needed sleep.

GARRETT WOKE JUST after six the next morning. He reached for Hope, but to his disappointment found the bed beside him was empty. The bunkhouse was exceptionally quiet. He found Hope sitting on the back porch, still in the clothes she'd had on the night before. She was seated on the glider, Max in one arm, bottle feeding him.

She cast him a beleaguered glance. "Don't start. My milk supply is low."

He moved toward them. "I wasn't going to say anything." Even though they both knew she needed more sleep than she was getting. Or had been getting for the past week.

"Good." She turned her attention to the sun rising in the east. A warm breeze ruffled her mussed, golden hair. Like last night, she was near tears. Mostly, he figured, of fatigue. "Because it wouldn't have been well received."

And with good reason, he thought. Hope was definitely still highly irascible and incredibly beautiful, despite the dusky shadows beneath her eyes.

Aware she seemed as fragile emotionally now as she had on the ride back from town the previous night, Garrett moved the stack of black-and-white photos and résumés she had spread out on the cushion beside her. He sat down. Max immediately propped a sleeper-clad foot on Garrett's forearm and stopped drinking from his bottle long enough to make flirty eyes and smile.

Affection flowing through him, Garrett smiled back.

Max resumed sucking down his breakfast, his innocent blue gaze moving from Garrett to Hope and back again.

"So what are you doing?" Garrett indicated the photos printed off her email.

"Looking for my new nanny. The agency is trying to pair me with a replacement for Mary Whiting."

"She isn't coming back at all?" This was bad news.

Hope released a shaky breath. "Her mother needs her, so she is taking a part-time position close by."

Garrett fanned through the applicants, trying to find the bright side. "All of them look nice."

Hope sighed. "Not to mention impossibly well trained. British nanny academies are the best."

"Then…?"

Hope's lip took on a troubled curve. "Something could happen to the next baby nurse—or her family—too. I don't want Max getting attached to a series of people. And his stranger-danger phase is coming."

He blinked in surprise.

"All six- to nine-month-old children go through it," Hope explained seriously. "Just as they usually start experiencing separation anxiety at nine to twelve months."

She never ceased to amaze him. "Did you memorize that?"

She blinked. "Doesn't everyone?"

Garrett draped his arm along the back of the glider. "I have no clue."

She settled into the curve of his body. "Well, they should."

He cuddled her close, drinking in the vanilla and lavender scent of her. He pressed a kiss to the top of her head. "What else is bothering you? And don't try and fib. I can tell something is really upsetting you."

Hope studied the golden sun rising slowly in the east then, settling even closer, looked up at him. "What if I do get another nanny and keep working these ridiculously long hours and Max bonds with someone else more than me? Because, let's be honest, Garrett—" she paused to look deep into his eyes "—life would have been a whole lot easier the last week if I hadn't had to cart Max everywhere with me. And fit his feedings in between work sessions."

Garrett studied the anguished expression on her face. Finally they were getting to the root of what had been upsetting her on the ride back from town the previous night. "Yeah, but the week would have been really dull without Max, too. I know for a fact every one of us has enjoyed having the little guy around." *Me, especially.*

"Yes, well, that's because right now Max

thinks that everyone is his friend. It was why I was able to leave him with Bess, and Wyatt and Chance yesterday for a little while."

Garrett snorted. "That also explains why Max took so readily to Chance and Wyatt yesterday."

Hope shifted toward him once again, her shoulder bumping his. "Speaking of your brothers... Do you know they wouldn't let me put Max down at all yesterday? They took turns wearing the baby carrier and passing Max back and forth." She shook her head in astonishment. "I've never seen two guys so over the moon." She gave Garrett a closer look. "Do all the men in your family have baby fever?"

Garrett exhaled in exasperation. "Don't lump me in with my cowboy brothers." *Especially when it comes to you and Max.*

"Please," she scoffed. "You've got the most acute case of baby fever of all!"

Noting it was time for Max to burp, Garrett held out his hands. "That's just 'cause Max is so darn adorable."

Smiling proudly, Hope shifted Max to his arms. "He is, isn't he?"

So was his momma. It didn't matter what she wore, or didn't, or what time of day it was. She was absolutely gorgeous, Garrett reflected. He couldn't stop looking at her.

A comfortable silence stretched between them.

Max burped loudly and grinned, then patted his hand against the side of the bottle as if to say *more, please.*

Hope handed Garrett the baby bottle. He settled Max in the crook of his arm, aware he could get very used to all this. It was definitely affecting his future plans.

But it was too soon to discuss all that.

That he knew.

"So," he said, turning the conversation back to something they *could* discuss. "No more British nannies?"

Hope lifted one hand. "I have to find some sort of child care because I have to work to support us. But I also need an arrangement that has very flexible work hours." She shook her head miserably. "You've seen how crazy it can be when I'm in the midst of trying to manage a crisis."

Hers was a demanding profession, for sure. He searched for a solution, and finally pointed out, "You get paid well enough to take fewer jobs."

Her delicate brows knit together. "It doesn't really work that way. You're either available at a moment's notice or you're not. Clients in the midst of a breaking scandal have very little time. They're not going to waste it calling someone who has a reputation for possibly not being available due to child-care issues."

He shrugged. "You could hire someone to assist you at Winslow Strategies."

"I'd have to train them, bring them up to speed. Again, something I don't have time to do right now. And care for Max. Plus..." Her lower lip trembled and her voice trailed off in distress. "What happens if I'm at work when

A Texas Soldier's Family

Max turns over for the very first time and I miss it? Or takes his first step? Or says *Momma* instead of *meh-meh-meh* when he wants to eat?"

Able to understand that—it was something he had ruminated over, too—Garrett tucked Hope into the curve of his arm. "It could still happen, anyway."

Scowling, Hope shifted so her breast pressed into his chest. "Whose side are you on, anyway?"

"Yours. And Max's. Always."

She sighed, slightly calmer.

He loved the way she felt cuddled against him. Tenderness flowed through him. Daring her wrath, he pressed another light kiss to the top of her head. "Sure you don't want to go back to bed?"

Hope rolled her eyes. "We have a house full of family, in case you've forgotten."

He liked the sound of that. *We.* Who would have thought? A week ago, all he'd wanted to do was avoid family. Now having everyone nearby felt really good.

He turned to Hope. "I meant you—alone—sweetheart. You could get another hour or two of sleep. The camera crews won't be here until the afternoon."

Her slender shoulders squared in fierce defiance. "No. I need to shower and get into work clothes, so as soon as Max goes to sleep, I'll be doing that."

Okay, then. "How about I watch him for you while you do all that?"

Gratitude shone in her eyes. "There are times like now when I don't know how I'm ever going to repay you."

Resisting the urge to really kiss her, he offered a wicked smile instead. "Not to worry," he whispered in her ear. "I'll collect."

This time she smiled back, just as mischievously. "I am sure you will."

HOPE CLIMBED INTO the shower and let the hot water pour over her. She knew she had been moody lately—that Garrett had attributed it to lack of sleep and hormones, when, in fact, what she was really worried and sad about was the fact that the job with the Lockharts was coming to a close. She and Max would be leaving, and she might never see Garrett again. Or she would see him, from time to time, but it wouldn't be the same. Hadn't she promised herself she wasn't going to do this again? Launch herself into a love affair that was only destined to end?

She had told Garrett—and herself—she could handle it. That this fling was all she wanted. Or needed. Now she was beginning to see it wasn't true. She did want to get married. She wanted a husband to share the good and bad times with. She wanted Max to have a daddy. And she wanted that daddy to be…Garrett?

Not because he was so good with Max.

Or because he seemed to genuinely like having kids around.

But because Garrett just fit into their lives. And their hearts.

Worse, her body tingled with need for him every time she was near him. It had been thirty hours since they had last made love, yet it felt like forever. Of course that was probably just her hormones. It had to be, Hope told herself, as she toweled off and dressed for work, then went out to the main living area of the bunkhouse. Max was on the counter in his infant seat, watching Garrett and Sage alternately cook breakfast together and jockey for space.

"I keep telling Max that the kitchen is mine," Sage joked, looking every bit as enthralled with Hope's son as her brothers and mother. "And Garrett should just go put his feet up somewhere."

"Hey," Garrett claimed, with an elbow to his sister's side, "I'm quite the chef in my own right."

Hope found herself leaping in to defend him. "He really is."

Sage scoffed. "You say that now, but you haven't tasted my food yet."

Lucille walked out, still looking wrung out and exhausted, despite over twelve hours of sleep. "It's true." The older woman flashed a wan smile. "Although both Sage and Garrett are excellent chefs."

Curious, Hope asked, "Did you teach them?"

Lucille, who—like Hope—had already dressed for the interview to come at noon that day, adjusted her pearls. "Oh, no, I can't cook at all."

"Gladys, our cook, taught us when Mom and Dad were out evenings," Sage explained.

Lucille reached for the coffee pot. Her hand was trembling slightly. "There was a serious lack of family dinners when our children were growing up."

Garrett had said as much. Hope found that sad. So did the Lockhart matriarch.

Sage and Garrett hugged Lucille simultaneously. Garrett soothed, "Not to worry, Mom. We're making up for it now."

Lucille's smile faltered.

"Lucille?" Hope asked, not sure what the sudden pale shift in the sixty-eight-year-old woman's color meant. "Are you feeling okay?"

Lucille gasped. "I…don't know…" She put her hand to her chest, winced, as if in horrendous pain.

"Oh, my God, Mom!" Sage rushed toward her mother.

Lucille staggered slightly. "I think I'm having a heart attack!" she said.

Garrett caught his mother as she fell.

"EXHAUSTION. DEHYDRATION. HYPERVENTILATION. All of which led to one heck of an episode of tachycardia," Laramie Community Hospital emergency room doctor Gavin Monroe pronounced, after examining Lucille. Her children gathered round.

"So it wasn't a heart attack?" Hope blurted out before she could stop herself.

She knew she wasn't family, but at this moment she felt like it.

"No. It just mimicked one," Dr. Monroe explained. "Given what Mrs. Lockhart has been through the last few weeks, it's not surprising she is at her limit."

"What's the treatment plan?" Garrett asked, still cradling Max in his arms.

Dr. Monroe said, "Sleep is the most important thing. We're giving your mother a sedative and admitting her for at least twenty-four…maybe forty-eight hours, depending on how she does. That will help enormously. So will getting her out of the previous stressful environment. Try to see that she follows a healthy diet and has lots of family support. Exercise. We'll also have her evaluated to make sure she's not suffering from anxiety or depression. If she is, those can both be treated medically."

A mixture of guilt and worry filled Hope. This was partly her fault for not being able to take enough of the burden off the shoulders of the Lockhart matriarch. And not listening to Garrett when he tried to convince her and his mother to get more sleep. She couldn't do anything about that now, but she could take extra strides to protect her from this point forward. "Should Lucille be admitted under a fictitious name?"

Brows lifted, all around.

Hope staved off interruption with a lift of her hand. "I know there are medical privacy laws to protect patients."

Sternly, Dr. Monroe said, "And we take them very seriously."

"I'm sure you do," Hope countered, "but Mrs. Lockhart has been in the news a lot lately, and not in a positive way. When there is an ongoing crisis of this nature, things like a 'nervous collapse' or 'sudden hospitalization' have a way of leaking to the press."

Gavin Monroe gave Hope a censoring look. "In Laramie, Texas, we take care of our own. And anyone who happens to be just passing through, as well. But," he continued kindly, "if you-all like, I'll speak to the staff. See that Mrs.

Lockhart is listed in the hospital visitor register under her maiden name, Henderson."

"We'd appreciate that," Garrett said.

Dr. Monroe nodded. "In the meantime, you all need to go home and let Lucille get some much-needed rest."

Reluctantly, they all returned to the ranch.

They'd barely gotten out of their vehicles when two news vans with satellite hookups attached to the roofs caravanned down the drive.

Sage gasped. "Oh, no. I almost forgot!"

Hope hadn't.

Sage swung around. "What are we going to tell the reporter about Mom?"

Garrett looked at Hope. "Why don't we let Hope tell us?" he suggested quietly.

Chapter Thirteen

It meant a lot to Hope, that Garrett—and his siblings—trusted her to protect their mother to the best of her ability.

"The goal here is to preserve Lucille's privacy. Keep what should be confidential out of the public domain."

Garrett kept his eyes locked with hers. "You're asking us to parse the truth?"

Hope did her best to contain the protective emotion welling up inside her. She'd come to care for Lucille, too. "I'm asking you to reveal only what you think would be okay with your mom. Right now, if we were to let the press know she had been hospitalized for exhaustion—"

"They'd be camped outside the county medical center. Trying to get shots of us coming in and out," Chance predicted grimly.

"Right," Wyatt chimed in. He placed an arm around his younger sister's shoulders. "And none of us want that."

Hope searched Garrett's face. Although his expression remained implacable, she could only imagine the conflict this was causing him, deep inside. "Look, I know you agreed to take the lead here, as the eldest son and the male head of the family, but if you're not comfortable with this, I can prepare a statement. We can cancel the interview and go with that."

He regarded her for a long, thoughtful moment. "Won't that stir up more interest, instead of less, since we've already agreed to do the interview?"

Hope sighed. "Probably."

"Then we really need to follow through as promised," he decided.

"Besides," Sage told Garrett, "you are a doctor. You're used to protecting a patient's privacy. This is no different than that, really."

It shouldn't have been, Hope thought. But she could tell he was uncomfortable with the whole idea of trying to hide things from the press. Nevertheless, he was first in line to meet the TV reporter, Nikki Lowell, who'd had the camera crew filming from the moment she stepped out of the news van.

Looking as handsome as ever, Garrett strode forward to shake Nikki's hand. Grinning widely, his sea-blue eyes crinkling at the corners, he turned on the full Lockhart charm.

Enough to make Hope feel a twinge of relief. She knew in that instant that Garrett was going to put his own personal feelings aside and step up to master the task at hand. Even if it wasn't anything he would have ever chosen to do.

Once all the introductions had been made, Nikki asked, "Where's Lucille?"

Garrett explained Lucille had been unavoidably detained, but sent her apologies. "The truth is, my mother is worn out from the events of the last week and a half. I'm sure you can understand how hectic a schedule she has kept, personally meeting with all the directors of the charities who were let down, making good on their long-delayed fiscal gifts."

"Why did she do that?" Nikki asked, signaling for the camera crew to zoom in on Garrett's handsome face. "I mean, she could have left it to anyone else, even the lawyers."

Not Lucille's style, Hope thought proudly.

"As CEO, she felt personally responsible," Garrett said.

"Do you think Lucille should have known what was going on a whole lot sooner?" Nikki asked.

"I don't deal in what-ifs," he said quietly.

Hope knew that to be all too true.

As much as she might wish otherwise, Garrett wasn't the kind of man who would spend time wishing that he and she had met and become involved under wildly different circumstances.

As far as he was concerned, their affair was what it was. Just as this confrontation with Nikki and the TV network news could not be avoided. They would battle their way through it, even if doing so meant uncomfortably parsing every word.

Nikki tilted her head, as if trying to figure out how to get under Garrett's skin and uncover what she suspected was being kept from her and the rest of the media. "Do you think your mom should have skipped out on the scheduled interview today, whether she felt up to being here or not?" Nikki asked.

Sage, Wyatt and Chance moved in close to the eldest Lockhart. United, they were an impressive front. Garrett folded his arms in front of him and stared down Nikki Lowell with a warrior's ease. "My siblings and I all agree our mother's health comes first." His brothers and sister nodded in support.

Nikki turned to Hope.

"When this family bands together there is no stopping them," Hope informed her. "I did discuss the possibility of rescheduling so we could have the interview conducted as originally planned, but they were anxious to let people know what's been discovered about the fraud."

"I can understand that," Nikki said.

Hope sighed in commiseration. "And with the Dallas Police Department now actively beginning an investigation into the embezzlement, as of late last evening, it's only a matter of time before some other news outlet discovers the scoop we're giving you, so..."

Reminded that she and Hope had worked with each other on previous scandals, and Hope had always been as straightforward as possible with her, Nikki regarded Hope, one professional to another. "You're right. We can always add to the story later. Let's do it."

Everyone sat down in the Adirondack chairs in the backyard. With the breathtaking view of the ranch behind them, Nikki started with a few easy questions, then asked, "How was it possible to have twenty-five million dollars stolen without anyone noticing?"

"My parents wanted to avoid spending a lot of money on overhead for the foundation, so the Lockhart Foundation had very little staff." Garrett went on to explain how the CFO had handled all the financial activities. "My mother signed all the checks, but she trusted Paul Smythe—who was also an old family friend—to handle the rest."

"In other words, your parents' noble intentions and generosity made fraud possible."

All four Lockhart siblings nodded.

"What now?" Nikki continued. "Are you going to close the foundation?"

"No," Garrett said firmly. "Absolutely not."

"But if the bank accounts have been emptied…"

The siblings exchanged looks. It seemed, Hope noted happily, they were all of one opinion.

"We'll find a way to keep it going," Garrett promised.

THE REST OF the afternoon was spent showing Nikki and her film crew the Circle H ranch. When evening came, the news crew departed and the family enjoyed a brief dinner together, then Sage went to the hospital to check on her mother. Wyatt and Chance left for their own ranches to tend to their herds. Only Hope, Garrett and Max remained at the Circle H.

"Did you mean that—about finding a way to keep the foundation going, as a family?" Hope asked, after putting a sleeping Max to bed. "And not just leaving it to your mother?"

"Yes." Garrett continued loading the dishwasher.

Seeing the opportunity to finally check this off her To Do list, she went to lend a hand. "Because there is something your mother hoped I would be able to talk you into doing," she continued bluntly, knowing it was a risk to even try and broach this subject.

She waited until his steady blue gaze met hers. "Becoming CEO in Lucille's stead."

He studied her in a weighted, awkward silence, looking anything but pleased. Then he scoffed and shook his head. "You really expect us to ask my mother to be the scapegoat in this mess and resign? After all she's been through? After how hard she's fought the last couple of weeks to make things right?"

Ignoring the temper in his tone, Hope worked to keep her cool. "She made the decision days ago." She paused, to let that sink in. "Lucille's reputation as a manager is tainted, most likely irreparably. She understands she can still be a member of the board and she can help out behind the scenes. But the reality is that unless someone like you—a doctor with a distinguished military background—takes over and becomes the public face of the foundation, gets everything back on track, the organization's chances of survival are not good. Particularly if, in order to continue, you-all are going to have to rely on fund-raising instead of family money."

Grimacing he picked up the recycling container and headed outside. "A couple of problems with that. I'm lousy at soliciting money."

She could see that. Garrett wasn't the kind of guy to go cap in hand to anyone.

She also noticed that he hadn't said he wasn't interested in the job at all.

She followed with a bag of regular trash. "You can hire professionals for that."

"With what?" Garrett dropped both in the appropriate containers. "There's no money left, remember?"

They turned and walked back toward the bunkhouse. The sun was setting in a streaky pink-and-purple sky. The summer air was fragrant with the smells of sunshine, flowers and freshly mown grass. "I'm assuming, like your siblings, that at least some eventually will be recovered. If not, where there's a will, there's a way. Charities do it all the time."

His look let her know there was an even bigger obstacle.

He dropped down onto the glider on the back porch, stretching his long legs out in front of him.

Hope left the back door slightly ajar so she'd be able to hear Max if he needed her.

Garrett massaged the back of his neck. "I don't want to work in Dallas."

Where Max and I live.

Another arrow to the heart.

Hope forced herself to be a professional and continued lobbying for her client. "So hire a staff you like, move wherever you like." *Even if it is thousands of miles from me and Max.* "Run the Lockhart Foundation from afar."

Garrett studied her. Finally he asked quietly, "Somewhere like Washington, DC?"

Hope wasn't sure whether the question was rhetorical—or a test. She did know she didn't want Lucille to lose out on a great solution to their problems because their scandal manager had bungled it by pushing too hard, or not enough.

"We did some checking," she told Garrett carefully, trying not to notice how handsome he looked in his pale blue button-down, jeans and boots. "You can work for any charity you like, while still on active duty in the military, as long as there is no conflict of interest with your service to our country, and we would have the lawyers make sure that there would not be. The same would be true if you were to take the hospital job in Seattle."

He shook his head. "I already turned that down."

Although she had known he was leaning that way, she hadn't realized he'd already made a final decision. Which made her wonder, what else hadn't he told her? Just how much *did* she know about him? And why was she suddenly so unnerved? They were involved in a fling, nothing more. So, at least from his point of view, it shouldn't really matter to her what his plans were, or vice versa.

Telling herself to cut both of them a break, Hope forced her thoughts back to the CEO position. "It wouldn't need to be a permanent situation, Garrett."

Just like their love affair, enthralling as it was, wasn't permanent.

"We just need a fresh face to go with a fresh start for the foundation. The board of directors can name you the interim CEO, to manage the implementation of new safeguards to prevent fraud in the future, and ease you out in a month or two, if you like."

His lips formed a more amenable line. "I can see where this would take a great deal of stress off my mother. Especially now, with her so exhausted." He turned to look at Hope. "But why didn't my mother broach this with me?"

A tricky point. Hope remained standing, her back to the wooden porch post, her hands behind her. "She was going to, eventually. But she thought the initial discussion might be better received coming from someone else."

Garrett waited, obviously sensing there was more.

With a reluctant sigh, Hope told him, "A pretty face."

He winced.

"Her words, not mine."

Garrett rolled to his feet. "You didn't mind being put in the middle of a family drama?"

Holding her ground, Hope shrugged. "Sometimes it's my job."

He ambled closer. "You're sure this is what my mother wants?"

He was so near, she had to tilt her head back to see into his face. "That, plus for all of her children to make good use of their inheritance from their father."

"I understand that for Chance and Wyatt.

They're ranchers. Although she's the last person to admit it, Sage needs to be closer to her family. But for Zane—who's in the Special Forces—and me...? My mom really expects me to *reside* in Laramie?"

Was that even a possibility? Over a week ago he had been going to sell both his Laramie properties as soon as possible and move on.

Unable to clearly read his mood or expression, Hope moved away from the post and paced to the far end of the porch, where gorgeous flowers had been planted in advance of the film crew's arrival.

Drinking in the sweet, sun-drenched floral scent, Hope turned back to face him.

"If Laramie County is where you see yourself settling down, why not? You've already become involved in the community, in supporting one nonprofit organization here that you obviously feel passionately about—West Texas Warrior Assistance."

He downplayed his largesse. "I wrote a check."

It was more than that; she knew it, deep down. And so did he, if he would just admit it to himself.

Irritated that he wasn't telling her what was on his mind, she walked slowly toward him and said, "Chance showed me the specs on the office building you inherited on his phone yesterday afternoon, when you were in town clearing the trash out of the Victorian."

Another shrug of those powerful shoulders. Another poker face. "It's got to be fixed up to be leased out again."

Leased, not sold. Hope moved even closer and dared to push a little more. "We all figured out what you were doing."

Abruptly, Garrett became cynical and guarded, similar to the man she'd first met on the plane from DC. "Yeah?" he challenged dryly. "And what is that?"

"You're turning the office building into a place to house the WTWA."

When he didn't react, she pushed even more.

"With what would appear to be an area for physical therapy and spaces on the upper floors for counseling and group therapy."

He remained where he was, legs braced apart, brawny arms folded in front of him. "So?"

"An undertaking that large is going to need a medical director to pull everything together. And my guess is you want it to be you."

GARRETT HAD NEVER met anyone who understood him the way Hope did. All week long he had been wondering if he was crazy, unrealistic, getting ahead of himself. Taking the guilt he felt over the way the foundation and his family had let Bess Monroe and the local former soldiers down by not fulfilling their promises, and turning it into what could be a life's mission for him.

He'd never been impulsive.

But here he was, after a little more than a week's time, taking his career objective and standing it on its head. And not just for the soldiers. No, there was a lot more driving this.

"It's true," he admitted carefully, letting his gaze rove over Hope. Because she'd been working in her official capacity as scandal manager all day—albeit in a rural environment—she was dressed in a black and sky-blue print cotton skirt that molded her hips and waist and ended just above the knee. A sleeveless white cotton blouse had been paired with a blue cardigan and flats. A heart-shaped gold necklace and earrings gleamed against the creamy alabaster of her skin. As the urge to make love to her again grew, his body tightened in response. How he wished he could simply take her to bed, instead of having this uncomfortable conversation.

But she wanted, needed to know where things stood with him, so...

He looked her in the eye. "Whether I'm active-duty military or not, I want to keep helping soldiers." *No matter what I'm doing, I can see myself still wanting you. And wanting to be a part of Max's life, too.*

"Which is why the job at Walter Reed held so much appeal to you, even if it meant reenlisting."

He walked close enough to inhale her sweet and sexy scent. "As much as I'd like to practice medicine there, I also know there will always be other doctors ready and willing to help out."

"You have good doctors and nurses here in Laramie County, too." They'd seen them in action—first caring for Max and then Lucille.

"What we don't have in Laramie County are programs designed exclusively for former military. In many ways, their needs are greater, because they are no longer in the armed services, yet many are still dealing with injuries and rehabilitation, and the process of making the transition back to civilian life."

Understanding lit her pretty emerald-green eyes. "You know you could make a difference."

He gently stroked her cheek with the back of

his hand. "Which maybe is what my dad wanted all along when he left me the two properties."

She leaned into his touch. "For you to settle here?"

The silky warmth of her skin sent another wave of desire roaring through him.

He nodded. "And to help the people in Laramie County, where he and my mom grew up. He knew I had no ties to Dallas. That I'd never really fit there."

"But you do here."

Her compassion warmed him from the inside out. He let his hands slide to her shoulders. "Not sure I want to breed horses or bulls, like my brothers, but yeah...I like the Texas countryside a lot. And I like the house in town, too."

Smiling, she lifted her chin. "It's close to the hospital. And the office building."

It would be a good place to settle down one day and bring up a family, he thought, his gaze roving the softness of her lips. But wary of getting ahead of himself, scaring off Hope, who thus far had only agreed to a temporary liaison with him, he reined in his innate need to just say whatever was on his mind, and kept silent about that. For now.

Garrett decided to show her what he felt, instead.

Chapter Fourteen

Garrett took Hope in his arms and kissed her until her abdomen felt liquid and weightless and her knees grew weak. He brought her against him, length to length. His tongue swept her mouth until her whole body was quivering with urgent need, her heart thumping so hard she could feel it in her ears.

And still he pressed her against him intimately, hardness to softness, until the last of her reservations regarding the wisdom of a short-term affair faded. She knew her task here would be over soon. But that didn't mean they couldn't make the most of what little time they had left.

Still kissing her ardently, he undid the buttons on her blouse, unfastened the front closure of her bra. He bent to kiss her chin, the arch of her neck, the uppermost curves of her taut, tingling breasts.

Around them, the sky grew dusky. The silence of the countryside as well as the warm, flower-scented air and faint summery breeze, provided a sensual setting.

It would be completely dark soon.

She didn't care. She wanted him.

Here. Now. Like this.

Spinning him around with a boldness she had not known she possessed, she pushed him beneath the overhang, up against the side of the house. Her eyes locked with his and she began unbuttoning his shirt.

He threaded his hands through her hair, watching. "And just when I thought you couldn't surprise me," he murmured.

She rose on tiptoe and, parting the edges of his shirt, pressed her bare breasts against the muscles of his chest. Wreathing her arms around his neck, she smiled wickedly. "Oh, I'm full of surprises."

Why not, since this was likely their last hurrah?

"Like this..." She fit her lips to his, opening her mouth, caressing his tongue, savoring the hot, masculine taste of him. Finding solace... finding strength...in tenderness.

Aware she had never felt as soft and womanly and empowered as she did with him, she unclasped his belt buckle and undid the zipper on his jeans. He moaned as she cupped the hard, velvety length of him in her palm. Stroking. Reveling. Enciting.

The next thing she knew, the back zipper of her skirt was coming undone, too. The floral fabric was sliding down over her knees. Pooling at her feet. A swift hook of his thumbs in the elastic and her panties followed.

"Hey. I'm supposed to be in charge here," she reminded him breathlessly.

He grinned and lifted both hands in ready and willing surrender. "Then I guess I'll have to let you have your way with me."

Deciding the only way to keep him where she wanted him was to trap him with her weight, she took his hand and directed him toward the glider.

A quick tug sent his jeans down his thighs. Leaving them at mid-knee, thus trapping him right where and how she wanted him, she settled on his lap, her arms encircling his shoulders, her thighs planted tight on either side of his.

"Now, where were we?" she murmured, kissing him again.

"Here?" The tip of his manhood pressed against her. "Or here?" Seconds later, his calloused palms moved slowly, lovingly upward over her ribs. "Or maybe here…?" Her nipples tingled as he bent and kissed her breasts. She moaned again, yearning to have him inside her.

This was torture.

Sweet torture.

But torture nevertheless.

"Maybe I will let you call the shots," she said, kissing him again, deeply, provocatively. "As long as it's—" she shifted wantonly to show him what she meant "—right now."

He grinned, his lips nipping at hers even as one hand slid between them. He refused to let her rush. "Not yet."

Gripping her buttocks with one hand, he spread her thighs all the more, stroked her inner thighs, made his way through the nest of soft curls to the softer petals hidden within. She shuddered, gasped as he sent her libido into overdrive.

And still he kissed her with maddeningly slow intensity until her blood flowed through her veins like liquid fire and her body pulsed and shuddered with exploding need.

With a groan, he brought her down over top of him. Pushed up into her, hard. Seeming to know, as always, exactly what she wanted and needed, he lifted her against him, thrust deep, let her settle, thrust deep again. Faster, then slower. Then perfect, so perfect. Her soul soaring as high as her heart, he possessed her on his terms. Refusing to let her run away, set unnecessary limits, he brought her to life. Again and again. Until at last his control faltered, too. They surged together, finding a pleasure so deep and profound it seemed impossible. And Hope knew that maybe—just maybe—she'd been wrong. This wasn't a short-term love affair, after all.

It was one that would last.

All she had to do was open up and take a risk. With her heart. With her life…

And maybe Garrett would, too.

MORNING BROUGHT WITH it a flurry of activity. While Hope cared for Max and responded to journalists inquiring about the theft at the Lockhart Foundation, Garrett went into town to meet with Bess Monroe and the other founders of West Texas Warrior Assistance.

At noon, he returned to the ranch with his siblings and recovering mother in tow.

Not that Lucille had apparently accepted her physician's advice to take it easy. A fact that appeared to be irking her own doctor son to no end.

Garrett squared off with Lucille as she called everyone to the long plank table. "Mom, you just got home from the hospital. Now is not the time for a Lockhart Foundation board meeting."

Hope backed Garrett up. "I agree."

Although Lucille had slept nearly nineteen hours straight in the hospital before being released, the older woman still looked exhausted in a way that would take weeks to recover from. But, for the moment, as Lucille waved off her eldest son's concern, she was as fiercely determined as ever. "Nonsense! There are things we need to talk about—and vote on. I won't be able to rest until we do. And since my doctor's orders were "rest, rest, and more rest..."

With a groan, everyone sat down.

Hope started to exit the room.

Lucille waved her back. "No, Hope, you need to stay." Reluctantly Hope returned. "The first order of business is that I want you to be the new director of public relations at the Lockhart Foundation. A move that takes board approval."

Taken aback, Hope looked at the shocked faces all around her. "We probably should have talked about this beforehand. And you should have spoken with the board, too."

Had Hope not fallen hard for Garrett, she would have jumped at the opportunity. The fact that she was intimately involved with him made it all far too complicated.

Lucille scoffed. "And give you a chance to refuse me? No way. You need a job with more flexible hours. Recovering from the scandal is going to continue to be an uphill climb and we require your expertise."

Hope slipped into the open chair next to Sage and looked across the table at Garrett. He was so still he could have been playing a game of statue.

That did not seem like a good thing.

She battled a self-conscious blush and swallowed around the rising ache in her throat. Suddenly, she had to know. "Did you instigate this?"

He let out a long breath, shook his head.

Disappointment roiled through her. Why, she didn't know. Since when did she want anyone propelling her into a job that would likely upend her life more than it already had been the past few weeks?

She had Max to consider.

Well, that and her heart, which suddenly seemed to be in jeopardy, too.

Garrett rubbed his hand across his jaw, as if it were taking everything he had to contain himself. Dropping his hand, he met the gazes of everyone at the table. "Hope's right," Garrett said in a low, clipped tone. "We probably should have spoken about this. Since finding the funds for her salary could be a problem, given the current state of foundation bank accounts."

"I have a solution for that, too," Lucille announced with a brisk smile. "I'm selling my home in Dallas. Half the proceeds will go into a trust to fix up the Circle H, where I now plan to reside full time. That, plus the money from my retirement account will see me comfortably into old age. The other half will go to the foundation."

She paused for effect as she glanced around the room. "But this time, I don't want to try and work with one hundred charities. I just want to work with one. West Texas Warrior Assistance. If Garrett is going to be the medical director, we need to support him."

No problem there, Hope noted. Garrett's siblings were completely behind the idea.

"Let's vote on it," Sage enthused. "All in favor of hiring Hope, say aye."

A chorus of "Ayes!" came from around the table.

"And focusing the foundation on West Texas Warrior Assistance?"

Once again, the support was unanimous.

Sage made a note in the meeting minutes.

Hope cleared her throat. When she had everyone's attention, she asked, "Shouldn't you ask me if I want the job?"

"Ah, not just yet." Sage turned back to her mother. "Obviously, Mom, you've given this a lot of thought."

Lucille smiled. "I have. And for the record, I also want to install Adelaide, since she was instrumental in helping us uncover the fraud, as our new chief financial officer."

Wyatt frowned the way he always did when his former girlfriend's name came up. "We definitely need to talk about that."

Lucille leveled a look right back at Wyatt. "Oh, we will," she promised.

Garrett shook his head as if that would clear

it. "Mom, what's gotten into you? You used to be so…restrained!"

"The last few weeks made me think about all the problems I couldn't solve, as well as the ones that we could, if we had just not swept problems under the rug and instead confronted them directly. And that brings me to my next agenda item." Lucille referred to her tablet. "Garrett, you've said you're willing to be CEO. Can you start immediately?"

He nodded, obviously willing to do whatever it took to allow his mother to concentrate on regaining her good health.

Lucille smiled her approval. "Everyone want to vote on the last two items?"

And with a quick vote the family gave its approval.

"Great." Lucille grinned at the four children gathered around her. "Now, what are we going to do about having Garrett, the new CEO, in Laramie, and Hope in Dallas? Hope, are you—

and Max—willing to relocate? As soon as it's convenient, of course."

The matriarch of the family was definitely a steamroller. And she had just run roughshod over Hope. With all good intentions, certainly, but Hope still felt shell-shocked and uncertain.

Knowing she had to get her life problems figured out and solved on her own, Hope ignored the intentions and focused on the assessing way Garrett was looking at her. She lifted her chin. "Lucille, I appreciate your confidence in me, but I haven't even said I'd take the job yet."

"If we meet all your demands—salary, living arrangements, work hours, responsibilities and so forth—would you?"

Hope looked at Garrett, still having no clue as to how he felt about all this. And that was the sticking point—not where she lived, or how much she made, or even how many job responsibilities she would have. She wanted to know what he felt. That he wanted to work side by side with her. Because if that wasn't the case...

and the maddeningly inscrutable look on his face said maybe it wasn't…then any further discussion was pointless.

She'd grown up feeling in the way. She wasn't going to do it again.

"I don't know what I'd do. All I know is that I can't give you an answer today, not like this."

For a second, disappointment reigned.

Hope realized she hadn't been the only one secretly wishing she could be a permanent part of all this…

Sage looked at Garrett with a mixture of starry-eyed envy and approval. "Maybe it would help if you came clean." She prodded her eldest brother in the unabashedly romantic direction she wanted him to go. "Told everyone the two of you are…um…"

Lucille put in hopefully, "Serious about each other…? Engaged?"

It was all Hope could do not to groan. If Garrett's mother only knew how far from any kind of commitment, never mind any lasting future, she and Garrett were...

Lucille would be so disappointed.

As disappointed as Hope suddenly felt.

What happened in the darkness of his bedroom was one thing, to have it scrutinized in the glaring light of day, with the people who meant most to him gathered around, was another.

Garrett looked at Hope as if trying to read her mind. This time, she gave him nothing of what she was feeling, putting him on the hot seat, too, right along with her.

"No," he said finally. "It's too soon for that."

Lucille harrumphed, her disapproval as sharp as the glare she gave her son. "But not too soon to sleep with each other."

A collective gasp was followed by a beat of silence.

Ignoring Garrett's dark scowl, Lucille turned and focused on the blush blooming in Hope's cheeks. "I know two well-loved people when I see them."

Funny, Hope thought. Until now, she'd felt that way. She looked into his eyes and saw regret, and wondered if it was as painful as the remorse filling her heart. But there was no clue in the watchful silence of the room.

Garrett swung back to the members of the board, squared his shoulders and tried again. "I get that you're trying to help, Mom, but what Hope and I have shared is *not* up for family discussion. Nor is any aspect of her life or mine. I thought I had made that abundantly clear."

Suddenly, Hope didn't want their relationship to be something that could not be acknowledged or talked about. Even, or especially, to his family. To her surprise, she wanted one heck of a lot more. And she wanted it right now. Because if he didn't feel what she did, if he didn't even come close, then Lucille's unspoken accusation was right. What were they doing?

And to think she'd been worried about a succession of nannies! This was so much worse for her baby boy than that! Max deserved stability, and it was up to her to give it to him. He could not be expected to love and depend on Garrett, only to have the only father he had ever known walk away without warning. She and Garrett both had career decisions that needed to be made.

She'd been thinking he would factor into hers. Just as she had hoped she was factoring into his.

Had she been wrong? About that, how he felt, how he might ever feel?

Hope pushed back her chair and stood. Hands on the table in front of her, chin high, she asked, "Then how would you define it, if we're not engaged—" and apparently not headed that way, judging by his continued stony reaction "—and not an item?"

Garrett shoved back his chair and moved effortlessly to his feet, too. They stared at each other across the wide plank table.

Aware the foundation board meeting had devolved into something else entirely, yet needing her questions answered, Hope put her usual decorum aside and pressed on without shame or discretion. "I mean if it's only a fling and you're okay with that…" And she wasn't, she realized far too late, not at all! "Shouldn't you be able to own up to that?" She gestured at their audience. "I mean we're all adults here. Right?"

An even tenser silence fell.

Lucille stared at her son, waited.

"Ah. Maybe we should call an end to the board meeting and leave." Sage scrambled to her feet.

"Or better yet, maybe we should get out the popcorn." With an ornery grin, Wyatt stayed put.

Chance rocked back in his seat, arms folded in front of him. "I'd like to hear this, too," Chance said. "Might learn something. About what not to do, obviously."

"It's *private.*" Garrett pushed the words through clenched teeth.

Hope's heart pounded as if she'd run a marathon, even as her spirits sank. She held Garrett's gaze, ready to put it all on the line for the very first time in her life. If only he would dare to do so, too.

But that, she could tell, would only happen if she forced him.

Fighting through her disappointment, she pushed on like a reporter in a hostile press conference, "*Private* as in doesn't exist?"

He gave her no reaction.

Fighting tears, Hope offered another choice. "Never happened? Never should have happened?"

Because ethically, morally, she knew the answer to that even if he hadn't hired her and couldn't fire her.

Oh, heavens above, what a mess they had made.

WHAT DID HOPE want from him? Garrett wondered, grinding his jaw in frustration. Without warning, he felt as if he'd been propelled back to his childhood. Filled with all those unspoken and implied expectations he couldn't figure out, never mind meet. When he'd unfortunately blurted out whatever came to mind and gotten himself in even more trouble. Every time.

Determined not to do this, and certainly not in front of his whole family, he stood there, silent, just waiting, just looking at Hope. Waiting for her to give him a clue as to what would fix this. Not just with his family, who were more confused than he was, but with the two of them.

Usually, she was pretty good about doing that. Not today.

And after the way they'd made love the night before? All night long? What was going on with her, with them? How had he managed once again to end up so completely blindsided and confused?

Giving her one more chance to fully illuminate this matter before he hauled her off to continue this discussion in private, Garrett finally asked with forced calm, "What do you want this to be?"

Another sad silence fell.

Hope, looking more disillusioned and disappointed than he ever could have imagined her, simply shook her head. She looked him right in the eye, long and hard, and said, "Not. This."

Chapter Fifteen

Two days later, Lucille Lockhart stood in the bathroom of the former rental home and gaped at her eldest son. She was recovering nicely from her bout of exhaustion, getting stronger and healthier every day.

Garrett felt his own life going in reverse.

"You were serious about cleaning the bathrooms yourself."

Garrett dropped his scrub brush into the bucket, stripped off his gloves and stepped back. The entire upstairs of the Victorian house reeked of hospital-grade disinfectant. But the hours he'd spent working out his aggression had left it sparkling clean from top to bottom.

Thanks to the help he had received at the local hardware store, he also knew a lot more about home maintenance than he ever had before.

Had Hope elected to stick around, that skill might have come in handy. Since she hadn't...

He gathered up the rest of his gear, headed downstairs. "Why would you think I wasn't serious?" *About becoming more family oriented? Learning skills that would help with that—in a very practical way? Settling down?*

"Maybe you had better things to do with your time?"

He slid his mother a glance. "Like what?"

"Speaking to Hope?"

If he'd thought it would do any good, he would have. "She made it pretty clear when she left the Circle H she had nothing more to say to me."

"And you're content to leave it at that?"

No, but it was what he had to do, needed to

do, to come out of this relationship with even a shred of dignity. Hope had been honest with him from the first. Told him her life was too chaotic and full, as it was. That she had her son, who was all she needed. That even if she wanted to embark on a relationship with him, which she clearly hadn't, she wouldn't have the time or the energy to be able to do so.

He should have listened to her, instead of seducing her into what was to be a strictly physical relationship with a firm expiration date.

He had agreed with her stipulations because he had thought, deep down, that he would be able to change her mind. That, as time wore on and they got closer—and they *had* gotten closer—she would come to want the same things he did.

Only she hadn't.

And he had to live with his crushed expectations, hopes and dreams. Because it was his fault he hadn't listened to her at the outset.

Garrett crossed over to the cooler and pulled

out a couple of icy-cold flavored waters. He wiped off the dampness with a paper towel and handed his mom one. "Hope and I had an agreement, Mom. What we had was going to be a short-term thing, and that was it."

Lucille took a small, dainty sip. "You don't think she changed her mind?"

He had a flash of the soft, sweet way Hope gazed up at him when they made love, and the fiercely determined way she had looked as she had left the Circle H to return to her life in Dallas. He knew his mother was invested in this, rightly or wrongly. She had tried to help them find a happy-ever-after, and even if her ploy hadn't worked she deserved credit for trying.

Garrett downed half the bottle in a single gulp. The hot persistent ache in his throat only grew. He shrugged. "She never said so if she did."

His mother edged closer. She studied him with an eagle eye, before asking the kind of question she would have been too refined to have voiced before. "Did you change yours?"

The ever-present heaviness inside his heart remained. What did it matter? "It takes two equally committed people to make a successful relationship, Mom. You and Dad taught me that." It was what he wanted, what he had to have.

Lucille gazed at him thoughtfully, looking glad that at least one of her life lessons had sunk in. "Hope turned down the job at the foundation. Not because it wasn't challenging enough or would require her to relocate to Laramie, Texas. She turned it down because of you, Garrett."

Was he that much of a pariah? Did she still feel he had treated her poorly? Garrett clenched his teeth. "She didn't want to work with me?"

"She said she couldn't bear to be that close to you."

He stared at his mother like a shell-shocked idiot. "Hope actually said that?"

His mother propped her hands on her hips. "While she was crying her eyes out."

He took a moment to consider that. It was both the saddest thing and the best thing he had ever heard. Finally he found his voice, demanded thickly, "Hope cried over me?"

Lucille scoffed, as if she couldn't believe how oblivious he was. "You broke her heart!"

The accusation stung. And more, was completely unfounded. What had he done, after all, but offer Hope everything of value he had to give? All within the parameters she had set. "She decimated mine!"

Lucille leaned closer. "So tell her."

If he hadn't already been turned inside out, he would have. But he had, so...

Forcing himself to be realistic in a way he hadn't been before, Garrett shook his head. A reconciliation wasn't in the script Hope had laid out for them. And she was a woman who always stuck to the plan, never more so than when times got stressful. It was the only way to survive and come out unscathed, she had said.

Garrett winced. "She'd never believe me."

His mother encouraged him kindly. "Then it's up to you to tell her what's really in your heart and change that, isn't it?"

ON SATURDAY, HOPE left Max at home with a sitter and walked into the Lockhart Foundation for the last time. Lucille had asked her to pack up her personal belongings in advance of the mover's arrival.

Hope had readily agreed. Not only was it a way to help the still physically rebounding former CEO, but a way to give herself desperately needed closure, too.

As promised, Sharla, Lucille's soon-to-be-ex assistant, greeted Hope at the door.

Like Hope, she was in casual clothing, suitable for packing and moving.

They chatted for a moment, about who was tasked with packing up what and how, and Sharla's need to leave shortly to pick up her daughter after her ballet class.

Sharla led Hope over to the unassembled book boxes, markers, tape and scissors. While the two worked to put some boxes together, Sharla chatted. "I saw the video you posted on all the social media websites. You did a great job giving the history of the foundation and really introducing the entire family. I especially liked the way you portrayed Garrett. Sometimes he comes off as grumpy rather than heroic, but you caught his true essence."

Maybe because I know who he is, deep down. One of the kindest, strongest, most gallant men on Earth.

"Thanks."

"I was surprised you didn't take the public relations job for the foundation. Things had been going so well, from the sound of it."

They had been, for a while, anyway, Hope thought. In fact, she easily could have imagined herself becoming an integral part of the family charity.

Sharla chatted casually. "Is it because, like me, you didn't want to move to West Texas?"

"I just wasn't sure it was a good fit." *With me crazy in love with Garrett, and him feeling, I don't know exactly what, about me...*

Hope held a box closed while Sharla taped it shut. "What about you? Lucille told me you have a fantastic new job."

Nodding, Sharla grinned. "I start Monday. I've got a bump up in salary and responsibility, and a much shorter commute. Lucille really pulled out all the stops to make sure I wouldn't spend any time unemployed."

"Sounds like her," Hope said fondly.

"I know. All the Lockharts have huge hearts."

Even more importantly, the Lockharts had shown her what it was like to have a loving, supportive family surrounding you. They'd made her realize what she wanted in her own life—a love that would last, a daddy for Max, a family like theirs. Moreover, they'd helped her see that, in insisting on forging on alone, she was settling for far less than what either she or Max deserved.

And that meant changes had to be made, Hope schooled herself firmly. No more dead-end love affairs. No more falling for guys who weren't falling for her just as hard.

Aware Sharla was waiting for more of an explanation, about how Hope could be so close to the family one week, and then working so furiously to distance herself from them, Hope said in a low tone, "Crises can bond people together intensely in the moment. Those feelings rarely last."

How often had she said those very words? And found them true?

Sharla fit bubble-wrapped pictures of her family into a box. "You're not friends with any of the people you've helped in the past?"

Hope began taking plaques bearing Lucille's

name off the wall. "Not the way we were when the scandal or situation was in progress, no."

"That's too bad," Sharla sympathized.

It was. She needed more concrete relationships in her life. More people she and Max could rely on through thick and thin. Otherwise, her son was likely to grow up feeling as alone as she had when she was a child.

"I thought you and Garrett were getting, well, close."

They had been, Hope thought ruefully. She'd actually started to put herself out there instead of sticking to the script. She'd made the cardinal sin of allowing the overwhelming emotion of the crisis itself to influence her actions, as they had Garrett's.

If they'd simply had a casual fling, and ended it when they'd agreed that they would, without complication or hurt feelings, maybe they could have remained friends. Maybe she would have been able to move to Laramie, and see and work with Garrett every day. Let Garrett be a constant, loving male role model in Max's life.

And that might have left open the possibility that maybe, over time, as life returned to normal, they would *both* realize they wanted to take a chance on each other, this time with no holds barred.

But that wasn't ever going to happen, Hope realized again with a pang as she said goodbye to Sharla and worked on alone.

When confronted by his family, Garrett had taken an immediate and decisive step back. A move that had, sadly, told her all she needed to know.

He'd decided to settle close to his family, after all, and make good use of his inheritance, just the way his late father had wanted him to do.

He'd found a way to open up his heart. Just not to her. Not the way she wanted.

And she knew now that she couldn't settle for half measures. Not when it came to Garrett. She wanted it all with him, or she wanted nothing at all. Twenty minutes later, Hope had taken the last of the awards off the wall when she heard the door to the suite open and close.

Thinking Sharla had forgotten something, Hope stepped out into the reception area. There stood Garrett. Handsome as ever, big as life. Like her, he was in jeans and sneakers, and a loose-fitting cotton shirt worn open at the throat.

He looked good, too.

Freshly shaven, his hair cut, blue eyes glinting with the masculine determination she found so appealing.

"This was a setup," she deduced, her heart squeezing hard.

He nodded. "Engineered by me." As he strolled toward her purposefully, his sexy grin widened. "I have to tell you, my mother did not want to help me."

Tears misted her eyes and joy rose inside her. Even though she knew it was too soon for that. Might not even be the right time.

She swallowed around the lump in her throat and did her best to appear cavalier. Tilting her head, she looked him up and down, as if she found him wanting. "Obviously, you convinced her."

"Once she listened to all I had to say." He squinted. "The question is, will you?"

Fear moved past the excitement roaring through her. She knew she couldn't bear it if he disappointed her again. She regarded him steadily, her guard up. "I think we said all we had to say during the board meeting." That she never should have been invited to attend, because then she wouldn't have heard all the questions, or seen him hedge.

Wouldn't have had everyone bear witness to her humiliation and heartbreak.

He came closer still, his eyes level on hers. "Not quite," he said softly but firmly.

Her heart pounded all the harder.

His eyes were full of things she was almost afraid to read as he took her hands in his. "I've never had trouble saying what was on my mind." The tips of his fingers caressed the back of her hands, eliciting tingles. "You may have heard," he continued, his voice a low, sexy rumble, "I'm blunt to a fault."

Hope hitched in a breath, suddenly afraid of where this might be going. "Except for the last time we saw each other," she reminded him, surprised she could sound so brave when inside she was on the verge of falling apart. *Again.* She lifted her chin. "Then you had no words."

Regret flashed on his handsome face. He nodded ruefully, his gaze narrowing. "Part of that was because I didn't want my family interfering in my life, or yours, and trying to engineer either of us into doing what *they* felt we should be doing."

Hope understood that.

The Lockhart clan had put them on the spot. Well-intentioned or not, the move had been a complete disaster.

Knowing he still had his own reticence to account for, she swallowed. "And the rest?"

"I was trying to follow your lead. Be sensitive. Discreet in a way I've never been before. Now, I'm here to lay my soul bare and tell you exactly what's on my mind," he said, his voice firm and strong. "First, I realize that holding back on what we are both thinking and feeling is never going to be right. Not for me, not for you, not for us."

She fought back a grin as her heart kicked against her ribs.

He wrapped both his arms around her waist. "I can still be tactful," he said, drawing her close, "but you need to tell me what's on your mind and in your heart, and I need to do the same." His voice dropped to a husky timbre. "So we're not caught off guard. Or left guessing what the other person is thinking or feeling."

"Agreed."

"So here's what's on my mind. No more scripts for either of us to follow. We both have to agree to wing it in the most genuine of ways to avoid miscommunication."

"You have given this a lot of thought!"

He waggled his brows as if to say *Just wait!*

"Next, as far as business goes, I want you to come to Laramie and work with me on both the WTWA and the re-launch of the much smaller but entirely laudable Lockhart Foundation. It will require you wearing two hats, being public relations director for both, but the hours will be entirely flexible to accommodate Max, and the offices are all going to be in the professional building I own, when the repairs are finished, which are apt to take about three months."

She splayed her hands across his chest. Felt his heart beating as hard as her own. "And until then…?"

"The WTWA will be working out of the Victorian. Renovations will be going on there, too, mostly on the weekends, but Max can come to work with you as much as you want, and there will be a place for you and Max at the Circle H bunkhouse, where you can live rent free."

It was nearly perfect. And yet…she knew she still had to have—they had to have—more.

But if that meant giving a little, too. Slowing down. Waiting to see what developed…

She could do that.

Yes, she could.

Because some things—some people—were worth waiting for.

"As family friends…?" Hope asked.

Because she and Max definitely fell into that category.

"No, sweetheart." Garrett shook his head. "As the woman I was meant to spend the rest of my life with." Raw emotion glimmered in his eyes. He wove his fingers through her hair and tilted her face up to his. "I love you, Hope," he told her hoarsely. "I have since the first moment you landed in my lap."

He pulled her up and into him. She rose even higher and met his lips in a searing kiss. Wrapping her arms around him, she tucked her face into the crook of his neck, shivering at the delight she felt being with him again.

"I love you, too," she whispered, drinking him in. His heat, his size, the brisk, masculine scent of him. She released a shuddering breath, savoring the feel of his hands moving over her. "I should have told you earlier."

He stroked a hand down her spine. His voice as tender as his touch, he asked, "Why didn't you?"

Hope drew back. Her arms resting on his broad shoulders, she looked deep into his eyes. It was time to let the defenses go. To dare the way he had. "It was all just so complicated." She shook her head with remembered misery. "I wasn't sure if what we had discovered was strong enough to last past the crisis."

A wry smile started on his lips and lit his eyes. "It is." He bent his head and kissed the top of her head, her temple. His thumbs caressed the line of her chin. "It definitely is."

He was so confident. She forced herself to admit with wrenching honesty, "Most of all, I was afraid to put myself out there all the way. Afraid of what would happen to us if I put it all on the line and you didn't love me back." Tears misted her eyes. "I didn't want to lose you."

His eyes crinkled at the corners, and he gave her a confident smile that she felt in every iota of her being. "You won't." He lifted his brow mischievously. "And to that end…" He reached into his pocket and drew out a velvet jewelry box, pressed it into her shaking fingers.

Inside was a beautiful diamond ring.

The sparkle of the gem was nothing compared to the brightness in his gaze. "Say you'll marry me, Hope," he rasped.

Was there any question? She grinned, a grin big as all Texas. "I will."

They shared another kiss. Long, lingering, sweet.

He cupped her face in his big, gentle hands, rested his forehead on hers. "So, it's agreed.

From now on—" he kissed her cheek, nose, ear, with the kind of slow deliberation that always preceded the most mind-blowing lovemaking "—to avoid future misunderstandings, we both promise to always speak our minds. And encourage each other to do the same."

Not following a preordained script suddenly felt very, very good. Her heart melted a little more. How had he gotten so wise? "I think I can handle that."

"Good." He tipped her face up to his and looked into her eyes until her knees went weak and joy bloomed within her. "Because I can't imagine a life without you and Max."

Hope kissed him back, promising, "You'll never have to…"

Epilogue

Six months later...

"Come on, buckaroo," Garrett crooned from the opposite side of the third-floor party room in the office building that now held both the Laramie Foundation offices and West Texas Warrior Assistance. Hunkered down affably, both hands outstretched toward their son, he encouraged cheerfully, "Walk to Daddy."

Eager to share what she had seen just a few hours earlier, Hope helped her wildly grinning nine-month-old son balance on the soles of his feet. "Show him what a talented boy you are." When Max seemed completely steady, she slowly and carefully released his hands.

Max let out a joyous whoop, swayed slightly and then shifted backward, landing squarely on his diapered bottom, as if that were the plan all along. He clapped his hands. And whooped again, Texas cowboy style.

His spirit was infectious. Hope and Garrett clapped and yee-hawed, too.

Max shifted quickly to his knees and crawled rapidly over to his daddy's side. Garrett scooped him up in his arms. "Good job, little fella!"

Max threw back his head and chuckled again.

Hope joined in the family hug. Briefly, she leaned her head on Garrett's chest. "I swear. Max was doing it earlier."

Garrett put a squirming Max back down so he could explore again. Immediately, Max crawled to a window ledge and pulled himself up to a standing position. "I believe you."

Hope put her hands on her hips, while Max

thought about walking sideways using the wall for balance, as he had been doing for a good two months now. Then he changed his mind, sat down, flipped and began crawling again.

This was ridiculous.

Hope shook her head, laughing. She met the indulgent arch of Garrett's brow. "No. You don't."

And probably with good reason. She was always jumping the gun and seeing progress that wasn't quite there yet.

Sage breezed in with a tray of goodies for their first annual Day Before Thanksgiving party. "Have you met this man?" She peeled back the plastic wrap and offered Garrett a taste. He gave the cranberry, pecan and cream cheese appetizer quiches a thumbs-up. Hope nodded her approval, too. Grinning, Sage put the tray aside. "All he does is brag about you and Max."

Darcy and Tank walked into the group meeting room. The usual circle of chairs had been pushed back to the walls to allow for maximum dining space. Winking, Darcy spread tablecloths over the double row of buffet tables in the center of the room. "I think Hope might have had a few kind words to say about her hubby, too."

With good reason, Hope thought. No longer afraid to say what was on her mind, she swept her son up in her arms and walked over to buss Garrett's jaw. "Sage's big brother is a wonderful husband."

Wyatt and Chance appeared in the doorway. A chorus of male groans sounded. "Tell me they're not getting mushy again," Wyatt complained, strolling in.

"Yeah, you-all have been married for three months now. Enough already!" Chance said with a mischievous wink. "The honeymoon is over."

"It'll never be over," Garrett vowed.

Everyone groaned again—in humorous approval.

Lucille walked in, a horn of plenty in one hand, a big basket of fruit in the other.

She set both down on a buffet table and turned to her beloved grandson. "Want to show your nana how you can walk?" she said.

"Not quite there yet," Garrett told her.

"Maybe it was an anomaly," Hope reluctantly admitted.

Max pulled himself up on Garrett's legs, turned around, balanced briefly on the balls of his feet and took off for his grandmother. One step, two. Everyone held their breaths. Then he swiveled and headed right back to Garrett and Hope.

Tears of joy pouring down their faces, they watched him toddle all the way to their sides. One arm wrapped around each of their knees, he chortled and looked up at them.

Everyone cheered.

Max pulled on their legs, his signal he wanted to be picked up. Garrett lifted their son in his arms. Hope kissed his cheek.

Puzzled, Max tracked the happy tears pouring down both their faces while smiles flashed all around. Then he tucked a fist in the shirts of each of his parents. "Mine," he said fiercely.

"You bet we are," Garrett said fiercely.

"No question," Hope murmured, going in for a joyous group hug. "We have so much to be thankful for!"

* * * * *

MILLS & BOON®

Why shop at millsandboon.co.uk?

Each year, thousands of romance readers find their perfect read at millsandboon.co.uk. That's because we're passionate about bringing you the very best romantic fiction. Here are some of the advantages of shopping at www.millsandboon.co.uk:

* **Get new books first**—you'll be able to buy your favourite books one month before they hit the shops

* **Get exclusive discounts**—you'll also be able to buy our specially created monthly collections, with up to 50% off the RRP

* **Find your favourite authors**—latest news, interviews and new releases for all your favourite authors and series on our website, plus ideas for what to try next

* **Join in**—once you've bought your favourite books, don't forget to register with us to rate, review and join in the discussions

Visit **www.millsandboon.co.uk**
for all this and more today!

ROSICRUCIAN
QUESTIONS AND ANSWERS
WITH COMPLETE HISTORY OF
THE ROSICRUCIAN ORDER

▽

ROSICRUCIAN

QUESTIONS AND ANSWERS

WITH COMPLETE HISTORY of the
ROSICRUCIAN ORDER

By H. Spencer Lewis, Ph. D., F. R. C.
First Imperator of the Rosicrucian Order
for North and South America

ROSICRUCIAN LIBRARY
VOLUME I

SUPREME GRAND LODGE OF AMORC
Printing and Publishing Department
San Jose, California

#4093784

FIRST EDITION
1929

SECOND EDITION
April, 1932

THIRD EDITION
July, 1941

FOURTH EDITION
1947

FIFTH EDITION
1954

THE ROSICRUCIAN PRESS, LTD.
SAN JOSE, CALIFORNIA

Library of Congress Catalog Card Number: 65–14964

SIXTH EDITION
1959
SEVENTH EDITION
1961
EIGHTH EDITION
1965
NINTH EDITION
1969
TENTH EDITION
1971
ELEVENTH EDITION
1973
TWELFTH EDITION
1975
THIRTEENTH EDITION
1977

PRINTED AND BOUND IN THE U. S. A. BY
KINGSPORT PRESS, INC., KINGSPORT, TENN.

DEDICATION

▽

To the Memory of

BROTHER JULIUS SACHSE, F. R. C.
Historian,

*last descendant of the First American
Rosicrucian Colony, whose History of
their achievements will remain as a
monument to the Faith and Love of their
great leader, Magister Kelpius,*

THIS BOOK IS DEDICATED

*that I may place a flower among
the many at the side of
his grave.*

▽

The Rosicrucian Library

▽ ▽ ▽

*(Other volumes will be added from time to time.
Write for complete catalogue.)*

CONTENTS

▽

CRO ✠ MAAT

The Ancient and Mystical Order

Rosae Crucis

*The True Name and Emblems of the
International Rosicrucian Order*

Registered in the U. S. Patent Office
exclusively in the name of AMORC

MODERN SPHINX PRESERVES AGE-OLD PRINCIPLES

The former Imperator of the Rosicrucian Order, Dr. H. Spencer Lewis, in full ritualistic regalia, upon the occasion of the dedication of the Rose-Croix Science Building in A.D. 1934, is seen here depositing for posterity a scroll which contains fifteen of the Order's most important philosophic principles. On his left are Dr. Clement Le Brun, Past Grand Master of AMORC, and an assistant.

EXTENSION OF JURISDICTION

A decree by the F.U.D.O.S.I. and International Council of the Rose-Croix of the world, issued August 13, 1934, at Brussels, Belgium, empowering the A.M.O.R.C., as the authoritative Rosicrucian Order of the Western world, to extend its jurisdiction to include the countries and territories of South America.

F. U. D. O. S. I.

Federatio Universalis Dirigens Ordines Societatesque Initiationis

PAX HOMINIBUS BONÆ VOLUNTATIS... SALUTEM NOSTRUM IN LUCE VERITATIS

Cathedra Fratris Magni Secretarii

Valle _Bruxellis_ (Belgia)

die _21 juni_ Vera Lucis

Libri Matricularis

Numerus :

Fratri Carissimo : Sâr H. Sp. Lewis Imperator

in Valle _San José California_

Trës Ill ∴ Fr ∴ Imperator

J' appelle sur votre prochain Convent la Lumière de l' Esprit-Saint et ses sept dons. Je prie le Très-Haut, Souverain Créateur et Maître de toutes choses de répandre ses grâces divines sur tous vos travaux.

Suivant sa promesse, qu' à l' appel de votre prière, le Christ soit au milieu de vous. -

Je vous bénis dans la Lumière resplendissante de la Sainte Rose et la gloire éternelle de la divine Croix..

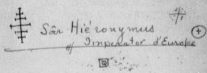

✠ Sâr Hiéronymus
Imperator d'Europe

SALUTATIONS FROM THE IMPERATOR OF EUROPE

A communication from Sar Hieronymus, Imperator of the Rose-Croix of Europe to the first Imperator of AMORC of North and South America, Dr. H. Spencer Lewis, extending greetings. The felicitations were written on the official stationery of the F.U.D.O.S.I., a federation of the authoritative, initiatory and mystical Orders of the world, AMORC being the only Rosicrucian movement of the Western world affiliated with it at that time.

Manifesto

Au Nom et Sous les Auspices de la PUISSANCE SUPRÊME

CONSEIL INTERNATIONAL
des ORDRES ORIENTAUX
PAIX — TOLÉRANCE — UNION !

It is decreed that :

Since the A⸫ M⸫ O⸫ R⸫ C⸫ with its S⸫ S⸫ and See in the Valley of San Jose, California, is the only authorized sector of the ancient Fraternity of Rosicrucians perpetuating the true traditions and principles of the R+C in North and South America, with authenticity recognized by all the ancient Initiatic Orders forming this Conseil International and Federation,

Therefore, the said S⸫S⸫ and its Imperator (ad vitam), Thr⸫ Ill⸫ Fratre H. Spencer Lewis, F⸫ R⸫ C⸫ 33°-66°-95°, S⸫ I⸫, and his hereditary successors shall be the exclusive representatives and Sover⸫ Officers for North and South Americas and their affiliated countries, of all the Initiatic Orders composing the FUDOESI, with authority to establish and maintain such Orders in the aforesaid countries.

This decree was unanimously endorsed by vote of all the Sov⸫ Officers and recognized delegates of the fourteen Orders composing the FUDOESI at its International Convention in Brussels, Belgium during the week of August 13th to 18ª 1934 A.D., and attested by the following principle officers of the said fourteen Orders who were personally present:

AUTHORITATIVE RECOGNITION

Manifesto issued and signed by the highest dignitaries of the International Council of the Rosicrucian Order for the world, at a conclave of the F.U.D.O.S.I. held in Brussels, Belgium, during the week of August 13 to 18, 1934 A.D. The Manifesto decrees that the AMORC, with See in San Jose, California, is the authorized sector of the ancient Rosicrucian fraternity in North and South America.

MEDITATION CAVE

Fleeing religious intolerance in Europe and looking toward America as a land of freedom of conscience, a group of Rosicrucians under the leadership of Master Johannes Kelpius settled on the banks of Wissahickon Creek in Pennsylvania in the year 1694. This was the beginning of the first cycle of the Rosicrucian Order in the New World. Johannes Kelpius, leading a life of celibacy, frequently lived as an ascetic for months at a time in the above cave. The cave is now part of the celebrated Fairmount Park in Philadelphia.

EARLY ROSICRUCIAN SETTLEMENT

In Ephrata, Pennsylvania, in the early eighteenth century, this settlement of Rosicrucians and mystics was established by Johann Conrad Beissel. The edifice to the left above is the *Saron,* or Sisters' House. Adjoining it is the *Saal,* or Temple. There are other edifices not shown, and there were others that have since passed with time. Many of the settlers were descendants of the earlier Rosicrucian colony established in Philadelphia in 1694 by Johannes Kelpius.

ANCIENT RITUALISTIC POSTURE

This ancient figure of a prince, possibly the son of King Mena of the first dynasty (3400 B.C.), assumes a ritualistic posture familiar to all Rosicrucian lodge and chapter members. The position of the hands and the wearing of the apron reveal the early origin of the symbolic gesture. The prince was undoubtedly attached to one of the mystery schools of the period. This rare figure, found in a tomb at Abydos, is one of several thousand authentic objects on display in the Rosicrucian Egyptian, Oriental Museum.

PREFACE

The mystery which has always surrounded the origin and history of the Great White Brotherhood has probably been one of its fascinating attractions, even with those who had no interest in its teachings or activities. The mystery is not eliminated by a revelation of the *real* as well as the *traditional* facts associated with its origin; and in its history one will find romance, intrigue, astounding achievements, fascinating exploits, and alluring inducements.

The history of the Brotherhood must be divided into two general classifications. First, that which is traditional, and which has come down to the present time by word of mouth, supported by more or less definite references in ancient writings or symbolical passages in the rituals or teachings; and second, that which is truly historical and supported by the records found in the various branches of the organization throughout the world.

It is realized that the traditional history of the organization is very often cast aside, or accepted with considerable doubt by those who hesitate to believe in the antiquity of the organization. Persons of this type prefer to have the history of the

organization begin with its first definite, printed records. They forget that everything of human construction had a beginning, and that there must have been an origin and beginning of the Order which antedates the first definite, printed or written records.

It was generally believed, several hundred years ago, that the *historical birth* of the Rosicrucians did not antedate the seventeenth century. It was likewise believed that the *traditional birth* of the Order began some time in the Christian Era, and ended at the time of the historical birth. In other words, the attitude was taken that all the stories, reports, and references to the Rosicrucians as existing prior to the seventeenth century belonged to the *traditional history* of the Order. But, the many discoveries of documents, books, manuscripts, and references of an authentic nature in the past century have taken the actual origin and existence of the Order backward step by step, year by year, into the very heart of the so-called traditional period.

The demand on the part of Rosicrucian students throughout the world, and the search on the part of thousands of others, for more facts regarding both the traditional and actual periods of the Order's existence, have warranted this history.

Parts of this history appeared for the first time in the official Rosicrucian magazine called the *American Rosae Crucis,* beginning with the January, 1916, issue. That history was, at that time, considered the most complete outline of the traditional part of the Order's existence ever presented, and has been widely utilized by other writers who found therein the clues which enabled them to verify many of the statements made. Since 1916 a number of other histories have appeared in the French, Dutch, German, and English languages by eminent officers of the organization. In most of these, the facts presented in the articles which appeared in the *American Rosae Crucis* have been utilized and appreciation expressed for the publication of hitherto concealed records.

The present history is an extension of the one published in the magazine, and is considerably augmented by documents, books, and papers sent to the author by other historians or members of foreign branches of the Order, who were able to find further details because of the clues given in the original articles. Credit must also be given to the researches made by the official historian of the Order in America, *Fra Fidelis,* who, through his editorial association with one of the largest newspapers in North America, and his connections with

the Order and with foreign libraries and records in many languages, has been able to make extensive researches covering a number of years, thereby bringing to light many important and intensely interesting facts.

Whether one accepts all of the points of the traditional history or not, one is certain to feel that the origin of what is now the Rosicrucian Order is found in the early mystery schools of the Great White Brotherhood. A study of the schools of philosophy and arcane wisdom in the Oriental lands preceding the Christian Era reveals that there is but one land in which the Rosicrucian organization could have had its birth. That land is Egypt; and even the casual student of Egyptian history is impressed with the probability of the birth of the organization in that land.

If one sets aside the traditional history entirely, and accepts only that which is based upon very definite records in printed or official manuscript form, one must reject the popular and entirely fictitious claim that the Rosicrucian Order had its origin in the seventeenth century in Germany. The very positive references to the Order in printed books dated centuries earlier in other lands prove conclusively that the Order was very old and very well

established when it had a form of revival in Germany in the seventeenth century. Likewise, one discovers at once that the romantic or symbolic story regarding *Christian Rosenkreuz* and *his* foundation of the first Rosicrucian body must be rejected, unless one associates that story with similar stories found in many earlier records.

The author, therefore, presents the following history as the most modern version, and perhaps the most complete outline of the history of the Rosicrucian Order, with the hope that the members of the Order will find between the lines the facts which are carefully concealed; and the inquiring mind, seeking for a mystery story and nothing more, will also find in the printed words a mystical romance prepared to his liking.

INTRODUCTION

It is no violation of secrecy to give the outer, objective details of the various activities of the Great White Brotherhood, but the genuine conservatism of the Eastern Councils until recent years has acted as a barrier against such publicity as we in America and the West generally believe necessary for the growth of any public or semipublic institution.

After twenty years' study of the doctrines and principles and a very careful examination of all matters pertaining to the history of the Order, one does not find a single prohibition against the general publication of the history except in such minor details as are closely associated with the working or manifestation of some of the R. C. doctrines. While these exceptions are few, although of vast importance to the higher students, they have undoubtedly caused the subconscious attitude on the part of all R. C. Fratres and Sorores that it is safer, in the face of their individual sacred oaths, to refrain from all mention of either the antiquity or progression of the Order.

cloaked with mystery. Its published history is very esoteric and mystical, although its actual history, as known to all advanced Rosicrucians, is a living testimonial to the truth of the notable principles of Brotherhood which actuate Freemasonry.

So closely are the two Orders allied in some lands that many of the great exponents of the one are active workers in the other. Freemasonry has acknowledged its debt to the ancient White Brotherhood by adding a Rosicrucian Degree to the Ancient and Accepted Scottish Rite.

H. Spencer Lewis, F. R. C.

ADDENDUM

The author of this work passed through transition (the Rosicrucian term for that change from mortal to immortal existence commonly referred to as death) on Wednesday, August 2, 1939, in San Jose, California, the See of the Rosicrucian Order. For a quarter of a century he devoted his time and genius exclusively to the furtherance of Rosicrucian doctrine in the Americas. He was unstinting in the sacrifices he made (as had been the venerable masters before him) that Rosicrucian idealism might survive and its heritage of wisdom be transmitted to the searching and inquiring minds of men and women, so that their lives might accordingly be bettered. Also, like the leaders of the Rosicrucian Order in past centuries, he was Cosmically prepared, if not ordained for his tremendous task, with a versatility of talents amounting to genius, and an abundance of dynamic energy.

There is no greater testimony of his abilities and powers of accomplishment, than that in so few years he should make an organization, the name and repute of which had been commonly confined to dusty tomes and the records of secret archives, come to command the attention and respect of thou-

sands of persons in every walk of life, and in every section of North and South America. There was hardly any realm of creative enterprise which his mind and personality did not touch. The technical diagrams used to illustrate the precepts of the Rosicrucian teachings, as well as the elaborate symbolical paintings which ornamented the periodicals of the Order, issued for membership and for public consumption alike, were the products of his artistic ability. Many of the Temples of the Rosicrucian Lodges throughout this jurisdiction of the Order are examples of his skill of design and mastery of color harmony in ornamentation. In the Sanctums and homes of members, and in some of the edifices of the See of the Order are large oil paintings executed by him. Likewise, the very architecture and structural design of these buildings are the results of his creative efforts.

Scientifically accurate, insofar as their technical employment of physical laws is concerned, are the instruments and devices he invented and constructed to demonstrate nature's phenomena, that men might physically perceive and come to comprehend the majesty of the Cosmic laws he so loved. Such instruments included the Luxatone, a color organ, which demonstrated the relationship of sound and color years before such present instruments were

[28]

constructed. The Planetarium projector, which he designed and erected for astronomical display and instruction, was the first instrument of its kind made entirely in America.

His knowledge of human nature, traits of character, and their relation to the everyday problems which beset people, made him much in demand as a *human engineer,* and a consultant upon personal welfare matters by societies and individuals. His executive ability and organizing genius made him, early in life, a success in the advertising and business worlds, a career which he forfeited for his higher obligation as Imperator of the Rosicrucian Order. He was much sought after by service clubs and business executives, as a counsellor in their respective fields. His literary talent is attested to in his numerous books on a variety of topics and his innumerable articles appearing in Rosicrucian periodicals throughout the world, and in technical and popular journals.

His self-sacrifices made him indifferent to wealth. His personal fortune and large sums of money which he came to command were devoted to furthering the Rosicrucian Order's expansion. Upon his transition, his personal estate was extremely modest in assets of any tangible nature. His sacrifices were not all material. The greatest he had to make

at times was his peace of mind. He was, with the rise of Rosicrucian doctrine to prominence in the Western world, the personal target of every individual, society, or group which was envious of the Order or sought to suppress the knowledge it preserved. Their machinations were centered upon him, for with the cessation of his activities, they conceived the abolition of Rosicrucian philosophy. These forces which conspired against the Rosicrucian Order of the Twentieth Century were parallels of the same interests that sought to extirpate knowledge in the Middle Ages, and, in fact, in every era of civilization. Their reasons for seeking to do so were in some instances superstitious fear, in others misguided religious zeal, and more frequently the desire for power. His ordeal was one of vilification of character, calumny, and malicious persecution and harassment.

These torments, however, became a crucible out of which came forth a strong, resolute character. He lived to be recognized throughout the world, by the preceptors of the Rosicrucian Order and profane historians alike, as the greatest authority upon and master of the Rosicrucian teachings in modern times.

In accordance with his wish, the traditions of the Rosicrucian Order, its Constitution, and the vote

of the Board of Directors of the Supreme Grand Lodge of AMORC, on August 12, 1939, authority was transmitted to his son, Ralph M. Lewis, to succeed him as Imperator.

All data and events chronicled in this work, subsequent to August 12, 1939, are by the incumbent Imperator of the AMORC for North and South America.

R. M. L.
February 10, 1941.

THE TRADITIONAL HISTORY OF
THE ORDER

THE Rosicrucian Order had its traditional conception and birth in Egypt in the activities of the Great White Lodge. In giving the story of the origin, the writer realizes that to an exceptional degree exactness will be demanded by the reader, and in return pardon must be granted for reiteration.

Space will not be used in describing conditions in Egypt as they existed at the time of the conception of so wonderful an organization as this. The reader is requested to read either a brief or extended history of Egypt, which will prove highly illuminating upon this subject.

One will find, however, that the Egyptians had reached a high state of civilization and advanced learning at the beginning of the XVIII dynasty, comparable only with the European Renaissance. Many were the means adopted to preserve the knowledge attained that it might be correctly given to future generations. The hieroglyphic markings on the pyramids, obelisks, and temple walls give us evi-

dence of the first desires to make permanent the knowledge and learning of the Egyptians.

The more profound secrets of nature, science, and art were not to be entrusted to the masses, however, nor were they susceptible to preservation through writing upon papyri. For this reason classes were formed by the most learned, attended by the select minds, and there the doctrines and principles of science were taught.

These classes or *schools,* as history refers to them, were held in the most isolated grottos at times, and again in the quiet of some of the temples erected to the many Egyptian gods.

Actually, it is extremely difficult to determine when these schools began. The search for knowledge among the ancient Egyptians was undoubtedly coeval with their conscious observation and analysis of the current happenings of their lives and times. The cyclical repetitions of certain phenomena in nature and in their own beings were the first *mysteries* of early man. In fact, these things, to a great extent, still remain mysteries today. The personal mysteries—or rather the intimate ones—were those of birth and death, and that strange resurrection that occurred periodically in nature, as a rejuvenation of plant life in the spring.

At first, the term *mysteries* must have been syn-

onymous with the unknown. Later it came to represent, to the Egyptian neophyte and priest alike, an uncommon or esoteric knowledge of the laws and purposes of life and being. Thus the appellation, *mystery school,* or place of imparting knowledge of the mysteries. Such first mysteries consisted of a matrix of mythology, founded on facts of observation and figments of imagination. From them evolved the indisputable truths of the inner comprehension of Cosmic law, just as there emerges from modern theories and hypotheses the eventual light of truth.

The first mystery schools were devoted principally to agrarian rites, such as the paying of homage to the fertility of the land, and the fecundity of domestic animals, and the offering of libations to the gods of the seasons. We might say that religion and learning formed the basic pattern of the instruction of the early mystery schools. The Osirian mysteries, deriving their name from the god, Osiris, of ancient Egypt, are credited with being one of the most popular expounded by the mystery schools. However, within its general ceremonies and rituals was the nebulous formation of *a vast philosophy of immortality,* for it sought to embrace the welfare and future of the dead.

Osiris was the god of earth, the first substance

from whence things sprang. He was likewise the symbol of *good* and was in constant conflict with the powers and forces of evil. The legends and myths declared that he was murdered by his brother Seth. He was later brought to life by the goddess Isis, and her son Horus, the latter symbolized by the bird, the hawk. Horus later, in turn, avenged Osiris by killing Seth. Crude as all of this may seem, in its telling, it had a far more important and mystical meaning. As Plutarch says: ". . . so the legend before us is a kind of reflection of a history reflecting the true meaning of other things; as is shown further by the sacrifices containing a representation of mourning and sadness; as also by the ground plan of the temples, in some parts spreading out into colonnades and courts open to the sky, and lightsome, in others having underground, hidden and dark galleries (like those at Thebes) and halls as well; . . ." In other words, the architecture of the temples of Egypt, the openness, the spaciousness, the lighted courtyards, on the one hand, and the underground passages, on the other, and certain dark and dreary places, represented the life and glory of Osiris, his death, his temporary stay in the nether world, then his glorious resurrection again.

Since Osiris was the judge in the after-world of the conduct of the dead who came before him, the plays

of the mystery schools (for their truths were revealed as mystical dramas) attempted as well to define that moral conduct which is essential for the greater life after death. The priests and preceptors sought to teach lessons in each act of the mystery dramas. At the ancient temple of Dendera, the ritual was performed with puppets, perhaps the earliest record of the use of puppets. Each had its part to enact; even a miniature bier was constructed, upon which the effigy of Osiris was placed. This temple was first erected by Khufu, in 2900 B. C. In other temples, some of the ceremonies were enacted by persons who were carefully chosen for the roles, and intensively trained. Those who were to be initiated, or inducted into these mysteries—in other words, those who were the tyros, or candidates—were brought to the temple to witness the plays, after assuming certain very strict obligations. Frequently the rites were performed on a great, highly ornamented barge on the sacred lake, usually in moonlight. Herodotus tell us: "On this lake it is that the Egyptians represent by night his sufferings, whose name I refrain from mentioning (Osiris), and this representation they call their mysteries. I know well the whole course of the proceedings in these ceremonies, but they shall not pass my lips."*

---

*Herodotus, from *The Euterpé*.

Astronomical observations, or the mysteries of the heavens, found their place in the legends of Osiris as well. The days numbering the phases of the moon were related to the purported age of Osiris. It is not that the Egyptians actually believed that Osiris was a deified individual, or that he actually lived on earth a certain number of years, but to round out the legend he was given an age, and the age was related to observable phenomena, revealing further the fact that Osiris was an allegorical character representing truths or *mysteries*. Plutarch states: "The number of years that some say Osiris lived, others that he reigned, was eight and twenty; for just so many are the lights of the moon, and for so many days doth she revolve about the circle."*

The mystery schools of the old and middle kingdoms gradually experienced a transition from symbolical rites and dramatic rituals, to what we may term a philosophical analysis of the "physics" of the earth and of man's material nature, as well as such considerations as life after death. In other words, physical philosophy, or what rightly may be termed *scientific conjecture* began to hold forth with religion and mysticism. For example, the sistrum is an ancient device consisting of an oval, or

* Plutarch—*Isis and Osiris*.

round frame, in which are inserted little movable beads or rods, and to which a straight handle is affixed at one end. When it is shaken, these beads and rods vibrate, and it serves as a rattle. In the earliest periods of Egypt's history, and later during its decadence when the custom revived, this device was shaken so that the noise it emitted would frighten off evil spirits. However, at the height of the greatest culture and *secret learning* of the mystery schools, it became a symbol of universal or *cosmic motion*. It was conceived that all things that are must be *shaken,* must be kept in *motion* by nature, if they are to generate themselves. If their motion ceases, so then shall they. We see here, then, that a thousand years before the earliest Greek atomic theories were advanced, a doctrine of *motion,* as the generation or cause of all matter, was expounded.

That portion of this vast knowledge which has been transmitted to us as inscriptions in stone, or on parchment, is a negligible part of the whole. There was a wealth of knowledge, an accumulation of perhaps centuries, the result of numerous investigations, tedious and heart-rending probing into nature's secrets, the significance of which the Kheri Heb (the High Priest or temple master) alone knew. The fear to entrust this knowledge to

any kind of tangible form that could be abased by wrongdoers, into whose possession it might fall, is one motive, and a most logical one, for imparting it only by *word of mouth*—to those worthy. Those who doubt that such a knowledge ever existed—and was transmitted by mouth to ear—because there is no original manuscript, papyrus, or stele to substantiate it, are themselves ignorant of the mundane, historic evidence which gives weight to this belief. No less an authority than Egyptologist Sir E. A. Wallis Budge states: "It is impossible to doubt that these were 'mysteries' in the Egyptian religion, and this being so, it is impossible to think that the highest order of the priests did not possess esoteric knowledge which they guarded with the greatest care. Each priesthood, if I read the evidence correctly, possessed a 'Gnosis', a 'superiority of knowledge', which they never did put into writing, and so were enabled to enlarge or diminish its scope as circumstances made necessary. It is therefore absurd to expect to find in Egyptian papyri descriptions of the secrets which formed the esoteric knowledge of the priests. Among the 'secret wisdom' of the priests must be included the knowledge of which day was the shortest of the year, i. e., the day when OSIRIS died and the new sun began his course, and the day when SIRIUS would rise heliacally, and the

true age of the moon, and the days when the great festivals of the year were to be celebrated."*

If the *secret wisdom* was imparted in any tangible form, it is to be found to exist in the symbolism of the Egyptians, namely, in such devices as were not an integral part of their language or common writing. In this manner, a symbol would exoterically depict to one mind one meaning, and to another a far different significance. This is not merely a supposition, but a fact borne out by such a vast number of circumstances and indications, as to remove them from the realm of coincidence. It will suffice to mention but one such example. The Egyptian ground plans of a temple were almost always oblong in shape. Likewise this sign ⬚ was a symbol in Egypt of the letter "M," or "Ma," implying the earth or *mother influence*. The powers, gods, or deities which were worshipped in the temples were conceived to transcend the earth, and therefore, by contrast, were *positive* in nature or spirit. "Ra" was one of the most celebrated masculine creative powers. He reached down to earth and impregnated it with life. "Ra" was frequently depicted as a solar disc or circle. Thus we have in these two symbols, the *oblong* and the *circle,* a lesson in

*Sir E. A. Wallis Budge, former keeper of the Department of Egyptian Antiquities, British Museum.

the creation of earth and creation of life by the combining of dual forces. We might say that one represented one polarity, and the other another.

Those who possessed such knowledge were under great oath not to reveal it wrongly, and would suffer dire consequences if they misused the *secret wisdom*. In a translation from the original hieroglyphic inscriptions in *The Book of the Dead,* by Sir E. A. Wallis Budge, we find these admonishments, "to allow no one to see it," nor was it to be recited to even a close friend, for further we find: "never let the ignorant person, or anyone whatsoever look upon it"; also "the things which are done secretly in the hall of the tomb are the *mysteries* . . ."

In some cases, classes of a very select nature were held in the private chambers of the reigning Pharaoh.

The members of such assemblies became more and more select, the teachings more profound, and the discussions so dialectic that there arose a most autocratic and secret society of the truly great minds of the day. Thus was laid the foundation of the Great White Brotherhood.

The first Pharaoh who conducted the class in his private chambers was Ahmose I, who reigned from 1580 B. C. to 1557 B. C. Because he was capable of

conducting the great school as well as ruling the people with more civilized and advanced principles (due to his training in the school, no doubt), he is referred to as the "deliverer of Egypt" by some historians.

He was succeeded as Pharaoh by Amenhotep I, who became a teacher in the secret school for three years.

On January 12 (approximately), 1538 B. C., Thutmose I was crowned succeeding Amenhotep I. He owed his position to his wife, Ahmose, who was the first woman to become a member of the class on equal terms with the men. The discussion regarding her admittance (preserved in the Rosicrucian Archives) forms an interesting story and reveals the origin of some of the doctrines of the equality of the sexes.

Thutmose I was succeeded by Hatshepsut, his daughter, who ruled as a "king" independently and as co-regent with her half-brother Thutmose II, a son of Thutmose I by his marriage to Isis.

It was Thutmose III who organized the present physical form followed by the present secret Brotherhood and outlined many of its rules and regulations. He ruled from approximately 1500 B. C. until 1447 B. C., and his reign is unimportant to us except for his establishment of the Brotherhood.

History relates a very strange occurrence, in the life of Thutmose III, that is mystically important to us. We are told of a great feast which, oddly enough, if that is the term to use, occurred about on the occasion of the Spring equinox. This great festival was being held in the Temple of Amen, one of the prevailing gods of the time, in the great Temple of what is now Karnak at Thebes, Egypt, the then great capital city. We can visualize this ceremony, if we will; the magnificent colonnaded halls of this splendid edifice, the balmy air of a March evening in Egypt, the Nile nearby, swaying palm trees, the heavy shadows, the flickering light of the torches, the colorful attire of the priests and the assembly, the chanting, the soft strains of the string instruments.

Thutmose III, as was his custom, was present at the feast. He, with his colleagues, was seated in the Northern Hall of the great Temple. The chief priests or Kheri Hebs were perambulating and carrying a little image symbolic of the god Amen. As they passed the different groups of personages they were acclaimed. But, strangely, the High Priest would walk over to each group and peer into their faces as though he were searching for someone, and then as if realizing that they were not the ones, he

would shake his head in the negative, and cross over to the opposite side and repeat the process. He knew all the time that Thutmose III was present, but finally when he reached the Northern Chamber of the Temple, he acted as though he had suddenly discovered the one for whom he had been searching. He placed at the feet of Thutmose III the image of Amen which depicted, in the customs of the time, that he, Thutmose III, had been chosen instead of his brother to succeed the father upon the throne, and the great assemblage broke forth in acclamation.

What interests us mostly, and which is recorded in history, is Thutmose III's explanation of his experience upon the occasion. He had no knowledge that he was to be chosen to become Pharaoh, because by right of accession, his brother should have been. But when the image was placed at his feet, he was seen to stand up; however, according to Thutmose III he felt "raised" as though his feet hardly touched the ground, and as though he had ascended into the heavens, and there he tells us God duly appointed him to serve his people. In fact, he felt as though he had been divinely ordained because of the mystical experience, and it became not even necessary for him to journey to

Heliopolis where the Sun Temple was located, as had been the custom, to be formally coronated.*

He appears to have been quite original in his application of the doctrines of mysticism, but held to the existing external form of religion, possibly because of political conditions. Egypt was not free from the danger of the "grasping hand" of adjoining nations and the life of this ruler was constantly tormented by outbreaks of war; the cooperation of his military forces depended considerably upon his permitting the populace to indulge in all its fanciful beliefs—especially the idolatrous religions. For this reason an immediate change in the fundamentals of their religion—such as was made by Thutmose's descendant, Amenhotep IV, in 1355 with such reactionary results—did not seem advisable or even necessary.

A gradual development in the existing mystical beliefs could be more easily and permanently accomplished by establishing a secret school of philosophy, the students of which would put into practice the high standards selected.

As in all ages there were those who might be called *advanced thinkers,* true philosophers, sages, and scholars. Many of these were students of the

---

*Breasted, *History of Egypt.* Chap. XV, p. 268.

mystical doctrines as taught by Thutmose's predecessors, and they evidently had great faith in the final success of the principles; for when Thutmose proposed that the "class" which had been meeting in his chambers become a closed and secret order, "there was no dissenting voice, and articles of limitations were established ere the assembly dispersed in the early hours of dawn."

This grand "Council Meeting," for such it is considered in all official records of the Order, occurred during what would be the week of March 28th to April 4th of 1489 B. C., according to our present calendar. It is generally conceded to have been on Thursday, April 1st, but this may be associated with *Maunday Thursday,* a later establishment. However, Thursday has become the usual day for Rosicrucian meetings, and "Maunday" Thursday has become the occasion for special Temple Convocations in many AMORC Lodges of the world.

Twelve known Fratres and Sorores were present at this first Supreme Council. The Sorores were the wife of Thutmose III, known in the Order as *Mene;* the wife of one of the Fratres; and another who was a descendant of one of the rulers of a preceding dynasty. Therefore, there were nine Fratres and three Sorores at this Council, a combination of numbers very significant.

No worldly name was decided upon for the Brotherhood, the records showing that the predominating thought was the maintenance of secrecy.* The organization had no publicity; it required no propaganda other than personal advice to those whose presence was desired, and as the one word, translated into *Brotherhood* (a secret, fraternal body), was sufficient name for all purposes, we do not find any other term. This accounts for the widespread diversity of the name as adopted later. In many of the documents issued to the Grand Lodges throughout the entire world, the name of the Order is seldom mentioned.

The idea of secrecy is so strong and predominant that the Order is referred to indirectly and sometimes erroneously (or perhaps diplomatically) as *it*, the *school*, the *brotherhood*, or the *council*. Furthermore many of these documents begin with the announcement: "*I, Brother of the Illuminati,* with power decreed, do declare this Manifesto," or with the Salutation: "I, F. Illuminati of the 12." (I, Frater Illuminati of the 12th degree.) Very often these official manifestoes are signed: "With Peace

---

*It must not be construed that the word *Rosicrucian,* or any variation of it, was used by, or applied to, this ancient brotherhood. This Egyptian Brotherhood was *not* Rosicrucian as we know the Order today, but rather the Order has its traditional roots in the ancient brotherhood. It derives its principles and objectives from it.

Profound" and sometimes "F, Profundis" or "F, 12."

These words not only show that the twelfth or last degree has been the last circle within the Order, and known as the *Illuminati,* even to this day, but they also explain why some references are made to these documents as "Instructions of the Illuminati," which may easily be misinterpreted as "Instructions to the Illuminati" as one sees them referred to in works published abroad in the 15th, 16th, and 17th centuries A. D., where the *Order Rosae Crucis* is designated solely by the term *Illuminati.*

Furthermore, if one considers for a moment the prejudice—even the prohibition—against such secret Orders, one will appreciate the very evident attempts at subterfuge. Not only did certain bigoted religious organizations condemn all secret orders as "works of the devil," but those orders or schools which claimed to have *rare knowledge* of the sciences were severely criticised by the various scientific bodies of the day. As soon as learning became so general that competition arose between schools and students, the secret orders were widely condemned even though many of the most unfair critics of some were oath-bound members of others.

Though the Order had no definite name, Thutmose saw that it had very definite principles, rules,

and modes of procedure, all of which have come down to us today without material change.*

At the close of his reign in 1447 there were thirty-nine Fratres and Sorores in the Council, and the meetings, which had become regular and systematic, were held in a hall of the Temple at Karnak, outside of which Thutmose III erected two obelisks bearing a record of his achievements.

Thutmose signed most of the decrees of the Council with his own *cartouche* and it became the Seal of the Order "in testimony of the great work of our teacher (Master) to be forever a mark of honor and loyalty." As was customary with these rulers when any event of national importance occurred, Thutmose issued a *scarab* bearing his *cartouche* on one side, plus a mark which has a special meaning to all mystics. One original scarab, which was used for hundreds of years in Egypt by various officials to impress the Seal of the mystic fraternity in wax on all official documents, was given to the Grand Lodge of America with other jewels and papers of an official nature. It is considered one of the rarest antiquities of Egypt now in this country.

The Order here is to be congratulated on having in its possession one of the *oldest,* if not the most

---

*It is understood, therefore, that the present name of the Order was not used during the formative period of the Egyptian mystery schools.

sacred, of all mystic jewels, one which has never been used by other than the Masters in Egypt. It means virtually the passing of the Master's Spirit from Egypt to America, as was planned by the founders centuries ago.

This Seal appears on the official documents of the Order of the present International Jurisdiction together with the American R. C. Seal, and its illegitimate use constitutes a forgery, according to the By-Laws of the Order throughout the world, punishable by a special decree of the Masters.

In this connection it may be explained that the Obelisk now in Central Park, New York City—one of the two erected in Egypt by Thutmose III and intended to stand some day in "the country where the Eagle spreads its wings"—bears this Cartouche, or Seal, as well as many other authentic and instructive signs now used by all Rosicrucians of the true Order. In Egypt today, the Rosicrucian Order, descending from very ancient lodges, uses this Cartouche as its official emblem above all others.

Before his transition, Thutmose III made his son (by Hatshepsut) co-regent. Thus Amenhotep II took up his father's work in the Brotherhood about the end of September, 1448 B.C. In the month of March—the seventeenth to be exact—1447 B.C., Thutmose passed to the Great Beyond, having been

king (pharaoh) for nearly 54 years and being but one week less than 89 years of age. His mummy was found in the Cachette at Deir el-Bahri, and history acclaims him "the greatest pharaoh in the New Empire if not in all Egyptian history."

Amenhotep II ruled from 1448 to 1420 B.C. and he in turn was succeeded by his son Thutmose IV, who ruled from 1420 to 1411 B.C. Amenhotep III, son of the preceding, occupied the throne from 1411 to 1375 B.C. and was the last of the truly powerful pharaohs or emperors.

Upon the transition of Amenhotep III the Empire fell to his son Amenhotep IV, with whose history all Rosicrucians are greatly concerned. He was the last Great Master in the family of the founders and the one to whom we owe the really wonderful philosophies and writings used so universally in all Lodge work throughout the world.

Amenhotep IV was born in the Royal Palace at Thebes, November 24th, 1378 B.C. His mother Tiy or Tia was of Aryan birth, but both he and his father paid the most sincere respects to her and were ever proud of designating her *Queen Tia* upon all monuments.

He was only eleven years old in 1367 B.C. when he was crowned and immediately began a career unequaled by any pharaoh of Egypt.

His father, having been the Master of the Order for a number of years, built the great Temple of Luxor and dedicated it to the Brotherhood. He also added to the Temple of Karnak and in many ways left "monuments of testimony and praise."

The Brotherhood numbered two hundred and eighty-three Fratres and sixty-two Sorores at this time, and at the time of the crowning of young Amenhotep IV, the Master was one Thehopset who remained in the office until 1365 B.C. Amenhotep's installation as *Master-by-Council-Decree* occurred in the Temple of Luxor, April 9th, 1365, at sunset, in the presence of his bride and her parents.

Amenhotep being the only descendant, it was deemed advisable that he marry as early as the customs then permitted in order that an heir to the throne would be assured. But Amenhotep's children unfortunately were daughters, and this proved disastrous to the throne.

The life of this great man is too easily found in various histories of Egypt, especially Breasted's, to warrant space here, but his accomplishments for the Order must be considered, at least briefly.

Since he was born in a country where people were given to idolatry, where the chief endeavors were those of building Temples to gods, it is easy to ap-

preciate his attitude toward the existing religion (or religions) after he had been thoroughly instructed in the secret philosophy. So keen was his understanding that in his fifteenth year he composed many of the most beautiful prayers, psalms, and chants used in the organization today, as well as contributing to the philosophy and sciences.

To him came the inspiration of overthrowing the worship of idols and substituting the religion and worship of one God, a supreme deity, whose spirit was in Heaven and whose physical manifestation was the Sun—the *Symbol of Life*. This was in accordance with the secret doctrines, and it changed the worship of the Sun as a *god* to the worship of *the God* symbolized by the sun. This was the beginning of monotheism in Egypt and the origin of the worship of a spiritual deity which *"existed everywhere, in everything,* but was *nothing of the earth"* i.e., had no physical existence on earth in the form of inanimate or nonspiritual images.

Arthur E. P. Weigall, Chief Inspector of the Department of Antiquities, Upper Egypt, in writing of the religion inspired by Amenhotep IV (Akhnaton), says: "Like a flash of blinding light in the night time, the Aton (the sun-symbol of the true God) stands out for a moment amidst the black Egyptian

darkness, and disappears once more—the first signal
to this world of the future religion of the West. . . .
One might believe that Almighty God had for a
moment revealed himself to Egypt. . . ."

We shall let a portion of one of a number of
hymns written by Amenhotep, and sung to the
glory of the sole God, speak for itself:

> *How manifold are thy works!*
> *They are hidden before men*
> *O sole God, beside whom there*
>   *is no other.*
> *Thou didst create the earth*
> *according to thy heart.**

Truly the religion of Amenhotep did not endure
for long. Compared to the years of darkness, it was
but a flash, for it ceased as a *public* and *general* religion when Amenhotep passed beyond the veil in
1350 B. C.

He, too, left many monuments to the glory of the
Brotherhood. First, he removed as far as possible all
"pillars to Ammon" and all references to Ammon
as a *god*. So thorough was his work that he did not
hesitate to mutilate the work done by his father, at

---

*The word *heart* may mean either *pleasure* or *understanding* here.
Compare this with Psalm 104:24, to see influence on early Hebrew
Psalmist.

Karnak and Luxor, by effacing all reference to the god Ammon—put there to appease the heathen priesthood—even to removing the name of his father and mother where they were connected with such idolatry. This naturally provoked the populace, especially since Amenhotep substituted beautiful monuments to the "living God."

In the fifth year of his reign—when he was only sixteen years of age—a sweeping reform was initiated throughout Egypt by his decree, which prohibited any other form of worship except that already mentioned. In one of his decrees he wrote: "This is my oath of Truth which it is my desire to pronounce, and of which I will not say: 'It is false,' eternally forever."

He then changed his own name so that it would not be inconsistent with his reform. Amenhotep meant "Ammon is satisfied"; this he altered to Akhnaton or Ikhenaton meaning "pious to Aton" or "Glory to Aton."

He built a new capital at El Amarna (Akhetaton) in the plain of Hermopolis on a virgin site at the edge of the desert and abandoned Thebes because it was the *magnificent city of Ammon*. At El Amarna he also built a large Temple for the Brotherhood, in "the form of a cross," and a large number of houses for his Council. Here was the

beginning of monastic life, for within the boundaries of El Amarna lived two hundred and ninety-six Fratres of the Order, each having taken an oath never to pass "beyond the shadow of the Temple."

These Fratres wore special costumes which included a "cord at the loins" and a covering for the head, while the priest in the Temple wore a surplice of linen and had his head shaved in a round spot on the top.

It is from this institution that all monastic orders, especially that of St. Francis, derive their methods, even their costumes.

During these years at El Amarna the Brotherhood was being made into a concrete organization, and the Fratres at this community outlined the initiations and forms of service as used today.

Akhnaton (Amenhotep IV) not only built his Temple in the form of a cross, but he added the cross and the rose as symbols and further adopted the Crux Ansata,* in a special coloring, as the symbol to be worn by all teachers (Masters). In fact, the last year of his life was spent in evolving a wonderful system of symbols used to this day, to express every phase and meaning of the Rosicrucian sciences, arts, and philosophies, and while

---

*The crux ansata is one of the earliest forms of a cross. It is an oval resting on a tau cross, or letter T. It was a symbol of life.

some of these have become known to the uninitiated through the researches of Egyptologists, many remain secret and all are understandable only to the initiated.*

As a ruler, our Master failed to check the desire for war. He foresaw the result of the approaching crisis and, sad at his neglect of political matters in his enthusiasm for the spiritual, he weakened his health and was finally forced to take to his bed in the month of July, 1350 B.C. Instead of using his mighty knowledge to regain his health it appears from his last dictated writings that his constant wish was to be spiritualized, that he might be *raised up to that plane* from which God's symbol shone down upon him. He fasted—practically starving himself— refused the services of the physician in the Order, and prayed constantly. Then, on July 24, late in the afternoon, with his right hand upstretched to God pleading to be taken into the *nous* he was seen by his Fratres and Sorores of the Order watching there, to be actually raised for a moment and then to drop back in "sweet repose with a smile of illumination upon his countenance."

Thus, passed to the beyond our Great Master, who

---

*The sciences and arts at the time, or the rituals, were not known as Rosicrucian. They descended to subsequently become a part of the present Rosicrucian traditions and rites.

did so much and left so much for our organization.

He may have neglected Egypt politically, but she will always remember her young Pharaoh whose twenty-eight years left her art and architecture, her sciences and philosophies so greatly changed and improved. His reign was like unto the Renaissance of France, and even the hieroglyphics and arts show a vast improvement based upon the principles of Truth. At the time of his crowning he took the title of "Amenhotep, King, *Living in Truth,*" which was the Rosicrucian phrase of fidelity as it is today, and he passed onward to the other life in *truth.*

Perhaps the most summary of all testimonies to Amenhotep IV found outside of the Rosicrucian literature, is that paid by James Breasted, Professor of Egyptology, University of Chicago, who says in his *History of Egypt:* "The modern world has yet adequately to value, or even acquaint itself with this man, who in an age so remote and under conditions so adverse, became the world's first individual."

APPENDIX

One unbiased authority, William Singleton, in the *History of Freemasonry* (Volume V, page 1327) says: "During A.D. 1118, some writers say 1188, according to a Swedish legend, 'the Rose Croix came

from the East into Europe.'" Again, on the same page: "To Ormesius, a priest of Alexandria in Egypt, is attributed the origin of the Order of Rose Croix." This priest of the mystery temple in Egypt and six of his companions embraced Christianity at the solicitation of St. Mark, the Evangelist, in A.D. 46.

"Many similar historical notations reveal the antiquity of the 'very secret and mystical Order of the Rose Croix (Rosy Cross).' Because it was not a sectarian religious order, its members and highest officers were permitted to embrace any religion. Its officers were often Priests or Masters in Oriental temples.

"That the Rosy Cross became the true esoteric symbol of not only the Rosicrucians, but of the inner circles of the Essenes, the Templars, and the Militia Crucifera Evangelica is due to the fact that all of these organizations were, and still are, channels for the work of the Great White Brotherhood. The secret ritual of the Templars contains many allusions to the significance of the Rosy Cross; likewise, the Militia contains definite explanations of its 'secret revelations.'"

CHAPTER II

THE GROWTH OF THE ORDER
IN THE ORIENT

T THE close of the first epoch of the Brotherhood's history, ending with the transition of Amenhotep IV (Akhnaton) in 1350 B.C., there was but one secret assembly, that which met in the Temple at El Amarna; and the Fratres and Sorores numbered four hundred and ten, including the Officers of the Lodge and the members of the Supreme High Council.

Plans had been made for years for the establishment of other assemblies or Lodges in various countries; but in those countries where a Lodge could have been established by one of the Egyptians who would have traveled there, war was raging and conditions were against any such institution.

Greeks were coming to Egypt to study its philosophies and become acquainted with its learning. Many of them sought entrance into the Order but it appears from various Council decisions that they were not admitted because of unpreparedness.

Benedictus Figulus, a Brother of the Order, who made a very exhaustive study of the growth of the Order, wrote: "About the year 1680 A.M.[1] the Greeks went to Chaldea and Egypt to learn this philosophy—but after learning a little they became so puffed up and proud, depending more than was meet on their own understanding."[2] This seems to have been the result most feared by the Council there, just as it is today. So many are ready to grasp at the first principles and then thinking their minds capable of building a philosophical structure upon the foundation, cease to be students and at once become teachers, each having a distinct, incomplete, and erroneous philosophy or "ism." Naturally there will be heretics in every school of thought; but a heretic is one who diverges from the established teachings only because of a *thorough knowledge* of such teachings, and to such we may turn for helpful criticism and suggestions at times. We must be delivered from the bigoted student who rises above his fellows and places his "superior" mind and judgment above the experienced understanding of his teachers.

---

[1] A. M. (year of the world—supposedly beginning at 4004 B. C.)
[2] "Dedicatory Speech to the Golden and Blessed Casket of Nature's Marvels," by Benedictus Figulus—p. 12. James Elliott and Company, London 1893.

For many years the Order progressed but little. Amenhotep IV left the work in the hands of competent teachers, and as the years passed by a few were admitted and initiated while the great teachings were being transcribed into symbolism and a special secret alphabet.

There being no male descendants of Amenhotep IV, he was succeeded by his son-in-law as Pharaoh, and at the close of the XVIII dynasty the religion of Ammon had been established once again, while the dreams and hopes of our Master were confined to the Order and its succession of teachers.

During the XIX dynasty under Seti I and Rameses II considerable tolerance was granted to the Order in Egypt; but gradually a feeling arose against its "secret power" and the lines of activity had to be drawn closer and closer.

Fortunately, in the Order at the time of the transition of Amenhotep IV, there was a sage named Hermes. So great was his learning and yet so mystical his many writings, purposely veiled so that they might be of value only to the future initiates, that the uninitiated minds of future years arose and acclaimed Hermes a myth, and there are those today who try to establish his identity with that of the Egyptian god "Thoth." However, it is the author's

pleasure to state now that which has never appeared in print before, and which has perplexed investigators for centuries—the birth date of Hermes Trismegistus—the Thrice Great Man.* He was born in Thebes, October 9th, 1399 B.C. He lived to the age of one hundred and forty-two years, dying in the Rosicrucian Monastery at El Amarna, on March 22nd, 1257 B.C., and his mummy lies among others in a cachette in the vicinity of El Amarna.

He was "thrice great" because he lived to attend the installation of Amenhotep IV as an R. C. Master, became Master himself upon the latter's transition, and in 1259 installed one Atonamen as Master of the Order.

It was at this time that Hermes completed his writings, especially the seven books and tablets which were found and brought to light in 400 A.D., and which were upon diverse chemical and physical subjects.

The following quotation from the text, *Poemandres, the Shepherd of Men,* is a Greek version of the ancient writings of Hermes, relating a cosmological vision which he had. Though the wording may

---

*Dr. Budge, eminent Egyptologist, says that the Egyptians often referred to Hermes as "Lord of Maat," i. e., Lord of Truth, and that he was regarded as the inventor of all arts and sciences. "Lord of Books" is still another title assigned him.

have been actually influenced by Greek philosophical thought, it does show the attempt to preserve not only the name but the wisdom attributed to this great man:

"But in a little while darkness came settling down in part, awesome and gloomy, coiling in sinuous folds so that methought it like unto a snake.

"And then the darkness changed into some sort of a moist nature, tossed about beyond all power of words, belching out smoke as from a fire and groaning forth a wailing sound that beggars all description.

"(and) after that an outcry inarticulate came forth from it, as though it were a voice of fire.

"(Thereon) out of the light—a holy word (Logos) descended on that nature. And upwards to the height from the moist nature leapt forth pure fire; light was it, swift and active too. The air, too, being light, followed after the fire; from out of the Earth-and-Water rising up to fire so that it seemed to hang therefrom.

"But Earth-and-Water stayed so mingled each with other, that Earth from Water no one could discern. Yet were they moved to hear by reason of the Spirit-Word (Logos) pervading them."

In 1203 several of the Fratres of the Order who

were of the *Illuminati* were commissioned to go into other lands and spread the secret doctrines by the establishment of other Lodges. It was quite apparent that Egypt was to be subjected to a devastation and that its great learning might be lost. Confidence seems to have been the keynote, however, for one may read a long argument, reminding one of a speech in Congress, delivered by one of the Fratres at a Council held in El Amarna on June 8, 1202 B.C., in which he reassures all present that the "stars shew naught but trial, and test, by air, fire, and water, which we hold to be the elements of the crucible from which the precious stone will bring forth its own." And again: "who among us will rise and predict defeat for that which our Masters have labored over 29 cycles (two hundred years)? Is not this *Truth?* Are we not assembled in *Truth?* Are we not living *Truth?* And, can *Maat* ever die?* Is not transition the gateway of progress? And can the crucible do more than bring about a physical and spiritual transition, a transmutation, of the principles for which we have pledged our lives?"

---

*As early as 3500 B. C., the word *Maat* appeared as the epitome of those values of the moral order which men conceived, such as *truth, justice,* and *righteousness.* Later the chief justices of the Egyptian courts, we are informed by Dr. James Henry Breasted, wore Lapis Lazuli emblems upon their breasts, symbolizing *Maat.*

It was finally decided that "no undue haste should be sanctioned in permitting the Fratres who have gone abroad to establish Lodges, but rather that those who travel here in search of the Light should be tried, and to those found qualified shall be given the commission to return to their people and establish a Lodge in the name of the Brotherhood."

It was this dictum—known as the *AMRA*—that in later years proved the wisdom of the Councilors at this meeting, for it not only became a hard and fast rule, but made for the success of the plans of propagation.

It was in this wise that the phrase "travel East for learning or Light" first came into use; for those who soon began to travel to Egypt came from the West.

About the year 1000 B.C. there came to Egypt a character whose name is recorded as Saloman but who was identified in later years with Solomon.

The records show that he had come from the *West,* had traveled over many lands and across waters. He was of a nation which was large and important, situated in some very distant land. All this is indicated from the report he made to the representatives of the fraternity whom he inter-

viewed at Thebes "whither he had gone immediately upon his arrival in Egypt accompanied by his slaves (!) and his *najah* (a word unknown to the translators)."

He desired instruction in the higher Egyptian sciences and philosophy, and was directed to El Amarna with a letter of introduction from the *intendant* at Thebes. He reached El Amarna on the 4th day of June, 999, under the name of Saloman, *the youthful seeker*.

Saloman did not complete his studies, for it is reported that he left El Amarna "before the fourth examination." He left with his Fratres and Sorores a definite feeling of love, wisdom, and virtue, and all were grieved at his sudden but announced departure.

The next word of him is as a resident at the *royal home* in Bubastis in the Delta where Shishak I (or Sheshonk) had established himself. This was in the year 952 B.C., and Saloman is referred to as an instructor to the Pharaoh's son. This is probably a mistake in translation, for in another place he is referred to as advisor in political matters, and this seems more probable in the light of future developments. Whether he had been at this residence all the intervening years from 999 to 952 B.C. is not definitely established, but there is a record of his presence

at Thebes in the year 980 when he visited some *games* in company with the *intendant* of Thebes, and a group of scholars with whom he seemed on the most intimate terms.

Saloman seems to have been greatly influenced in Thebes and Bubastis by the religion of Ammon and conceived a form of philosophical religion which was a mixture of the Rosicrucian monotheism and the Egyptian idolatry. To him the *sun* became more than the mere symbol of a God; it was the living vital spirit of God, and while not the God, it was God's ethereal body. This would indicate that Saloman conceived God as being (a) personal, rather than *impersonal* as the Rosicrucians taught, and (b) dual, body and spirit, Father and Holy Ghost.

When Shishak I secured Thebes he appointed his son priest in the religion of Ammon, and gave his daughter, Aye, to Saloman to wed. Then within a year or so Saloman departed for Palestine where he became a mighty power, and by a prearranged plan, permitted Shishak I to rule over his people. The history of Saloman or *Solomon* in Palestine is too well known to warrant any further comment except on one point.

Five years after Saloman began his rule in Palestine he completed a Temple there in which to

house a "society" or brotherhood such as he had found at El Amarna. An examination of the plans and cross-section views of the so-called Saloman's Temple shows it to be not only typically Egyptian in architecture and decoration, but copied after the mystic Temple at El Amarna, even to the location of the Altar, with the exception that the side structures which made the original building a *cross* were eliminated in Saloman's plans.

Saloman had the assistance of two who had traveled in Egypt as architects and artists—Hu-ram-abi of Tyre and one Hiram Abif.

The Saloman brotherhood was closely watched by the fraternity in Egypt, which had removed its headquarters to Thebes again because of political changes and the warring invasions in the territory of El Amarna, which eventually reduced the entire community to ruins.

It was found that Saloman restricted his order to males and adapted a great many of the details of the Rosicrucian initiations and services. At first it was believed that he would apply to the Grand Lodge in Thebes for a charter and make his work a branch of the R. C., but it became apparent before the first assembly was held that he was not adhering to the

Rosicrucian philosophy, for he used the sun as the exclusive symbol of his order.

Of the growth of the Saloman brotherhood, as it was officially called in all ancient documents, one may read in all literature bearing upon Freemasonry. It has evolved into a semi-mystical, speculative, secret, fraternal order of power and great honor, gradually altering the principles laid down by Saloman, it is true, but doing so for the greater benefit of man.

The Greeks were now coming to Thebes to study, and it was at this time that the world-wide spread of the organization began.

Pythagoras is very often mentioned as one of the earliest Messiahs of the order, but in truth there were many who preceded him. Among the first to become worldly famous in the order was Solon, who became the first chaplain who was not an Egyptian. He entered the order in 618 B.C., and remained a true Messiah until his transition in 550 B.C., leaving for our use some of the most beautiful and inspiring prayers ever spoken by a yearning soul. His sagacity is also seen in the counsel he gave those who sought his advice. The following has been given us by Diogenes Laertius, in his biography of Solon:

"Put more trust in nobility of character than in an oath."

"Do not be rash to make friends, and, when once they are made, do not drop them."

"In giving advice seek to help, not to please, your friend."

"Learn to obey before you command."

Contemporary with him was Anaximander, who came from Miletus to study at Thebes preceding the coming of Pythagoras.

Pythagoras was born in Samos on November 26th, 582 B.C. He entered the Order at Thebes on the second of April, 531, and having passed through all the initiations and examinations he entered the Illuminati, October 16, 529, and left at once for Crotona (Krotono), Italy, with jewels and documents to found a Grand Lodge there. There were a few so-called secret cults in existence at that time in Italy, and when Pythagoras began to promulgate his plans and admitted that women might not only become members, but could hold office, he attracted the attention of the most advanced thinkers of the day. Theano, the wife of Pythagoras, was one of the principal officers for three years. The Grand Lodge eventually had 300 brothers and sisters and issued

many charters for local lodges of the order throughout Italy.

From this time onward toward the Christian period, great minds from many countries journeyed Eastward and Westward and *Crossed the Threshold,* and having completed the work and studies, passed again into the world's darkness to spread the *light* as they interpreted it.

As a historical record and a guide to the student who delights in research and antiquarianism, there will be given the names of those who came to Thebes to study, became Masters of Rosicrucian Lodges in other lands, and during their lifetimes published at least one book, an official work, treating on the Rosicrucian philosophies or sciences.

Many of the books or manuscripts to be listed are still extant in the original, or translated, and quite a few of them are in America. A perusal of any one of them convinces one of the author's real knowledge and experience in Rosicrucianism.

Chapter III

THE WORK OF THE DISCIPLES

OUTER activities of the Great White Brotherhood, during the pre-Christian Era, were centered in a number of branches controlled by one group of supreme officers who constituted the Rosicrucian Fraternity of Brethren of the Rosy Cross. The Supreme Masters of the Great White Brotherhood withdrew from public activity and with a council of eminent advisors constituted the esoteric body known thereafter as the Great White Lodge.

The first spread of Rosicrucianism to the Western world was from the great seats of learning of ancient Egypt, namely, Tell el-Amarna, Thebes, Heliopolis, and Alexandria. The great masters, sages, or Kheri Hebs (high priests), who presided over the instruction, were initiates of the Great White Brotherhood. They authorized eminent scholars as disciples to go forth and disseminate the light under various organization names. Even those in authority, who were not initiates, acknowledged the greatness of the Secret Wisdom in the archives of the order, and appealed for its release to the worthy, as we shall

see. Philadelphus, the Ptolemy principally responsible for the establishment of the first great university at Alexandria, Egypt, about 305 B.C., sought
in the beginning, it is believed, to create a center of eclectic philosophy. For this purpose, he
had the Athenian orator and statesman and his
personal friend, Demetrius, invite the great minds,
the philosophers of Greece, to teach or impart
their knowledge to Alexandrian students. It
was apparently the intention to classify such
knowledge and select that which, in the opinion of Philadelphus and his associates, merited
dissemination. The enthusiasm which the great
school inspired in the seeking minds of the
day altered the plans. The policy changed to research and advancement of knowledge, on the one
hand, and on the other hand, a careful preservation in the great library of all the wisdom of
all ages. Philadelphus became aware of the vast
knowledge of natural law and of a Cosmic philosophy had by those who were *initiates* of the mystery schools. Much of such knowledge seemed to
parallel that which he was having introduced
in Alexandria from the West—from Athens.
His consequent actions prove that he realized
that much of the Western knowledge was syn-
cretic, and had formerly come from Egypt. In

fact, Plato tells us that Solon got his information from the priests of Sais, who told him that all of the records were preserved in the Temple of Neith. A further tradition relates that Solon, Thales, and Plato all visited the great college at Heliopolis, and that the last mentioned studied there.

A contemporary of Philadelphus was Manetho, a High Priest at Heliopolis, and a learned man, also a prominent scribe of the Great White Brotherhood, who had access to the secret teachings of the Order. Manetho was also master of the ancient Egyptian writing, or Hieroglyphics, which, in the Third Century B.C., was becoming archaic and could not be generally read. The Egyptians were at that time reading a modern version of the ancient writings, the Demotic, and Greek was becoming still more popular. Philadelphus commissioned Manetho to compile a history of Egypt, and particularly a text of the *mystic philosophy* of the Secret Schools of the Great White Brotherhood and Rosicrucians. This knowledge, we are told, was mainly contained in the Hieroglyphic inscriptions in the library of the priesthood at Ra. It will be recalled that Amenhotep IV (Akhnaton) declared Ra, the sun, to be a physical manifestation or symbol of the great *sole God*. This library, there-

fore, must have contained the great truths of his monotheistic religion, and the truths which the thinkers with which he surrounded himself at Tell el-Amarna discovered. Much that we know of the outer or profane history of Egypt came about through this compilation by Manetho. In fact, it is generally conceded that Plutarch acquired much of his information from this source. In a book of Manetho's, called *Sothis,* of which fragments only are to be found in the writings of others, appears the following letter to Philadelphus, from Manetho, telling of his efforts to compile the ancient wisdom:

"We must make calculations concerning all the points which you may wish us to examine into, to answer your questions concerning what will happen to the world. According to your commands, the sacred books, written by our forefather, Thrice-greatest Hermes, which I study, shall be shown to you. My Lord and King, farewell."

Manetho's greatest work was his Egyptian history, which was done in three books, and in the Greek language. It is famous because it is the only work in Greek based upon a full knowledge of the Egyptian sources. Fragments of these works come to us today in the writings of Fla-

vius Josephus and Julius Africanus. The former is a more reliable authority and refers to Manetho in his treatise, *Against Apion*. In the *History of Egypt* by Manetho, there is an interesting reference to Moses, which shows him also to have been an initiate of the Great White Brotherhood of Egypt, and to have transmitted their knowledge in a veiled manner to his people. The excerpt reads:

"Moses, a son of the tribe of Levi, educated in Egypt and initiated at Heliopolis, became a High Priest of the Brotherhood under the reign of the Pharaoh Amenhotep. He was elected by the Hebrews as their chief and he adapted to the ideas of his people the science and philosophy which he had obtained in the Egyptian mysteries; proofs of this are to be found in the symbols, in the Initiations, and in his precepts and commandments. The wonders which Moses narrates as having taken place upon the Mountain of Sinai, are, in part, a veiled account of the Egyptian initiation which he transmitted to his people when he established a branch of the Egyptian Brotherhood in his country, from which descended the Essenes. The dogma of an 'only God' which he taught was the Egyptian Brotherhood interpretation and teaching of the Pharaoh who established the first monotheistic religion

known to man. The traditions he established in this manner were known completely to only a few of them, and were preserved in the *arcanae* of the secret societies, the *Therapeutics* of Egypt and the *Essenians."*

Nearly five centuries later, during what might be said to be a period of decline of mysticism, or the mystic philosophy in the Western world, an emissary was sent from Egypt to Rome to capture the hearts and minds of the peoples, with a true mysticism free of the superstitions of the cults, and tempering the cold intellectualisms that were flourishing there. The world generally calls his great work *Neo-Platonism,* but it corresponds to the Rosicrucian doctrines of mysticism before as well as subsequent to his time. This master teacher was Plotinus. He was born in Lycopolis, Egypt, in 205 (?) A.D. For eleven years he was the personal student of Ammonius Saccas, at the great school at Alexandria. Ammonius Saccas related to him the doctrines of Plato, and he was instrumental in having Plotinus initiated into the inner circles of the Great White Brotherhood. He was carefully trained and prepared to introduce an aspect of the Platonic philosophy, with which the world was generally familiar, combined with the true mysticism and occult philosophy of the Secret Schools. This combi-

nation was necessary, for if he had attempted to present the latter in its true form during his time, it would have been rejected. By making it appear a new kind of Platonic teachings, people investigated it and were intrigued by the subtle beauty of these Eastern teachings.

Plotinus travelled extensively, as part of a military expedition in Persia, so that he could learn firsthand the Persian religion and philosophy. The influence of their beliefs is found in his dualism of good and evil as a single force, which is recognized in the mystical teachings of the Rosicrucians today. He entered Rome in 244 A.D., and founded his school as part of the great outer activity of the Great White Brotherhood. He was universally revered, not alone for his learning, but for his character. He was held in high respect by Emperor Gallienus and his consort Salonina.

Notable among the phases of the spread of the work of the Rosicrucians to other lands was the establishment of two branches known as the *Essenes* and the *Therapeuti*. The Essenes constituted that branch which went into Palestine and adopted a distinct name in order to veil its preliminary work while the Therapeuti was a similar branch established for the same purpose in Greece.

In Palestine the Essenes established a community of members and associate members at Galilee where they had many homes in this non-Jewish, Gentile part of the country, and built their principal monastery and temple on the top of Mount Carmel where Elijah, as one of the descendants of the Great White Brotherhood, had previously established a retreat and had taught many of the mysteries of the Brotherhood.

Just before the Christian period, the Great White Brotherhood had also established a new monastery and temple and other structures for a great central point of their activities at Heliopolis, and the temple here was known as the Temple of Helios, or sometimes called "the Temple of the Sun." The intercourse between the temple at Heliopolis and the one on top of Mount Carmel was intimate and frequent, and many of the philosophers who journeyed from European points to Egypt to study spent some of their time at Mount Carmel.

Just about the time of the birth of Jesus the great library and archivist records maintained at Heliopolis were transferred to Mount Carmel, and the Essene Brotherhood in Palestine together with other branches of the Great White Brotherhood were preparing for the coming of the great Avatar who was

to be the reincarnation of Zoroaster, a famous Avatar of the Brotherhood in centuries past.

The birth of Jesus in a family of Gentiles living in the Essene community at Galilee fulfilled the expectations of the Brotherhood, and from this time on the outer and inner activities of the Brotherhood became centered around the ministry of the great Master Jesus. The details of the birth, preparation, ministry, and culminating events of the Master Jesus are all set forth in a separate volume entitled *The Mystical Life of Jesus* wherein are given details from the records of the Essenes and the Great White Brotherhood and which have never been published before.* Therefore, I will not take space in the present record to recite these many and important matters.

At the close of the life of Jesus the Christ, the disciples of Jesus and the high officers of the Great White Brotherhood planned to carry on the new cycle of illumination and revelation of doctrines as presented by him, and an outer congregation or public movement was established known as the Christine Church. This movement gradually evolved into a more or less independent public organization. While it was sponsored by the Great White Brotherhood, and all of the principal workers like unto the

The Mystical Life of Jesus, by H. Spencer Lewis, Ph.D.

original Apostles were men chosen from the Essene Gentile community at Galilee, the Great White Brotherhood did not establish the Christine Church as a part of its activities, because it was interested in the work of all religious movements in all lands, and did not become a part of any of them.

Several hundred years after the foundation of the Christine Church, and while it was being actively promulgated by the representatives of the Great White Brotherhood in those lands where the doctrines and teachings would do the utmost good, the Supreme Temple and monastery, as well as the library and archivist records, were transferred from Mount Carmel to new structures built in an isolated section of Tibet where the Headquarters of the Great Masters of the organization was maintained for some time.

During the time of the organization of the Christine movement, and throughout all the centuries thereafter, the inner circle of the Great White Brotherhood continued to function as a nonsectarian, nonreligious school of mystical, occult, and scientific teachings. All of the outer activities such as the Essene movement, the Christine movement, and similar bodies in various lands, represented the outer congregation of the Great White Brotherhood while

the secret schools and temples with their high priests and instructors and large membership of students represented the inner congregation. All through the ages up to the present time the Great White Brotherhood has continued to function in this dual manner.

It was during the period of contentions and strife which the Christine movement faced, that the Great White Brotherhood found it advisable to establish another organization composed almost exclusively of men, and called the *Militia Crucifera Evangelica*. Its purpose was to protect the cross as a mystical symbol, against its misuse by those who attempted to carry on crusades of persecution against others who would not accept a sectarian interpretation of the symbolism of the ancient emblem. It was in the foundation of this Militia that we find the origin of all the militant organizations which became defenders of the faith in later years. It is notable, however, that the Militia Crucifera Evangelica never became an active body of prosecutors or crusaders, but merely of silent defenders who were pledged never to unsheathe the sword except in absolute defense. The organization became greatly enlarged in later centuries, not as a true military organization, but as a group of those who defend the Rosicrucian emblem and

the cross with their moral strength rather than with any physical strength.

The Militia Crucifera Evangelica continues today throughout the world as a small but courageous and active body perpetuating its traditional ideals. In July of 1940, the members of the American jurisdiction, authoritatively established by European decree, met in San Jose, California, in their first *official* conclave for the Western world. The principal purpose of the convention was the adoption of a means to defend Christianity and mystical concepts at a time when humanity was again afflicted by a second World War.

Throughout the centuries preceding the Christian Era and thereafter, the Great White Brotherhood and its centers of learning, its libraries and monasteries, became the centers for pilgrimages on the part of great minds seeking illumination and the highest advancement in culture and ethics. The records of the Brotherhood are replete with the life stories of many eminent characters known in general history who became students in the mystery temples of the organization in Egypt, at Palestine, or elsewhere. They later presented outlines of modified philosophies and principles which the public could understand and apply, and became authors of

books which have been valuable contributions to the advancement of learning.

Among the very earliest of the philosophers who contributed to the Rosicrucian philosophy were: the fellow workers of Hermes—Mena, Busiris, Simandius, Sesostris, Miris, Sethon, Amasis, Adfar Alexandrinus, and King Calid.

Then there was "Maria Hebraeae," a Hebrew woman supposed to have been Miriam, a sister of Moses.

After the journey of Pythagoras to Italy many came from Greece and other lands to be initiated in Egypt and from there returned to their native lands or elsewhere to establish branches of the mystic school and become Masters and Officers therein.

Most of these—whose names are listed below, published during their lifetimes one or more papers dealing with various principles of the Rosicrucian philosophy and science.

Some of these writings were kept secret—others were written for public reading with the true doctrines carefully veiled. In order that the Rosicrucian students may study such writings as are extant today these philosophers' names are given and sometimes the name or title of their work which is especially recommended.

Solon, c. 639-c. 559 B.C.

Anaximander of Miletus, 611-547 B.C.

Anaximenes of Miletus, 520 B.C.

Heraclitus of Ephesus, 520 B.C.

Parmenides, 515 B.C.

Empedocles of Agrigentum, 500 B.C.

Democritus of Thrace, 460 B.C.

Socrates of Athens, 470?-399 B.C.

Euclides of Megara, 450?-374 B.C.

Plato of Athens, 427?-347 B.C.

Aristotle of Thrace, 384-322 B.C. (Read *De Anima* and the *Metaphysica*.)

Epicurus of Athens, 342?-270 B.C.

Metrodorus, Hermarchus, Colotes, Leonteus and his wife Themista, and Leontium—all pupils of Epicurus in his R.C. Lodge in Athens, 306-301 B.C.

Philo of Alexandria, 110 B.C.

Antiochus of Ascalon, 100 B.C.

Cicero, 106-43 B.C.

Nigidius Figulus, 70 B.C.

Seneca, 54 B.C.?-A.D. 39

Plotinus, A.D. 205?-270

THE CHRISTIAN PERIOD

After these came philosophers from the Christian period beginning a new line of writers.

From this time on the work spread very rapidly throughout many lands and only a brief list of the most prominent can be given. The following not only contributed interesting writings to the future R.C. literature, but were either Masters of various Lodges or assisted in bringing the mystic fraternity into their respective countries.

Geber, or Jabir, Arab scholar, fl. 721-776. (*The Sum of Perfection*)

Charlemagne, king of the Franks, 742-814.

Al-Farabi, 870-950, compiler of encyclopedia of R.C. Science and Arts.

Avicenna of Bokhara, Persia, 980-1037.

Raymond VI, Count of Toulouse, defender of the Albigenses, 1156-1222.

Albertus Magnus, German scholastic, 1193?-1280. (*De Alchimia*)

Jean de Meung of France, 13th century. (*Roman de la Rose*)

Roger Bacon of England, 1214?-1294. (*Opus Majus*)

Thomas Aquinas, Italian theologian, 1225?-1274.

Arnold of Villanova of Catalonia, 1235?-?1312. (*Rosarium Philosophorum*)

Raymond Lully of Spain, 1235?-1315. (*Anima artis transmutationis* or *Clavicula*)

Dante Alighieri, 1265-1321. (*Divine Comedy*)

Nicholas Flamel of France, 1330?-1418. (*Exposition of the Hieroglyphical Figures*)

HISTORY OF THE ORDER

Thomas Norton, 15th century. (*Ordinall of Alchemy*)

Johannes Trithemius, 1462-1516.

Pico della Mirandola, Italian humanist, 1463-1494. (*Oration on the Dignity of Man*)

Cornelius Heinrich Agrippa, German physician, theologian, and writer, 1486?-1535. (*De occulta philosophia*)

Sir George Ripley, c. 1490. (*Twelve Gates*)

Paracelsus, Swiss alchemist and physician, 1493?-1541.

Dr. John Dee, English mathematician and astrologer, 1527-1608. (*Hieroglyphic Monad*)

Simon Studion, 1543-?1605. (*Naometria*)

Giordano Bruno, Italian philosopher, 1548?-1600. (*Concerning the cause, principle, and one*)

Johann Arndt, German theologian, 1555-1621. (*Zweytes Silentium Dei*)

Heinrich Khunrath, 1560-1605. He established the first R.C. library in Germany.

Sir Francis Bacon, past Imperator of the Order, 1561-1626. (*New Atlantis*)

Tommaso Campanella, Italian philosopher, 1568-1639.

Michael Maier, Grand Master of the R.C. Order in Germany, 1568-1622. (*Themis Aurea*)

Robert Fludd, English physician and Rosicrucian apologist, 1574-1637. (*Tractatus Apologeticus*)

Jacob Boehme, German theosophist and mystic, 1575-1624. (*Three Principles* and *Mysterium Magnum*)

Jean Baptiste van Helmont, Flemish physician and chemist, 1577-1644. (*De vita aeterna*)

Dr. William Harvey, 1578-1657.

Johann Valentin Andrea, 1586-1654.

Jan Amos Komensky (Comenius), Czech theologian and educator, 1592-1670.

René Descartes, French scientist and philosopher, 1596-1650. (*Discours de la Méthode* and *Meditationes de Prima Philosophia*)

Sir Robert Moray, 1600?-1673.

Benedictus Figulus, c.1608.

Elias Ashmole, 1617-1692. His collection of rarities, presented to Oxford, contained a manuscript copy of the *Fama Fraternitatis*.

Irenaeus Agnostus, c.1619. (*Portus Tranquillitatis*)

John Evelyn, 1620-1706.

Thomas Vaughan, a Welshman, who wrote under the name of Eugenius Philalethes, 1622-1665. He translated the early R.C. papers into English. (*Euphrates: or The Waters of the East* and *Lumen de Lumine*)

Jane Leade, English mystic, 1623-1704.

Dr. John Frederick Helvetius, 1625-1709. (*Golden Calf*)

Robert Boyle, British physicist, chemist, and natural philosopher, 1627-1691.

John Heydon, a Master in the English R.C. Order, 1629-1667. (*English Physitians Guide: or A Holy Guide*)

Baruch Spinoza, 1632-1677.

Sir Christopher Wren, English architect, 1632-1723. He designed and rebuilt St. Paul's Cathedral after the Great Fire in London of 1666.

Sir Isaac Newton, 1642-1727. An English natural philosopher and mathematician, who conceived the idea of universal gravitation set forth in his *Principia*.

Gottfried Wilhelm von Leibnitz, German philosopher and mathematician, 1646-1716. (*On the True Theologia Mystica*)

Johannes Kelpius, 1673-1708, Grand Master of the R.C. Order in its first cycle in America in 1694.

Dr. Christopher Witt, 1675-1765.

Conrad Beissel, 1690-1768.

Benjamin Franklin, 1706-1790. American statesman, scientist, and philosopher, he was associated with the Rosicrucians of Pennsylvania during the Order's first active cycle in America.

Peter Miller, 1710-1796.

Martínez de Pasquales, Portuguese mystic, 1715?-1779. He founded a society of mystics later led by Marquis Louis Claude de Saint-Martin.

Count Alessandro Cagliostro of Sicily, 1743-1795. Became a Master and established many R.C. lodges in Europe. (*Rituel de la Maçonnerie Egyptienne*)

Thomas Jefferson, 1743-1826. Statesman, scientist, philosopher, and third President of the U.S.

Louis Claude de Saint-Martin, 1743-1803. This French mystic and philosopher carried on the work of Martínez de Pasquales. His society became known as the Martinists.

Johann Wolfgang von Goethe, German poet and mystic, 1749-1832. (*Die Geheimnisse*)

[92]

John O'Donnell, 1749-1805.

Karl von Eckartshausen, 1752-1803. (*Cloud on the Sanctuary*)

William Blake, English artist, poet, and mystic, 1757-1827.

Dr. John Dalton, English chemist and physicist, who arranged the table of atomic weights, 1766-1844.

Marshal Michel Ney, 1769-?1815.

Michael Faraday, English chemist and physicist, 1791-1867.

Honoré de Balzac, French mystic and writer, 1799-1850. (*Louis Lambert*)

Edward George Bulwer-Lytton, English mystic and writer, 1803-1873. (*Zanoni*)

Eugene Sue, French novelist, 1804-1857. (*Wandering Jew*)

Giuseppe Mazzini, 1805-1872.

Anton Rubinstein, Russian Jewish pianist and composer, 1829-1894.

Dr. Franz Hartmann, 1839-1912.

Julius Friedrich Sachse, historian of the Rosicrucian movement in America, 1842-1910.

Ella Wheeler Wilcox, American poet, 1850-1919.

Elbert Hubbard, American writer, printer, and philosopher, 1856-1915.

Claude Debussy, French composer, 1862-1918.

Marie Corelli, English writer of mystical fiction, 1855-1924.

Nicholas Roerich, Russian-born mystic, artist, and philosopher, 1874-1947.

François Jollivet Castelot, d.1937.

△▽△

When the Rosicrucian movement reached what is now France, early in the Christian Era, it found there its greatest welcome.

The pilgrims to the Holy Land had brought back to the Counts and Lords of the South of France reports of the activities of a certain secret society devoted to science and brotherhood. Charlemagne was at the time conducting his great school of learning. History will tell the lay mind a great deal regarding his famous school. He realized that through education alone could he build his power and hold the reins of government. He gathered around him the brightest scholars of the day, the learned men of many countries, and offered them excellent remuneration if they would devote all their time to the teaching of the pupils in this school. The pupils included himself, his family, his relatives, and a few of his appointed officials.

Nor were these learned men limited to teaching. Charlemagne desired to promote learning. He gave his tutors every opportunity to make extensive researches in every field and provided them with an experimental laboratory. The philosophers—among them was the famous Alcuin—were permitted to

travel to other lands to bring back the cream of all knowledge. In this school, St. Guillem, a nephew of Charlemagne, received his education.

One of these philosophers, Arnaud, was directed to go to Jerusalem in A.D. 778 to learn all he could about this wonderful secret society which possessed the key to all science and all art. Arnaud journeyed to Jerusalem and was there directed to Egypt. It is recorded that he made humble application for admission into the Order in Thebes, and then, in accordance with the Law AMRA, applied for permission to establish a branch Lodge in France [then the Frankish Empire].

Arnaud completed his study in Egypt in approximately two years and one month. Because of the difficulty of communication his several letters and reports to Charlemagne failed to reach their destination, and in France he was given up as dead— a fate which befell many who journeyed far in those days. One of his letters to Charlemagne, written on a papyrus in Thebes, was afterward found in a monastery near Millau in France, where it had been deposited in a vault among other rare papers for some unknown reason. In it Arnaud makes a very glowing report of his discoveries, and refers to the body of "silent students clothed in white as pure and spotless as their characters but diligent in their

mastery of God's laws and privileges." In closing his report he says: "Should it be my privilege,
my great honor, to bring to our land the seal and
signs of this great school, we shall have in our midst
the power which our beloved Master may use in
destroying all ignorance, provided, of course, our
Master shall deem it wise and beneficial to humble
himself, not to those who ask it, but to God, and
thereby become as one of the disciples of our Lord
Jesus."

The significance of this closing sentence will be
brought to mind when it is recalled that the religious feeling in Charlemagne's school was very
intense and sincere. Bear in mind, Arnaud was
trying to state diplomatically and respectfully that
it would be necessary for Charlemagne to become
a humble supplicant for admission into the Order
if he wished to become a Master of the Order
in France—a position and honor which Arnaud
and his colleagues would certainly have insisted
upon.

Arnaud returned to France in 802, however, and
was given a very interesting ovation in the chamber
of Charlemagne's throne. Charlemagne did not
become a Master in the Order, but after two years'
delay permitted a Lodge to be established in Toulouse. The original Lodge was founded in a tem-

porary monastery on the outskirts of Tolosa—the ancient city—which is now in ruins some little distance from the present city of Toulouse. Part of the Altar of this first Lodge in France was still preserved by the archivists of the Order in France in 1909, though it was much the worse for very severe handling during the many religious wars in the Provinces.

Arnaud became the Master in that first Lodge which held its opening convocation about 804-805. (The difficulty with exact dates is due to the many changes in the calendar and in interpreting the various methods of keeping records in those days.)

The first Grand Master of France was Frees, who reigned from 883 to 899 A. D. Until that time Grand Masters were not appointed. There was to be only one Lodge in any country, according to the original plans, and the Master of that Lodge held no other power or authority than rule over the one Lodge. The granting of charters was still in the hands of the Supreme Council. But it was Frees who brought before the Council the advisability of establishing Grand Lodges in certain countries and giving to the Masters the right to grant charters to other Lodges within the same national confines. It was only one year before Frees passed to the beyond—898—that he received his

authority and instructions to establish other Lodges in France and the second Lodge was immediately established in Lyons.

There were many devout students of the Order in Toulouse who lived in Lyons and they lost no time—after years of waiting—in getting a very flourishing Lodge established there. Many years later—1623—the Freemasons in Lyons organized a Rose Croix degree in the same city to please the many Rosicrucians who were Masons. The Masonic body was organized at a Council held there July 23rd, 1623.

In the meantime the Order in France had spread very rapidly and had attracted wide attention. Some of the Monks in the various monasteries in the South of France became interested, and without mentioning names at this time—let it be known that some of these Roman Catholic persons, devout and sincere, rendered a great service to the upbuilding of the sanctity of the Order by contributing many beautiful moral and spiritual creeds and dogmas.

Finally in 1001—the year when all the South of France was expecting the end of the world—according to an old Biblical prophecy—the Order in France established a Rosicrucian Monastery—the

first in the world—in the old Roman city of Ne-
mausus, now Nimes.

This Monastery became the nucleus for the great
Rosicrucian College or Ecole R. C. which flourished
in France from the twelfth century to the middle
of the sixteenth and which was revived again in
1882 in Montpellier.

The history of the Order in France is very interesting. The most minute facts of the early history were recorded by Phonaire, who was the
Official Historian of the Order in 1132 to 1134. The
later history was compiled by a number of Masters
of the R. C., R. F. and preserved in the archives in
the Dongeon at Toulouse. This latter city has been
the meeting place of the French Supreme Council
since 1487. France held second place in strength of
number of members, Germany holding first place,
and England third. Egypt of course was the great
Supreme Center, but had only a comparatively small
number of members.

In France, the loss of membership through the
great war was enormous.* Of the French Supreme
Council of twenty-five, there were living in December of 1915 only seven. But the loss in Germany had
been even greater. Many of the Brothers of the Or-

*This refers to the first World War.

der in France were called upon to bear arms; yet all did not reach the front, for some were classified and placed in offices and laboratories. Then, again, a great many of the French Brothers were older men, some of whom held high offices in the army, navy, and general government. Thus it was that all the Brothers of the Order in France did not participate in the actual conflict.

The Order spread into Germany shortly after the Grand Lodge was established in France. Charlemagne himself was the first to introduce the Order in Germany, for by his command one Mause settled somewhere along the Rhine near Coblenz and there began propaganda for members in a quiet dignified manner. He never lived to see his work bear fruit, however, for the restrictions placed around membership were severe and too stringent, but in 1100 a Lodge was established in Worms, and this became the Grand Lodge.

The work grew rapidly in Germany during the twelfth century, but it remained so secret and so inactive in its outward manifestations during its 108 years of inactivity that little was known of the Order or its members. Toward the beginning of the fifteenth century a spell of quietude—of dormancy —came again to the Order and as its members passed

on few were admitted. Religious controversies and other troubles not of interest here threatened the complete destruction of the Order. At the beginning of the fifteenth century there were only about seven hundred Brothers and Sisters of the Order living within the jurisdiction of the German Grand Lodge at Leipzig.

But in the fifteenth century—at almost the last moment—the great revival came again. While this revival brought new life, new vigor and new hope to the Order in Germany, it has proved to be the most perplexing one that ever came to the Order anywhere throughout the world. It has left a question, a doubt, unanswered and unsettled, in the layman's mind and has caused more misunderstanding of the Order's true history and ancestry than this humble attempt by me will ever be able to make clear.

THE 108-YEAR CYCLE AND "C.R-C."

———

T IS necessary, just at this point in the history, to refer to one of the very mysterious and puzzling laws of the organization, the origin of which is lost in the traditional history, but the general acceptance of which accounts for many of the peculiar breaks in the activities of the organization.

It appears from many ancient writings that in the first centuries preceding the Christian Era the organization complied with a regulation which may have been established centuries before, or may have been tried at this time as a new regulation. This regulation called for a periodicity of active and inactive cycles, each of 108 years. The number of 108 is significant in itself to all occult students, but just why this new regulation was brought into effect is not known.

According to the terms of this regulation, every branch jurisdiction was to select a certain year as the anniversary of its original foundation, and from that year onward operate in accordance with the periodicity of cycles.

A complete cycle of existence from birth to re-birth was to be of 216 years. Of this cycle, the first 108 years was to be a period of outer, general activity, while the second period of 108 years was to be a period of concealed, silent activity, almost resembling complete dormancy. This period of inactivity was to be followed by another 108 years of outer activity, just as though a new Order of the organization was born without any connection with the previous cycles. This regulation seemed to be a close analogy to the cycles of birth and rebirth for the human family, except that the number of years in each cycle was different. Just as man's rebirth on earth was considered a reincarnation of his previous existence, so each new birth of the organization in each jurisdiction was to be considered the birth of a new organization as a reincarnated soul in a *new body*.

So we find in the first few centuries preceding the Christian Era the Order seemed suddenly to disappear from all outward existence and all outward activity in some of the older branches in the Orient. So far as the uninitiated were concerned, and so far as the casual historians recorded the events, the older branches forming a part of the foundation of the Rosicrucian Order suddenly ceased to exist without any explanation, or any in-

dication that they would be revived. The members of the branches, and the great leaders, did not cease to carry on their *individual* activities, and we know from the records of the organization that, according to the rules and regulations regarding these periods of silence, during the 108 years of inactivity the members of the organization privately initiated their own descendants in their immediate families, but accepted no new members from the profane world. Thus several generations of Rosicrucians, initiated within the privacy of homes or secret temples, continued to carry the heritage of the Order in some lands, while outwardly and in all of its general activities the Order seemed to have gone out of existence. Then for several years preceding the time of the new birth, many prepared themselves by getting in contact with an active branch of the organization in other lands, and at the proper time announced in their own land the birth of a new cycle of the Order.

In most of the foreign lands the periods of dormancy and the periods of activity were not coincidental. Therefore, we find, for instance, that Germany was in the midst of a period of dormancy as far as the outer activities of the Order were concerned, during a time when the Order was very ac-

tive in France and Holland. Again we find that the Order was inactive in France just at the time that the Order had its new birth in Germany, and the Order in England was in the very center of its period of activity.

The Mystery of C. R-C.

As the time approached for each jurisdiction or country to have its new birth of the Order, arrangements were made for the usual issuance of a manifesto or pamphlet setting forth the beginning of a new cycle. Just when this custom was adopted it is difficult to say, and of course in the early pre-Christian days, the issuance of pamphlets or printed matter was impossible, and so a decree was promulgated or disseminated by word of mouth and by the display of a certain symbol among the people. This manifesto, decree, or symbol, announced the opening of a "tomb" in which the "body" of a great master, C. R-C., was found, together with rare jewels and secret writings or engravings on stone or wood which empowered the discoverers of the "tomb" to establish the secret organization once again.

We will find later on in our history that when the time came for the new birth in Germany, the incident of the opening of the "tomb" was given

wider circulation than had ever been given to a similar incident in any land before. This was due to the invention of the art of printing, which made possible the distribution of the manifestoes and the announcements in the form of pamphlets issued in five different languages, and disseminated through many nations at the same time. Coming at a crucial hour, as we shall see, in the evolution of religion and philosophy, and being so widely distributed, the pamphlets of the seventeenth century attracted such universal attention among persons who had never heard of the organization before that a common impression was created and recorded to the effect that a *new* organization, never known in the world before, had come into existence through the discovery of a tomb, and the body of a person unique in history. This false impression was recorded in so many later histories, that even today we are required to explain the misconception.

It must be apparent to the reader of this history that the discovery of a "body" in the "tomb," or the finding of the "body" of a person known as C. R-C., is allegorical, and is not to be taken in a literal sense. In the first place, the word "body" in the language in which it was first used, was symbolical of something entirely different than the

physical body of a man. In the second place, the initials C. R-C., did not mean *Christian Rosenkreuz,* except as the words represented by those initials were translated in the *German* language. The initials C. R-C., standing for the *Christus* of the *Rosy Cross,* may be translated into the Latin, French, and other languages without any change; therefore the initials C. R-C., when first used were not the initials of either *German* or *French* words, but of Latin words.

Those writers of mystical and fantastical stories who have tried to present the story of C. R-C., by stating that these initials were those of an individual, are wholly unacquainted with the facts. Even if the spiritual person represented by the "body" of C. R-C., were the same in each cycle, through a series of reincarnations, such a reincarnated person would be a different *earthly individual* in each incarnation. For that reason it must be understood that there was no one earthly person who was *uniquely* and *exclusively* known as C. R-C., in any cycle of the Order's existence. Our records refer to at least twelve discoveries of "tombs" containing the "body" of C. R-C. in different lands preceding the greatly popularized incident in Cassel, Germany, in the seventeenth century. There have been similar incidents in the his-

tory of the Order since the one in the seventeenth century.

Therefore, when the student of the history of the organization finds the various breaks in the outer activities of the organization he soon notices that there is a periodicity to the breaks, and almost unconsciously sets down the dates of the cycles of activity and dormancy. We shall note a few of these dates as we proceed with the history in the different lands.

However, everyone who reads in some of the modern mystical books, and even in those that claim to be Rosicrucian, the story of "Christian Rosenkreuz" being the *original founder* of the Rosicrucian Order in Germany (speaking of C. R-C. as though he were an earthly person who invented and established the first lodge of Rosicrucians anywhere in the world) will know at once that the writer of the account is unfamiliar with the facts and has mistaken the allegorical story for an actual event. The other explanation of the Rosicrucian work, by an author of this calibre, may be easily placed in the same category of unreliability. And, when the seeker comes in contact with a mystical organization, or a "Rosicrucian" group, that claims that it has its *authority* and *power* derived from the organization started by

"Christian Rosenkreuz" in Germany, or that it is a *descendant from the original lodge* established by C. R-C. in Germany, he will know also that the claim must be fictitious and wilfully misleading; for the facts contained in this history will show that the Order was in existence in many lands before the popular new birth of the Order in Germany in the seventeenth century, and that any Rosicrucian student—and most certainly any leader of Rosicrucian activities connected with the genuine organization—would have the correct story and the correct facts which are available to all of those who are truly affiliated with the real organization.

CHAPTER V

THE POPULAR REVIVAL IN GERMANY

A S INTIMATED in previous paragraphs of this history, the most popular and puzzling incident in the whole history of the Rosicrucian Order is in connection with the third or fourth revival of the organization in Germany. Coming as it did, at a critical time in the awakening of the religious consciousness of the people, and when various reforms were being instituted and attacks were being made upon older institutions, with a promulgation of ideas for newer ones, the announcement of the birth of the Rosicrucian Order for the new cycle in Germany was considered by many as a part of the general reform taking place throughout that country and other lands. The revival would never have become so popular nor attracted so much attention if it had not been that for the first time in the history of the Rosicrucian Order, the art of printing was freely used.

Such a use of printing was almost unique, and it naturally attracted the attention of persons who were easily convinced that great wealth and great

power were back of this national and international program, and for this reason other pamphlets and booklets were written criticizing, commenting upon, and attacking the organization, as well as praising it and endorsing it.

The mass of literature resulting from the opening announcements of the German revival constitutes one of the very dependable sources of historical information regarding the Rosicrucians, and at the same time constitutes one of the deplorable problems that confronts every seeker for real information.

Many of the pamphlets and booklets issued by critics or by enemies of the organization—or even in some cases by persons who merely wished to attain prominence or attract attention through writing about the organization, without any real knowledge of the subject—resulted in a mass of misinformation, a great deal of which eventually found its way into encyclopedias and general histories. To this very day, the average newspaper, or magazine writer, or seeker for information regarding the organization, who turns to one of the standard encyclopedias or histories of literature, religion, science, or art, is very liable to come in contact with misleading statements based upon the critical essays written about

the organization during this period of the German revival.

It is not my intention to take space in this present history to review the facts relating to the revival in Germany, but merely to call attention to the outstanding points connected therewith, because the real history of the revival, as well as the theoretical and misleading history, has been published in many books and can be found in many articles and essays dealing with Rosicrucianism.

The opening salute of that revival was the sudden and mysterious publication of a book briefly called *The Fama*. In just what year the original pamphlet entitled *The Fama Fraternitatis* was issued in Germany is really unknown; for there were so many editions in so many languages appearing in a number of different cities at slightly varying dates. Judging from copies which have been collected, one may see that the pamphlet appeared during the years 1610 to 1616, or even later. It is generally conceded that most of these were printed at Cassel, in Germany, although the English edition and the French edition were probably printed in other countries. As is natural with all of the ancient Rosicrucian literature, the authorship was veiled with a symbolic name, and a great deal of the literature of the period of revival in Germany

was signed with the name of *Christian Rosenkreuz* if the pamphlet was in German, or with a similar name translated into other languages if published in foreign lands; or else the principal character telling the story in the announcements or proclamations bore this symbolical name. Of course, the name translated into our English means "a Christian of the Rosy Cross."

The pamphlets were addressed to the learned persons of the world, particularly of Europe, and appealed to the educated and cultured. It is very doubtful if any of the learned persons in Germany or other lands who read those pamphlets believed that the name *Christian Rosenkreuz* was the actual bona fide name of any person. However, today throughout the world we find thousands of persons, and especially those who have attempted to write misleading articles about the Rosicrucians, or who have attempted to found and organize commercial propositions selling so-called Rosicrucian books, who really seem to believe that the name *Christian Rosenkreuz* was the name of an individual, and that this individual was the real author of the *Fama* and other pieces of Rosicrucian literature, and likewise the *founder of the entire Rosicrucian Order* which had its beginning, according to their belief,

in this very establishment during the years 1610 to 1616.

The other general opinion regarding the authorship of these pamphlets is one which was born in the minds of a great many persons who criticized the organization during the seventeenth century. They believed that an individual by the name of Johann Valentin Andrea was the real author of the *Fama,* and the later book called the *Confessio Fraternitatis R. C.*

In the year 1614, the *Fama* had attained nation-wide popularity in its way, and had created a real public sensation, and at that time Andrea was but a young man of twenty-eight years. He was born at Würtemberg, on August 17, 1586. He was of a family devoted to the Lutheran form of reformation, and although Andrea was raised according to strict orthodox religious principles, he did come under the influence and instruction of a group of theologians and philosophers, two of whom were mystically inclined, and one of whom was one of the high officers of the Rosicrucian Order in Germany. The public knew nothing of his studies under this Rosicrucian teacher, but it knew or heard something of his mystical viewpoints, and this was sufficient to make some start the

story that Andrea was the real author of the Rosicrucian pamphlets.

As has been explained heretofore, the Rosicrucian Order has always been subject to the law established by itself; one hundred and eight years of activity and one hundred and eight years of inactivity. We now have sufficient record, in the form of manuscripts, documents, and official papers not available or known to the German public in the seventeenth century, to show conclusively that the Rosicrucian Order was not born for the first time in the history of the world in Germany, in 1610 or 1614, but had existed in many lands for many centuries previous thereto, and had had cycles of activity and inactivity in Germany for several centuries before the revival to which we are referring. Even the *Fama* itself referred to the fact that the symbolical author of the manuscript, or the symbolical characters in the story, had been members of the organization centuries previous. All of this has been overlooked by those who still claim, especially in America, that a German whose true family name was *Christian Rosenkreuz,* invented and established the Rosicrucian Order, for the first time in the history of the world, in the years 1610 to 1614, in Germany.

One of the many well-established facts regarding the history of the Order, which proves the existence of the Order of the Rose Cross or Rosy Cross throughout Europe before 1610, is the story of the founding of one of the branches of the Rosicrucian activities.

Throughout Rosicrucian literature, reference will be found to peculiar initials and strange names usually connected with the title *Militia Crucifera Evangelica*. The "M. C. E." has always been a puzzle to those who have not worked through the complete history of the Order, and at the same time it has continued to be one of the most essential forms of Rosicrucian activities in many lands.

It may be that the following facts regarding the "M. C. E." will interest those of my readers who have never had the privilege of learning the real facts before, and it will probably set at rest the hundreds of questions that have been in the minds of Rosicrucian research workers for many years.

As stated above, the revival of the Rosicrucian work in Germany in 1610 to 1614, which constituted the beginning of one of the new cycles of one hundred and eight years, occurred when most of Europe was being torn by various forms of religious reformation and strife between church and state. Throughout each of the countries of Eu-

rope, various secret societies or military organizations had been formed to protest against the established activities of the larger church, or to stamp out the growing freedom of religious thought and practices of the so-called heretics. Thus we find that for many years before the revival of the Rosicrucian Order there had been established, in 1511 for instance, as typical of the many secret religious bodies, a *Holy League* composed of those persons who had pledged themselves to support the church against its critics, even to the extent of taking up arms and carrying on warfare in "the name of the cross." The *Holy League* was perhaps the most famous or powerful of these organizations, but there were so many others, and with so many different purposes or ends in view, that historians have been incapable of classifying them or even determining the real part that any of them played in the changes that were made. During all these years of strife and contention, the *cross* either as a Christian symbol or as adopted by the early Crusaders in the eleventh, twelfth, and thirteenth centuries was used as the standard under which the wars and other forms of persecutions were conducted. To the worshipper of the ancient cross, who had its *real symbolism* in his mind and heart, the use of the cross in the

manner in which it was being employed by these contending organizations brought grief and deep sorrow.

Our records show that the Rosicrucians early protested against the cross being carried on staffs or painted on flags that were carried into the battles and into the fields of bloodshed, as well as into the plans and schemes for tortures and persecution. To the Rosicrucians, the use of the cross for such destructive work was not only irreligious and a sacrilege, but a mystical insult and a spiritual crime. It is easy to believe that the Rosicrucians, wherever they could avoid doing so, took no part in any of these religious strifes and contentions, and it is easy to believe that they never permitted themselves to carry any standard that bore the cross in public affairs.

Matters became so bad in connection with the use of the cross in this sorrowful way that finally the Rosicrucians decided to revive an ancient organization to defend the cross against its misuse. The idea of re-establishing this organization was born in the mind of the Grand Master of one of the inactive branches in Germany. His name was Simon Studion, and he was born at Urach in the state of Würtemberg in 1543, and later attained the high degree of Imperator in Germany. Dur-

ing the year 1586 he planned an international convention for the purpose of organizing a special body of Rosicrucians to defend the cross against its misuse in destructive and sorrowful activities. After communicating with the leading Rosicrucian officers in various lands, and receiving their wholehearted approval, a convention was called in Hanover, where was located the "silent" Grand Lodge of the Rosicrucians for that part of the country. The meeting was officially called "Cruce Signatorum Conventus," and its opening session was held on July 27th, 1586. Studion himself made the opening speech, reading the history of the original *Militia* formed in Palestine soon after the founding of the first Christian churches; and then introduced the high representatives from many lands and the legates from the many thrones which gave support to the movement. The records show that the convention and its plan was sponsored particularly and specifically by Henry IV, king of France and Navarre, who had received the "arms" of the ancient Militia through direct authority from the Militia in Palestine, Queen Elizabeth I of England, and the king of Denmark, as well as the nobility of other lands. The organization thus formed used the ancient name, *Militia Crucifera Evangelica,* and was established as an organiza-

tion of loyal Rosicrucians who would defend the cross, not especially the Rosy Cross, but the ancient and much loved cross of all times, against its use in religious persecution, religious warfare, or destructive contests of any kind. Each who signed the great scroll at that convention became titled or knighted as a *Chevalier* and a secret worker to *protect* the Rosicrucian organization in its constructive activities, revive the pure mystical teachings of the Pristine Christians and Rosicrucians, and prevent persecution of any kind because of freedom of religious and scientific thinking. A few years later, when the records of activities of this great organization had been gathered from all lands, Studion compiled a great book of nineteen hundred and ninety-five (1995) pages, dedicated to Frederick, the Duke of Würtemberg, who was a Grand Master of the Rosicrucians. This book was called *Naometria,* and it was completed in 1604. This book is still in existence, and has been examined by eminent historians and quoted from quite freely. A Rosicrucian manuscript, entitled the *Wirtembergis Repertorum der Litterator,* a history of Rosicrucianism and alchemy, published in 1782-3, says, in part, of the *Naometria:* "Its reflections on the renewal of the earth and a general reformation to come breathe the Rosi-

crucian spirit—and it embodies real Rosicrucian doctrines."

A great part of the book is devoted to a history of the cross and its real spiritual and mystical significance, to the rose and its symbolical meaning, and to the special significance of the rose and the cross when united. In fact, on page 271, of the *Naometria,* there is an illustration of the joining of the two—the Rose and the Cross—and accompanying it the Latin phrase "Hierichuntis Rosa ex quotour ins Partes." The book contains also a complete outline of the Rosicrucian doctrines, reviving the ancient teachings of the Essenes, the first Christians, and the Rosicrucians, giving emphasis to the spiritual and mystical significance of the Rosicrucian ideals. It has never been copied or republished in any form, and constitutes one of the secret publications that has been examined only by eminent historians who have sought positive proof of the existence of such a book or such a Rosicrucian movement before the year 1610.

The *Militia Crucifera Evangelica,* as a defensive body within the Rosicrucian Order, still exists, and is the real secret organization within the Rosicrucian Order. Membership in it is limited to those who are well trained in the fundamentals of

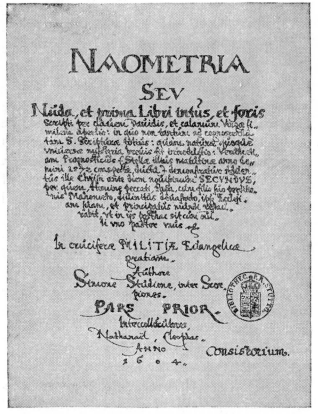

The above is a photograph of the original title page of the *Naometria* manuscript by Simon Studion. The original manuscript is in one of the large state libraries of Europe, where it is treasured as a rare possession. Note the reference to the Militia Crucifera Evangelica and the date 1604. This is the first text of Rosicrucian history in which this title page has ever been reproduced.

the Rosicrucian teachings, and to those who have pledged their entire lives in devotion to the Rosicrucian ideals, and especially to the support of the individual Imperator in each country where the Militia exists. It is the existence of such an organization that makes possible the continuous protection of the Rosicrucian Order, and it enables the Order itself to carry on its national and international secret activities in a conservative, uniform manner, to the glory of the Order and the preservation of the true, secret doctrines of Jesus. To be admitted and titled as *Chevalier* of this Militia is to receive one of the highest honors and highest acknowledgements in the Rosicrucian Order. The ranks of the Militia are open to both men and women who have been individually tested and tried for a number of years by the Imperator of the jurisdiction where each member lives.

An interesting point in connection with this is the fact that this organization and this convention of Rosicrucians was brought about by the cooperation of thousands of well-trained, tried, and tested Rosicrucians, and the first convention and meeting of establishment was held on July 27th, 1586, which was several weeks before Johann Valentin Andrea was born. The statement, therefore, on the part of those unacquainted with Rosicru-

cian history that Andrea was the author of the books that "established the first and only Rosicrucian Order in the world in Cassel, Germany, in 1610," appears ridiculous.

The real author of the pamphlets that brought about the revival in Germany was none other than Sir Francis Bacon, who was Imperator for the Order in England and various parts of Europe at the time. His other Rosicrucian writings, and especially his book the *New Atlantis,* admittedly his own work, clearly indicate the connection between Bacon and the publications issued in Germany between 1610 and 1616.

Conventicles, or special conclaves, of the Militia Crucifera Evangelica are held biennially at Rosicrucian Park at San Jose, California, U.S.A., the official See of the Supreme Grand Lodge of the Ancient and Mystical Order Rosae Crucis, the modern continuation of the ancient Rosicrucians. These conclaves are attended by chevaliers of the M.C.E. from throughout the world.

THE BIRTH OF SEMI-ROSICRUCIAN ORGANIZATIONS

HE SPREAD of Rosicrucian activity throughout many lands and the attraction to its ranks of many notable characters brought the organization before the attention of men of other associations and affiliations. It was but natural that other secret societies or fraternal Orders would investigate the increasing activities of the Rosicrucian Order, and attempt to discover whether there was any invasion of their sacred rites by the Rosicrucians, or anything of value in the Rosicrucian work that might be added to their own rituals and forms of operation.

We will not consider at all the attempts made by various persons at various times to institute "Rosicrucian" lodges or bodies solely for the purpose of attracting the gullible or misleading the unwary. A number of such organizations came into existence in France, Germany, and England, but in each case their existence was very short and they left no records of importance.

We do find, however, that preceding the year 1870 the development of Freemasonic activity in England, with an increasing desire on the Continent to add more and higher degrees to the existing Masonic degrees, tempted many men of that organization to establish separate secret bodies or societies composed entirely of Masons, and in some cases new Orders or organizations were established with many degrees based upon Masonic symbols and requiring Masonic affiliations as a pre-requisite for affiliation in the new organization. The histories of Freemasonry deal extensively with this unfortunate situation throughout Europe, for these many bodies attaching themselves to Freemasonry or attempting to associate themselves with the Freemasonic ideals caused endless trouble and confusion. A few of the bodies thus formed became recognized eventually and carried on a very excellent work. It must be stated, however, that the average Freemasonic enthusiast of that period was a true seeker for *light* and arcane wisdom, and while he found much in the Freemasonic teachings to gratify his desires or satiate his hunger, many seemed to feel that there was more *light* and wisdom to be found elsewhere and especially in the secret, *mystic* schools which had their origin in the Oriental philosophies. Probably in those

days, as today, many of those in the Freemasonic fraternity did not realize the vast amount of wisdom that is contained in their symbology and in their carefully veiled teachings. However that may be, the fact remains that many of the most prominent Freemasons congregated at different times in different places, and formed research bodies or groups devoted to the sole purpose of unearthing such additional teachings or arcane knowledge as might be found in the various *mystic* schools of the day.

It is not surprising, therefore, that a number of these men were attracted to the Rosicrucian Order, especially the English lodge, and were admitted therein and became enthusiastic students and workers. The time came, however, when some of these believed that further research of an independent nature might be carried on outside of both the Rosicrucian and the Freemasonic circles, and that members of both organizations might come together in a more social and informal manner at stated periods for the purpose of discussing the work and teachings found in both bodies.

Out of this belief was born a new organization in England, the activities of which, and the imitation of which, have caused considerable confusion in the

minds of those persons seeking to trace the origin and development of the Rosicrucian Order.

It appears from definite historical records that some men of learning, and with minds adapted to research, united to establish what they intended to be a *Masonic* Rosicrucian Society. During their first discussion of the plans of organization it was clearly stated that application for membership in this new body would be limited to Freemasons, in good standing, who had mastered the elementary work of Freemasonry and were desirous of such philosophical knowledge as was available just beyond the limited teachings of their organization. The transactions of this organization, with minutes of its meetings, are to be found in the British Museum in London, but the most definite statements regarding its purposes and activities are found in a small historical treatise prepared by the Supreme Magus of the body, Dr. W. Wynn Westcott. It appears that after much discussion they decided to call their new society the *Societas Rosicruciana in Anglia,* which name, translated, would mean the *Rosicrucian Society in England,* and the initials of this title were used as a brief form of name in their literature. Hence the initials S.R.I.A. became significant among Freemasons during that period, and have contributed to

considerable confusion in Rosicrucian records ever since.

It seems that the prime mover of the formation of this new society was Robert Wentworth Little, who is referred to in the records as a clerk at Freemason's Hall, and subsequently secretary of the Royal Institution for Girls. Freemason's Hall at that time was the national headquarters for the Freemasonic Brotherhood, and it contained a large library and archives of ancient books and manuscripts, to all of which Mr. Little had access. Nowhere in the early literature of this organization or in its early histories as published by them is there any reference to any of the organizers of the S. R. I. A. being initiates or members of any other Rosicrucian body or organization anywhere in the world. *This is a very important fact,* and its significance is emphasized by the statements of this society regarding the methods or means of its foundation.

In its official history, this S. R. I. A. says that the society was "designed" by Robert Wentworth Little, who "rescued" some rituals from the storerooms of Freemason's Hall. In other places there are statements indicating that Mr. Little found and *borrowed,* or as Mr. Waite, the Masonic historian, states it *abstracted* certain papers containing Rosi-

crucian ritual information preserved in the Grand
Lodge library of Freemason's Hall, and that these
papers had been discovered before him by William
Henry White, who was Grand Secretary of the
Freemasons until 1857. According to Dr. Westcott, Mr. White had received some "Rosicrucian"
initiations in an English "Rosicrucian Lodge," but
had never made any use of the ritual manuscripts
which he had discovered in the Masonic Grand
Lodge library. Waite calls attention to the fact that
other records intimated that after Mr. White's retirement from the office of Grand Secretary, wherein
he had charge of such secret or private manuscripts as were not a part of the Masonic work,
Mr. Little *borrowed* the Rosicrucian papers and
called to his assistance a year or so later one Ken-
neth R. H. McKenzie, who claimed that while
he was in Germany he had been admitted by
some "German adepts" into *some* of the "Rosicrucian system," and had been licensed to form a
group of Masonic students in England "under a Rosicrucian name."

To the sincere and careful student of Rosicrucian history, the claims made by Mr. McKenzie
seem peculiar, to say the least. Why some *German
adepts* should admit an English person into just a
part of the Rosicrucian work and then *license him*

to establish a group of *Masonic* students in England under a *Rosicrucian* name, while there was a superior Rosicrucian body already active in England, is certainly incomprehensible. It would appear to be the first and only instance in Rosicrucian history where the Rosicrucian Order "licensed" anyone to establish a Masonic Rosicrucian body. And it is as inconsistent with Rosicrucian principles as would be the *licensing* of a Freemason to go into a foreign land and establish a Masonic body composed of Rosicrucians.

Dr. Westcott states also that the peculiar Rosicrucian papers that were taken from the Masonic archives were used to reconstruct a branch of the *Red Cross of Rome and Constantine,* as well as the foundation of the S. R. I. A.

The important points in this brief sketch of the foundation of the S. R. I. A. are: First, the fact that the Society was started by an individual without any charter or authority from the local Rosicrucian lodge in London, or any other superior Rosicrucian body in Europe; and second, that with some manuscripts of an indefinite nature a society was formed which did not adopt the universal name of the Rosicrucian Order or the universal symbol as used by the rest of the Rosicrucian fraternity throughout the Continent. In no other Rosi-

crucian records do we find any reference to any German branch that *licensed* Mr. McKenzie, and, therefore, we may believe that Mr. McKenzie's contact with the Rosicrucians, if real at all, was a contact with some of the temporary, clandestine, or imitation societies that flourished for short intervals in foreign sections.

Mr. Waite, in his English history of the Rosicrucian Order, gives little credence to Mr. McKenzie's Rosicrucian connections, and emphasizes the fact "That in 1866 McKenzie was a Mason only under some foreign and apparently unacknowledged Obedience." Mr. Waite, who is not only a Rosicrucian historian but an eminent Masonic historian and writer as well, plainly indicates the cloud that seems to cover the origin and foundation of the S. R. I. A., and shows that while it became a very worthy, learned, and highly respected organization of gentlemen seeking for arcane wisdom, enjoying a banquet and social evening once a month, it was not in any sense a part of the Rosicrucian organization throughout the world.

However, the S. R. I. A. in England continued to grow and called its first branch the *Metropolitan College*. We find that its principal officers were well-known Freemasons, and included a number

whose names we shall mention later. Mr. McKenzie visited Paris some years later and there met one who was deeply interested in the Rosicrucian work and teachings, as a member of the regular Rosicrucian organization, known as Eliphas Levi, but whose name was Alphonse Louis Constant. Levi was invited to become a part of the S.R.I.A. in England, and did so with the belief that the founders were really sincere in their desire to delve deeply into Rosicrucian lore, and become neophytes of the Rosicrucian organization. A few years after his acceptance into the S. R. I. A., Levi evidently felt that his connections therewith were not proper in the face of his affiliation with the regular Rosicrucian Order, or else he discovered reasons for withdrawing. It is indicated that he had many arguments with the founders of the new English society, and disagreed with their viewpoints in many ways, and finally withdrew his membership. The records of the S. R. I. A. state that Levi incurred their displeasure by the publication of his several books on magic and ritual, but since these books have proved to be excellent and highly endorsed by mystics of many periods, such explanation does not seem to be justifiable. Levi passed through transition in 1875, and in the last

years of his life was not connected with the S. R. I. A. in any way.

Other branches of the S. R. I. A. were established at Bristol, Manchester, Liverpool, and Yorkshire, and finally a branch was established in Canada. All of these branches were strictly limited to Freemasons. In fact, the ritual adopted by the S. R. I. A. for its initiations and ceremonies was quite distinct from the Rosicrucian ritual of the regular Order, and the fantastic names for the various grades were designed to appeal to Freemasons. The highest of these grades were limited to Freemasons who were in the higher grades of their own organization.

Prior to the establishment of a branch of the S. R. I. A. in Canada, which was intended to be under the British or English jurisdiction of the organization, a branch was authorized in 1880 to be known as the *Societas Rosicruciana in U. S. A.* According to some records, a few Freemasons living in Pennsylvania were granted permission to establish this American branch, but there is no record of its having existed very long in Pennsylvania, and in the meantime the Canadian branch carried on very successfully among the Freemasons in that part of North America.

We have seen the official copies of the charters issued by the Canadian branch which was known as the *Societas Rosicruciana in Canadiensis*. These charters were preserved in the House of the Temple of the Southern jurisdiction of the Scottish Rite of Freemasonry in Washington, D. C. They were issued by the Canadian branch of the S. R. I. A. to Brother Albert Pike and several others of the American Freemasonic organization, particularly because Albert Pike, the honored and respected writer of American Freemasonry, was a very thorough Rosicrucian student. The charter grants to Brother Albert Pike and others the privilege of establishing a Southern College of the S. R. I. A. in the United States, and it is worded as though the Canadian branch was unaware that a similar warrant for an American branch had been issued previously to the Freemasons in Pennsylvania. However, a controversy arose over the establishment of a second North American branch, and thereby hangs a very interesting story.

It must be borne in mind that these S. R. I. A. branches were not operating as a part of the ancient Rosicrucian Order, and by their own admission did not have the Rosicrucian rituals and teachings nor any warrant, charter, patent, or authority from the Rosicrucian Order of Europe

and other lands. American Rosicrucian students were well aware of the fact that the Rosicrucian Order of Europe had previously authorized the establishment of true Rosicrucianism in America in the year 1693, and there were many living descendants of those first official Rosicrucians who objected to the establishment of Rosicrucianism in America in connection with any other organization and without warrant or proper rituals. But nothing was done to prevent the S. R. I. A. of England from maintaining a branch of its English work in America, especially in connection with Freemasonry, since it was recognized that the Masonic Rosicrucian society thus being established in America would cooperate with the desires of many of the Masons in giving them that additional light or knowledge along certain arcane lines which they desired, and which was highly praiseworthy. This did not in any way infringe the rights of the Rosicrucian Order. In fact, there was no conflict or discussion in that one regard, because the S. R. I. A. did not claim to have the *genuine* Rosicrucian teachings or ritual, and was, therefore, entitled to establish a branch of its English body in America.

The controversy referred to started between the various officials and members of the S. R. I. A.

and gradually involved the interest of all Rosicrucians; because the argument in regard to two establishments of S. R. I. A. under two different warrants was bringing the subject of Rosicrucianism and the Rosicrucian activities into unfavorable light among those who did not understand the situation. It appears that the gentlemen who were granted the privilege by the Canadian branch to operate in the United States finally withheld any action on their part, while the Brother who held the charter direct from England for the State of Pennsylvania, proceeded to organize a branch, and some spasmodic meetings of this branch were held without attempting to practice the Rosicrucian rituals or introduce the true Rosicrucian teachings. This was the situation existing in the United States when a third effort was made to establish the S. R. I. A. in America, and the third effort proved more successful, as we shall see from the following facts:

A number of Freemasons in America were admitted into the S. R. I. A. of England in its branch known as the *York College.* They petitioned the English headquarters for permission to continue the work in America under the charter that had been granted for Pennsylvania. They established a branch at Philadelphia and another in New York

City in 1880. Eventually these two American branches established a High Council of the society for the United States. This Council then chartered branches in Boston and Baltimore, in the spring of 1880, and another one in Vermont. Practically every officer connected with these establishments was a Freemason, and we must quote here the words of Dr. Westcott, the Supreme Magus of the English headquarters of the organization, who said in an address: "I have been asked to speak on the Rosicrucians because I have the pleasure to hold a high office in the *Rosicrucian Society* of England, so might reasonably be supposed to have studied the history of the Order. But to avoid misconception, I wish to say that *the S. R. I. A. is a Masonic body*—it is composed of Freemasons who have associated themselves in order to study the old Rosicrucian books in the light of history, and to trace the connection between Rosicrucianism and the origins of Freemasonry, the connection which has been alleged to exist by many historians belonging to the outer world." This statement by Dr. Westcott is taken from biographical sketches in the official literature of the S. R. I. A.

In September of 1889, after nine years of operation as a literary society with banquets, the new branches of the S. R. I. A. in America decided to

reform and reorganized their body with the distinctive title "Societatis Rosicrucianae in the United States of America" (S. R. I. U. S. and not S. R. I. A.). Under this new form of name and constitution, the various branches accomplished very little, and the New York and Baltimore sections seemed to pass out of existence. One of the prominent characters initiated into the S. R. I. U. S. in Boston was Sylvester Clark Gould, who became the publisher of a small Rosicrucian magazine, and who sincerely sought to learn and master the real Rosicrucian teachings. We read in the official literature of this organization the following significant statement: "Membership in these Colleges was limited to Freemasons of the 32nd degree; quarterly meetings were held, and their sessions were devoted principally to banquets, with an aftermath of a literary and philosophical nature, with little if any attempt to exemplify the Rosicrucian degrees with the philosophy they embodied."

In other words, the society had nothing more of a Rosicrucian nature connected with it than the word *Rosicrucian* which they arbitrarily adopted in their title. This was practically true of the national headquarters of the organization in London, and records of this society show that when Rosi-

crucians belonging to the Rosicrucian Order became affiliated with the S. R. I. A. or the S. R. I. U. S., they did not continue to remain active for a very long period.

According to the literature of the branch established in America, Mr. Gould, who was their most illustrious American member, became "thoroughly awakened to the omission of the real Rosicrucian work, and having received the eighth degree of the society constituting him a provincial magus of the fraternity, engaged in special research work to recover the original rituals of the fraternity." He succeeded in corresponding with some Rosicrucian officers in Europe, and then undertook to revive the American branch of the S. R. I. A., which had become inoperative for a time. It was his intention to make the S. R. I. U. S. a typical Rosicrucian organization if he could secure the permission and authority of the Rosicrucian Order in Europe. According to the records of the S. R. I. U. S., the transition of Mr. Gould occurred on July 19, 1909, preventing the fulfillment of his personal ambitions in regard to the society, and the work of reorganization devolved upon a few of the other members who were still interested.

It should be noted that in the very month in which Mr. Gould passed to the Great Beyond, an-

other American proceeded to Europe to secure permission to pursue the Rosicrucian work of the international Rosicrucian Order, and made his plea to the regular Order of Europe instead of petitioning the Masonic Rosicrucian society in England. The success of this plea we refer to in a future section of this history.

Those who followed Mr. Gould, after his passing, in trying to re-establish the S. R. I. U. S. in America, finally organized a new body with a different name. According to their official papers, they adopted the name *Societas Rosicruciana in America,* which gave them the old familiar initials S. R. I. A. as their official title. They adopted a revised constitution under this new name in 1919, which became effective January 1st, 1920. Their constitution stated that they were incorporated under three different classifications: first, as a church; second, as an academic institution; and third, as a fraternity. In their general literature, they stated: *"The Societas Rosicruciana in America,* therefore, is a continuation in direct succession from the High Councils of Anglia." In other statements it is said that the society "works in complete harmony and close association with the Masonic fraternity, and constitutionally its major officers are Masons of all rites and degrees." Fur-

thermore, "the society, deriving from the English fraternity, was incorporated in 1912, and is therefore the active American branch of the Rosicrucian fraternity." These statements have been refuted by published articles in various magazines, and of course it is well known to all Freemasons and others that no other organization of any kind can be a part of Freemasonry unless it is operating under the Freemasonic title and symbolism. And, in regard to the S. R. I. A. in the United States being derived from the English fraternity of the same name or charter, or authorized by the same society in England, an article was published in the *Occult Review* of England in recent years, wherein the *Societas Rosicruciana in Anglia* denied that the society in America was sponsored by it or officially recognized by it. This denial was later acknowledged as correct by the American S. R. I. A., which leaves the American organization standing as a distinctly separate institution operating without any charter from the general Rosicrucian Order of Europe, or any Masonic Rosicrucian body of England.

This organization has, therefore, continued as an independent body, establishing a few branches in different cities, and continuing to make its appeal to Freemasons who enjoy purely philosophical dis-

cussions without any of the rituals or teachings as used in the various branches of the Rosicrucian Order of Europe and other lands.

Among several other American institutions using the name *Rosicrucian* in about the same manner that the S. R. I. A. of England and America have adopted it, is one which has also caused considerable confusion in the minds of those who attempt to trace the history and activities of the Rosicrucian Order. Since the name and term *Rosicrucian* is not protected by any patents or copyrights of any kind, it may be used in connection with other words for various purposes. Hence there may be Rosicrucian societies, Rosicrucian clubs, or Rosicrucian churches without having any authority from the Rosicrucian Order. It is interesting to note, however, that only one organization throughout the world uses the ancient title of *Rosicrucian Order* and this organization maintains its active branches in all lands, under the abbreviation of AMORC.

It appears from some historical records that a man by the name of Dr. P. B. Randolph, who was a student of the occult and mystical, came in contact with some Rosicrucian literature or essays prior to the year 1856 while in America. It appears that Dr. Randolph visited London in 1858 and

there met a student of mysticism known as Mr. W. G. Palgrave, who claimed to be a member of some esoteric Order in Europe, which was operating under a charter issued by a "Council of Seven." Through this man he was introduced to Mr. Hargrave Jennings, Eliphas Levi, and several others who eventually formed the High Council of the original S. R. I. A. in England. Dr. Randolph was initiated into this Masonic Rosicrucian body and as an honorary member continued his tour, and returned to America. While in America he wrote a number of books dealing with the subjects of health, marriage, love, and sex hygiene, and in one of them introduced a story about the mystic Rosicrucians, intimating that he was planning to establish some of the Rosicrucian Masonic work in America on the basis of that which was being carried on by the S. R. I. A.

Because of the nature of his books, dealing in unusually plain language with subjects not generally discussed in American literature, and certainly having none of the goodness and high idealism of the S. R. I. A. (London) teachings, he was tried in courts for such publications, and eventually abandoned his entire work because of the condemnation of his writings. Mr. Arthur Waite, the eminent Masonic historian of England, has this to say re-

garding Randolph's form of "Rosicrucian" activities as considered by him:

"In respect of deception there is no question that he was his own and his first victim if he thought that his views and lucubrations might stand for authentic Rosicrucian teachings. But in a judgment which makes for justice it must be added that he revoked his own claim on a vast antiquity. . . . It does not appear that in the matter of the Rosy Cross he did more than give a fresh circulation to some of the old reveries, to the extent that he was acquainted with these by common report and otherwise. . . . In other and more hectic stories, he paraded flaming accounts of the Brotherhood, its immemorial antiquity, its diffusion throughout the world, with suggestions that its ramifications extended to unseen spheres . . . . I have worked through such of his volumes as are available here in England, . . . and have concluded that, mountebank as he was, he believed in all his rant and was not lying consciously when this stuff of sorry dreams was put forward unfailingly as the wisdom of the Rosy Cross. This is how it loomed in his mind, and this is what it was in a dream, for it was a thing of his own making. On this subject, he is his own refutable witness, affirming that 'very nearly all which

I have given as Rosicrucian originated in my own soul'."

Randolph eventually signed himself in some letters and papers as the "Supreme Grand Master of Eulis for the world," and a few of his friends tried to explain after his unfortunate transition through suicide that he believed himself to be a Grand Master of the "Triple Order." This term is not an official part of Rosicrucian terminology, and there are no documents or papers to be found in Europe indicating that he was ever authorized to establish anything of a Rosicrucian nature in America or elsewhere, and none of the historical records of the Order mentions his name or his branches as a part of the Rosicrucian history.

Randolph was succeeded by a Mr. Dowd, who tried to continue operating some of the branches which Randolph had established on the Pacific Coast and in several eastern cities, but, *according to their own records,* these branches constantly disbanded when the members thereof discovered that there were no real Rosicrucian teachings or rituals in the work, and insisted on withdrawing from the Randolph work and uniting with the regular foreign branches of the Rosicrucian Order. Mr. Randolph and his successors claimed that such actions constituted "treason," and for many years there

were bitter quarrels and arguments within his branches over this point, with the branches disbanding and remaining inactive for years at a time. Mr. Dowd was succeeded by a Dr. Edward H. Brown, who likewise was unable to secure any of the Rosicrucian teachings, or maintain Randolph's scheme against the common criticisms and the bad reputation which his writings had brought upon their activities.

In a statement signed by Mrs. Randolph, and which appeared in a fraternal publication as a biographical sketch of the life of Dr. Randolph in 1917, it is said that Dr. Randolph was born in New York City on October 8th, 1825, and that his transition occurred in Toledo, Ohio, on July 29th, 1875; and she further stated that although he organized some branches as late as 1874, they "have long since become extinct."

According to Sedir, the well-known Rosicrucian historian, the work of Randolph was simply a society of "editions"—referring to the significant point that his work was mostly that of publishing various *editions of books* claiming to be Rosicrucian. This point is one which should be impressed upon the minds of every student of Rosicrucian history. The Rosicrucian Order has never been exclusively, or even primarily, a book publishing business, and a

careful examination of the historical writings connected with the Rosicrucian Order shows that none of the books now famous as Rosicrucian manuscripts or official publications ever contained a complete outline of the secret teachings or rites of the Rosicrucians, and what is more important, never *claimed* to contain such things.

It has been a serious and universal law with the Rosicrucian Order that its secret teachings should never be published in book form, or offered for sale to the public, and there is no violation of this law that has ever been brought to our attention. On the other hand, there have been many who were not a part of the Rosicrucian Order, or even initiated in its teachings, who have attempted to commercialize the desires of seekers by the printing and selling of books which *claimed* to be "Rosicrucian textbooks" or books of Rosicrucian doctrines or teachings. It is a notable fact that *none of these books* has made any valuable contribution to mystical literature, and all have passed into oblivion and can hardly be found in the best libraries of Europe or America. This is true of Randolph's books, which claimed to be wonderful revelations of Rosicrucian teachings, but which today have no place in the real occultist's library and have not been considered worthy of preservation even in the great ref-

erence libraries of the world. Such books as these, catering to the gullibility of the seeker, and often misleading the worthy inquirer, are being published and sold in America today very freely, while Europe most naturally fails to support such publications. We have, for instance, in America, a book called *The Rosicrucians and Their Teachings*. This book was written by a New Thought leader, who has written many other books on various subjects and who is *not* a member of the Rosicrucian Order. The book contains none of the Rosicrucian teachings. Such books are harmless in themselves, and perhaps interesting to casual students of mysticism; but they have no place in any list of authoritative publications. It is for this reason that Sedir made his satirical remarks regarding Randolph's society of "editions." The good that Dr. Randolph did as a New Thought pioneer will live for many ages, but the failure of his Rosicrucian movement was due to a complete lack of authority, and no understanding of the Rosicrucian teachings.

Dr. Randolph's work was later taken up again by a Dr. R. S. Clymer, who claimed to be the "successor" to Randolph and to have inherited and acquired the Rosicrucian "authority" which Randolph had. Clymer followed the same plans adopted by

Randolph and conducted an organization consisting wholly of books, a number of which deal with love, marriage, and "sex regeneration," the latter being in such language as to be condemned in any Rosicrucian assembly, if not in any general assembly of ladies and gentlemen. He proceeded to carry on his work first under the name of a publication company, then under various names, avoiding the use of the complete name, or correct name, of the Rosicrucian Order, and devising entirely new and unique symbols for his Rosicrucian literature without infringing upon the correct symbols in any way. Dr. Clymer * continued to operate his sale of books and presentation of personal, "Rosicrucian" teachings under different names from his home in Pennsylvania, without having established any typical Rosicrucian temples anywhere in America, and without having any connection with the regular Rosicrucian Order and lodges of Europe.

It would be expected that Dr. Clymer's representations and maladroitly presented "teachings" and attacks on other movements would eventually attract the attention of the Supreme Council of the Rosicrucian Order of the World and the dignitaries of the Rose Croix of Europe. One of the first to voice a protest was the eminent F. Wittemans, avocat—

---

* For further details see page 156.

at the time, a member of the Belgian Senate—and renowned European historian of the Rosicrucian Order, his works on the Order being published in several languages. In a letter addressed to the Imperator of A. M. O. R. C. of North America, dated December 16, 1928, and referring to Dr. Clymer's writings, he said:

"I criticize very much such writings, which should not be issued by an occultist and prove by their self their hollowness. I will thus not mention them in my work—"

The combination of Dr. Clymer's synthetic Rosicrucian teachings and his insidious campaign of vilification and libel of the A. M. O. R. C., in the American jurisdiction aroused a spirit of defense and indignation on the part of the affiliated Rosicrucian bodies abroad. Coeval with Dr. Clymer's campaign of machinations against A. M. O. R. C., various individuals were establishing mystical and occult societies in America and elsewhere, having no true arcane or authoritative background, and misappropriating the time-honored signs, words, and terms of the esoteric, traditional, hermetic orders of Europe. This wholesale plagiarism was especially disastrous where the welfare of the humble seeker and the neophyte was concerned, for the protagonists of these movements were inept at presenting the mys-

tical knowledge in a proper way, not having been initiated or prepared. Their "teachings" were a distorted and disorganized accumulation of certain of the noble precepts, damaging to the interests, and often the mentality of those who studied them. As nearly all of the true *Initiatory Orders* of the world functioned in harmony with each other, and as their concepts were based upon eternal truths, to a great extent paralleling each other, they were brought closer and closer together by the pressure of this rape of their Sacred Truths. What had been under way for some time finally came to pass, namely, a Federation of these societies and orders, for their mutual defense and the protection of their heritage. The Federation was duly instituted at Brussels, Belgium, on the 14th of August, 1934. It became officially known as the Federation Universelles des Ordres et Societes Initiatiques, known generally by the abbreviation, F. U. D. O. S. I. It consisted of the fourteen oldest arcane and mystical orders, each having as part of its rites certain initiations, which, because of their esoteric nature, produced mystical effects in the consciousness of the initiate.

The A. M. O. R. C. of North America was the only Rosicrucian body, of the few on this Continent so styling themselves, which was invited to become

a member of this august Federation. The invitation was extended on the basis of such documentary authority and evidence of authenticity of the A. M. O. R. C., revealing its connection with the ancient fraternity of Europe, as existed in the archives of the Order in Europe, as well as in America. At the close of the conclave, which was attended by the highest officers of the respective Orders and the Imperators of the Rose Croix of the different jurisdictions, there was presented to the Imperator of North and South America, a document, signed and sealed with the emblems of the Orders participating, which reads, in part:

"(4)—that the only North American section of the A∴A∴O∴R∴R∴A∴C∴, duly authorized and recognized by the International Rosicrucian Council, and affiliated with the Supreme Council of the G∴W∴B∴ is that known in the Western world as A∴M∴O∴R∴C∴, with its S∴S∴ in the Valley of San Jose, California, of U. S. A., duly perpetuating the North American foundation of the Brotherhood, established in the City of Philadelphia in the year 1694, and having exclusive jurisdiction in North America."

Arthur Edward Waite, celebrated Masonic and Rosicrucian historian, in his history of the Rosy

Cross, also said of Dr. Clymer and his organization:

"It would serve no useful purpose to enlarge upon later foundations, like that of Dr. R. Swinburne Clymer, who seems to have assumed the mantle laid down by Randolph, or Max Heindel's Rosicrucian Fellowship of California. They represent individual enterprises which have no roots in the past."

The *Journal of the American Medical Association,* in its issue of December 15, 1923, said of Dr. Clymer: "Our records fail to show that this man was ever regularly graduated by any reputable medical college. In a paid notice that appeared in Polk's Medical Directory for 1906, Clymer claims the degrees of 'Ph.G.' and 'M.D.' He is classified as a 'Physio-Medicist' and a graduate of the 'Independent Medical College,' Chicago, 1898. The Independent Medical College was a diploma mill which sold diplomas to anyone who sent the cash. It was finally declared a fraud by the federal authorities and put out of business."

In 1939, Dr. Clymer, after making what appears to have been his *first* trip to Europe, although claiming for years previously that his organization was affiliated with the authoritative Rosicrucian Order of the World, said in correspondence: "I have

just returned from Europe, where a meeting of the International Confederation was held in Paris, and articles signed by the many European organizations." It will be noted that the *International Confederation,* to which Dr. Clymer referred, appears to have been modeled after the F.U.D.O.S.I., established in 1934, to which Dr. Clymer and his organization were *not invited* because of ineligibility. Five years later, therefore, or in 1939, Dr. Clymer either had another existing body of equal dignity, tradition, and authenticity recognize his small association, *or* he went to Paris *to invent* such a body and *to confer upon himself* the European recognition which he did not have and needed.

That the latter was the case is borne out from the following evidence: Hieronymus, the Imperator of the Rose Croix of Europe, and Jean Mallinger, an avocat of the Belgian Court of Appeals and Secretary of the F. U. D. O. S. I., through the Corresponding Secretary of the Order in France, wrote to the Imperator of the A. M. O. R. C. of North America that they officially had no knowledge of any such *International Confederation of Rosicrucians,* to which Dr. Clymer referred, of its meeting in Paris, or its purported signing of articles. In essence, however, they stated that if such a meeting were held, it was *clandestine,* and any articles which

those attending adopted and signed would have no more legal weight with the Rosicrucian Order throughout the world than the mere blank paper upon which they were written.*

Dr. Clymer's claims that his organization was the only true representative body of Rosicrucian philosophy in the Western world have been challenged upon numerous occasions by the executive officers of A. M. O. R. C. He was asked to meet the Chief Executive, or Imperator, of A. M. O. R. C. in public debate, at a place and at a time of his own selection. Upon such occasion, he was to be permitted to introduce all materials, documents, and papers, decrees and charters, which he might have in his possession, to substantiate his claims; and A. M. O. R. C. would do likewise. As a gesture of good faith in making the challenge, A. M. O. R. C. offered to pay all the expenses incident to such debate.

Dr. Clymer's refusal, *in writing,* a number of times, is part of the evidence which A. M. O. R. C. possesses of his *disinclination* to bring about a fair and final solution of this problem and disputatious matter. In essence, he stated in his correspondence

---

*See statement about Clymer and his international Confederation appearing in the Manifesto issued by the F. U. D. O. S. I. in Brussels in 1939.

and in books which he wrote upon the subject, that no purpose would be served by such a *public* disclosure. On the other hand, he continued to make one-sided, distorted misrepresentations of the facts in books, which he himself circulated to public libraries, institutions, organizations, and societies. I leave it to the reader, therefore, to judge the *conduct, fortitude,* and *motives* of Dr. Clymer.

In considering other semi-Rosicrucian movements in America, we find little in any of the Rosicrucian histories of Europe to support their claims to Rosicrucian association. That which was most popular in past years was the Rosicrucian *Fellowship,* established by Mr. Max Heindel. Mr. Heindel was at one time a student of the occult. In his desire to learn more about the Rosicrucian teachings, he went to Europe to seek affiliation with the Order. He became discouraged by the many obstacles presented, and finally became a personal student of Mr. Rudolph Steiner, the eminent *Theosophist,* who was an unaffiliated student of Rosicrucian history and principles. Mr. Steiner was at that time inaugurating the work of a new organization of his own creation, and Mr. Heindel became one of his enthusiastic students. Mr. Heindel claimed that in addition to this short period of study in Europe, he had a *"psychic initiation"* into the

Rosicrucian Order during a *dream* or a *trance,* whereby he was *authorized* (!) to proceed with the work of bringing Rosicrucian philosophy to America and later given permission through the same unnamed and unknown Masters to write a personal outline of his opinions of the Steiner teachings and issue this to the American public in regular book form.

These claims to authority by Mr. Heindel, and his subsequent organization, have been refuted by the Grand Master of the Rosicrucian Order of Germany. In a document, dated in Berlin on June 3, 1930, and now in the archives of the A. M. O. R. C. of America, and which was signed not only by the German Rosicrucian Grand Master, but by high Civil authorities of the German Government, there appear the following statements in both the English and German languages: "The irrevocable proof that the claims of the above-mentioned leaders of the Rosicrucian Fellowship, of Oceanside, are false can be ascertained by a perusal of the Rosicrucian Fellowship publications, which have also appeared in German translation. . . . Max Heindel has no connection with this only authentic German Rosicrucian Fraternity, whose origin goes back to their forefathers, the Deutsche Gottesfreunde, a brotherhood of high adepts, of the 13th and 14th centuries,

from whom our tradition descends in direct and continued line through descent and the ties of the Order. . . . An initiation through psychic-spiritual-istic manipulations of the kind Max Heindel claims to have received is not recognized by the true German Rosicrucian Fraternity."

He returned to America, and in 1911 established his printing plant and offices in a very small city of Southern California, and before his transition in 1919 had written a number of books dealing with an outline of his personal "Rosicrucian" beliefs, which are claimed to be a form of "Christian philosophy." So, once again, America was presented with a representation of so-called Rosicrucian doctrines through commercialized books, selling to anyone who had the price, dealing with many subjects not taught in the regular Rosicrucian lodges of Europe or elsewhere. Mr. Heindel made no attempt to establish lodges throughout the country, as is customary with the Rosicrucian Order in every land, for, of course, he had no authority from the Order in Europe to do so, and he in no way conducted the work as it is conducted by the Rosicrucian Order.

Unquestionably, the work of Mr. Heindel was inspirational and added to the interesting mystical literature of America, but the name of his personal

organization, and the fact that all his work was conducted through the sale of books, plainly indicated to the Rosicrucian seeker that the work of Mr. Heindel, like that of several others, was unofficial from the Rosicrucian point of view, and "Rosicrucian" only in name. His widow attempted to continue the Fellowship after his transition, but internal difficulties arose and she withdrew from all connection with the Fellowship in the early part of 1932, while a few of its former students attempted to hold together the remnants of an organization that reduced itself to a mere personal interpretation of Christian teachings.*

Thus we have written of the various semi-Rosicrucian, or unofficial, organizations existing in America, including the "Masonic" Rosicrucian activity which started in England and made many attempts to establish itself in the United States. All of these bodies have done good work in their particular fields, and, aside from the objectionable sex teachings that are found in a few of the books issued by some of these organizations, their publications undoubtedly start many casual students of occult science on a path that leads eventually to the higher teachings.

---

* Apparently because dissension might have meant dissolution of the Fellowship, an accord was reached with the Board of Directors and Mrs. Heindel returned.

CHAPTER VII

THE FIRST ROSICRUCIANS IN AMERICA

WE HAVE just been speaking of semi-Rosicrucian bodies in America, but we must not overlook the first *genuine* Rosicrucian body to come to America. The brief facts given herewith are taken from two excellent books. First, that by Mr. J. F. Sachse, who was an heir and descendant of the first Rosicrucians to establish an official branch of the work in the United States, and second, from Mr. Arthur Waite's history of the Rose Cross Order. According to these two books, and the many other books quoted by them in their histories, a movement was started in Europe in 1693, as a result of previous plans to send a colony of leaders in the Rosicrucian work from the principal European branches to America, not only to found a Rosicrucian colony but to establish the Rosicrucian sciences, arts, and trades. The plan had its inception in the book called the *New Atlantis* written by Sir Francis Bacon while he was Imperator of the Rosicrucian Order in Europe, and which plan was later worked out in detail by the principal lodge of the Rosicrucian Order in London known

as the *Philadelphia Lodge* or the *Philadelphic Lodge,* named after the city in the East where one of the original mystery schools was located.

In the fall of 1693, the tourists started out in a specially chartered vessel called the *Sarah Maria* under the leadership of Grand Master Kelpius, who was connected with the *Jacob Boehme Lodge* of the Rosicrucians in Europe, and with other officers from the Grand Lodge of the Rosicrucians in Heidelberg. They reached the city that is now known as Philadelphia, and to which they gave that name, in the first months of 1694, and built many buildings in what is now known as Fairmount Park, and later they moved further west in Pennsylvania.

Mr. Sachse, in his monumental work on these early Rosicrucians, says of this event: "Ten years later June 24th, 1694, Kelpius and his chapter of Pietists or true Rosicrucians landed in Philadelphia, walked to Germantown, and finally settled on the rugged banks of the Wissahickon."*

Many of their own books and manuscripts prepared in their own printing plant are still preserved in the historical collections of various historical societies of Pennsylvania, and by the descendants of

The German Pietists of Pennsylvania, by Sachse, page 4.

early governors of the state. Mr. Sachse and Mr. Waite have examined many of these manuscripts and books and find in them the undoubted connections with the Rosicrucian Order, and the presentation of the true Rosicrucian teachings. Mr. Waite discusses at length the Rosicrucian manuscripts used by these American pioneers and shows that they were the genuine secret teachings of the Order, and that the activities and regulations of the men and women forming the colony coincided with the standard activities of other Rosicrucian branches. It was here that many important American institutions were established, and that valuable contributions to the scientific and art foundations of the United States were laid. The list of eminent Americans who became affiliated with the Rosicrucian activities during the first century of its existence in Philadelphia reads like the roster of American patriots and leaders. Benjamin Franklin and Thomas Jefferson were but two of the outstanding figures in the activities of this national headquarters of the Rosicrucians in America.

"In that retired valley beside the flowing brook the secret rites and mysteries of the true Rosicrucian Philosophy flourished unmolested for years, until the state of affairs brought about by the American Rev-

olution, together with pernicious Sunday legislation which also discriminated against the keepers of the scriptural Sabbath day, gradually caused the incoming generation to assimilate with the secular congregations."*

It would take too many pages in this history even to outline the many unique forms of activities which they created in a spirit of assisting to build up a new nation in a new land.

We must call attention again to the fact that this first colony came to America in accordance with the rules and regulations of the 108-year cycle of the Rosicrucian Order. Having started their movement toward America in 1693, it was only natural that 108 years later, or in 1801, this first American movement should close its outer public activities and start its cycle of 108 years of retirement and secret activity. So we find, according to the records, that in 1801 the large colony of Rosicrucians in Philadelphia dispersed and proceeded to various parts of the United States where small branches had been prepared even as far west as the Pacific Coast. The principal buildings in Philadelphia were abandoned, and the members continued to carry on their work in silence. Children were carefully trained in the teachings, and as they reached adult-

*The German Pietists of Pennsylvania, by Sachse, pages 7-8.

hood were initiated secretly into the organization so that their descendants might also carry on the work.

It was well known that as the 108-year cycle of silence and secrecy closed in the year 1909, the Order would again be authorized and chartered in a public manner and therefore, documents, papers, seals, and jewels were carefully handed down from one generation to another in anticipation of the coming of the year 1909. And, just as Mr. J. F. Sachse became the custodian of many of the manuscripts and jewels, so other descendants, notably those who assisted in the re-establishment of the new Order in 1909, possessed certain papers or "keys" which were useful in re-establishing or bringing to birth again the Rosicrucian Order in America, in its new cycle.

Thus we close this section of the history, but call attention to the fact that during the years 1800 to 1900 the Order in France, Germany, England, Switzerland, Holland, Russia, Spain, and in the Orient, was carrying on with increasing activity, but under very difficult conditions. It was found necessary, in most foreign lands, to continue the extreme silence and secrecy originally established because of the political persecution that was directed toward every sort of secret organization devoted to the pro-

mulgation of advanced knowledge and the higher laws. Despite such difficulties, the records show that in France, England, and Germany especially, the organization operated a great many branches with ever-increasing membership; and as the year 1909 approached, many men and some women journeyed to Europe to contact the Rosicrucian Order. Among these were a few eminent Freemasons, who sought to revive the "Masonic" Rosicrucian studies, and others who sought permission or authority to assist in the new birth of the 1909 cycle. The success of their missions, and the result of their activities, will be referred to in the next section of this history.

THE PRESENT ROSICRUCIAN ORDER
IN AMERICA

I N WRITING this section of the history, I find that I cannot avoid using the first person pronoun because of my own intimate connection with the activities to be described, and I trust that the reader will understand this and overlook the personal element.

I have said that as the year 1909 approached, many men and women journeyed to France or other parts of Europe seeking not only initiation into the Order, but some official permission to aid in the establishment of the Order again in the United States, for its new cycle.

In France, during the years from 1880 onward, the Order became very active, because the year 1880 was apparently the beginning of a new cycle of the Rosicrucian activities for several of the countries, and records show that in the years 1900 to 1909 the Rosicrucian branches were many, and very active indeed, especially in France. It was only natural, therefore, that those students of Rosicrucian history, and those who had been partially

initiated into the work as descendants of earlier members of the Order, should look to France and its high development in the Rosicrucian activities for aid in their plans and desires. As in other lands at other periods, a number of semi-Rosicrucian bodies had come into existence in France during the early part of the twentieth century, and many of these gradually affiliated with the Rosicrucian Order and adopted the strict rules and regulations of the ancient fraternity. A few of them, however, continued to use their previous titles even after affiliation with the Order, and this caused some confusion in the minds of those who journeyed to France seeking the genuine movement.

Many veiled stories regarding the Brotherhood had appeared in France, notably those by Eugene Sue, and Émile Zola. These informed the seekers of the existence of certain Rosicrucian activities which contained clues that enabled the determined seekers finally to contact the proper officials. From the seventeenth century onward, the Order in France had adopted the French term *Rose Croix,* in preference to the Latin term *Rosae Crucis.* We find even in Wassenaer's *Historisch Verhael* published in 1623, mention of the *Ordre de la Rose Croix* in France, with connections with members and other branches

of the Order in Spain, Italy, England, Switzerland, Germany, Flanders, and other lands; and many prominent persons are mentioned in several French histories as having been active in the Order previous to the new cycle of 1880. I refer to such persons as Garasse, Gaultius, Naude, Richelieu, Louis XIII, king of France; and many others, even Descartes. Other records show that Jacques Rose organized before his transition in 1660 one of the newest and largest branches of the Rose Croix, and of course there were such famous leaders of the work in France as *le Comte de Gabalis,* Martínez Pasquales, and Louis Claude de Saint-Martin.

The very complete history of the Rosicrucian Order written in French and other languages by Brother Wittemans, a member of the Belgian Senate, and an honorary member of our Order here in America, contains very interesting facts regarding the activities of the Order in France during the twentieth century. Among the independent organizations in France after 1900 were a branch of the S. R. I. A. of England, the "Masonic" Rosicrucian society referred to previously, the Hermetic Order of the Golden Dawn founded in 1887, and *l'Ordre Cabbalistique de la Rose-Croix.* The latter organization contained a number of officers connected with

the regular Rosicrucian Order, and this cabalistic body devoted itself to a limited list of subjects for scientific research and did not claim to be a part of the regular Rosicrucian Order. It was therefore never considered a clandestine body.

There was also an independent organization known as *la Rose Croix Catholique,* which attracted the interest of many Roman Catholics who were misled into the belief that it was a separate organization for them. On the other hand, there was also a Rosicrucian group quite independent under the leadership of Frater Castelot, who was, and remained until his transition, a member of the regular Order in France, and one of the honorary members of our Order here in America.

Frater Castelot was one of the most eminent and dearly beloved workers in the art of alchemy, devoting his time and interest to the study of alchemical problems with the few who were in his independent organization. He demonstrated in their group laboratory the possibility of transmutation in accordance with the Rosicrucian teachings and succeeded in producing gold, as told in a story published by our Order in our official magazine, the *Rosicrucian Digest.*

However, the real Order, as established throughout the world, had several official branches in

France as national headquarters. One of these was the "Secretariat" in Paris, while another was a College of Rites at Lyons, originally established by Cagliostro, and the national Council Chambers and temple, with the national archives in the environs of Toulouse, the ancient site of the first Rosicrucians established in Europe.

The meetings that were held in the various special branches of the Order in parts of France were as secret and veiled as were the activities at the larger national offices. It was difficult to locate a Rosicrucian lodge or identify a Rosicrucian member anywhere in Europe, a situation which has greatly changed in the last twenty-five years.

A survey of the history of the various occult movements that find moral and psychic support from the Great White Lodge shows that in the year 1909 more of the mystical movements of the world were reborn, revised, or changed in their form of activity than in any other year of occult history. It was in this year that Mr. Heindel of the semi-Rosicrucian independent society in America went to Europe to attempt to secure Rosicrucian information, and instead became a student of Mr. Rudolph Steiner, and his revised form of theosophy. It was also in the year 1909 that Mr. Gould planned to go to Europe to secure the true Rosi-

crucian rituals and teachings for his branch of
the S. R. I. A. in the United States. And other leaders of other movements journeyed to Europe during
this year, or received instructions from foreign
branches in this year, to revise or renew their activities.

It was in 1909, also, that I made my visit to
France for a similar purpose. For many years I had
held together a large body of men and women devoted to esoteric and metaphysical research along
Rosicrucian lines. As editor of several esoteric magazines, I had made contact with various Rosicrucian manuscripts and had discovered that I was
related to one of the descendants of the first Rosicrucian body in America—that which had established itself in Philadelphia in 1694. This gave me
access to many of their old papers, secret manuscripts, and teachings. These we discussed, ana-
lyzed, and attempted to put into practice. Among
ourselves, the society, composed of several hundred
persons in professional life, was known as *The
Rosicrucian Research Society*. Among the many
prominent persons then affiliated and holding active
positions as officers were I. K. Funk, president of
the Funk and Wagnalls Publishing Co. (publishers
of the *Literary Digest*), "Fra" Elbert Hubbard, of
the famous Roycrofters, who was deeply interested

in the work to the very day of his transition, and
Ella Wheeler Wilcox, the famous mystical writer,
who later became a member of the Supreme Council of AMORC, which position she held until the
time of her transition. Others of equal prominence,
who were active members, are still members in high
degrees of the present AMORC. The meetings of
the Society were held monthly from 1904 to 1909 in
New York City. Realizing that we were not yet
chartered or authorized to use the name *Rosicrucian,* the society operated publicly under the
name of *The New York Institute for Psychical
Research.*

Just before 1909 there applied for membership in
our society one who presented papers proving ap-
pointment as "Legate" of the Rosicrucian Order
in India. Many weeks of close association with this
member revealed the fact that I might be successful
in my search for some form of authority to introduce the true Rosicrucian work in America at
the right time. Every means of communication with
any official of the Order in foreign lands was
denied to me until early in the year 1909 when I
was informed that the year for the public appearance
of the Order in America was at hand and that
definite arrangements for the new cycle had been
completed. The Legate from India encouraged

me to follow the urge that had actuated me for six or more years, regardless of any obstacles or trials that might tend to discourage my unselfish aims.

Therefore, I went to France in the summer of 1909 and after a brief interview with one who refused to commit himself very definitely, I was directed to various cities, and in each case redirected until I finally approached a definite contact in Toulouse. There I eventually found that my plans and desires had been anticipated and known for some time. I was permitted to meet not just one of the officers of the French Rosicrucian Order, but a number, as well as some who were members of the international Council of the Rosicrucian bodies of various European nations. At a regular Council meeting, and at several special sessions of the Order in other cities held in the months following, I was duly initiated and given preliminary papers of instruction to present to others whose names had been given to me. I was also instructed to arrange to hold preliminary foundation meetings for the purpose of organizing a secret group of workers, who would receive further instructions from Legates of the Order in India and Switzerland. These instructions were signed by Count Bellcastle-Ligne, the secretary of

the international Council, and the venerable La-
salle, the well-known author of many historical
Rosicrucian documents, and Grand Master of the
Order Rosae Crucis or *Rose Croix of France.* Before leaving France I had the pleasure of meeting
several of the highest officers, and met in America,
on my return, the Legate from India, who presented to me the jewels and papers which had
been preserved from the early American foundation.

Throughout the years 1909 to 1915, many official
Council sessions were held in my home and the
homes of others, with men and women present who
were descendants of early initiates of the Order, and
a few of whom were initiates of the Order in France
during the years 1900 to 1909. In 1915 the first official public *manifesto* was issued in this country
announcing the birth of a new cycle of the Order,
and immediately thereafter the first Supreme Council of the Order was selected from among hundreds
of men and women who had been carefully selected
during the preceding *seven years.* At the first official
sessions of this American Supreme Council, officers
were nominated and I was surprised to find that
the Legate from India had been instructed to nomi-
nate me as the chief executive of the Order because of the work I had done during the seven

years in organizing the new foundation. Well-qualified persons were elected to other executive positions in the Order, and copies of the French constitution of the Order and official documents were presented to committees for translation and adoption in a form to fit American conditions.

These meetings were followed by the first initiation of new members, the report of which to the French High Council brought a document of sponsorship for the American branch signed by the principal French officers. As with every new cycle in each land, the first years of its activity are under the sponsorship of some well-established jurisdiction, and so for a time this new cycle of the American Order operated under the sponsorship of the French jurisdiction.

It must be noted that from the very start, and with the issuance of the first public manifesto, the correct name of the international Rosicrucian organization was used, namely, the *Ancient Mystical Order Rosae Crucis*. This is a slightly abbreviated form of the original Latin name, *Antiquus Arcanus Ordo Rosae Rubeae et Aureae Crucis,* and the initials AMORC were immediately used as well as the true and original symbol of the Rosicrucian Order—the golden cross with but *one red rose* in its center.

At this time, and especially during the years 1915, 1916, and 1917, there were in existence in America several forms of semi-Rosicrucian movements, namely, the S. R. I. A., and the Rosicrucian *Fellowship* founded by Mr. Heindel. One will note that the S. R. I. A. was using the unique independent name of *Society* of Rosicrucians, rather than the ancient name of the Rosicrucians, which body always used the name *Rosicrucian Order* as used by us; and the S. R. I. A. symbol was very different from the symbol used by us. The Rosicrucian *Fellowship* likewise had adopted a name that was not that of the regular organization throughout the world, and for its symbol had created a new and independent device consisting of a cross with a *garland of seven roses* around it instead of only *one rose* in its *center*. Both of these organizations were publishing their teachings in book form, and were carrying on a work that was undoubtedly of value to students of general occultism. The very earmarks of their organizations—their distinctive names and symbols—differentiated them from the ancient organization, and the fact that they published and sold books claimed to contain the Rosicrucian teachings, put them in a different category from any of the

other Rosicrucian Branches of Europe or elsewhere.

Therefore, the AMORC proceeded with the ancient customs and practices by publishing no books of teachings, but insisted that all who desired to study the work of the Order must join with and help form regular lodges or chapters in various localities.*

So successful was this form of activity during 1916 that branches were established from coast to coast, and from Canada to Mexico. By the summer of 1917 there were so many branches of AMORC in existence and carrying on the work with such enthusiasm that a National Convention was called for one week at Pittsburgh, Penna. Here hundreds of delegates from the branches, and members of the Order, assembled officially to acknowledge the existence of the Order and to finally adopt a National Constitution.

A committee was selected, composed of ten or more well-known Freemasons, who were eminent in the sciences and professions and who were *fa-*

---

*The books which the A. M. O. R. C. publishes, on various mystical, philosophical, and metaphysical topics, do not contain the official teachings of the Rosicrucian Order.

miliar with ritualistic and fraternal law, to examine the translated and revised French constitution of the Order, for adoption in America. This committee rendered its report, and the National Constitution of AMORC was adopted at the sessions of the convention, paragraph by paragraph. The Committee later signed a document stating that their experience with the work as members of the Order, and their familiarity with the claims and teachings of the Order, proved to them that the Rosicrucian work as issued by the AMORC was distinctly different from anything that they had contacted in their other affiliations, and worthy of the deepest and most profound study on the part of every seeker for the greater light. Other matters were officially established by this great convention, and thereafter the organization continued to grow throughout the United States, Canada, and Mexico.

This increasing activity resulted in a proclamation being issued at the International Convention of Rosicrucians held in Europe, establishing North America as a complete jurisdiction of the international organization, and it was then no longer

necessary to operate as a branch of the French body.*

Eminent Rosicrucian officers of France, notably Monsieur Verdier, the commander-in-chief of the Illuminati of the Rosicrucians in France, visited the Order in America and left papers of approval and recognition. These were followed later on by a document issued by the International Convention held in Switzerland, appointing the national headquarters of the Order in North America as a branch of the international body. This latter document is one of the most important in the archives of the American headquarters.

During the years 1918 to 1925, the Imperator for the Order in America was honored with various degrees in the French organization, and in 1926 attended the next session of the International Conventions held both in Toulouse and Switzerland, receiving other appointments and honors; and finally in Paris during the same year, at a high reception given by a Congress of the most notable

*The international jurisdiction of A. M. O. R. C. has since been increased to include all of the countries of the world. The original jurisdiction was by authority and proclamation issued during the 1934 International Convention and Congress of the Rose-Croix of Europe and affiliated bodies held in Brussels, Belgium. See page 150 for further details of International Conclaves of Rosicrucians, in which the A. M. O. R. C. of America was the only Rosicrucian participant from the Western world.

of all the Rosicrucian officers of Europe, he was acknowledged as one of the highest officers of the Rosicrucian work. At the same time these high officers of the French Order, who are also high officers of other fraternal organizations in Europe, were made honorary members of the American Order, and official papers exchanged to verify these appointments.

The Order in America, known by the general international name of the Order as AMORC, continues to function strictly in accordance with the ancient traditions and in affiliation with all other recognized branches. The Imperator of the AMORC in North America is the only official American delegate to the International Rosicrucian Conventions. After the Great World War of 1914-17 the Order in various parts of Europe, Asia, and Africa had to operate under strict surveillance and with great secrecy, while here in America conditions were favorable to an open and frank operation of all Rosicrucian activities.* Hence the

---

*This refers to the first world war. During the second world war an edict existed prohibiting the continuation of any secret, philosophical, or mystical fraternal orders and societies in France and in all of the countries occupied by the Nazis. They particularly sought to suppress the Rosicrucians and Freemasons. Once again, therefore, there was the attempt to extinguish the light of truth. Communications from the French Grand Secretary of the Order were irregular, veiled, and most of the time transmitted by means of the underground.

principal propaganda of the Rosicrucians may be carried on in this country without interference; for this reason the work in North America has grown to such an extent that the American AMORC today is the largest metaphysical and mystical organization in the Western world.

Adhering to the ancient traditions, the AMORC sells no books claiming to contain the secret teachings and does not sell its services at any price. Membership is limited to those who are carefully examined and tested with preliminary studies for many months and then finally admitted into regular membership. The teachings are given freely to those who are members, and no fees are charged for degrees or titles as with organizations operating on a commercial basis. An official magazine called the *Rosicrucian Digest* is sent from the international jurisdiction of AMORC to all members, thereby keeping every one of its many thousands of students well acquainted with the general activities of the Order in America and affiliated lands. The Order now owns Egyptian temples and lodge rooms throughout the United States, Canada, the British Commonwealth, Mexico, Central and South America, Europe, and Africa. It possesses property devoted exclusively to the great work, and carries on a number of humanitarian activities under various

names in order to avoid publicity in connection with such matters as are of no public concern.

The Supreme Temple was first located in New York City, but in 1918 was moved to the Pacific Coast because of property secured there which had been originally owned by the first organization established in America, and which was eventually transferred to the present Order. After establishing administration offices and a Supreme Temple in San Francisco, the executive offices were moved, in 1925, for a period of two years, to Florida, in order to help strengthen the work in the Southeastern part of the United States. An agreement was made with the large membership on the Pacific Coast that the Grand Lodge would return within two years to the West, and so in one day less than two years the organization, with the entire executive staff returned to the Pacific Coast to occupy its own property at its present site in San Jose, California, where the Order maintains a beautiful park and instruction facilities which include the following: a large Egyptian Museum and Art Gallery built upon authentic Egyptian designs and which contains the finest collection of Egyptian and Babylonian antiquities in Western United States, a beautiful Egyptian-styled Supreme Temple, a modern Planetarium that houses the latest in planetarium equipment, a Science Museum, a University

complex with laboratories and classrooms, a sound Studio in which films and sound recordings are made, a Research Library, an Auditorium, and extensive administration buildings. Unlike other secret organizations of a mystical nature, the AMORC in North America during its entire history has had very little unfavorable publicity purporting to discredit its teachings and practices. It has never been involved in any political disputes.

THE PILGRIMAGE TO EGYPT

Early in 1928, the Imperator for North America received official notice of several important national and international meetings that were to be held by the various Rosicrucian bodies of Europe and Egypt during the spring of 1929.* Desiring to have the highest officers of the organization in North America meet many of the high officers of the Order in foreign lands, the Imperator planned a pilgrimage to Egypt and proceeded to select members from the various groups and lodges throughout North America who could accompany him on his trip. The members finally selected represented thirty-one different cities in North America, covering nineteen jurisdictions and every grade and degree of the work. Among these were

*The Imperator here designated was Dr. H. Spencer Lewis.

seventeen of the highest officers of the Order in Canada, United States, Mexico, and the Latin-American jurisdictions, as well as a number of officers representing many of the secret and allied activities of the organization.

The pilgrimage started from Supreme Head-quarters in San Jose, California, on the evening of January 4th, and proceeded in special railway cars across the United States in a unique route touching Southern and Mexican cities and north into Canada to pick up members from various cities and take them to New York. The large party proceeded by boat to the Mediterranean and, after visiting many of the ancient cities, spent considerable time in Palestine, visiting the holy shrines of the Essenes and the Great White Brotherhood, and finally reached Egypt, where the Rosicrucian Order there prepared a number of interesting features for entertainment and instruction, including a series of initiations conducted in the ancient Rosicrucian manner, beginning at the Sphinx and the great Pyramids, with ceremonials at Lake Moeris, and culminating in a special initiation ceremony arranged by the oldest Rosicrucian lodges in Egypt in the Temple of Luxor on the Nile. From this place, the tour continued through Europe, giving the members and officers an opportunity to visit the Rosicrucian land-

marks in Switzerland, France, Germany, and England. The officers of the North American jurisdiction had the pleasure of visiting, secretly and privately, the oldest of the Rosicrucian temples in Europe and meeting with many of the high officers.

This unusual pilgrimage not only afforded the Imperator an opportunity to attend the official sessions, but the officers also an opportunity to make contacts seldom made by American mystics; and the initiation ceremony in Egypt whereby a Rosicrucian Egyptian lodge was instituted, composed solely of American members, was the first of its kind ever held in Egypt and will not be held again for one hundred and eight years.

The results of this pilgrimage will become highly significant as the years pass; but the one outstanding fact is that the AMORC is today the only Rosicrucian movement anywhere in the world whose principal officers and active representatives in so many jurisdictions *actually journeyed to Egypt* as in the pre-Christian Era, receiving in the ancient temple of Amenhotep IV at Luxor Rosicrucian *initiation* and Rosicrucian *acknowledgment* at the hands of officials of the oldest Rosicrucian lodges in existence anywhere in the world.* This gives the

---

*Subsequent Rosicrucian tours to Europe and Egypt were conducted by Rosicrucian officers in 1937, 1960, 1962.

AMORC a special power and an international standing which no other metaphysical organization in North America has ever had or probably ever will have.

In 1936, the Rosicrucian Order, A.M.O.R.C., sent a motion-picture camera expedition throughout Asia Minor, Palestine, Egypt, and the countries of the Levant, to film professionally the sites of the mystery schools, the great temples, and the remains of ancient civilizations as a matter of record for the Order. A few of the places filmed included the Great Pyramids, Karnak and Luxor Temples, the Valley of the Kings and Queens, the tombs of the nobles, the great palaces of the Rameses, antiquities of ancient Thebes; the ruins of Babylon, Baalbeck, Biblos, Ctesiphon, and the Island of Lesbos in the Aegean Sea; splendid mosques of Istanbul and Pera, and centers of early culture in Italy. This was the first time that any school or society of mysticism had ever made an effort to introduce its students and members to the magnificence of the great work of these early peoples, from whom we derive so much benefit in useful and inspiring knowledge.

In 1948-49, the Supreme Council of AMORC sent three officers of the Order on a film expedition on behalf of the cultural activities of its extensive

Egyptian and Babylonian Museum. This journey took the members of the expedition to China, Thailand, India, Egypt, and Europe. By means of the Rosicrucian affiliation, temples and monasteries in India and inside Tibet were filmed. These color and sound films, as a public relations activity, have been shown to thousands of members and the public throughout the world. The Imperator wrote articles on his unique experiences in connection with the journey, not only for Rosicrucian publications but also for outside periodicals of wide public circulation.

In 1953, 1957, and 1962, further camera expeditions to the philosophical and archeological shrines of Greece, the Aegean region, the Holy Land, and the area of the Dead Sea Scrolls were conducted by the AMORC Technical Staff.

CHAPTER IX

THE INTERNATIONAL JURISDICTION
OF THE ORDER

HE original jurisdiction re-established in the United States, in 1915, has grown to become a world-wide organization. In 1934, after a meeting in Europe composed of representatives of the Order throughout the world, the jurisdiction in the Western world was extended to include North, Central, and South America. The following year, complying with the new responsibilities of the jurisdiction, the Latin-American Division of the Order was transferred to San Jose.

During the second World War, many Rosicrucian groups in Europe became inactive. In many countries, rituals and teachings had been destroyed, and these groups became dependent upon the North and South American jurisdiction. In 1946, the British jurisdiction consolidated with it* and gradually others followed, until today the international jurisdiction of the Order centers in Rosicrucian Park, San

---

*See following chapters for details.

Jose, California. This international jurisdiction now includes The Americas, Australasia, Europe, Africa, and Asia.

The Supreme Grand Lodge of AMORC is therefore the supreme body of the Order for this international jurisdiction, and various Grand Lodges in many parts of the world are subordinate to it. The Supreme Grand Lodge of AMORC in the United States is incorporated as a nonprofit, educational organization, and is so registered in many other countries throughout the jurisdiction.

The Order throughout the world is known by the initials of the full name of the Order, A.M.O.R.C., which are the first letters of the words composing the full name, Ancient Mystical Order Rosae Crucis. The universal symbol of the Order is a gold cross with a *single red rose* in its center. Another symbol frequently used is an equilateral triangle with one point downward, enclosing a cross with a red rose in its center. These symbols are registered in the patent office of the United States by the Supreme Grand Lodge of AMORC, and only official Rosicrucian movements approved by the Supreme Grand Lodge may use these symbols. These symbols and the word *AMORC* are also registered in many countries throughout the free world.

After Dr. H. Spencer Lewis had been authorized to re-establish the Rosicrucian Order in the Western world, and his powers had later been confirmed by the European jurisdiction, the responsibility for the growth of the new jurisdiction rested entirely with itself. Intercourse was continued with the International Supreme Council of the Rosae Crucis throughout the world. Teachings were transmitted in document form and by other means, from the European Order, to the A. M. O. R. C. of America, but the labors of development and expansion were confined strictly to the American administration. New policies had to be adopted to conform with conditions in the Western world, which were entirely extraneous to Europe. America knew a freedom which Europe in its most liberal period and countries never enjoyed. The secrecy, such as the European jurisdiction of the Order employed to veil its activities against abasement of its principles, was not necessary in America, and, if attempted, would arouse suspicion as to the motives of the Organization.

There existed in America, therefore, an opportunity for the advancement of the Rosicrucian teachings, with their consequent benefit to humanity, which the Rosicrucian movement had never experienced since its inception during the time

of the early mystery schools. To establish and maintain lodges in just the larger cities or centers of population, as had been the custom of the Order in Europe since the time that Grand Master Frees reigned in A. D. 883-899, would be to deprive thousands of sincere American seekers of the knowledge and *light* which they sought. In every little hamlet or village, there were some who were duly prepared *inwardly* for initiation and for the Rosicrucian mystical philosophy. It would have been impossible to establish a lodge or temple in every little community, and completely furnish and equip it with the necessary ritualistic appurtenances.

At the first Convention of the A. M. O. R. C. in America, held the week of August 2, 1917, at Pittsburgh, Pennsylvania, after due deliberation by officers of the various lodges, and official delegates, a resolution was passed, establishing the *National Rosicrucian Lodge*. This Lodge was intended as a solution to the problem of expansion. It provided certain requirements, whereby a probationary, or introductory phase of the Rosicrucian teachings might be sent by correspondence to the inquirer who had met definite qualifications

of membership. During the next few years considerable work was done in determining the best manner of presenting these time-honored teachings, even the elementary aspects, in a dignified and an appropriate way. From this research, there developed a system of instructions that became highly successful and won the approval of educators for its perspicuity in introducing profound subjects. The new method was accepted by the seekers for mystical truth and knowledge, in a manner far beyond the expectations of the Imperator and the Supreme Grand Master of the A. M. O. R. C. of America.

The rise and spread of Rosicrucian teachings in America became positive and rapid. Eventually, the completion of the elementary studies by the isolated Neophyte, and his desire to advance further and participate in the teachings of the Temple Degrees, as given in established Rosicrucian Lodges, renewed the old problem. A Lodge could not be established in each community where there were a few who had successfully qualified for the Postulant Degrees of the Order. Neither could these Neophytes journey with regularity to distant lodges. In 1926, Dr. H. Spencer Lewis, illustrious Imperator of A. M. O. R. C. at the time, presented the

matter to a Congress of Rosicrucian dignitaries in Switzerland.*

The result was that the teachings and doctrines of the higher degrees of the Rosicrucian Order could be extended in like manner, if each Neophyte assumed certain obligations and complied with traditional ritualistic rites. After this further decision and approval, the expansion of the Rosicrucian Order of North America was still more rapid. Individuals in foreign lands, which as yet were not part of an established or recognized jurisdiction of the Rosicrucian Order, sought admission in the A. M. O. R. C. of America by this unique means. The method of maintaining a Sanctum, or "a lodge at home" was appealing. The infant American jurisdiction of the Rosicrucian Order was now able to express itself in a manner that amazed, and yet caused the Masters and Hierophants of the other jurisdictions to rejoice.

Extensive yet dignified campaigns of a public nature were conducted to draw seekers to the portals of the Temple; in other words, to shorten their time of search. In 1927, in Tampa, Florida, which was then the See of the Supreme Grand Lodge of the A. M. O. R. C. for North America, a large radio broadcasting station was erected by the Order. It

*See page 178.

was assigned the call letters of WJBB by the Federal Bureau of Communications of the United States Government. Cultural programs were extensively broadcast. Though the station was the largest in the state of Florida, no commercial activity or sale of time was conducted by it. Lectures on scientific and philosophical subjects, classical and popular music, drama, public service, addresses by prominent Government officials and educators, and a form of social service constituted its daily programs. The transmission range of the station was several thousand miles, making the name *Rosicrucian* further known, and identifying it with enlightenment and civic progress.

In 1934, the first great International conclave of the Rosicrucian Order in modern times was held in Europe. The following are excerpts from the *Rosicrucian Digest,* of November, 1934, the official publication of the A.M.O.R.C. of North America, reporting the event:

"This was not to be merely a huge assembly of initiated members of the world's oldest mystical groups. On this special occasion, only the highest officers—Imperators, Hierophants, Grand Masters, or members of Supreme Councils were to come together to meet with the representatives of the Great White Brotherhood."

"Such a great convention or congress had been an-

ticipated for many years. It was decreed for this cycle of world activities many years ago. The first attempt in 1914 was purely of a preliminary nature, merely continuing the preliminary efforts of 1908 and earlier. In 1921 and 1927 larger preliminary sessions were held, in which our Imperator participated. In 1931 various national conventions in Europe crystallized the plans for the 1934 Congress, and again our Imperator was an important delegate."

"The opening address, made by the Venerable Imperator (of Europe) was translated into English, and it contained many and elaborate compliments to our Imperator and the work he has accomplished in North America."

"The high objects of the Convention were stressed and urged by each speaker. Among these was Fra. Wittemans, a member of the Belgian Senate, an eminent law authority, and a well-known author of a very complete history of the Rosicrucian Order, published in several languages."

"Of the many direct results, the following are the outstanding ones, of special interest to our members:" (here followed eight points, but for brevity we quote but one)

"That the Supreme Council of AMORC at San Jose, California, shall continue to be the exclusive repository for North and South America of the genuine and authorized rituals, rites, teachings, and findings of the Rosicrucian Order or Fraternity, and its allied organizations."

This, then, was another ratification of the work which the A. M. O. R. C. was accomplishing in the jurisdiction of North America, to perpetuate the ancient Rosicrucian teachings. It was further substantiation of A. M. O. R. C.'s claims to its authority, and its right to represent itself to be the perpetuator of the authentic Rosicrucian teachings in the Americas.

Of momentous importance was the Manifesto issued in 1934, which reads in part:

"Be it known that at a Convention of the Supreme Officers of the various ancient Rosicrucian Orders and affiliated bodies of the world, composing the F. U. D. O. S. I., held in Brussels, Belgium, August 13 to 18, 1934, it was unanimously decreed the S . . . . S . . . . of the A.. M.. O.. R.. C.. of North America is hereby empowered and authorized to extend its jurisdiction and exclusive authority to South America as well as to the territories and dependencies of the United States, Canada, and other possessions of North and South American countries; and that the said S. . . . S. . . . of A.. M.. O.. R.. C.. for North and South America shall have the right and authority to act as a sponsor for the establishment of Rosicrucian Lodges and Chapters, in such countries of the world not governed by any recognized Grand or Supreme Lodge or S. . . . S. . . . ,——"

This document was attested to by the signatures and seals of each of the Masters and Hierophants and dignitaries and official delegates of the august societies convening.

La Rose+Croix magazine, published for forty years, and being the official "Organe de la Société Alchimique de France et de l'Ordre Antique et Mystique de la Rose-Croix," directed by the renowned Rosicrucian alchemist, F. Jollivet Castelot, announced in its issue of January, 1935, this successful convention and the formation of the F..U..D..O..S..I.., as a victory for the mystical and hermetic orders.

In July of 1934, at an annual convention of the A. M. O. R. C. of North and South America, the Imperator, Dr. H. Spencer Lewis, dedicated the first unit of what became known as the Rose-Croix University of America.* The large, handsome, colonnaded building, of Egyptian design, housed chemistry, physics, and light and photography laboratories, classrooms, and study hall. In June of 1935 the first term of the Rose-Croix University of the American Jurisdiction began, with students enrolling in its "College of Humanities," "Fine and Mystic Arts," and "Arcane and Mundane Sciences."

---

* This and subsequent chapters of this book, excepting the Question and Answer section, were written after the transition of Dr. H. Spencer Lewis, the original author.

Rosicrucians who wished to specialize in material sciences or certain aspects of Rosicrucian arcana were given the opportunity under duly qualified instructors. Since the above date, the original building has had several annexes, which include added classrooms, a cinema studio, and a biology laboratory.

After several years of experimentation and a visit to the leading planetariums in Europe, Dr. H. Spencer Lewis had built in the year 1936 the first Planetarium containing an apparatus which he himself had designed. The magnificent domed building, with its many ingenious mechanical devices, made possible a realistic reproduction of the movement of the stars and the planets for the study of astronomy. He named it the *Theater of the Sky,* and it is indeed an appropriate title, for it portrays the cosmic roles of the cosmic bodies.

In August, 1936, the Supreme Secretary of A. M. O. R. C., Ralph M. Lewis, while on a cinema and still-camera expedition through Asia Minor, Egypt, and North Africa, attended a conference of the officers of the F. U. D. O. S. I., in Brussels, Belgium, in behalf of the Rosicrucian Order of America. He had conferred upon him an esoteric degree of the Rose Croix of Europe. The venerable Imperator of the Rose Croix Order of Europe presided at the

Initiation. He was likewise inducted into the rites of the Traditional Martinist Order of France, receiving initiation both in Brussels, Belgium, and in Paris, France. Certain Martinist documents were entrusted to him to transmit personally to the Imperator of A. M. O. R. C. of America upon his return.

Again, in August of 1937, another International Convention of the Rose Croix was called for Brussels, Belgium, and the F.U.D.O.S.I., with its allied bodies, convened at the same time. The sessions were presided over by *three Imperators*. Signal honors were conferred upon many of the various dignitaries. Dr. H. Spencer Lewis, having had conferred upon him the various degrees of the Traditional Martinist Order years previously, was now appointed Regional Sovereign Legate for the Martinist Order in the United States and its territories and dependencies. He was given charters empowering him to re-establish the rites of Martinism in the United States, as they had descended from its Illustrious Venerable Grand Master, Louis Claude de Saint-Martin. The charters and decrees were signed by the rightful successor to *Papus,* first president of the Supreme Council of the Traditional Martinist Order, with Sanctuary in France.

The versatility and organizing genius of Dr. H. Spencer Lewis is also seen in the fact that he organized and directed the establishment of the Rose-Croix Research Institute and Sanitarium, which first accepted patients in the Spring of 1939. For years, he relates in Rosicrucian literature, he had dreamed of having a center for healing, where the various established systems of treatment could be used in conjunction with the Rosicrucian methods of healing for the alleviation of suffering and, by study and research, to advance the therapeutic arts. Through the financial assistance of Rosicrucian members throughout the world, the Institute was equipped with the latest instruments and apparatuses for the treatment and study of disease. Many Rosicrucian principles were employed in the design and lighting of patients' and treatment rooms and in the development of unique facilities.*

In June of 1939, the Supreme Secretary, Ralph M. Lewis, on behalf of the Imperator, dedicated the Rosicrucian Research Library. Of Egyptian design and modern in every respect, the library employs the latest systems of filing and contains several thousand volumes on such subjects as occultism, mysticism, Rosicrucian philosophy, the arts, history, and the

*This activity was suspended a few years after the transition of Dr. H. Spencer Lewis.

sciences. It is for the exclusive use of Rosicrucian members, who, even though they cannot attend, can avail themselves of its research facilities by correspondence.

In August of 1939, the Scandinavian Lodges of the Rosicrucian Order held an International Convention in Malmo, Sweden, under the jurisdiction of the A. M. O. R. C. Grand Lodge of Sweden. A National Convention of the Danish Grand Lodge preceded this in Copenhagen by a few days.

In the same month, officers of the F.U.D.O.S.I. convened for the consideration of important pending matters, one of which was Dr. R. Swinburne Clymer's false claims to Rosicrucian authority and a renewal of his scurrilous attack on the Imperator and the organization of A.M.O.R.C. of North and South America.

The delegates to these two respective conclaves representing the A. M. O. R. C. of North and South America were the Imperator's personal representative, James R. Whitcomb, who had on previous occasions met with officers of the F.U.D.O.S.I. in their Congresses, and the Sovereign Grand Master of A. M. O. R. C. of America.

On August 13, 1939, in Brussels, Belgium, a Decree, written in the French language, was signed and sealed with the esoteric emblems and insignia of

office of the Imperator of the Rose Croix of Europe and given to James R. Whitcomb to transmit to the Imperator of A. M. O. R. C. of America. It is now in the repository of the Order in San Jose, California. The document reads in part:

"It is inevitable that the AMORC, the only Organization in the Western world perpetuating the teachings of the R+C that have been transmitted by written or spoken word by the R+C instructors, become the target of evil forces working through isolated individuals or organizations, who would attempt to put obstacles in its way and to curtail its progress.

"Therefore, in due Assembly in Brussels, Belgium, on this 13th day of the month of August, in the year 1939, we, members regularly elected of the Supreme Council of the F.U.D.O.S.I., after due examination of the elements of appreciation in the case that has been submitted to us, do proclaim that Reuben Swinburne Clymer, who does profess to perpetuate the true and ancient Rosicrucian teachings in America and who assails the character of the Hierarchy of AMORC, and who seeks to stalemate its progress, is in no wise recognized by us as having any Rosicrucian authority.

"We do also proclaim that the so-called International Confederation of Rosicrucians which R. Swinburne Clymer purports to exist in Europe, and with which he claims to be associated and deriving certain articles of authority, is in no wise recog-

nized by the R+C Orders and Fraternities of Europe that are affiliated to the F.U.D.O.S.I. In our opinion, the above-mentioned Confederation, is a clandestine organization that is illegitimate in its function, and does not give any initiatique guaranty."

The Convention of the Rosicrucians in Sweden concluded about one month prior to the beginning of the second World War. It made possible the putting into order of their affairs, before the anticipated calamity which befell them. They presented several documents, or Manifestoes, to James R. Whitcomb, delegate of the Imperator of America, attesting to their unity with the Rosicrucian Order, A.M.O.R.C., of North and South America, and deploring the clandestine movements which sought to interfere with the work of the authentic Order. A manifesto signed by the Grand Master and Grand Secretary of the Rosicrucian Grand Lodge of Denmark, in Copenhagen, on the 14th of August, 1939, on the occasion of their National Convention, and referring to the above-mentioned delegates of A.M.O.R.C. from America, states:

"Their stay, even though brief, has done much to cement the two jurisdictions—theirs of North and South America and ours of Denmark—into closer understanding and mutual support, for the spread of

the ancient Rosicrucian teachings, which we perpetuate as a Sacred Heritage."

The Supreme Council of the Martinist Order and Synarchy of the United States was legally incorporated on the 3rd day of August, 1938, in the State of California. Having been fraternally affiliated with the Rosicrucian Order in Europe for nearly two centuries, it was proper that it should also be closely aligned with the Rosicrucian Order's activities in America. The transition of the Illustrious Imperator of America, Dr. H. Spencer Lewis, occurred on Wednesday, August 2, 1939, at 3:15 P.M., Pacific Standard Time, in San Jose, California, the Sovereign Sanctuary of the A.M.O.R.C. for North and South America. It therefore became necessary that his authority as Sovereign Legate and Supreme Grand Master of the Traditional Martinist Order be transferred to another. By order of the Supreme Council of the Traditional Martinist Order of France, which was the sponsor of the American jurisdiction, the charters and manifestoes of authority granted to Dr. H. Spencer Lewis were then transferred to his son, Ralph M. Lewis. Ralph M. Lewis was his traditional and *elected* successor as Imperator for the Rosicrucian Order, A.M.O.R.C., for North and South America. He was duly elected and proclaimed Imperator by the Board of Directors of

the Supreme Grand Lodge of A∴M∴O∴R∴C∴, on Saturday, August 12, 1939. He had served as Supreme Secretary of the Order for fifteen years. On this same occasion, Cecil A. Poole, who had been the former Director of the Latin-American division of AMORC, was elected the Supreme Secretary and Treasurer of the Rosicrucian Order, AMORC, for North and South America. A proclamation to the entire membership of the Grand Lodge of the Order, announcing these changes, was made in the October, 1939, issue of the *Rosicrucian Digest,* the official periodical of the A.M.O.R.C.

On March 7, 1940, in an official communication to the Imperator, Ralph M. Lewis, the Acting Secretary of *The International Supreme Council of the Order Rosae Crucis,* Mademoiselle Jeanne Guesdon, notified him as to the results of an election held by that body, as follows: "I must say that they are all unanimous in their wish to have you, Ralph M. Lewis, as President of the International Supreme Council."

DEVELOPMENT AND EXPANSION
IN FRANCE

THE traditional Rose-Croix of France, following its custom of small secret bodies meeting as Rosicrucian lodges scattered throughout the nation, was rapidly diminishing by its own admission. The two great World Wars had taken their toll of the members. The economic plight in which France found herself following these catastrophes had made it impossible for the Order of the Rose-Croix to conduct even the most conservative program for rehabilitation and expansion. Furthermore, at the International Conventions held in France and Belgium, which are referred to in the previous chapters, it was expressed by the Venerables of the Rose-Croix that the more liberal times, the growth of population, and the increasing opposition to the enlightened tenets of the Order by materialistic movements necessitated changes in its policies.

The seclusion in France of the Rose-Croix was denying many persons worthy of the teachings knowledge of where it existed and how to contact

it. The Venerables, therefore, realized the need for a revitalization of the Rosicrucian Order in France. They had previously given the AMORC of the International Jurisdiction, with its See in America, their approval to extend the teachings privately to qualified initiated members for study in their home sanctums (p. 196). They desired that the same modern methods used by AMORC in America be adapted to France. However, they believed themselves not prepared to accomplish this purpose. Consequently, it was decided that the AMORC of America should establish a Grand Lodge of its own in France and extend the Order's activities in like manner in that nation. This modern activity would be concomitant with the remnants of the old Rose-Croix.

For some years, Mlle. Jeanne Guesdon, a native of France, residing in Villeneuve-Saint-Georges, a suburb of Paris, had been a member of the Rose-Croix, France, and a scholar of the traditional esoteric orders. She was recognized as a brilliant student of mysticism and metaphysics and had functioned for several years as liasion officer between Dr. H. Spencer Lewis and certain of the mystical bodies of Europe. In addition to these activities, she was also a member of the AMORC of America and was highly enthusiastic about its expansion program

and its preparation and manner of presenting the Rosicrucian teachings.

Dr. H. Spencer Lewis, the incumbent Imperator of AMORC, conferred with Mlle. Guesdon with regard to her assisting in the voluminous and tedious work of translating the modern form of the teachings and rituals into the French language. She agreed to undertake this task and immediately began her voluntary labor of love. The Imperator's transition occurred before much of this work could be accomplished. Following this, World War II and the Nazi occupation of France further inhibited Mlle. Guesdon's efforts. After World War II, the newly presiding Imperator, Ralph M. Lewis, journeyed to France to confer with Mlle. Guesdon, and preparation for the AMORC in France was renewed with vigor.

In July, 1954, Mlle. Guesdon attended the International Rosicrucian Convention in San Jose and conferred with the Supreme Council there. She passed through transition suddenly in March, 1955, after a short illness. The work of AMORC in France had, nevertheless, been established by her sacrifice, with the full cooperation and further direction of the Imperator, Ralph M. Lewis.

Although a tremendous amount of effort had been expended, the organization of AMORC in

France was still in a rudimentary stage. The transition of Mlle. Guesdon produced a temporary state of confusion. She had clerical assistance but no one as yet qualified to succeed her as Grand Secretary of AMORC, France. The Imperator was obliged to fly to France from America to try to surmount the difficulties. He was able to engage the voluntary services of the illustrious Grand Master of Sweden, Albin Roimer, who generously divided his time between his own jurisdiction and that of France in order to administer the latter's affairs temporarily. This he did with true Rosicrucian fraternal spirit. It became obvious, however, that this arrangement was not expedient and would actually interfere with the functioning of both the French and Swedish jurisdictions.

For some time, Mlle. Guesdon had been impressed with the sincerity, intelligence, and dynamic personality of a young frater of the Order, Raymond Bernard, who lived in southern France. She had corresponded with the Imperator of AMORC with regard to him, expressing the hope that sometime she might prevail upon Frater Bernard to assist her with the burdens of the growing Order in France. She passed through transition before realizing this hope. The Imperator, conscious of the necessity of a permanent direction for AMORC France and a

need to release the Grand Master of Sweden from his burden, approached Frater Bernard. In 1955, they met in conference with Grand Master Roimer in France. Not long after this conference, Frater Raymond Bernard assumed the office of Administrator of AMORC France. But with the transition of Mlle. Guesdon, there was now actually no official officer of AMORC in France.

The confidence in Raymond Bernard which Mlle. Guesdon had expressed, as well as the favorable impression he had created upon the Imperator, were substantiated by his efforts. He not only had a highly evolved mystical consciousness and mentality, but an excellent academic education and administrative ability. He followed the instructions of the Imperator of AMORC explicitly, adopting the modern methods proposed to him. As a result, the AMORC France membership grew rapidly. AMORC France now has a Grand Lodge and includes in its jurisdiction Switzerland, Belgium, and the French-speaking countries of North and West Africa and elsewhere throughout the world. Pronaoi and chapters of enthusiastic members soon grew into lodges.

Mlle. Guesdon began the work of AMORC in France in her own home and even constructed a small administration office on her property. She

bequeathed this property to AMORC France, in trust for the Supreme Grand Lodge of the Order. The AMORC in France, however, soon outgrew the original facilities and has since acquired much adjoining property at Villeneuve-Saint-Georges. It has beautifully landscaped these properties and built modern administration buildings, as well as an attractive temple for ritualistic and ceremonial work.

In July, 1959, Frater Bernard, with his wife Yvonne, who has ably assisted him, attended the International Rosicrucian Convention in San Jose. While there, he was duly vested with the honorable title and authority of Grand Master of AMORC France. The ritualistic stole and emblems of office were conferred upon him in the Supreme Temple in Rosicrucian Park. Subsequently, in 1962, in company with other officers of the Order, he again journeyed to the International Convention in San Jose. Also, he has traveled extensively throughout Europe and Africa, speaking to subordinate bodies of AMORC France.

With the growth of AMORC membership in Europe and with the realization that comparatively few of the many members could journey to America for an International Convention, a similar convention was decided upon for Europe. The first of

these modern conclaves was held in Geneva, Switzerland, in October, 1960. The second of these biennial conventions was held in Paris (1962), with hundreds of Rosicrucians from throughout Europe in attendance. Grand Lodge officers of Sweden, Denmark, Holland, England, and Italy were present. The Imperator presided at the memorable event. A similar function of magnitude was held in Paris in September, 1964.

The World Convention of AMORC was held in Montreux, Switzerland, in September 1973. There were 2,000 members from every continent in attendance. World Conventions were subsequently held at the See of the Order in Rosicrucian Park, San Jose, California.

In August 1977, the largest World Convention of the Rosicrucian Order, AMORC, was held in Paris with an attendance of 8,000 members. At the Convention Frater Christian Bernard, formerly Grand Secretary of the Grand Lodge for the French-speaking countries, was installed as Grand Master of the same jurisdiction. He succeeded his father, Raymond Bernard. The latter, however, retained the exalted office of Supreme Legate of AMORC for Europe. Raymond Bernard also remained as a member of the Board of Directors of the Supreme Grand Lodge of the Ancient Mystical Order Rosae Crucis.

·OTHER WORLD-WIDE ROSICRUCIAN ACTIVITIES

N February 1976 the Nordic Grand Lodge of the Rosicrucian Order, A.M.O.R.C., was legally established in Sweden. This resulted in a merger of the Grand Lodges of Sweden and of Denmark-Norway, and included in the expanded jurisdiction Finland, Iceland, and Greenland which had not previously been served in this way. This unity resulted in a central administration office which provided much greater efficiency and service to the members in their respective languages. Frater Irving Söderlund directed the administrative office, at first in the capacity of Secretary General, but was elevated to the office of Grand Master at the world convention held in Paris in August 1977.

There are a number of subordinate bodies in the newly combined countries of this Scandinavian jurisdiction.

In recent years several books of the Rosicrucian Library have been translated into Swedish and other Nordic languages, and are beautifully printed and publicly circulated.

Following World War II, an effort was made by the Imperator of AMORC to reactivate the defunct Rosicrucian Order in Italy. The former illustrious Grand Master, Dunstano Cancellieri, a true venerable, resided in Tunisia during World War II. While there, he translated many of the English monographs into Italian. It was also his intention to rehabilitate the Order in Italy along the lines of AMORC elsewhere. He passed through transition before accomplishing his splendid purpose.

In more recent years, the work of the Grand Lodge of Italy was reactivated under the guidance of the Supreme Legate for AMORC in Europe, Frater Raymond Bernard. With the decline of religious opposition in Italy, the work began to make progress.

In August 1974 the Imperator installed Soror Irene Zaccaria as Grand Master of AMORC Italy. She had previously served as Administrative Secretary of the Grand Lodge in Rome. The installation took place in the beautiful temple of the Geneva Lodge of AMORC in Switzerland. The Rosicrucian Grand Lodge of AMORC in Italy is excellently administered by Soror Zaccaria. It has published Rosicrucian books, bulletins, and periodicals in the Italian language. The official monographs are also in Italian

and correspond to those authorized by the Supreme Grand Lodge.

During World War II, the eminent Grand Master of AMORC in Great Britain, Raymund Andrea, found it impossible to continue the activities of the Order in that jurisdiction. It was not possible to prepare and disseminate the teachings. The Imperator then decreed that the Grand Lodge in the United States should assume the responsibility of forwarding all Rosicrucian instructions to the members throughout the British Isles. At that time, British members could not remit dues to the United States because of government restrictions on exporting funds from their country. Upon an appeal from the Imperator, American members rallied to the cause and personally donated an amount sufficient for defraying the expense of carrying the memberships of the British fratres and sorores for several years.

At the conclusion of the war, correspondence between the Imperator and Grand Master Raymund Andrea revealed the fact that the British jurisdiction was not able to continue its prewar activities. Consequently, in the fall of 1945, the Imperator journeyed to Bristol to confer with Frater Andrea on this momentous matter. After a thorough analysis of the situation, a manifesto was signed on

October 25, 1945, which stated in part: "The juris-diction of the Rosicrucian Order (AMORC) of Great Britain and the Ancient, Mystical Order Rosae Crucis (A.M.O.R.C.) of North and South America, shall, after the date finally appearing below, coordinate, for the joint dissemination of the Rosicrucian teachings and the rehabilitation of the Rosicrucian Order in England, Ireland, Scotland, and Wales."

Subsequently, administrative problems made it necessary that an administration office be estab-lished in London by the Supreme Grand Lodge for the better servicing of members' needs. By 1965, the work had grown to such proportions that the office in London was moved to Bognor Regis in Sussex, where the Order enjoyed a greater expanded area for work in a modern office building. In a new location in Colchester it later became known as the United Kingdom Administration Office. Frater Ian Clegg was appointed Secretary-Administrator.

Although there were many subordinate bodies of AMORC in Great Britain, none were ritualistically qualified to confer all of the traditional full degree initiations. Therefore, this essential phase of the Rosicrucian work in modern times was being neg-lected, a condition which the Imperator greatly de-plored. A ritualistic initiatory team for Great

Britain was finally established in London by the Imperator. This team has conferred the beautiful initiations upon several hundred members in recent years. The meticulous manner and observance of details in the performance of these initiations have been most creditable to the team.

Since the beginning of the middle of the twentieth century, conclaves of the Order, as conventions, have been held annually in London. Because of excellent organization and programming, these conventions have become exceptionally successful. They attract Rosicrucians not only from throughout the British Isles, but also from elsewhere in Europe and from America and Africa.

The Grand Lodge of Holland has gone through a complete reorganization. Under the leadership of Grand Master E. van Drenthem Soesman its membership has considerably increased, and it now has numerous subordinate bodies. Its Administration Office and Temple are located in its own building in The Hague.

In Germany the traditions and historical aspects of the Order gave impetus to its regeneration after World War II. It is now one of the most progressive Grand Lodges in Europe. The Grand Lodge is located in scenic Baden-Baden. It is most efficiently directed by its Grand Master Wilhelm Raab.

CHAPTER XII

PROGRAM OF DECENTRALIZATION

———

ROSICRUCIAN activity in Latin America had increased considerably. The Latin-American peoples were generally psychologically more disposed to the study of mysticism and the philosophical teachings of the Order than most other nationalities. Pronaoi, chapters, and lodges sprang up throughout Central and South America in the decades following World War II. Extensive promotional campaigns of a dignified and educational nature further stimulated interest in the Rosicrucian Order on the part of the general public. The entire Rosicrucian library of books was eventually translated into Spanish and disseminated throughout the Latin world. All the teachings, rituals, and instructions of the Order were made available in the Spanish language.

The Imperator and Frater Cecil A. Poole, then the Supreme Secretary, made numerous journeys to Rosicrucian subordinate bodies in the Latin countries. They took part in their conclaves (conventions) and conferred with their officers. Qualified members were selected as Grand Councilors voluntarily

to assist officers and members in the respective countries of Latin America.

With the increased political turbulence throughout the world in the middle years of this century, the Supreme and Grand Lodges of AMORC were faced with many administrative problems. It became more and more difficult to serve the members in some of the distant countries. A serious inconvenience to student Rosicrucians was the delay of surface mail for many weeks. The difficulty of exporting monies from some countries imposed an additional economic problem upon the member and the Grand Lodge which served him from the United States. The high cost of labor for administration in the United States, plus the need to maintain dues at a much lower rate for members in countries elsewhere, made a program of decentralization advisable.

Membership in Brazil had grown rapidly. However, its distance from the Grand Lodge and its dependence upon the facilities of that body increased administrative problems. The Imperator, accompanied by the Grand Regional Administrator, Arthur C. Piepenbrink, made a journey to Brazil to confer with officers of the lodges in Rio de Janeiro and São Paulo. As a result of these conferences, two Brazilian members, Maria Moura and

Jose de Oliveira Paulo, were delegated to translate the monographs and all doctrinal and ritualistic materials into the Portuguese language, a truly stupendous undertaking.

Finally, in 1956, the Grand Lodge of Brazil was regularly organized and established. It became subordinate to the Imperator and the Supreme Grand Lodge. Notwithstanding a number of serious economic cycles within Brazil, AMORC flourished. Maria Moura was duly appointed Grand Secretary of AMORC Brazil and Jose de Oliveira Paulo, Grand Treasurer. Under their capable direction and organization, with the full cooperation of the Supreme Grand Lodge, a magnificent administration building was erected to house the growing staff in Curitiba, in the State of Paraná.

In September, 1964, adjoining the Brazilian administration building of like size and design, a splendid Grand Lodge temple of Egyptian-style architecture was completed. Officers of the Supreme Grand Lodge in San Jose personally participated in the formal and inspiring dedication ceremony of the temple upon the occasion of the Brazilian National Rosicrucian Convention, held for the first time in that same year. Grand Secretary Maria Moura (later Grand Master) had journeyed to San Jose in 1963 to attend the International Convention of the Order.

While there, she conferred with other Grand Lodge officers from throughout the world and made arrangements for the temple dedication. In October, 1970, the Imperator again visited Brazil, this time to dedicate another addition to the growing building complex in Curitiba, a large and beautiful auditorium, named for Dr. H. Spencer Lewis. The World Convention of AMORC was held in Curitiba, Brazil in 1975 with 2,000 members in attendance from throughout South, Central, and North America as well as Europe.

Similar circumstances which had necessitated the establishment of the London Administrative Office and the Grand Lodge Administrative Office in Brazil now existed in other parts of the world. Members in Australasia, that is, Australia and New Zealand, were likewise plagued with long mail delays because of distance and complicated international regulations. It became apparent that some immediate relief must be provided them if the Order is to grow in those countries. The Imperator and other officers had on several occasions visited Australia and New Zealand officially. Their conferences with officers of the Order in those lands emphasized the urgency of the need for remedial measures.

Facilities for transmitting monographs and other membership materials to Australia and New Zea-

land were eventually established by means of air freight and subsequent special distribution in each of said countries. This met with the full approval of the membership because it eliminated previous excessive delay in the receipt of study materials. This was accomplished in 1976.

Further conferences of the Supreme Council of AMORC during 1964 resulted in resolutions passed by that body that other administrative offices should be established in such areas of the world as circumstances required. Thus the international aspect of the Order was intensified, its single legal jurisdiction being retained even though a decentralization of its activities was necessary. But no longer could one central headquarters provide all of the facilities for world-wide membership. However, the See of the Order in San Jose for many reasons would need to conduct exclusively certain activities which could not be duplicated elsewhere.

On May 4, 1966, the Order suffered the loss of Mrs. H. Spencer Lewis who passed through transition on that date. She had carried on a great number of labors begun by her husband, Dr. H. Spencer Lewis, and served to complement his mission in giving impetus to the Order's growth in the twentieth century.

Her absence left a vacancy on the Board of Directors which was subsequently filled by Raymond

Bernard. Upon his election, he was assigned the coordination of Rosicrucian activities in Europe, assuming the role of Supreme Legate for Europe.

Frater Cecil A. Poole retired as Supreme Treasurer but remains on the Board of the Supreme Grand Lodge as Vice President. By September 1977, the full complement of officers at the See in San Jose read as follows:

SUPREME GRAND LODGE

Ralph M. Lewis	Imperator
Cecil A. Poole	Vice-President
Arthur C. Piepenbrink	Secretary, Treasurer
Raymond Bernard	Legate for Europe
Gladys Lewis	

GRAND LODGE

Robert E. Daniels	Grand Master
Leonard J. Ziebel	Grand Secretary
Edward L. Fisher	Grand Treasurer
Mario Salas	Grand Regional Administrator

A FEW WORDS TO THOSE WHO ARE STRANGERS

If you, Reader, are not a member of the Rosicrucian Order, we wish to take this opportunity to greet you, and to thank you for the opportunity of placing in your hands this history of the organization with the questions and answers which further explain the ideals and purposes of the Rosicrucians.

HISTORY OF THE ORDER

There are two ways by which this book may have come into your hands: first, through the courtesy of some member or interested person who has believed that you would be interested in its contents; second, through your own acts whereby you have either purchased this book or borrowed it from the shelves of some public library. If the book is in your hands through your own act, it is an indication of your curiosity or your interest.

We hope, therefore, that you have found in the history of the organization such information as satisfies your desire for facts, and that we have introduced ourselves to you sufficiently well to have you know us better and appreciate the real traditions of the Order as compared with the false beliefs and misunderstandings which have been so prevalent in the past centuries. There is, perhaps, no other organization in the world that has been so greatly misunderstood as the Rosicrucians.

We cannot say that all of this is due to a brief or mysterious presentation of the history, for much is also due to the writings of many novelists, who have found in the history and traditions of the Order the basis for many weird, fantastic, and romantic plots. As stated in the Introduction to this history, there was a time when such stories as *Zanoni*, by Bulwer-Lytton, served their purpose in revealing the existence of the organization, but surrounded

it with a cloak of mystery and fantasy, which left the seeker for its portals doubtful of any success in his search. For almost a century, the fictitious mystery which enveloped the Rosicrucian Order has been dispelled by the illumination of research and publicity.

Today, nearly all modern and comprehensive encyclopedias give an accurate account of the purposes and history of the A.M.O.R.C. Even abridged dictionaries refer to it, and the veil of mystery as to its existence and activities has fortunately been lifted. Excellent accounts, brief but authoritative references to the Rosicrucian Order of the past and present, may be found in the 14th Revised Edition of the *Encyclopaedia Britannica, New Standard Encyclopedia, Winston's Cumulative Loose-Leaf Encyclopedia and Dictionary, Modern Encyclopedia, Webster's Unabridged Dictionary, Funk & Wagnalls' Unabridged Dictionary,* and many others.

The Rosicrucian Order today throughout the world represents a movement of high idealism and high purpose. It has become a public movement among men and women of repute and wide affairs and is no longer the closed council for restricted membership. Its work has broadened into many channels and its place in the evolution of modern civilization has become fixed and well recognized.

If you are interested in knowing more about the

organization or desire to share its teachings and practices, you are cordially invited to make further inquiry; and if your expressions are sincere and it is apparent that more than curiosity prompts your inquiry, you will receive that encouragement which will enable you to have your desires fulfilled.

In order that the Secretary may competently take care of your inquiry and know that you have already read this book and are familiar with the facts contained therein, he would thank you to address your letter to the department name given below.

Scribe R. Q. A.

Rosicrucian Order, AMORC

Rosicrucian Park, San Jose, Calif. 95191, U.S.A.

PART TWO

QUESTIONS

AND

ANSWERS

IMPORTANT INSTRUCTIONS

The questions presented in the following pages have been carefully selected from among the many hundreds asked by those who are interested in the activities and principles of the Rosicrucian Order. Such questions constitute a large part of the correspondence sent to the General Secretary of the Order in America, and from his records a list of questions from among those most frequently asked was carefully compiled.

The answers to the questions given in the following pages have been prepared by those who are most familiar with the points covered by the questions, and represent official, authentic statements. In most cases the questions have been answered more elaborately and in more detail than they are usually answered in correspondence.

The reader of this book will find these questions and answers a valuable aid in the comprehension of the nature of the Rosicrucian Order, its activities, principles, ideals, and doctrines. Even members of the organization will find these illuminating and helpful, especially since they represent official viewpoints.

The subjects have been indexed and cross-indexed for ready reference, and the information contained

therein, in conjunction with the history of the organization, gives one of the most complete outlines of the nature and work of the real Rosicrucian Order ever presented to the public.

QUESTIONS AND ANSWERS

No. 1

Q. Do the Rosicrucians constitute a religious cult?

A. The Rosicrucians do not constitute a cult, either religious or otherwise. They constitute a fraternity of men and women like any other fraternity or brotherhood. The members of the organization are of every religious denomination, and are not asked to change their religious beliefs in any way. Therefore, the organization is not a cult.

No. 2

Q. Do the Rosicrucians in each country have a great leader or founder who is their absolute ruler, and to whom allegiance must be pledged?

A. The organization in every country is physically formed like a society or other organization of men and women, with chief executives equivalent to president, vice-president, secretaries, treasurers, and recorders. There are no national or international founders, leaders, or discoverers, to whom personal allegiance must be pledged at any time or in any manner. All officers are elected and do not hold their positions by any super virtue or

Divine decree that is unique to each as an individual. The chief executives of each branch in each land are on an equal basis, constituting an international advisory council like the Board of Directors of a business concern.

No. 3

Q. Are there any secret oaths or any form of allegiance to individuals which must be subscribed to before or after joining the organization?

A. There are no real "secret oaths" in connection with the organization whatsoever. There are no oaths or pledges which contain secret agreements or implied penalties for violations. No pledges are asked by the brotherhood in behalf of allegiance to any individual except obedience to the rules and regulations of the organization, its constitution, and the executive decisions of the officers who are its representatives.

No. 4

Q. Is one bound for an entire lifetime to the Order by taking any oaths or pledges?

A. You are freely permitted to partake of the benefits of the Order and share in its great work, and just as freely are you permitted to resign from it and sever all connections. Of course, the promise to keep secret the few passwords or signs by which

members may be easily identified is to be respected by every man and woman as a moral obligation even after he believes it desirable to withdraw from the organization. It must be said in fairness to all concerned that the few who do drop out of the ranks of the Order for one reason or another in each country have generally held in high esteem the ethical and moral ideals of the organization and have, therefore, kept their promises in regard to the secret elements of passwords, grips, signs, and so forth.

No. 5

Q. Are there any secret agreements or binding obligations on the part of members which may interfere with their religious, political, social, or business activities?

A. Nothing is ever asked of a member in the Order, or before he becomes a member, which will force him to do anything that will interfere with his righteous beliefs and moral obligations to God, the members of his family, or his country. Certainly, there is nothing in the work of the organization that will interfere with any person's activities in connection with legal and proper business matters, or with the proper ethical and moral social relations in the world. When any special work of any kind is to be done that calls for a personal sacrifice of time

and interest in behalf of a member, volunteers are asked to serve that purpose, and no one is obligated to do that which he cannot easily do, or do without injury to his own interests.

No. 6

Q. Are the members of the Order bound in such financial manner as to make them obliged to meet assessments or special taxes of any kind?

A. No assessments have ever been made and no *obligations* other than the nominal monthly dues are required in each lodge to meet the incidental expenses and general operating accounts.

No. 7

Q. Why are there any monthly dues when one has always been told that the high spiritual teachings are given without a price?

A. This question is based upon the assumption that the nominal dues universally charged by the Rosicrucian organization constitute payment for the teachings. This is a mistake. The dues have nothing to do with the instruction work whatsoever. Every branch of the organization must have general assembly rooms in which the classes can come together for their lectures, discussions, and general activities. Some means must be devised for the payment of the monthly rent, electric light, and general operating expenses.

QUESTIONS AND ANSWERS

Who will pay these monthly dues? The master of the classes, who is giving all of his spare time to helping in the work because of his enthusiasm, or the students themselves on the basis of an apportionment of the actual amount involved? No organization can avoid incurring operational expense.

If any lodge could meet in a proper hall or assembly place, properly equipped with necessary paraphernalia, without having to buy any equipment or having to pay carpenters, electricians, painters, decorators, and others for making the necessary equipment, and without paying any rent or paying for any electricity or heat, then the members might come together without any cost to themselves. Since this is not possible, dues are charged by each Lodge or Chapter and the amounts of the monthly dues vary in accordance with the operating expenses of the individual bodies. Since no salaries are paid to the masters, teachers, or secretaries in these lodges, the dues are nominal.

To make the instructions available by correspondence, it was necessary to devise some means for defraying the cost of postage, stationery, typewriting, and the printing of such forms and pieces of literature as are necessary to make the seeker acquainted with the Rosicrucians. In addition to this, the investment in automatic machinery for the

addressing of envelopes, filing of reports, as well as the rent and lighting of the many offices necessary for such correspondence work, requires some form of proportionate division of operating expenses. Nominal monthly dues constitute the only logical manner to take care of this matter; but, again, such dues do not pay for the teachings. If those who desire personal instruction could travel from the various parts of the world to the Grand Lodge and thereby save the necessity of postage and stationery, and if they would be willing to meet out in an open valley where the officers and teachers could come without any expense for travelling, and if all other incidental expenses could be avoided in this way while the teachers gave personal instruction to the seekers, there would be no necessity for monthly dues in connection with personal instruction. Granting that the lessons and teachings are absolutely free, there still remains the problem of getting these instructions from the various central points to the students. In this, also, lies an element of cost.

No. 8

Q. Do not some organizations extend membership on a purely voluntary donation basis, permitting the member to pay as little or as much as he chooses?

QUESTIONS AND ANSWERS

A. Yes, there are several esoteric organizations in America which claim that they are operating solely upon a voluntary donation basis. An investigation of these movements revealed, however, an entirely different system than that used by the Rosicrucian Order. These others extend membership upon a purely voluntary basis, and that means that the member may donate anything from twenty-five cents a month to five dollars a month. But, in exchange for this voluntary donation, the member receives nothing but affiliation with the organization and perhaps an occasional letter of greetings, which is a stereotyped letter sent to all members that reads identically the same for all. If such members desire to take up the studies and teachings of the organization to which they belong, they find it necessary to buy the many books published by the organization, and they find that these books are *not* given or offered on a voluntary donation basis, but sold at a definite price. We see, therefore, that the voluntary donation merely covers membership, while the instructions and teachings must be paid for by the purchase of books. The Rosicrucian Order sells no books containing its private teachings. The nominal monthly dues—which are hardly more than any sincere member would voluntarily offer as a donation—cover every benefit of member-

ship, which means more than merely a monthly letter. The magazine is sent monthly to every member, and throughout the year hundreds of personal, especially dictated and written letters of advice and instruction are included in the general membership benefits, as well as the privilege of attendance at lodges and affiliation with the various activities of the organization. In addition, the biweekly private instructions are given to the members without requiring the purchase of any books or pamphlets. It is a fact demonstrated to practically every member of the Order that the amount of money paid in a year as dues is less than what the average seeker spends in the purchase of books, and yet the organization offers many benefits in addition to the teachings, which could not be expected or asked for if the student were merely the purchaser of books from a publishing company.

No. 9

Q. Has the Order ever tried to operate on a voluntary donation basis?

A. After the Order in North America had been operating for a number of years with nominal monthly dues, the matter of adopting voluntary donations as a basis for supporting the general operating expenses was submitted to every lodge of the organization and to every member in every

lodge. The vote showed that ninety-seven per cent of the members believed that the definite monthly amount decreed by the individual lodges was the better system inasmuch as it put every member upon an equal basis in sharing the expense of the operating expenditures and did not throw the burden of a monthly deficit upon the several leaders in each group. The members themselves proclaimed that the knowledge that their voluntary donations left a deficit to be met by those who were giving so freely of their services in addition to a proportionate donation to the general funds made them feel uneasy, undutiful, and guilty of a lack of appreciation of the benefits they were receiving.

It was found from the records and reports of other organizations that those who insisted upon the voluntary donation were those who sought to take advantage of the liberal method to contribute less than their proper portion. If it were not for the sale of books and paraphernalia by many organizations that operate on a voluntary donation basis, they would not be able to carry on their work with any system or degree of efficiency.

No. 10

Q. Are the members required to buy robes, paraphernalia, or devices of any kind?

A. The general members *are not required* to buy

robes, equipment, devices, instructions, or material things of any kind. Everything that is necessary for the study of the teachings and the proper development of the work is supplied without cost by the Order. Where there are lodges carrying on the Egyptian ritual ceremonies and the demonstrations of the natural and divine laws, the officers wear Oriental robes which they furnish themselves voluntarily, and the equipment is generally supplied by voluntary donations on the part of those most interested in the work.

No. 11

Q. Who prepares the teachings and the lessons given by the Order?

A. Since the teachings are not the discovery of some self-appointed leader or founder of the organization and since they are not the personal opinion of some philosophic individual, the lessons are impersonal and prepared not by a single individual, but by groups of individuals in the highest grades of the teachings in the various lodges of the Order throughout the world. The teachings are, therefore, not stereotyped or in fixed form, but continually evolving and becoming enlarged and improved through newer discoveries, newer tests, and newer demonstrations in the many lodges. This gives us another excellent explanation of why the Order has

never permitted its teachings to be put into books or other printed form. Such books would soon become obsolete so far as the revised teachings are concerned, and could not possibly be kept up to the minute in such matters as are of the utmost importance to the individual student. International conventions discuss the great problems of the teachings, as well as the great problems of the affairs of man, and bring forth additional instruction and advice to be added to the lectures for the benefit of all.

An International Research Council in every jurisdiction contributes freely to the teachings and the extension of various systems of help and advice. Likewise, scientific research is conducted by the Order in its own laboratories. Therefore, the teachings are uniform and free from personal opinion and personal bias. There is probably no other system of instruction as flexible, as modern, and as progressive as this.

No. 12

Q. Is it necessary for the members to memorize a great many laws and principles as well as the many lessons?

A. Except for the ritualistic parts, dramatized by the officers in the various lodges, there is nothing to be memorized by any member. The lectures and

lessons are so worded and so interestingly presented with arguments, demonstrations, illustrations, analogies, and similes that the student's interest is held without conscious effort on his part, and he absorbs the knowledge which becomes a part of his memory without becoming aware of the process of memorizing.

The Rockefeller Foundation for education has stated that this sort of instruction is the most ideal and typifies the perfect method of conveying knowledge from one mind to another. Notebooks are kept by members who wish to aid their memory and in them notations are made of important principles and laws as they are given. Reference is made to these notes at times when daily problems call for the application of the principles taught by the Order.

No. 13

Q. Do the Rosicrucians teach astrology or any other method of fortunetelling?

A. The Rosicrucian organization does not teach astrology or any other method of prognosticating the future. It considers astrology to be an imperfect science and not an art in the true meaning of the word. Being evolved through ages of experimentation and testing, at the present time astrology is far from being efficient in predicting all the affairs of life. The fundamental principles involved in

astrology are referred to in various lectures and lessons pertaining to the nature of the planets and the nature of our talents and dormant tendencies, but the making of horoscopes and the study of astrology are not included in the work because the absoluteness of the art is not demonstrable.

The Rosicrucians do not teach or include anything in their teachings that cannot be demonstrated by the individual members as absolute and dependable. Organizations claiming to be Rosicrucian or mystical, which include astrology as a prerequisite or as an important part of their work, are merely taking advantage of the fascination which astrology holds for so many. Although teaching astrology would help to meet the financial necessities of the organization, the Rosicrucian Order will not deal with crystal gazing or any other form of necromancy.

No. 14

Q. Do the Rosicrucians deal with spiritualistic demonstrations or means of communication with spirits?

A. The Rosicrucians do not teach anything that pertains to spiritualistic demonstrations or such doctrines as commonly understood. In fact, the Rosicrucian Order deplores the popular tendency to hold seances and dark room sessions, advising against the

systematic or occasional attempts to enter the trance state or any other state of an abnormal nature for the purpose of trying to communicate with so-called spirits.

No. 15

Q. Do the Rosicrucians believe that man has many forms of spiritual bodies and that he lives in these various bodies at various times?

A. The Rosicrucians teach that there are two planes of existence upon which man lives; namely, this earth plane with its material earthly problems and activities and another plane which is not this one. It does not attempt to explain how we live or how we function on the other plane. It has no knowledge to offer regarding a number of ethereal, spiritual, psychic bodies possessed by man which function on various planes; and it does not attempt to divide the nonmaterial or spiritual plane into various subdivisions and hypothetical, super subdivisions, as taught by various complex mystical systems which are devoted to the dissemination of puzzling philosophies.

No. 16

Q. Do the Rosicrucians believe that there are spirit entities, large or small, which hover in space and which may take possession of an earthly individual and influence him for good or bad?

QUESTIONS AND ANSWERS

A. The Rosicrucians have never taught the existence of elemental entities or evil spirits that may take possession of human beings. These teachings are a remnant of ancient Oriental superstitions and are revived in these modern days by schools of thought which cater to the credulous and the unlearned.

No. 17

Q. Do the Rosicrucians believe in black magic or the ability of one mind to injure another at a distance?

A. The Rosicrucians have said in all ages that the only power that black magic has is the fear which the unlearned have of it. The Rosicrucian teachings make most plain the fundamental fact that the cosmic space which intervenes between two humans at a distance from each other will not carry destructive thought vibrations since such vibrations are inharmonious and incongruous to its own constructive, divine nature. Evil thoughts directed toward another person do not leave the mind of the individual conceiving them and are reactive upon the individual attempting to radiate them. The teaching of the possibility of black magic by some modern schools has created a fear of it in the minds of those who do not understand the true cosmic laws, and this fear causes much suffering and dis-

comfort, which is immediately attributed to the thoughts of others and black magic.

No. 18

Q. Do the Rosicrucians still practice the art of alchemy or transmutation of base metals into gold?

A. In some of the higher lodges of the organization where complete laboratories are maintained for testing and proving many of nature's fundamental laws, the art of transmutation has been tested and a small amount of gold made from baser metals after a great many hours of diligent work and at a tremendous cost that was out of proportion to the value of the gold manufactured. In France, one of the great laboratories of the Order has been very successful in demonstrating to the scientific world the feasibility of the Rosicrucian principles of alchemy.

The Rosicrucians have always been accused of being the makers of gold because throughout the history of the organization it appears that its members and branches have always been well qualified to meet their financial obligations and enjoy many of the luxuries of life.

The progress and advancement which the members make as they go through the higher teachings of the Order impress strangers with the idea that some means of securing material wealth is given

to the students of the organization. The real art of alchemy practiced by every Rosicrucian organization, and every member of the organization, consists of transmuting the baser metals of a material, mental, and spiritual nature into the pure gold products of efficiency in action, prosperity in result, and happiness in attainment. This is the greatest of all the processes of transmutation and enables each member to master his own problems successfully and bring about such realizations of his dreams as may seem miraculous or mysterious to the uninitiated.

No. 19

Q. Do the Rosicrucians constitute a body of healers or a healing organization?

A. Throughout all the ages, many of the leaders of the Rosicrucian work have been valuable contributors to the art of physics, as it was originally called; or the science of therapeutics, as we understand it today. Many of these eminent men were discoverers of fundamental principles in connection with physiology and anatomy, as well as chemistry, thereby helping to establish the many great fundamental principles of healing, as well as revealing the real nature of disease and health.

The Order today teaches its members how to prevent disease through proper living. It also teaches how to cure and correct the violations of nature's

laws which generally result in disease or suffering and pain.

Many of the members of the organization become so fascinated with these principles dealing with health and the cure of disease that they make a special study of this branch of the teachings and take it up in addition to their regular profession. Such persons generally are physicians of other schools and add the Rosicrucian principles to their regular practice in order to secure more lasting results and more immediate changes in any physical condition.

But the Order does not specialize in the healing work by attempting to make healers of all its members or encouraging them to go out into the world as healers or practitioners. Throughout the entire studies, the members are advised to consult only the very best physicians in regard to any physical problem. *Neither medicine nor surgery is condemned by the Rosicrucian teachings,* but all systems are given their proper places in the world of therapeutics.

The Rosicrucian Order realizes that a real healer must be trained in the various systems of therapeutics to be highly efficient and that such physicians, using the Rosicrucian principles in addition to the other principles they have learned, will become the very best physicians. In the winter of 1939, the Rose-Croix Research Institute and Sanitarium was es-

tablished as a subsidiary activity of the Rosicrucian Order, A.M.O.R.C. This modern institution included the latest therapeutic equipment, such as X-ray, fluoroscope, metabolism apparatus, electrocardiograph, short wave, and dynotherapy instruments. In addition to the generally accepted systems of treatment, it employed the tried and tested Rosicrucian principles of healing.

No. 20

Q. Does the Order offer its healing services to its members?

A. For those members who cannot come in contact with physicians of the regular schools who are connected with the local branches of the Order, the organization itself offers to use the metaphysical principles taught by it to help those who are in mental or physical need. Such work is done gratuitously in a scientific manner, without any criticism or antagonism toward the regular schools of medicine and surgery.

It is a notable fact, however, that the members of the Order generally continue to improve in health as they go through the various lectures and lessons. It is also true that many finally reach a point where the need for special treatments of any kind is rare. The organization does have ways and means of doing those things which science

might call miracles and of helping in such cases where all other systems seem to have failed or where the problem is not understood in its right terms. Such service is given freely, and thousands of members in all parts of the country take advantage of it in emergencies for themselves or for members of their families. This service is one of the outstanding benefits given to the general membership.

No. 21

Q. Does the Rosicrucian Order insist that its members refrain from eating meat and become vegetarians; also, that they refrain from smoking and drinking?

A. The Rosicrucians do not attempt to change the habits and methods of living on the part of their members by *revolutionary reforms* or autocratic decrees. They recommend moderation in all things. The teachings gradually make plain to each member the nature of his own health and physical condition, and reveal to him what is best for him to eat under any or all circumstances.

Each member soon discovers whether he may, with any consistency, eat a diet exclusively of vegetables or a diet composed of vegetables and meat. When a member discovers the effect that his diet has upon his individual constitution and upon his individual stage of development, he will be better pre-

pared to adjust his method of living. He will do it with greater efficiency than if some universal, arbitrary rule were established for all members regardless of their individual needs. The same may be said in regard to fasting, smoking, drinking, or indulging in any of the other attractions or seeming necessities of the mind, body, or soul.

No. 22

Q. Is it true that the eating of animal flesh adds lower vibrations to the human system?

A. Such an idea is purely theoretical and there is nothing in the sciences or the esoteric laws that shows that the eating of cooked meats adds vibrations of a lower kind than does the eating of wheat, rye, eggs, or milk. Milk contains as much of the animal nature as cooked meat. And the same may be said of butter and of cheese.

Many persons who believe the theory that meat lowers the rate of vibrations of the human body do not hesitate to drink milk or to eat cheese and eggs. This reasoning is completely inconsistent and unrealistic. It is an extremist's viewpoint. It is true however from a chemical point of view, that the eating of raw meat or meat that is very rare will add a great deal of the chemical nature of the animal blood to the human blood, but this is not true of well-cooked meats.

QUESTIONS AND ANSWERS

No. 23

Q. Is it true that the eating of meat interferes with the spiritual vibrations of the human body?

A. Some modern schools of thought have added this idea to their teachings in order that they may have another peculiar idea to present to their students. Many of these modern schools have had to invent a complete set of new ideas and new teachings in order to make their systems quite distinctive and unique. In their ambition to be very original with their teachings, they have promulgated ideas that are not only unsound, but ridiculous and contrary to natural law. However, the very uniqueness of such systems attracts the attention of those persons who are ever seeking new ideas, and especially peculiar ideas; and, of course, we find such persons usually fanatical and irrational in much of their thinking and acting. The truth of the matter is that man is born essentially spiritual, with as much divine essence in his soul as he will ever acquire. There is no way by which the soul essence in the human body can be added to or subtracted from in any way. The soul of man is something so infinite, so immortal, and so superior to conditions and elements of this earth plane, that nothing of a material nature can affect it. Neither disease nor sin affects the soul as far as its essential divine essence is con-

cerned. Man's consciousness and his character may be contaminated by sin and by disease of the mind or body; but these things cannot affect the infinite soul within him, for this infinite soul is ever and continuously a part of the Divine Soul of the universe and a part of God Himself. Therefore, the statement that certain exercises or certain actions will add to the "development" of the soul, in either essence or quantity, is absurd, as also is the statement that anything we eat or anything we drink may subtract from or change or modify the divine essence of which the soul is composed. The development of spirituality in a man or woman is the development of comprehension and understanding; it pertains to self-domination and man's relationship to the universe. It is not a development of the soul essence. Therefore, food cannot affect this divine essence, and only those leaders, teachers, or schools which are seeking to take advantage of the misconception of these facts on the part of seekers for the real truth will teach such an idea. Furthermore, your spiritual development will be indicated to others more clearly by what comes out of your mouth than by what goes into it, as the very true statement in the Bible explains, where we are reminded that more important than the food that passes through the mouth are the expressions which come out of the mouth. Then,

again, we have the words from that famous Sermon on the Mount, which may be read as:

"Be not anxious for your life,

What you shall eat and drink,

Or wherewithal you shall be clothed;

Is not the *life* more than the meat, and

the body more than the raiment?"

No. 24

Q. Do the Rosicrucians believe that there are millions of individual souls in the universe or just one soul?

A. The Rosicrucians believe and have always believed that there is but one soul in the universe, and that is the universal soul or the universal consciousness of God. Furthermore, the Rosicrucians have always taught that the essence of that universal soul resides in each being that possesses soul. And this essence is never separated from the universal soul nor is ever an entity in such a sense as to make it independent and individual. The soul expression of each person or, in other words, the expression of the soul in each of us, through the medium of the physical body and through the channel of our education and comprehension of things, may be quite different and thereby give us those characteristics or traits of personality which we interpret as individuality. These distinctive traits are not of the soul,

but of the characteristics or traits of personality that manifest through the physical body. We interpret these as individuality. In this sense, mankind is one universal brotherhood, being Sons and Daughters of God through the Fatherhood of God. This is the fundamental principle upon which universal brotherhood is understood by the Rosicrucians. All modern mystic teachings and even some popular *personal* conceptions of the Rosicrucian teachings which claim that man has an individual soul are inconsistent with the real and original teachings of the Rosicrucians.

No. 25

Q. Has man only one body and one soul?

A. As has been intimated, the Rosicrucians have always been rational and scientific in their postulations, and they say that so far as actual knowledge of conditions is concerned, they know of only one body and that is the physical body. We may stretch the use of a term and call the soul a spiritual body within man if we choose to do so, or we may call it the psychic body or astral body. In this case, man would possess two bodies, the physical body and that which is not physical. But to say that man has a physical body, an astral body, a desire body, a mental body, and several others is simply to state a theoretical postulation devised solely to confound

the acts of life and present a very puzzling and mysterious system of mysticism to keep the student ever trying to fathom the unfathomable and continuously blaming his lack of comprehension of the teachings for his lack of mastership.

It is an incontrovertible fact that no teacher of this sort of complex existence has ever been able to demonstrate his ability to function exclusively or partially in any one of these numerous bodies, nor has he been able to teach his students to function in one of these bodies successfully enough to enable them to prove to their own satisfaction that there are such bodies.

The Rosicrucians hold fast to the sane and rational law that that which cannot be demonstrated by another or which is not demonstrable to oneself cannot be classed as knowledge or fact. This keeps Rosicrucian students from sailing into the clouds of ethereal, hypothetical principles and away from the sane and solid facts of life.

No. 26

Q. Do the real Rosicrucians teach that it is possible for a man to live eternally in the same body?

A. The true Rosicrucians do not teach this and have never taught it as a physical possibility. They understand too well the universal laws of na-

ture, which include the divine laws as well. They know that one of the fundamental laws of all material manifestation is the law of change. Nothing that exists at this moment is identically as it was an hour, a week, a month, or a year ago. Man's body is susceptible to this law and governed by it just as is all other matter with which we are acquainted. The soul of man, or the divine essence which animates him, is the only part of man which is immaterial and not subject to the law of change.

It is impossible for man to live continuously or eternally in the same physical body. In fact, the physical body which man now occupies is not the same physical body in all of its elements which it was five years ago, or ten years ago. Every part of the body is being remade to replace that which is worn out or discarded. Sooner or later the breaking-down processes of the human body work more rapidly than the constructive processes, and eventually the physical body is cast off and rejected.

This is an inevitable law of nature, and there is absolutely no record to be found in any of the sacred, mystical, occult, or scientific teachings of the world which disproves it. Many of the popular teachers, who twenty or thirty years ago promulgated the idea of the possibility of very long life in the same physi-

cal body, have passed through transition and are gone from this plane. Most of them either sold secret, private courses of instruction which were claimed to teach one how to live without transition, or they sold secretly and privately to their students innocuous remedies which they claimed to have invented, which were supposed to prevent old age. Those modern teachers or lecturers who advocate this idea at the present time are simply catering to the gullibility of persons who believe it is possible to prevent old age or transition. No Rosicrucian of the true school, with his thorough understanding of nature's many laws, could possibly accept such statements.

No. 27

Q. Do the Rosicrucians believe that since transition is inevitable disease is a natural thing?

A. No, the Rosicrucians do not believe that disease is a natural thing. While it is a fact that transition is inevitable, on the other hand, disease, pain, and suffering of the physical body are not inevitable. It is possible and ideal for man to live to such a ripe old age without disease or pain that eventually the body will gradually weaken and, at some propitious time in the scheme of things, he will go to sleep, never to awaken again in earthly consciousness. That is the ideal ending of earthly life.

It is the way that the transitions of many advanced masters and teachers of the Order have occurred, and it is the way that the Rosicrucians would have transition occur in the lives of all of its members. Therefore, the way to live to prevent disease and pain and methods for remedying and removing the cause of any disease or pain are thoroughly taught by the organization.

No. 28

Q. Does the organization sell any remedies or devices which it claims will help to prolong life or prevent disease?

A. The true Rosicrucian Order has never sold such remedies, nor does it sponsor or tolerate the use of devices of this kind. Many occult or mystical schools, claiming to be Oriental and represented in America by foreign teachers, have fraudulently and successfully introduced under great secrecy and through insidious methods the sale of chemical combinations, drug preparations, or mystical charms or talismans which are purported to give immunity against disease and old age. The literature of such teachers or organizations is filled with misleading statements regarding the ideas being promulgated, and it is unfortunate indeed that America has proved to be the happy hunting ground of such charlatans.

QUESTIONS AND ANSWERS

No. 29

Q. Do the Rosicrucians of today attempt to practice or teach the Yoga principles or the other Hindu or Oriental teachings?

A. The Rosicrucian Order has never taught the Yoga principles except possibly in some branch of the Order located in India centuries ago. The Yoga teachings are distinctly the teachings of a special and limited sect of one part of the Orient. They were never considered universal teachings, applicable to all nations; nor are they, as a whole, of any value in the Occidental world to modern people. The fact of the matter is that the Yoga teachings were recognized long ago as of little value except to those persons living in that part of the world where they originated. That is why the attempt on the part of some schools or movements to introduce the Yoga principles in modern lands in modern times has proved futile.

To derive benefit from the Yoga principles connected with meditation—Bhakti Yoga—it was necessary for the Oriental devotee to spend many hours each day sitting in certain postures in absolute relaxation and profound meditation upon things unconnected with his material existence and unassociated with the practical duties and obligations of everyday life. Even the serious student of such

[264]

teachings in modern lands finds it impractical to give this much time to the development of a side of his nature that will be of no practical advantage in his daily life. Thus, there was an adjustment to be made.

On the other hand, the benefits to be derived from breathing exercises which constitute the branch of the teachings known as Hatha Yoga have found expression and application in more modern and simplified teachings, forms especially adapted to our needs and the complexity of present-day life.

No. 30

Q. Is the Rosicrucian organization in any way connected with the Roman Catholic Church or with the Roman Catholic Jesuit movement?

A. The Rosicrucian Order has never been connected in any way, outwardly or inwardly, publicly or secretly, with any church. The Rosicrucian organization is not a religious cult or sect in the sense that it teaches any sectarian theology or operates as a church in any sense. In the past, some important Roman Catholics have belonged to the fraternity. The historical records of the organization show that at one time one of the Popes and in previous periods many of the Jesuits were students of the Rosicrucian work. Because some of the great Protestant leaders were also Rosi-

crucians, it has often been claimed that the Rosicrucian Order contributed a part of the Protestant propaganda during the reformation period. Naturally, an organization could not be religiously biased in both directions. The organization has kept itself free from religious and political revolutions and campaigns.

No. 31

Q. Has the Rosicrucian Order ever been criticized or persecuted by any of the great religious organizations?

A. Just as Freemasonry has been attacked by the Roman Catholic Church, so has our Order been attacked. Because of its aggressiveness and its growth, the Order Rosae Crucis of America, as well as in all other countries, has been condemned by the Roman Catholic Church as being destructive to its principles.

The Roman Church has issued what are popularly called *bulls* against the Order, and it was no surprise to learn that it had done so in America just as, in earlier eras, it had decreed against the Order in every other country of the globe where the A. M. O. R. C. had been spreading the light. The attack upon Rosicrucians is continuous by priests of the various Orders of the Roman Church and in Catholic newspapers and periodicals.

QUESTIONS AND ANSWERS

No. 32

Q. Have the Rosicrucians ever been publicly condemned or prosecuted for any of their activities?

A. Neither justly nor unjustly has the Rosicrucian Order ever been publicly condemned for its teachings or activities. It has been peculiarly free from censorship by state and civil authorities. From time to time, it has received favorable publicity in newspapers commenting upon its activities. Even when the Order has had to defend itself in the courts of the land against individuals or groups who sought to attack it for malicious reasons or because of misconceived rivalry, the press has been most sympathetic in relating the circumstances. In all such litigation, the Rosicrucian Order, A. M. O. R. C., *has always been* victorious.

Even in modern times when so many mystical and metaphysical organizations have been ridiculed by the newspapers or in magazine articles for their sensationalism or for the purpose of increasing the circulation of such periodicals by creating morbid reader interest, the Rosicrucian Order has usually been treated with respect. The sincere inquirer can find in nearly every large encyclopedia and unabridged dictionary an account of the Rosicrucian Order, A.M.O.R.C., stating accurately its origin and

purposes. Such a record is one of which each member can be justly proud.

No. 33

Q. Is it true that some of the principal officers of the Rosicrucians in America today are associated with the Roman Catholic Church?

A. So far as the Rosicrucian Order, AMORC, is concerned, the chief officers of the International Jurisdiction are in no way connected with the Roman Catholic Church, nor have they ever been of that religious denomination.

The first Imperator[1] for North and South America was educated as a Protestant, and so was his wife. The incumbent Imperator is nonsectarian. The Supreme Secretary is also a member of a Protestant faith, and the Grand Masters of the various jurisdictions are generally of Protestant denominations. Some are members of the Jewish faith, and it is possible that an occasional officer may have been educated in the Roman Catholic Church. The present Grand Master of England is a member of the Anglican Church, while those of the Spanish-speaking branches are of various religious denominations. Some of the teachers of Grand Lodge Staffs of the Supreme Council, being of foreign birth, are

---

[1] Dr. H. Spencer Lewis.

of the Buddhist, Hindu, or other religions of the Orient.

No. 34

Q. I have been told that the Bible condemns the taking of oaths and the joining of secret societies. Is this true?

A. The injunction in the Bible against the taking of oaths pertains to making sworn statements in which the name of God is used to give emphasis to the statements made. We are reminded by this injunction that we should not use the name of God in this way, but let our aye be aye and our nay be nay. There is no injunction *anywhere* in the Bible against the joining of private *societies of learning*. In fact, we find from a careful reading of the Christian Bible that private societies of learning existed in the Bible days, or in the early Christian days, and they were not condemned.

The fact of the matter is that Jesus, as well as all the other great teachers of learning, appreciated the fact that not everyone is ready or qualified to receive all the facts and knowledge of life. Those who are ready should be given private and separate instruction from that given to the masses. In Matthew, Chapter XIII, we find that Jesus gave his great teachings by two different

methods. To the masses, he revealed the principles in simple stories and parables; and in private to his disciples he explained profound laws and principles in detail. His disciples realized that there was a reason for this, and so we find the following two verses especially interesting:

"And the disciples came, and said unto Him: Why speakest Thou unto them in parable?

"He answered and said unto them: Because it is given unto you to know the mysteries of the Kingdom of Heaven, but to them it is not given."

Ministers, clergymen, priests, and rabbis of the various religious denominations and churches of the world have been members of the Rosicrucian Order, as are many today. None has found anything in the work of the organization or its teachings that is inconsistent with the high ideals of Christianity or the principles and teachings of any other religion.

No. 35

Q. Why is the Rosicrucian Order believed to be a secret organization?

A. Because the average member makes it so. The organization itself has never attempted to make the Brotherhood a secret, nor has it ever attempted to conceal itself so completely that it could be classified as a *secret society*. Certainly, its ideals

and purposes are not secret, nor any of its pledges to the members or pledges of the members to the organization. It has no great secret oaths which members must accept or make which have not been dealt with at length in histories and other books, or which cannot be printed or exposed to public examination even today. It does not work through secret channels, nor have any secret or ulterior motives. Its meeting places and its propaganda are not secret. Nor do its officers and members hide in secrecy. If the Rosicrucian Order could have its way or have its dreams materialized, it would give its teachings and all it has to offer freely and without limitation to every man, woman, and child in the world. It is constantly seeking ways and means of spreading its teachings to the masses. The difficulty which the fraternity has to face is that only those who need what the Rosicrucians have to offer are really ready to accept the help that is available through the many activities included in the Rosicrucian work. The average member is so conscious of the fact that not all are ready or willing to give a little time and thought to their own improvement that he is careful and conservative in his remarks and in his invitations to others to accept the Rosicrucian offerings. This attitude on his part tends to make the

organization more or less private or secret, and constitutes the only reason for the seeming secrecy of its activities.

No. 36

Q. Why is it said that you must be invited to join the Rosicrucian Order and cannot ask for membership of your own volition?

A. It is a traditional custom with the Rosicrucian Order for the organization or its members to *invite* a seeker or a worthy person to come into the circle of its activities and share in its unusual benefits. In foreign lands, for many ages, it has been considered a great honor to receive a formal or informal invitation to unite with the Brotherhood. In the days of long ago, it would have seemed presumptuous for anyone to have made voluntary application or petition to join the organization. In America and Europe today, the ancient system is respected and applied with some modification.

Therefore, it is now customary for the organization or one of its members to invite the seeker or inquirer to make application for membership and have his application examined and passed upon. That is why all of the propaganda work is carried on in the form of invitations being sent to those who have manifested worthiness, interest, sincerity,

special qualifications, or a real desire to step ahead of the nonprogressive ones in life and become real masters of their affairs.

This method does not prevent the seeker or interested investigator from writing to any of the branches or to the international jurisdiction and asking for further information regarding the Rosicrucian teachings and activities.

If the inquirer's letter shows a sincere interest and a genuine desire for self-improvement, he is immediately invited to make application for membership, and a question sheet is sent to him to fill out and sign. The answers to the questions thereon are carefully considered by a committee, and if it is found that the inquirer is more than casually interested in the work and really of a progressive trend of mind, he or she is at once accepted into the neophyte or probationary form of membership.

No. 37

Q. Are all new members placed in the probationary or neophyte classification without regard to any of their previous studies or their intellectual comprehension and attainments along similar lines?

A. All new members are placed in the same category for a short period, during which time certain fundamental principles are given to them and

an opportunity afforded each member to indicate his or her special fitness for the studies. Thereafter, the member finds that his personal advancement is in accordance with his own ability and qualifications. No two members find the work identical and very soon after uniting with the organization, each member develops along lines particularly suited to his individual needs and previous education and training.

No. 38

Q. Is any special education or training needed to constitute qualifications for membership?

A. The ability to read and write and to concentrate the mind for a moment or two upon each paragraph or sentence as it is read are the preliminary educational requisites. Anyone with an ordinary education will be able to understand and apply even the most profound parts of the Rosicrucian teachings.

Higher education will not be of any material benefit in the general comprehension of the work. The most simple language and the most simple methods of presentation are used in all of the lecture work. Experiments are given to the members to try, whereby they can demonstrate and prove certain laws and principles for themselves. They are of the most simple form so that the average man or woman will

have no difficulty whatever in performing them. No memorizing, difficult mental tests, or extensive written examinations are required anywhere throughout the work.

No. 39

Q. Are persons past middle age too old to take up the work?

A. Many who are far beyond middle age have united with the organization and found in it the start of a new life, the beginning of a new career, and the openings of channels and paths to happiness, prosperity, and health, which they had believed were closed to them. It is not uncommon to find in the various jurisdictions of the Order men and women who are seventy, eighty, or ninety years of age, who have been affiliated only a year or two.

The usual statement made by these persons is that they regret that they did not contact the organization fifty years earlier in their lives. It is no more difficult for an elderly person to understand and master the teachings than it is for a young person, and there are just as many opportunities in life for the elderly person to bring a new world before his comprehension and enjoy the unknown marvels of life as there are for the young person.

No. 40

Q. What is the minimum age for membership in the Rosicrucian Order?

A. There never has been a definite minimum age established in a universal sense, and each country or each jurisdiction has certain rules in this regard which it has found compatible with the conditions to be dealt with. In most lands, young people of legal age may become members after being carefully examined as to their sincerity and serious attitude of mind. Persons above eighteen years of age find the work intensely interesting because of the new start it gives them in life.

No. 41

Q. What has the Rosicrucian Order done toward teaching and instructing children in the right way of living and the right way of thinking?

A. The Rosicrucian Order has created and continues to sponsor the Junior Order of Torch Bearers, an organization for all children between the ages of 6 and 18, whether of AMORC parentage or not. This junior organization sends to its members four child-guidance lessons monthly, one to be read at home each week during leisure hours. These lessons contain material especially written for boys

and girls of grammar-school age and for young men and women in their teens. The lectures and lesson stories are intended to guide the formation of character and direct their mental interests into cultural channels. The lectures inculcate a friendliness toward all races and people. They offset the bigotry and prejudices to which nearly all children are subjected.

Through these studies the juniors come to realize the need of self-reliance, truthfulness, honesty, and mental vision. The young men and young women members (from 13 to 18 years inclusive) are known as CRUSADERS, the intermediate group (from 10 to 13 years inclusive) are known as TORCH BEARERS, and the younger (from 6 to 10 inclusive) as KINDLERS—implying that they are kindling the allegorical Torch of idealism which they will carry throughout their lives.

The Rosicrucian Order also conducts a subsidiary body known as the Child Culture Institute, which carries on special courses of instruction for mothers who are attempting to give cultural and ethical training at home to children from the date of birth to six years of age. These courses include stories for the preschool age. In addition, there is a course of instruction for expectant mothers.

No. 42

Q. Must a member join a lodge and attend lodge meetings in order to receive the instructions and teachings of the Rosicrucians?

A. Years ago, this question became an important one in North America because of the great distances between the cities where the principal lodges were located. By a special vote of the national convention of the organization in 1916,* a national lodge to cover the entire North American continent was organized and empowered to offer a special series of graded instructions in manuscript form for home study.

Since the Rosicrucian Order never prints its teachings in books that are publicly sold and does not put its teachings in permanent printed form, the lessons offered are especially prepared from time to time, every effort being made to maintain the high standard and progressive work of the Order. The instructions in the form of monographs are sent to all Sanctum Members. Included are experiments, exercises, and tests designed to make each member proficient in the application of Rosicrucian principles. Thousands of members throughout the world today are pursuing their Rosicrucian studies

---

* Since that time, this activity has been greatly extended to serve members throughout the world.

at home in this manner with great success and efficiency.

Sanctum Members may form Pronaoi, Chapters, and Lodges in cities and localities where there are a sufficient number to conform to the requirements of a Lodge, Chapter, or Pronaos. All members of Lodges, Chapters, and Pronaoi are Sanctum Members, and all members are privileged to visit these subordinate bodies of the Order.

A monthly magazine issued by the Supreme Council of the Order (in several languages) goes each month to all members as well as to nonmember subscribers. In this way every member is kept informed of all the national and international activities of the Order. In addition, a bimonthly magazine on a subscription basis is issued for *members only*. This publication presents the latest findings and additions to the teachings and an analysis of Rosicrucian principles and viewpoints.

Members do not have to buy any additional books or special paraphernalia from the organization.* There are no heavy expenses of any kind, and the teachings are given freely. There are no commercial features, nor are fees charged for the work.

Sanctum Membership means *membership by cor-*

---

* Special books on a variety of subjects are available but need not be purchased unless desired.

respondence. All members of AMORC are members of the Grand Lodges in their respective language areas. Their membership privileges are formally defined in the *Constitution and Statutes of the Grand Lodge,* which is available to all members of the Order.

No. 43

Q. Do the thoughts of evil-minded persons create such powers or energies as will become destructive to land and property as well as to individuals? In a book entitled, *Realms of the Living Dead,* it is stated that mighty storm winds are made up of the embodied evil and malignant thought forces generated by mankind. They become entities like demons of destruction, sweeping on with tremendous power. Is this true?

A. Such an idea as that expressed in the book you have read is absolutely contrary to all sensible and rational mystical thought. Storms and winds, cyclones and hurricanes, thunder and lightning, and all such manifestations of nature and the results therefrom, good or bad, are parts of the creative process of evolution.

In the early formation of this earth, great disturbances of land and sea—undoubtedly in the form of

great storms, earthquakes, and other manifestations —resulted in the formation of continents, mountains, valleys, lakes, seas, and rivers. Certain animal life may have passed from existence, and other forms of living things may have changed their nature, but it was all for good. Every storm that blows and every cataclysmic occurrence which man interprets as destructive are part of the process of reconstruction. Only through intolerance, ignorance, or irrational thinking can man come to the conclusion that these things are evil.

As for the thought forces coming from embodied evil minds or malignant thinking on the part of man, affecting the earth and its elements or human beings and their lives, this is a superstitious idea continuing from the days when the ignorant minds of men believed that anything which was unpleasant to them or disturbing to their individual peace and contrary to conditions as they would have them emanated from demons or from evil, earthly minds or evil powers of the heavens. Everything that is, is good. However destructive natural manifestations may seem to be, all is part of the Cosmic's plan for harmony.

That we may be upset in our plans, disturbed in our tranquility, or denied our self-indulgent activities by nature's forces is no reason for us, individually or

collectively, to believe that our judgment of what is good and evil is right. The true mystic will not believe that because he, individually, apparently loses or suffers through a natural law, the law is evil or the manifestation of it is a manifestation of evil. What is loss to one is gain to another. What is a suffering to one must be a blessing to someone else if the cause of these things is a natural cause directed by the benevolent, merciful, omnipotent Mind of the Creator of all things.

No. 44

Q. What position do the Rosicrucians take in regard to the Christian doctrines?

A. Collectively, as an international organization composed of members of every religious thought and denomination, the Order takes no definite stand in regard to the religious doctrines of any church or religious movement. Naturally, there is nothing in the real teachings of the Rosicrucians which would make a devout Christian unhappy in his orthodoxy; nor is there anything in the teachings which would make the Jew or the Moslem unhappy. The real teachings of the Rosicrucians can be completely studied, assimilated, and put into practical application without in any way interfering with the religious beliefs of anyone. It has been stated by thousands of students of our teachings that the con-

tinual reference to divine principles and the exposition of many ideas expressed in Biblical literature have caused them to do more Bible reading and more reading of the sacred literature of their particular religious denomination.

No. 45

Q. Why is it that some writers of so-called Rosicrucian literature present the Rosicrucian teachings as a version of Christian mysticism?

A. For the same reason that so many cults and movements, particularly in America, use some of the terms of the Christian religion in connection with their work. Whenever propounders of a new form of philosophy wish to attract attention to secure a large following, whether in America or Europe, they organize their work as a *form of religion** and generally make it appear to be a *revelation of Christian principles*. By this means they are reasonably assured of a large and profitable business.

There is no reason for this so far as the Rosicrucian teachings are concerned, and books or pamphlets claiming to be Rosicrucian, which present a form of Christian mysticism based upon some individual or personal interpretation, are not Rosicrucian in any sense. They are simply designed to appeal to Chris-

---

* In America this is often done to gain property tax exemption.

tians without giving them the very important and valuable instructions of the Rosicrucian Brotherhood.

No. 46

Q. Can strictly orthodox Christians belong to the Rosicrucian Order without compromising their position in the Christian church?

A. Orthodox Christians of the most devout kind can belong to the Rosicrucian Order and study and follow its teachings with the utmost good to their lives and personal affairs just as they may study law or music, art or chemistry without compromising or conflicting with their position in the Christian church.

Our records show that not only are there as many Christians in our Order as there are members of other religions, but many leading Christian divines and eminent representatives of the Christian church are members and even officers of the Rosicrucian Order. Some of them have written at length about the Rosicrucian teachings, and others have presented many of the Rosicrucian principles in their Sunday services and radio broadcasts. All have found the teachings helpful.

No. 47

Q. If the Rosicrucians present no teachings that are contrary to the Christian teachings or the teach-

ings of any other church, then why should the Order claim to have new knowledge?

A. The teachings of the Rosicrucians deal with the practical things of life, and divine principles are included because they make plain to man the operation of natural laws. While it is true that none of the Rosicrucian teachings contradict any positive statement that may be found, for instance, in the Christian Bible, that does not mean that the teachings do not contain *new* knowledge that will not be found in the Christian or any other Bible.

In the teachings of the various churches, we are implored to live rightly, to serve God and our fellow man, and to lead a useful life. But nowhere in these sacred writings do we find *practical* instructions that will tell us precisely *how* we are to follow the advice that is given. We are not told how we can make our lives useful and of service to God and man.

Books on philosophy and ethics explain to us the *need* for right living and right thinking, but they do not contain the practical examples, illustrations, and methods for meeting the multiple problems of our earthly life, nor do they give us exercises and problems to work with whereby we may develop such latent faculties and functions as we possess to enable us to master the obstacles in our path

and attain the highest degree of usefulness and success.

The Rosicrucian teachings do not philosophize but state definite laws and give specific instructions for their application to our daily needs. This is why the Rosicrucian teachings are distinctly different from the abstract teachings of the many cults and philosophical movements which merely inspire the mind to seek to live better or more happily without giving the definite instructions for accomplishing the desired end.

No. 48

Q. Are the Rosicrucian teachings of today merely a rehash of the ancient teachings of the various schools of mystery?

A. Not at all. A compilation of the ancient mystery teachings has been attempted in many books and many encyclopedias and has never made a strong appeal except to scholarly, analytical minds who love to read about the ancient accomplishments without any thought of fitting them into the scheme of things today. The Rosicrucian teachings have been evolutionary in their development and progressive in their spirit. They have not merely kept abreast of the times but have anticipated the needs of each new generation and each new race of people and have forged a pathway

through the turmoil of civilization to the new land, the new life, and the new goal which was just beyond the horizon. In all ages and in all times, the master teachers and workers in the organization have contributed to the development and progressive nature of the teachings and instructions, and many of the revelations made in the teachings have been hundreds of years in advance of the discoveries of science.

The teachings in the organization today deal with the affairs of the lives of men and women of modern times, and only such principles taught in the past as are in the form of universal truth are to be found in the present-day teachings. Truth never becomes obsolete, and a law never changes its nature, but only its form of application. To study teachings with references to ancient applications would be of little value to the person of the modern world. This is why the cults and schools that teach the ancient philosophical principles of India and other Oriental lands without modification or modernization have failed to render practical service in the Occidental world.

No. 49

Q. Does one have to believe in *reincarnation* in order to master the teachings and principles of the Rosicrucians?

A. No one is asked to believe in any abstract or positive principle in order to continue with the practical teachings and benefits of the Rosicrucian Order. In fact, the organization seeks to have its members refrain from accepting anything on faith, or adopting any principle before it has been demonstrated to be a truth. The doctrine of reincarnation explains many of the mysteries of life, but the doctrine itself need not be adopted by any student of the Rosicrucian teachings unless he or she has found from personal experience that the doctrine is true. Aside from this doctrine, the other teachings of the organization will be found of such practical help and of such logical and reasonable presentation that the doctrine of reincarnation may be set aside by the student without interfering with his progress or mastership. Whether the doctrine of reincarnation is true or not is of no importance to the student of the practical teachings of the Rosicrucian Order. Those organizations which insist upon the acceptance of the doctrine of reincarnation greatly interfere with the freedom of the student's individual thinking.

No. 50

Q. Do the Rosicrucians teach that man evolved from an animal and that if he does not live properly he may be born again in some animal form?

QUESTIONS AND ANSWERS

A. The Rosicrucians teach no strange philosophy of this kind. The Rosicrucians know that the
soul personality of man is ever progressing and ever
evolving to a higher and higher standard of pureness
of thought; it never recedes or retrogrades. Therefore, it would be impossible for the soul of a human
ever to be born again in the body of a lower animal.
Such teachings as this are remnants of ancient superstitions and are easily disproved by scientific and
cosmic revelations. Man may be punished in various ways for his transgressions, but such punishment
is to enable him to purge himself of his evil tendencies and rise to a higher standard. To cast the soul
personality of a sinner back into a lower form of
animal life might serve as a punishment, but it
would not contribute to his evolution and progress
and his development into a higher spiritual being.
The Cosmic, carrying out the will of God, does not
seek to punish us for our sins independently of its
desire to make us better and more perfect in our
living. Therefore, such retrogression of the soul
personality as is indicated by the above question
would mean a defeat of the very purpose of the
cosmic principles.

No. 51

Q. I have read in some occult books that there
exist in the universe some peculiar kinds of spirits

called elementals or nature spirits, such as those which haunt forests, mountains, cataracts, rivers, and so forth, and are classified as dryads, naiads, elves, and so forth. It is said by several writers that these elemental spirits can seize humans and make slaves of men and women or affect their lives. What do the Rosicrucians say about this?

A. Of all the leading occult and metaphysical schools of the Orient and other lands, only two of them include this fantastic theory of elemental spirits in their teachings. So fantastic, alluring, and attractive was it to some Occidental readers of Oriental literature that they deliberately seized upon this weird idea and elaborated upon it because it made an excellent foundation for that sort of propaganda known as "fear propaganda," which is always profitable to those who intend to write and sell a number of books.

In one such book, the author intimates that everyone should be fearful of the influence of these elementals. At the same time, however, he is assured that he will be given formulas and methods whereby they may be kept at a distance and good spirits invoked. Nothing is explained in such books as to how one may protect himself against these elementals, but the intimation is there that by further inquiry or the buying of more books, the

great protective knowledge may be obtained. This is what might be called high-pressure salesmanship, or seductive advertising, of the mystical literature of the Occident.

The Rosicrucians know that no lesser form of beings has either the power or privilege of enslaving the human being or even influencing or endangering the normal, natural course of human existence. If it were otherwise, life would be so illogical, cosmic laws so unsound and unsystematic, and nature's principles so haphazard and undependable that there would be no need to study her laws and principles or attempt to cooperate with them or use them. Most certainly there would be no need to try to find formulas or methods to protect oneself against these invisible spirit elementals since they would have the advantage, through their invisibility, minuteness, and mystical powers, and so could overcome us and control us despite all of our efforts. Only the ignorant, superstitious minds of a few Oriental countries and only the grossly ignorant and gullible students of popular forms of fantastic beliefs in the Occident will give more than a passing thought to such theories; but rather they will smile with toleration at the fact that a few writers can turn such fearful ideas into means and methods for filling their coffers.

No. 52

Q. What is the relationship between the Great White Brotherhood and the Rosicrucian Order?

A. The original activities of the Great White Brotherhood when first established in Egypt consisted almost exclusively of secret sessions held in very secret places for the purpose of bringing together the most illustrious minds of the period, and for the discussion and classification of such unusual knowledge as had been discovered through experimentation, notation, observation, or revelation. The high motive in mind was to prepare teachers and workers to disseminate secretly among the seeking minds of the populace such seeds as would take root and have a very beneficial effect upon the cultural trend of their thinking. As time passed, eminent Avatars born in the organization or coming into it at an early age and being properly prepared were sent forth into other lands to quicken the reception of a new cycle and awaken the minds of the people to the higher aspects of life. To carry on the worldwide activities better, various forms of movements were organized by the Great White Brotherhood under various names, and these movements in several lands were wholly and enthusiastically supported by the Great White Brotherhood which, as a governing body, remained secret in its central loca-

tion. Among these organizations thus sponsored by the Great White Brotherhood were the Essene Brotherhood and later the Rosicrucian Brotherhood which evolved out of the Essene and Therapeuti movements.

Many of the eminent Avatars born in various parts of the world, who were conscious of the inspiration given to them to bring light to the masses, came under the observation of the Great White Brotherhood and through the Masters thereof received direct support and further inspiration. Some of these Avatars were permitted to organize movements of their own befitting the time and development of the people with whom they were dealing. One typical instance of this was the work of Madame Helena Blavatsky, who throughout her childhood was a subject of cosmic inspiration and preparation. She submitted to the cosmic urge to establish an independent organization, which she called *Theosophy* because of its appeal to the class of people with which she believed she would have to deal. As she more completely attuned herself with the Cosmic, she eventually came in contact with the Masters of the Great White Brotherhood, and in the latter part of her life her work was sponsored by the Great White Brotherhood as one of its channels of operation. At her transition, her work as an Avatar of

the Great White Brotherhood was completed. Madame Blavatsky's writings and teachings will remain as a monument to her contact with the Brotherhood and to the great good that such other activities can accomplish. The organization she had founded had accomplished its definite mission, and there seemed to be no need for its continuance under the name and form used by her.

In fact, the very rapid growth of the Rosicrucian Order throughout the world gave the Great White Brotherhood every possible channel and every opportunity it could utilize for the dissemination of its power and knowledge. With the Great White Lodge and its ashramas and monasteries in several lands of the Orient providing a place for the most evolved workers of the organization to come together and devote their lives to the inner work of the Brotherhood, there was no reason for the maintenance of many movements or schools under various names divided against themselves under opposing leaders. Thus the Rosicrucian Order throughout the world today represents the general inner and outer activities of the Great White Brotherhood and is the most extensive Western world channel for the dissemination of the secret doctrines and teachings of the great Masters.

No. 53

Q. What is the necessity for initiation ceremonies?

A. A question of this kind usually arises in the
mind of a person who is unfamiliar with the real
purpose of true initiation ceremonies. Very often
such persons have in mind an elaborate ritual, bombastic in its settings and pretentious in the formali-
ties and expressions. True initiation is rather of the
inner self than of the outer self. Ceremonialism may
be divided into two classifications: First, that which
is incidental to preparation for certain definite steps
about to be taken; second, a dramatization and
illustration of principles and ideals inwardly appre-
hended but outwardly incomprehensible. In regard
to the first of these, we may say that any preliminary
steps taken before beginning a definite course might
be considered as *initiatory steps,* and any procedure
wherein conditions are arranged and the individual
prepared to adjust himself to the conditions may be
properly called an *initiation.* In this sense, if a student of the higher teachings receives his first lesson
and decides that in order to do justice to the work
at hand and receive the utmost from the lesson to
be studied he should have privacy, quietness, and
the facilities for concentration, he is closely follow-

ing the procedure of initiation. If he takes himself off to a quiet room of his home and arranges a comfortable seat and adjusts a proper light to read by and softens other lights in the room or removes things that would distract his attention, closing himself against intrusion and interruption, we may properly say that in doing these things he is *initiating himself* into the work or labor at hand. If in doing these things he does them with a sense of the sacredness, importance, and influence that they will have in his life, and reverently sits down in his room and proceeds to meditate a while before starting the lesson in order to clear his mind of intruding impressions and irrelevant thoughts, he is *performing a ritual* or *ceremonial* in connection with his initiation. It is absolutely necessary that the student of the higher laws and principles who is seeking to have these things become a part of his inner self should proceed with a realization that the objective or outer self, with its burden of worries, thoughts, and concerns regarding the material things in life, must be quieted and made peaceful in order that it may not interfere with the attunement on the part of the inner self. The true value of initiation lies in the attunement it brings to the inner self with the Cosmic Mind and the Universal Intelligence. Any ceremony or ritual that aids the student or the adept

QUESTIONS AND ANSWERS

to bring the inner self to a higher phase of apprehension and comprehension is of unquestionable value and has its place in the course of study and development. Processes or rituals called initiations which do not do this, but merely elaborate on the importance of the work to be accomplished, are of little value indeed. Therefore, the Rosicrucians have only such ceremonies or forms of initiation in their work as to enable the student to attune himself with the Cosmic and quicken his inner comprehension. Such ceremonies are peaceful, quiet, and very often conducted privately and without elaborate ritualism by the student himself.

No. 54

Q. Are the Rosicrucian activities related in any way to the various religions or religious-fraternal movements of the Hindus, Persians, or others?

A. The Rosicrucian Order is not affiliated with any other outer or inner movements associated with religious activities, and is distinctly different from such movements as are indicated in the question. There are a number of organizations devoted to the unification of religions and religious ideas such as the *Bahai* movement, but the Rosicrucian Order is devoted exclusively to the dissemination and demonstration of such principles and laws as are applicable to the requirements of our everyday life. While

many other organizations are devoted to the spread of the idea of a universal brotherhood, with the altruistic purpose of bringing all races and all beliefs together under one symbol of cooperative thinking and acting, the Rosicrucians are quietly and efficiently going about the unification of the races of man and the minds of man by teaching practical principles to enable men and women to live more useful lives in harmony with others everywhere. Those organizations which do not attempt to teach such practical things are simply holding an ideal before the minds of men and inspiring them to work toward that ideal. The Rosicrucian Order, on the other hand, is showing all men the very practical ways to bring this about. In this way, the Rosicrucian organization is distinctly different in purpose and practice from any other international fraternal body in the world.

No. 55

Q. Why is the subject of mysticism of interest to progressive minds?

A. Because there is an inherent desire in the consciousness of every progressive thinker to inquire into the origin of things, the mystery of life, and the ultimate purpose of our existence. In the early history of civilization, such inquiries as these constituted the delving into the mystical side of our

existence, and mysticism became an eminent and profound school of thought. In the unlearned minds, mysticism today is erroneously associated with modern mysteries and with magic; but there is no magic in mysticism, and the only mystery therein is that which is unanswered and unsolved. Mysticism represents the highest expressions of Truth, and the study of mysticism is a study of Truth in all of its pristine purity and uncontaminated manifestations. Mysticism is not a religion, although it reveals and explains the greatest and most profound of the religious mysteries. It is not an unscientific study, although it does not depend upon the findings of science for its knowledge and accepts as many of its truths through cosmic revelations as it does through the analytical observation of the objective minds, utilizing every scientific process known to man. It is not a philosophy, for it directs the mind to the practical application of its principles as urgently as it emphasizes the need of inspirational meditation. It is generally conceded by every eminent theologian that the essence of religion is its mysticism; and it is likewise conceded by every artist, musician, architect, inventor, or creative artisan that mysticism is the fabric out of which he weaves the inspired impressions for objective comprehension. In this we see that mysticism is the very

essence of our higher thoughts and higher living, and without it as an element of nature and a school of instruction, man is only partially educated and not wholly cognizant of the beauties, powers, and blessings of existence.

No. 56

Q. In what way does a mystical comprehension of the things of life enable man to enjoy life?

A. The mystical understanding of all things that exist brings man to a closer attunement with the natural laws of the universe and removes from his consciousness the fear of the unknown and the fear of the misunderstood. This results in greater peace to his soul and mind, greater power of will, and greater determination to cooperate with the laws he knows to overcome the obstacles and limitations of his life here on earth. The study gives him a broader view of life and its miracles and mysteries and enlarges his horizon of comprehension as well as widens his realm of sympathy and attunement. It enables him to anticipate the inevitable results of certain actions in his life and to prepare for them. It removes the doubt regarding the consequences of other acts and gives him the power to proceed with greater sureness and security. It attunes the physical body to the creative principles and thereby brings better health and a greater freedom

from the influences of disease and contamination. It quickens man's perceptive faculties, awakens and develops the intuitive functionings of his consciousness, and makes him fortified in many ways to master the trials and situations of his everyday affairs, bringing greater success and happiness. The mystic is ever alert to the finer things, the higher things, the better things, and the more real things of life, and he finds enjoyment, pleasure, contentment, and peace in conditions and circumstances where another is depressed, distracted, and discouraged.

No. 57

Q. Are not the great truths of our existence obtainable through *revelation* rather than through study?

A. Even if this were so, it would be necessary for the average person to learn how to prepare himself for the revelations, and unquestionably the influx of cosmic revelations would necessitate the invention of some system for the proper classification and analysis of the knowledge thus revealed. Great truths have undoubtedly been revealed to unprepared minds in the past, and through the partial comprehension of these revelations, man has been able to advance civilization and to improve the conditions under which the races of man have lived. It

is also true, however, that those revelations which have come to prepared minds have been more comprehensible and more perfectly transmuted into benefits and blessings. The whole purpose of the Rosicrucian Order is to acquaint the seeking mind with an understandable explanation and analysis as well as a logical classification of all the revelations that have been made to man in the past so that those that may come to the seeker in the future can be instantly and properly related to the known truths and properly appreciated and comprehended. The teachings of the organization are not presented as dogmatic doctrines which must be accepted on faith, but as understandable principles susceptible to application and analysis, with such demonstrations as will bring conviction and remove the necessity for faith. The acquirement of this knowledge naturally and gradually attunes the student for the reception of further knowledge through his own experimentation and study and through cosmic revelation.

No. 58

Q. Why is not such knowledge published in books and disseminated freely to the public instead of being held for limited dissemination among members of a private organization?

A. Neither the Rosicrucian fraternity nor any other world-wide movement in the past or present

that has possessed a knowledge of the great truths of life has attempted to limit the dissemination of such knowledge. The great problem and serious struggle on the part of all such movements has been to discover ways and means for the widest possible distribution of the teachings and information at their disposal. If the present-day Rosicrucian fraternity could do so, it would have the teachings introduced into all of the public schools where the foundation of education is laid in the minds of young men and women, and the teachings would be expounded as part of the preachments in every church. In fact, if the Great White Brotherhood could realize its dream of universal dissemination of this knowledge, there would be no need for the Rosicrucian Order or any of the schools of mysticism or mystical philosophy. But the masses do not want this sort of education at the present time, and this is proved by the fact that only one person out of many thousands is interested enough in the improvement of his own welfare and the development of his best interests to pause a moment in the mad rush of material affairs to read a pamphlet or lesson or listen to a few words spoken by an enlightened one whom he may meet. This condition necessitates the dissemination of the knowledge in a limited way and in a manner that will appeal to those who are seeking for it; not the

projecting of it into the affairs of those who have no time for it, and who would actively protest against its dissemination as an unnecessary consumption of valuable time and effort. The Rosicrucian Order does not operate as a *secret* organization, but merely as a *private* organization. It does everything within its power to bring its work and its offerings before the attention of the public in a dignified and efficient manner. Every form of ethical procedure is used to apply the knowledge possessed by the organization to the betterment of mankind, in addition to the dissemination of the teachings; and for this reason many private forms of humanitarian and altruistic activity are conducted by the organization under various names so that great good may come to many without having it appear that it is for the purpose of promulgating the teachings or appearing to be a subtle form of proselyting.

Thousands of dollars are spent annually by the subordinate bodies of the Rosicrucian Order, AMORC, to conduct public meetings and present radio broadcasts consisting of fine music, interesting lectures, and illuminating discussions in order to scatter as widely as possible such seeds as may fall into the fertile minds of seekers and perhaps awaken an interest in these matters. Large sums of money are also spent in the dissemination of literature, in the

presentation of motion pictures and plays that teach an ethical or mystical principle, and in the dissemination of books and magazines containing helpful instruction. Nothing of a dignified nature is left undone to propagate the teachings of the organization in as efficient, economical, and impressive a manner as possible; and national congresses are held every year for the purpose of discussing ways and means of spreading the work as widely and as freely as is consistent with the awakening of the mass consciousness.

No. 59

Q. Why do we not hear more about the Rosicrucian Order in the speeches and writings of eminent persons?

A. The answer to this question is found in the reluctance on the part of prominent persons to speak of their personal affiliations for fear of appearing to be either boastful or seeming to bring their personal, philosophical connections into matters that have no connection therewith. On the other hand, many of the most eminent writers and public workers in America, Europe, and other lands today are members of the Order. In their writings, speeches, and general activities they apply the Rosicrucian principles and in many ways make themselves known to the understanding ones as students of the Rosicru-

cian work. In one case, in the North and South American jurisdiction for years the general manager and controller of one of the largest newspapers and every one of the heads of the important editorial and producing departments of the paper were members of the Rosicrucian organization until the newspaper was eventually sold. Rosicrucians reading that paper analytically would discover in each issue hundreds of earmarks indicating that the ethical ideals and sympathetic understanding of a real mystic entered into the make-up and editorial policy of that paper. The fact that the leading editorial articles and the news of the activities of the churches and the various educational institutions and humanitarian bodies always gave emphasis to the ethical and mystical side of the things of life and that the advertisements and offerings were free from all obscene or depressing pictures and statements indicated that the paper was being carefully edited and directed by those who understood the principles taught by the Rosicrucians. Even the business policy of this newspaper and its dealings with its advertisers and subscribers contained many unusual features that attracted attention to the paper as one having philosophical ideals of a very high standard. And yet only occasionally did there appear

a news item about the Rosicrucians, and when there did there was no reference to the fact that the newspaper knew anything more about the Rosicrucians than was contained in the item.

A number of eminent feature writers whose articles appear in magazines and Sunday editions of the newspapers are members of the Order, and their writings are often clipped and preserved by our members who recognize in the stories and the articles extracts and principles from our teachings, carefully presented so as to sow seeds of thought without the objectionable feature of appearing to be some form of propaganda. In courts of law, judges who are members of the organization adhere to the principles taught by the Rosicrucians in the administration of justice and the tolerant, sympathetic consideration of the cases brought before them. Many physicians, scientists, professors in colleges, and tutors in schools who are members of the organization are devoutly demonstrating the practical nature of our work and sowing seeds that must eventually produce distinct results. On the other hand, more and more of the popular books on religion, philosophy, morals, and ethics do make reference to the Rosicrucians; and the Rosicrucian Order in the United States has had in the past few years

more widespread publicity in the form of feature articles telling of its activities, its teachings, and the lives of its principal workers than any other humanitarian movement of its kind.

The Order has always tried to avoid such forms of bombastic propaganda as would make it appear to be a *cult* or a *sect* appealing for members to join some unique school of reformation and extreme fanaticism. Its unusual increase of members and students is more the result of the personal recommendation on the part of enthusiastic members than the result of any of its outer forms of propaganda. A Rosicrucian is generally known more by the life he lives and the happy, contented, successful manner in which he enjoys his life and carries on with his affairs than by any other sign; and often a number of Rosicrucians may be united in one church or in one service club or civic body for many years before any of them discover that there are other members of the Rosicrucian organization with them.

No. 60

Q. How do the Rosicrucians deal with the subject of hypnotism?

A. Rosicrucian teachings do not deal with hypnotism as a science or an art. In explaining and presenting all of the laws that pertain to various psychological states of consciousness, it is but natural

that reference would be made to sleep, whether induced or natural, and in this manner the so-called state of hypnosis is explained scientifically and properly. Likewise, the possible or probable benefits resulting from any induced state of semi-consciousness are fully dealt with as well as the false claims made for the so-called state of hypnosis. There was a time, a few years ago, when it would have been necessary to expound considerably on the dangers of experimenting with the popular formulas for attempting to produce the state of hypnosis; but those days have passed, and the real dangers associated with such experimentation are of little consequence as a result of the more popular understanding of other laws and principles of a superior efficiency. The popular craze for the study of hypnotism rightfully passed into oblivion as men and women came to understand the real principles of psychology and the application of them to our mental and physical requirements. Perhaps the greatest danger that was associated with the idea of hypnotism was the *fear* of it that existed in the minds of the unlearned. Hypnotism is not used in connection with the Rosicrucian teachings because the Rosicrucians can obtain the same psychological and physiological results by the use of their principles without resorting to hypnotism. However, we do recognize the impor-

tance of hypnotism when therapeutically used and in connection with psychiatry, but it is not included as a part of the teachings of the Order.

No. 61

Q. Will not a thorough study of practical psychology cover all the benefits to be derived from the study of the Rosicrucian teachings?

A. A thorough study of practical psychology will make the student familiar with the fundamental principles of the functioning of the mind and cast some light on the relationship of the mind to the soul. This knowledge constitutes but a fraction of the knowledge included in a complete study of mysticism, metaphysics, psychology, and ontology. Certainly the Rosicrucian teachings embrace more important and more practical knowledge than is contained in a thorough course on psychology. Furthermore, no course on psychology deals with all of the practical problems of everyday life with solutions for them and methods whereby men and women can master the serious situations in life and accomplish the things which lead to contentment, perfect health, peace, happiness, and prosperity. Hundreds of books have been written on the subject of psychology and hundreds of lecturers have conducted public and private classes dealing exhaustively with psychology, and yet the average student

of these courses and classes discovers that he has been merely touching the edge of a field of knowledge that becomes more and more alluring. Many thousands of the members who unite with the Rosicrucian fraternity have spent years in the study of psychology and come to the Rosicrucian organization seeking more knowledge and more *practical* help than they have had; and the fact that they retain their membership and become enthusiastic regarding the work and teachings of the Rosicrucian Order indicates that they did not find in psychology the complete presentation of the principles which are necessary for a comprehensive understanding of life and all of its problems. For a number of years, America was enthusiastic about the subject of practical psychology, and this study was offered as a solution to all of the ills and problems of humanity. The study of this science was considered by many to be the *last and ultimate key* to life and its enigmas. The fad has waned solely because the thousands who devoted their time and money to the study of psychology discovered that it was not the great panacea that it was claimed to be, despite the excellent help it has been in many ways.

No. 62

Q. Cannot anyone secure just as complete an outline of the Rosicrucian teachings from any of the

popular books on Rosicrucian principles as by taking
the course of study from the Rosicrucian Order?

A. The Rosicrucian teachings in their entirety
and even in a fairly comprehensible outline have
never been published in any books sold on the open
market, *and never will be*. It is true that a number
of publishers have been tempted by the demand on
the part of thousands of seekers for such books to
publish pamphlets and books *claiming* to contain
the Rosicrucian secrets, teachings, rituals, symbols,
and so forth. It is notable that in every case the most
bombastic of these claims and the most alluring of
these books are issued by publishing companies or
individuals having absolutely no connection with
the Rosicrucian Order and not operating as a part of
the Rosicrucian Order. Furthermore, a casual examination of the eight or ten books published within
the past fifty years in America claiming to contain
some of the Rosicrucian teachings shows that no two
of these books contain the same fundamental principles, use the same terminology, have the same viewpoint on essential principles in life, or offer the same
explanations. Certainly, therefore, all of them cannot be Rosicrucian presentations. There cannot be
and never has been any diversity of opinion on the
part of the real Rosicrucian instructors in regard to
the principles, laws, and teachings of the Rosicru-

cian work, and whether a man or woman unites with the Rosicrucian Order in Egypt, South Africa, Australia, Argentina, United States, England, France, or Germany, the teachings are identical, and the uniformity of understanding and practice of these principles is one of the strong features making for cooperative action and universal brotherhood. Differences of opinion on the part of teachers or writers of popular books in regard to the same science would not only cause confusion in the minds of the students, but lead to endless speculative theories and inconsistent consequences. This is precisely what one finds in the books offered on the open market as outlines of Rosicrucian teachings. In every case, these books have been written by men or women who have had some course of reading in metaphysical or occult subjects and have attempted to write a personal opinion of what the Rosicrucian teachings may be like or should be like without any real knowledge of them. No Rosicrucian student who has completed the course of study and is proficient and successful in his application of the principles and the mastery of his life has ever written or attempted to write a book presenting these teachings to the public for a commercial consideration. We say it has never been done, and we further say it never will be done; for every such student knows

that it would be inconsistent and improper and, therefore, *impossible* in the light of his understanding and development. Several thousand men and women, among the others who unite with the Rosicrucian Order every year, before becoming Rosicrucian students spend large sums of money in the purchase of such books with the hope of economically and conveniently learning the principles which they believe will produce the utmost benefit in their lives. Such students finally discover that the purchase of these books becomes a costly proposition and that more money can be spent in this way in one year than in several years in the proper manner of study. They find that they receive no benefits but are becoming constantly confused by the differences of opinions on the part of these authors and by the continual issuance of new books with new ideas written to tempt the seeker to continue to buy books in the hope that his search will eventually come to an end. The more alluring and tempting and the more *inclusive* are the titles of any of these so-called Rosicrucian books, the surer one can be that the books contain nothing of real value and are designed solely to appeal to the susceptibility of the unguided seeker.

Those books which claim to be an exposition of the Rosicrucian mysteries or a presentation of the Rosicrucian *rites and rituals,* or of the *secret doctrines*

of the Rosicrucians, are not only misleading in their titles, but deceptive in the claims set forth, inasmuch as such books do not and cannot contain what is claimed for them.

Attention is called to a section of the history of the organization published in this book, which explains how and why a number of pseudo-Rosicrucian movements have attempted to carry on the impression of being a part of the Rosicrucian Order by the adoption of misleading names or by simulating emblems while doing nothing more than publishing and selling useless books.* Everyone with common sense will appreciate the fact that a book claiming to be a complete presentation of the *secret teachings* and *secret ritual* of the *Freemasons,* would be unworthy of purchase at any price, for one would know instinctively that the contents of the book could not possibly fulfill the claim made by the title. The same may be said of books dealing with the subject of Rosicrucian philosophy.

No. 63

Q. Is it not true that the Rosicrucian Order in America and Europe has published some books dealing with Rosicrucian doctrine, even though they say that the Rosicrucian teachings are never published in any public books?

---

* See Chapter VI.

QUESTIONS AND ANSWERS

A. The Rosicrucian Order in America, Great
Britain, Sweden, and France, like the Order in other
jurisdictions, for many centuries has published certain books which present the real ideals and philosophical standards of the Rosicrucian fraternity.
None of these books, however, has ever borne a title
that would indicate that it contained the *secret
teachings* or an outline of all the teachings, or a
presentation of the complete teachings, rituals, practices, and work of the organization. In checking up
on the largest Rosicrucian bibliography, compiled
in Europe a few years ago, it was found that not one
of some three thousand eight hundred books
contained a title or a subtitle that was misleading.
Not one claimed to be a presentation of the *secret
teachings* or the *complete teachings,* or the practices
and arts, of Rosicrucian doctrine. This in itself
distinguishes these official books from the pretentious offerings and subtle inducements put forward
in the titles of books published by concerns not connected with the Rosicrucian Order and unfamiliar
with the real Rosicrucian teachings. The Rosicrucian Order in America, for instance, has published
a book dealing with the Rosicrucian principles for
home and business. This book does not present the
secret teachings of the Rosicrucians, nor does it claim
to do so. It distinctly states in its introduction that

the book presents only a few of the Rosicrucian principles with an enlargement and elaboration of their application to business and social affairs. Everyone who reads such a book and derives unmistakable benefits from the principles presented is continuously made aware by the statements therein that the more extended and varied teachings of the Rosicrucian work are not contained in the printed pages.

In another book published by the Rosicrucian Order, dealing with the subject of reincarnation in story form for the sake of those who want to know what reincarnation deals with, and in books dealing with the mystical life of Jesus, the history of the Order, the early manuscript writings of the Masters of Tibet, and similar publications, only such subjects are dealt with as are not a part of the secret teachings or the practical teachings of the complete course of Rosicrucian study. Even though the Rosicrucian Order were to publish a complete library of several hundred books, which it intends to do in the coming years, none of them would contain the complete course of study as given by the Rosicrucian Order in all the lands where it exists. Such books are helpful, inspiring, and of practical benefit to members and nonmembers alike, and are issued and sold at an economical price. They should be

classified as valuable contributions to the occult and metaphysical literature of the world and not claim to be expositions of the secret Rosicrucian teachings.

No. 64

Q. Why is so much being said about the Rosicrucian Order at the present time if it has existed in all lands for so many centuries?

A. A study of the history published in the other part of this book will show that the Order has had a public and private existence in alternating periods of one hundred and eight years each. There was a time when the Rosicrucian Order was as well known in America among the populace of this country at that time as it is known today, but this period was followed by one hundred and eight years of dormancy in the organization during which the public knowledge and interest in the organization passed away. In order to understand this better, the attention of the reader is called to the section of the history dealing with "The One Hundred and Eight Year Cycle and the Mystery of C. R-C." (See Chapter IV.)

No. 65

Q. What are the moral requirements of membership in the Rosicrucian Order?

A. The only moral requirements necessary for

membership in the Rosicrucian Order are that the applicant express a sincere desire to carry out the high ideals of the Order—make a commitment to pursue the study of Nature, practice good moral behavior, build character, and gain a more intimate awareness of a Supreme Being, or God—and to submit to such investigation after invitation to join the Order as may be decided upon by the Supreme Grand Lodge and eventually become duly elected to the Order, pass through its initiation in sincerity and humility, and profess allegiance to the Constitution and Statutes of the Grand Lodge. Those who are engaged in any practice or hobby contrary to the laws of the land or in any profession or study that is unethical and tends toward fanaticism, radicalism, or extreme unconventionalism are not permitted to unite with the organization. Religious differences of opinion, so far as sectarianism is concerned, have no consideration in the qualification of an applicant. Each applicant must promise before being accepted to *obey the laws of the country in which he lives,* and he or she must also promise to be *a good and useful citizen* in the upbuilding of a better nation. This naturally eliminates the objectors to law and order and those who pretend to be conscientious objectors to the upholding of the nation's best interests in the time of peace or

war. The sole purpose of the work of the Rosicrucian Order is not to make better beings out of individuals *in a selfish sense,* but to make better citizens in every country to the betterment of the nation. With each jurisdiction in each land having the same motive and the same purpose, the organization is building up a race of men and women of all nationalities, who see beyond national bounds and limitations and are united in one grand Brotherhood for the perfection of all races of mankind.

No. 66

Q. Do the Rosicrucians have to wear any particular garb, robe, or emblem, or conduct themselves in any outward manner so as to distinguish themselves from other citizens?

A. The Rosicrucian Order does not require its members to wear anything or act in any manner that would designate them as being different from other persons except insofar as their mental attitude of tolerance, sympathy, and understanding, and their success and happiness in life would indicate them to be advanced persons, familiar with and applying a philosophy and system of living that enables them to achieve the utmost and receive the bountiful blessings of this universe.

No. 67

Q. Do the Rosicrucians read the Christian Bible

and attend churches of any denomination?

A. It is but natural that the studies of spiritual and natural laws would lead to the close study of the Christian Bible as well as many other sacred books that have been written in the centuries past. Many Rosicrucians are devout students of the Christian Bible, for they find therein many expressions of the early comprehension of cosmic laws. They are generally members of various churches of various denominations, for there is nothing in the teachings that would lead them from the church; but there is much to make them appreciate the work that the churches have done in the past and are doing today which calls for their hearty support and co-operation.

No. 68

Q. Do the Rosicrucian teachings include *all* knowledge and *all Truth?*

A. It would be impossible for the Rosicrucian teachings to include all Truth and all knowledge. The study of facts known about *bacteria,* for instance, constitutes a long and serious course, but is not included in the Rosicrucian teachings because it has no place in its system even though it does represent Truth. All the laws of *art* and *music* are not included in the Rosicrucian teachings, regardless of the fact that they also represent Truth. There is

much knowledge in the universe generally known and much that is only secretly known that is not included in the Rosicrucian teachings because it has no place in the scheme of things as outlined by the practical purposes of the organization. But all knowledge of metaphysical, occult, psychological, mystical, natural, spiritual, and mental laws that pertain to man's being, his development and mastership of the conditions around him, is included in the course insofar as it is of *practical value* and enables him actually to *do things* in this material world for his own betterment and the betterment of others. The teachings are inclusive enough to contain all that is good and practical that is based upon Truth as presented in the teachings of the other metaphysical and mystical schools of India, Egypt, Persia, and other lands. The fact that the Rosicrucian Order is represented in all of the Oriental lands and that the greatest teachers of the individual philosophies and mystical teachings in these other lands are officers and enthusiastic workers in the Rosicrucian Order, and have been so for many centuries, should plainly indicate that whatever is good and practical and true of these other teachings would become a part of the Rosicrucian studies. The Rosicrucian work continues to be as it has been in all centuries the most complete and most inclusive of all schools.

As rapidly as any laws and principles of nature are discovered and evolved by experimentation and test on the part of Masters and highly developed individuals in any land, in any school of thought, and in any race of people, they are immediately brought before the national and international congresses of the Rosicrucian Order. If found of practical value in either the Oriental or Occidental worlds, they are added to the Rosicrucian instructions in a form to be most easily understood and most efficiently applied. Not being bound by any creeds or dogmas, or limited by any traditions of antiquity, the Rosicrucian Order can logically and rightfully add to its teachings and modify them continuously in keeping with the evolving consciousness and requirement of all men and women.

No. 69

Q. Are the Rosicrucian teachings of today the same ancient teachings as those promulgated centuries ago?

A. The very fact that men and women of the Western world find the teachings of *practical value* in their everyday affairs would indicate that the teachings of the Rosicrucian Order today cannot be those which were given in the schools of centuries past.

Truth is never changing, and a law or principle

that was sound and proved a thousand or ten thousand years ago must be sound and true today; but it may be a principle requiring no application on the part of men and women of modern times. Therefore, it would not be a practical one from the standpoint of modern thought and development.

Many of the ancient principles in regard to diet and fasting, which were sound, logical, and of practical help several centuries ago, are of little value today because of the improvements and modifications in man's living, especially in the matter of eating. Therefore, the study of the ancient philosophies in their original form includes many principles and practices that are of no value today.

This fact is overlooked by many who seek knowledge from ancient sources and is ignored by publishers of ancient books. On the other hand, many of the profound principles that served man so well in years gone by have their application today in a modified form or in relation to activities and practices on our part not known to ancient peoples. In addition to this, every year sees the discovery or evolution of a new principle or law partially known —or perhaps unknown—to the ancients, but always existing in the Cosmic as a universal principle. These discoveries or evolved principles are tested and tried by the highest members of the organiza-

tion in all lands and are gradually added to the teachings of the fraternity in order to provide the students with the very best and most modern application of the fundamental principles which are helpful to all.

For this reason, the teachings and lessons of the Rosicrucian organization are continuously revised, modified, and augmented by its officers and members of its Research Council. The revisions and modifications do not set aside any truth that is of a practical value, nor do they make untrue that which was and always will be true. The revisions and modifications usually apply to the wording, presentation, or utility of the principle or law. The Rosicrucian teachings of each year are the most advanced presentation of these things to be found in any school or system, and they are always in keeping with man's actual requirements.

No. 70

Q. Do the Rosicrucian teachings follow in the wake of science in their revelations, or do they anticipate them?

A. The Rosicrucian teachings have often been many years and even many centuries in advance of the findings of science. This is not a reflection upon science, for science acknowledges and gives voice to principles and laws only after it has tested them

in its own way and reduced them to certain measures and methods of observation. This unique standard of evaluation and judgment established by science causes it to hold back in the acceptance of any law or principle long after many of such principles have been known and used by other progressive minds.

The Rosicrucians, on the other hand, do not depend alone upon the rules of science for the discovery and test of natural laws and principles. They have their own methods by which they can prove the truth or worthiness of a principle, and these methods permit them to come to the proper conclusion quickly and often with less likelihood of misjudgment. This is proved by the fact that many principles and laws tested and proved by the Rosicrucians and adopted by them have been rejected or denied by science for centuries and then later found by science to be true.

Another interesting and particularly noteworthy fact is that at no time in the history of the Rosicrucian Order has it ever had to *retract* or *subtract* from its teachings any law or principle expounded as true. No principle taught by the Order has ever been discovered to be untrue and inconsistent with other laws and principles. This cannot be said of the material sciences, which are constantly retract-

ing and correcting statements made or conclusions reached by their own methods.

In this connection we say that scientists and philosophers have often called attention to the fact that the Rosicrucians have made important contributions to scientific knowledge because of their unique methods of securing information and their freedom from doctrinal limitations, which permit them to accept new knowledge that is proved true regardless of its uniqueness or astounding nature. New facts discovered by science, which do not fit nicely into the theories established by science, must of necessity be laid aside when there is a possibility of such new knowledge contradicting that which has been promulgated for some time. Rosicrucian doctrine has never been in this predicament and is not likely to be since it has no theories but deals only with facts and truth. No discovery or revelation of a truth, therefore, can be inconsistent with what is already known to the Rosicrucians, nor can it be so unique that it will not fit into the woven fabric of principles and laws already established and in use. In an article in the Sunday edition of the *New York World,* a former magazine editor writing on religious, scientific, and philosophic subjects stated that, "If my scientific friends think their labors are based on accuracy, this is nothing to the accuracy and the painstaking final-

ity of the mystics who anticipated science, who announced discoveries in science centuries before they were worked out externally."

He calls attention to the fact that certain discoveries of Einstein, Millikan, and Eddington deal with laws and principles well known to the mystics and used by them for many centuries. This probably explains why several eminent discoverers of great principles in physiology, anatomy, biology, chemistry, electricity, astronomy, medicine, music, and art have been advanced students of the Rosicrucian studies. It explains, too, why today the leading experimenters in many if the greatest scientific laboratories of the world are also advanced students of the Rosicrucian work.

No. 71

Q. Is the Rosicrucian work only of benefit to the very learned and those engaged in scientific and professional occupations?

A. The larger part of the membership of the Rosicrucian Order consists of men and women who are *not* engaged in scientific or professional pursuits. The average member is a man or woman engaged in business or job interests or solely in looking after a home, caring for children, and bringing joy and happiness into the lives of a family. The organization would fail in its great aim if its work were not

directed to give the utmost of benefit to the layman or to the average individual in life. It is with the multitude and with the masses that the great work must be accomplished and where the greatest benefit can result.

For this reason, every man or woman who is capable of reading and comprehending the meaning of the average words of the languages in which the instructions are presented can easily master and succeed in the application of the principles taught in the Rosicrucian teachings. The work becomes so fascinating, the study so tempting and attractive in its revelations and applications, that men and women who have little time for other studies or who cannot devote evenings to unnecessary things are happy to set aside a part of one evening each week for the study of the monographs so that in spare moments during the other days of the week, the principles can be applied and benefits can be derived in every one of the daily affairs.

INDEX FOR PART ONE

QUESTIONS AND ANSWERS

QUESTIONS AND ANSWERS

QUESTIONS AND ANSWERS

QUESTIONS AND ANSWERS

QUESTIONS AND ANSWERS

QUESTIONS AND ANSWERS

QUESTIONS AND ANSWERS

INDEX FOR PART TWO

QUESTIONS AND ANSWERS

QUESTIONS AND ANSWERS

Explanatory

THE ROSICRUCIAN ORDER

ANTICIPATING questions which may be asked by the readers of this book, the publishers wish to announce that there is but one universal Rosicrucian Order existing in the world today, united in its various jurisdictions, and having one Supreme Council in accordance with the original plan of the ancient Rosicrucian manifestoes. The Rosicrucian Order is not a religious or sectarian society.

This international organization retains the ancient traditions, teachings, principles, and practical helpfulness of the Brotherhood as founded centuries ago. It is known as the *Ancient Mystical Order Rosae Crucis,* which name, for popular use, is abbreviated into AMORC. The International Jurisdiction of this Order has its headquarters at San Jose, California. Those interested in knowing more of the history and present-day helpful offerings of the Rosicrucians may have a *free* copy of the book entitled, *The Mastery of Life,* by sending a definite request to SCRIBE S.P.P., Rosicrucian Park, San Jose, California 95191, U.S.A.

The Rosicrucian Library

consists of a number of unique books which are described
in the following pages, and which may be
purchased from the

ROSICRUCIAN SUPPLY BUREAU
SAN JOSE, CALIFORNIA 95191, U.S.A.

Eternal Fruits of Knowledge

By CECIL A. POOLE, F.R.C.

Truths are those thoughts which have a *continuous value* to man in inspiration and service. Down through the ages have descended the illuminating ideas of philosophers, mystics, and profound thinkers that are as realistic today as when conceived centuries ago. It has been rightly said that we stand upon the shoulders of those who have gone before.

Unfortunately, however, we often are not aware of the knowledge that has stood the test of time. Such knowledge can serve *you* as well in our time as it did men of the past. There are points of experience and understanding which are ageless in their benefit to mankind. What these golden gems of wisdom are, this book reveals clearly, concisely, and interestingly.

This volume deals with such subjects as the nature of the Absolute; Body, Mind and Soul; Good and Evil; Human and Universal Purpose, and many other interesting topics. It is a well-printed paperbound book.

∇

Rosicrucian Questions and Answers with

Complete History of the Order

By H. SPENCER LEWIS, F.R.C., Ph.D.

THIS volume contains the first complete, authentic history of the Rosicrucian Order from ancient times to the present day. The history is divided into two sections, dealing with the traditional facts and the established historical facts, and is replete with interesting stories of romance, mystery, and alluring incidents.

This book is a valuable one since it is a constant reference and guidebook. Questions that arise in your mind regarding many mystical and occult subjects are answered in this volume.

For many centuries the strange mysterious records of the Rosicrucians were closed against any eyes but those of the high initiates. Even editors of great encyclopedias were unable to secure the strange, fascinating facts of the Rosicrucian activities in all parts of the world. Now the whole story is outlined and it reads like a story from the land of the "Arabian Nights."

The book outlines answers to scores of questions dealing with the history, work, teachings, benefits, and purposes of the Rosicrucian fraternity. It is printed on fine paper, and indexed.

Rosicrucian Principles for the

Home and Business

By H. Spencer Lewis, F.R.C., Ph.D.

This volume contains such principles of practical Rosicrucian teachings as are applicable to the solution of everyday problems of life, in business and in the affairs of the home. It deals exhaustively with the prevention of ill-health, the curing of many of the common ailments, and the attainment of peace and happiness, as well as the building up of the affairs of life that deal with financial conditions. The book is filled with hundreds of practical points dealing especially with the problems of the average businessman or person in business employ. It points out the wrong and right way for the use of metaphysical and mystical principles in attracting business, increasing one's income, promoting business propositions, starting and bringing into realization new plans and ideals, and the attainment of the highest ambitions in life.

Rosicrucian Principles for the Home and Business is not theoretical but strictly practical. It has had a wide circulation and universal endorsement not only among members of the organization, who have voluntarily stated that they have greatly improved their lives through the application of its suggestions, but among thousands of persons outside of the organization. It has also been endorsed by business organizations and business authorities.

The book is of standard size and indexed.

$$\nabla$$

The Mystical Life of Jesus

By H. Spencer Lewis, F.R.C., Ph.D.

This is the book that thousands have been waiting for—the real Jesus revealed at last! It was in preparation for a number of years and required a visit to Palestine and Egypt to secure a verification of the strange facts contained in the ancient Rosicrucian and Essene records.

It is a full account of the birth, youth, early manhood, and later periods of Jesus' life, containing the story of his activities in the times not mentioned in the Gospel accounts. The facts relating to the immaculate conception, the birth, crucifixion, resurrection, and ascension will astound and inspire you. The book contains many mystical symbols, fully explained, original photographs, and an unusual portrait of Jesus.

Here is a book that will inspire, instruct, and guide every student of mysticism and religion. It is one of the most talked-about books ever written on the subject. Read it and be prepared for the discussions of it that you will hear among men and women of learning. Indexed for quick reference.

The Secret Doctrines of Jesus

By H. Spencer Lewis, F.R.C., Ph.D.

Does the Bible actually contain the unadulterated words of Jesus the Christ? Do you know that from 325 A.D. until 1870 A.D., twenty ecclesiastical or church council meetings were held in which *man* alone decided upon the context of the Bible? Self-appointed judges in the four Lateran Councils expurgated and changed the sacred writings to please themselves. The Great Master's *personal* doctrines, of the utmost, vital importance to every man and woman, were buried in unexplained passages and parables. *The Secret Doctrines of Jesus*, by Dr. H. Spencer Lewis, eminent author of *The Mystical Life of Jesus*, for the first time *reveals* these *hidden truths*. Startling, facinating, this book should be in every thinker's hands. It is beautifully bound and illustrated.

"*Unto Thee I Grant*

By Sri. Ramatherio

This is one of the rarest Oriental mystery books known. It was translated by special permission of the Grand Lama and Disciples of the Sacred College in the Grand Temple in Tibet.

Here is a book that was written two thousand years ago, but was hidden in manuscript form from the eyes of the world and given only to the initiates of the temples in Tibet to study privately.

Out of the mystery of the past comes this antique book containing the rarest writings and teachings known to man with the exception of the Bible. Hundreds of books have been written about the teachings and practices of the *Masters of the Far East* and the adepts of Tibet, but none of them has ever contained the secret teachings found in this book.

The book deals with man's passions, desires, weaknesses, sins, strengths, fortitudes, ambitions, and hopes. It contains also the strange mystic story of the expedition into Tibet to secure this marvelous manuscript.

∇

A Thousand Years of Yesterdays

By H. SPENCER LEWIS, F.R.C., Ph.D.

HERE is a book that will tell you about the real facts of *reincarnation.* It is a story of the soul, and explains in detail how the soul enters the body and how it leaves it, where it goes, and when it comes back to earth again, and why.

The story is not just a piece of fiction, but a *revelation of the mystic laws* and principles known to the Masters of the Far East and the Orient for many centuries, and never put into book form as a story before this book was printed. That is why the book has been translated into so many languages and endorsed by the mystics and adepts of India, Persia, Egypt, and Tibet.

Fascinating—Alluring—Instructive

Those who have read this book say that they were unable to leave it without finishing it at one sitting. The story reveals the mystic principles taught by the Rosicrucians in regard to reincarnation as well as the spiritual laws of the soul and the incarnations of the soul.

An attractively bound book, worthy of a place in anyone's library.

Self Mastery and Fate with the
Cycles of Life

By H. Spencer Lewis, F.R.C., Ph.D.

This book is entirely different from any other book ever issued in America, dealing with the secret periods in the life of each man and woman wherein the Cosmic forces affect our daily affairs.

The book reveals how we may take advantage of certain periods to bring success, happiness, health, and prosperity into our lives, and it likewise points out those periods which are not favorable for many of the things we try to accomplish. It does not deal with astrology or any system of fortunetelling, but presents a system long used by the Master Mystics in Oriental lands and which is strictly scientific and demonstrable. One reading of the book with its charts and tables will enable the reader to see the course of his life at a glance. It helps everyone to eliminate "chance" and "luck," to cast aside "fate," and replace these with self-mastery.

Here is a book you will use weekly to guide your affairs throughout the years. There is no magic in its system, but it opens a vista of the life-cycles of each being in a remarkable manner. This book is beautifully bound.

▽

Rosicrucian Manual

By H. Spencer Lewis, F.R.C., Ph.D.

This practical book contains not only extracts from the Constitution of the Rosicrucian Order, but a complete outline and explanation of all the customs, habits, and terminology of the Rosicrucians, with diagrams and explanations of the symbols used in the teachings, an outline of the subjects taught, a dictionary of the terms, a complete presentation of the principles of Cosmic Consciousness, and biographical sketches of important individuals connected with the work. There are also special articles on the Great White Lodge and its existence, how to attain psychic illumination, the Rosicrucian Code of Life

with thirty laws and regulations, and a number of portraits of prominent mystics including Master K. H., the Illustrious.

The technical matter in the text and in the 100 or more diagrams makes this book a real encyclopedia of Rosicrucian explanations, aside from the dictionary of Rosicrucian terms.

The *Rosicrucian Manual* has been enlarged and improved since its first edition. Attractively bound, and stamped in gold.

▽

Mystics at Prayer

Compiled by MANY CIHLAR

THE first compilation of the famous prayers of the renowned mystics and adepts of all ages.

The book *Mystics at Prayer* explains in simple language the reason for prayer, how to pray, and the Cosmic laws involved. You come to learn the real efficacy of prayer and its full beauty dawns upon you. Whatever your religious beliefs, this book makes your prayers the application not of words, but of helpful, divine principles. You will learn the infinite power of prayer. Prayer is man's rightful heritage. It is the direct means of man's communion with the infinite force of divinity.

▽

Behold the Sign

By RALPH M. LEWIS, F.R.C.

WHAT were the *Sacred Traditions* said to have been revealed to Moses—and never spoken by the ancient Hebrews? What were the forces of nature discovered by the Egyptian priesthood and embodied in strange symbols—symbols which became the everliving knowledge which built King Solomon's Temple, and which found their way into the secret teachings of every century?

Regardless of the changing consciousness of man, certain signs and devices have immortalized for all ages the truths which make men free. Learn the meaning of the Anchor and

Ark, the Seven-Pointed Star, ancient Egyptian hieroglyphs, and *many other age-old secret symbols.*

Here is a book that also explains the origin of the various forms of the cross, the meanings of which are often misunderstood. It further points out the mystical beginnings of the *secret signs* used by many fraternal orders today. This book of symbolism is *fully illustrated,* simply and interestingly written.

▽

Mansions of the Soul
By H. Spencer Lewis, F.R.C., Ph.D.

Reincarnation! The world's most disputed doctrine. The belief in reincarnation has had millions of intelligent, learned, and tolerant followers throughout the ages. Ringing through the minds and hearts of students, mystics, and thinkers have always been the words: "Why Are We Here?" Reincarnation has been criticized by some as conflicting with sacred literature and as being without verification. This book reveals, however, in an intelligent manner the many facts to support reincarnation. Quotations from eminent authorities, and from Biblical and Sacred works substantiate reincarnation. This volume *PROVES* reincarnation, placing it high above mere speculation. Without exaggeration, this is the most complete, inspiring, and enlightening book ever written on this subject. It is not fiction but a step-by-step revelation of profound mystical laws. Look at *some* of the thought-provoking, intriguing chapters:

The Personality of the Soul; Does Personality Survive Transition?; Heredity and Inheritance; Karma and Personal Evolution; Religious and Biblical Viewpoints; Christian References; Souls of Animals and the "Unborn"; Recollections of the Past.

Over 300 pages. Beautifully printed, neatly bound, stamped in gold—a valuable asset to your library.

▽

Lemuria—the Lost Continent
of the Pacific
By Wishar S. Cervé

Beneath the rolling, restless seas lie the mysteries of forgotten civilizations. Swept by the tides, half-buried in the

sands, worn away by terrific pressure, are the remnants of a culture little known to our age of today. Where the mighty Pacific now rolls in a majestic sweep of thousands of miles, there was once a vast continent. This land was known as Lemuria, and its people as Lemurians.

We pride ourselves upon the inventions, conveniences, and developments of today. We call them modern, but these ancient and long-forgotten people excelled us. Things we speak of as future possibilities, they knew as everyday realities. Science has gradually pieced together the evidences of this lost race, and in this book you will find the most amazing, enthralling revelations you have ever read. How these people came to be swept from the face of the earth, except for survivors who have living descendants today, is explained. Illustrations and explanations of their mystic symbols, maps of the continent, and many ancient truths and laws are contained in this unusual book.

If you are a lover of mystery, of the unknown, the weird—read this book. Remember, however, this book is *not fiction*, but based on facts, the result of extensive research. Does civilization reach a certain height and then retrograde? Are the culture and progress of mankind in cycles, reaching certain peaks, and then returning to start over again? These questions and many more are answered in this intriguing volume. Read of the living descendants of these people, whose expansive nation now lies within the Pacific. These descendants have the knowledge of the principles which in bygone centuries made their forebears builders of an astounding civilization.

The book, *Lemuria—the Lost Continent of the Pacific,* is beautifully bound, well printed, and contains many illustrations.

▽

The Symbolic Prophecy of
The Great Pyramid

By H. SPENCER LEWIS, F.R.C., Ph.D.

THE world's greatest mystery and first wonder is the Great Pyramid. It stands as a monument to the learning and achievements of the ancients. For centuries its secrets were closeted in stone—now they stand revealed.

Never before in a book priced within the reach of every

reader have the history, vast wisdom, and prophecies of the Great Pyramid been given. You will be amazed at the Pyramid's scientific construction and at the tremendous knowledge of its mysterious builders.

Who built the Great Pyramid? Why were its builders inspired to reveal to posterity the events of the future? What is the path that the Great Pyramid indicates lies before mankind? Within the pages of this enlightening book there are the answers to many enthralling questions. It prophesied the World Wars and the great economic upheaval. Learn what it presages for the future. You must not deprive yourself of this book.

The book is neatly and attractively bound, and contains instructive charts and illustrations.

$$\nabla$$

The Book of Jasher

THE SACRED BOOK WITHHELD

BY WHAT right has man been denied the words of the prophets? Who dared expunge from the Holy Bible one of its inspired messages? For centuries man has labored under the illusion that there have been preserved for him the collected books of the great teachers and disciples—yet one has been withheld—*The Book of Jasher*, discovered by Alcuin in 800 A.D. Later it was suppressed and then rediscovered in 1829, and once again suppressed.

Within the hallowed pages of the great Bible itself are references to this lost book. As if by Devine decree, the Bible appears to cry out to mankind that its sanctity has been violated, its truth veiled, for we find these two passages exclaiming: "Is not this written in the Book of Jasher?"—Joshua 10:13; "Behold, it is written in the Book of Jasher"—2 Sam. 1:18.

An actual photographic reproduction of this magnificent work, page for page, line for line, unexpurgated. Bound in its original style.

Herbalism Through the Ages

By RALPH WHITESIDE KERR, F.R.C.

VERY FEW things in human experience have touched the whole being of man as have herbs. Not only did they provide man's earliest foods and become remedies and medicines for his illnesses, but they also symbolized certain of his emotions and psychic feelings. Further, herbs are one of Nature's products that we still depend upon for their virtues, even in our modern age.

The source of our first foods has a romantic and fascinating history. This book reveals man's discovery of natural foods, herbs, and their various uses through the centuries. Most medicines prescribed or purchased today owe their healing or pain-relieving value to the properties of herbs or herbal products. Certain herbs are a natural medicine; they have a health-giving essence. Modern medical science uses many herbs whose real identity is obscured by technical medical terms. This book lists many of these herbs and tells their history and use.

▽

Mental Poisoning

THOUGHTS THAT ENSLAVE MINDS

By H. SPENCER LEWIS, F.R.C., Ph.D.

TORTURED souls. Human beings, whose self-confidence and peace of mind have been torn to shreds by invisible darts—the evil thoughts of others. Can envy, hate, and jealousy be projected through space from the mind of another? Do poisoned thoughts like mysterious rays reach through the ethereal realm to claim innocent victims? Will wishes and commands born in hate gather momentum and like an avalanche descend upon a helpless man or woman in a series of calamities? Must humanity remain at the mercy of evil influences created in the minds of the vicious? Millions each year are mentally poisoned—are you safe from this scourge? *Mental Poisoning* fearlessly dis-

closes this psychological problem. Read its revelations and be prepared.

This neatly bound, well-printed book has been economically produced so it can be in the hands of thousands because of the benefit it will afford them.

▽

Glands—Our Invisible Guardians

By M. W. KAPP, M.D.

YOU NEED not continue to be bound by those glandular characteristics of your life which do not please you. These influences, through the findings of science and the mystical principles of nature, may be adjusted. The first essential is that of the old adage: "Know Yourself." Have revealed the facts about the endocrine glands—know where they are located in your body and what mental and physical functions they control. The control of the glands can mean the control of your life. These facts, scientifically correct, with their mystical interpretation, are presented in simple, nontechnical language, which everyone can enjoy and profit by reading.

Mystics and metaphysicians have long recognized that certain influences and powers of a Cosmic nature could be tapped; that a Divine energy could be drawn upon, affecting our creative ability, personality, and our physical welfare. For centuries there has been speculation as to what area or what organs of the body contain this medium—this contact between the Divine and the physical. Now it is known that certain of the glands are governors which speed up or slow down the influx of Cosmic energy into the body. This process of Divine alchemy and how it works is explained in this book of startling facts.

Dr. M. W. Kapp, the author, during his lifetime, was held in high esteem by the medical fraternity, despite the fact that he also expressed a deep insight into the mystical laws of life and their influence on the physical functioning of the body.

INTRODUCTION BY H. SPENCER LEWIS, F.R.C., Ph.D.

Dr. H. Spencer Lewis—first Imperator of the Rosicrucian Order (AMORC), of North and South America, for its present cycle of activity, and author of many works on mysticism, philosophy, and metaphysics—wrote an important introduction to this book, in which he highly praised it and its author.

What to Eat—and When

By STANLEY K. CLARK, M.D., C.M., F.R.C.

"MIND over matter" is not a trite phrase. Your moods, your temperament, your very *thoughts* can and *do* affect digestion. Are you overweight—or underweight? Appearances, even the scales, are not always reliable. Your age, your sex, the kind of work you do—all these factors determine whether your weight is correct or wrong for *you.* Do you know that many people suffer from food allergy? Learn how your digestion may be affected even hours after you have eaten.

The author of this book, Dr. Stanley K. Clark, was for several years staff physician at the Henry Ford Hospital in Detroit. He is a noted gastroenterologist (specialist in stomach and intestinal disorders). He brings you his wealth of knowledge in this field, *plus* his additional findings from his study of the effects of the *mind* upon digestion.

What to Eat—and When is compact, free from unnecessary technical terminology. Includes complete handy index, *food chart,* and *sample menus.* It is not a one-time-reading book. You will often refer to it throughout the years. Well printed, strongly bound.

▽

Sepher Yezirah—A Book on Creation

OR THE JEWISH METAPHYSICS OF REMOTE

ANTIQUITY

DR. ISIDOR KALISCH, Translator

AMONG the list of the hundred best books in the world, one might easily include this simple volume, revealing the greatest authentic study of the secret Kabala. For those averse to fantastic claims, this book is truly *comprehensible*—for the wise student who does not care for magical mumbo-jumbo, it is *dynamic.*

The phantasies of those baffling speculations of other writers become unimportant when the practical student of mysticism reverently thumbs through these pages and catches the terse and challenging statements. The woolgathering of many so-

called authors of occultism is brought to nothing by this simple volume which makes a pattern for honest mystical common sense.

The *Sepher Yeziah* contains 61 pages with both Hebrew and English texts, photolithographed from the 1877 original edition. For anyone interested in the best—also, considered by some, the most ancient—in Hebrew mystical thought, this book will be a refreshing discovery.

The careful reader will be attracted to three characteristics of this edition of the *Sepher Yezirah:*

(1) A clear English translation of a most ancient work, almost unavailable up to the present.

(2) A simple exposé of fundamental aspects of the ancient Kabala without superstitious interpretations.

(3) An inexpensive translation of the world's oldest philosophical writing in Hebrew.

Attractive and convenient, paperbound edition.

▽

Whisperings of Self

By VALIDIVAR

Whisperings of Self is the interpretation of cosmic impulses received by a great mystic-philosopher, Ralph M. Lewis, who in this work writes under the pen name of Validivar.

The aphorisms in this collection have appeared singly in copies of the *Rosicrucian Digest* over a period of forty years and comprise insights into all areas of human experience—justice, war and peace, ethics, morals, marriage, family, work, leisure, and countless others.

Ralph Lewis' frank and direct style provides much food for thought in each brief impression. A reader develops the habit of using a thought a day, and there are more than two hundred from which to choose.

This is an attractive, hardcover book that makes an attractive gift as well as a treasured possession of your own.

▽

The Conscious Interlude

By RALPH M. LEWIS, F.R.C.

How many of the countless subjects which shape your life are inherited ideas? How many are actually yours? Would you like to have your own mind look at itself in perspective for

an analysis? In this book, Mr. Lewis, Imperator of the international Rosicrucian Order, AMORC, outlines the culmination of years of his original thought. As you follow him through the pages into broad universal concepts, your mind too will feel its release into an expanding consciousness.

You will be confronted with and will answer such questions as: Is consciousness something innate or is it generated? What is the reality that you experience *actually like?* What are your own conscious interludes? This work belongs to every seeker after knowledge. Indexed and illustrated, this is a volume of more than 360 pages.

▽

Essays of A Modern Mystic

By H. SPENCER LEWIS, F.R.C., Ph.D

THE writings of a true mystic philosopher constitute cosmic literature. The ideas they contain are born of *inner experience* —the self's contact with the cosmic intelligence residing within. Such writings, therefore, have the ring of conviction—of *truth.*

This book, *Essays of A Modern Mystic,* will disclose the personal confidence and enlightenment that mystical insight can give an individual.

The essays are a compilation of the private writings by Dr. H. Spencer Lewis which have never before been published in book form. Dr. Lewis is not only the author of many literary works but also was a contributor to publications and periodicals with world-wide circulation.

This book is not hastily put together. It has a hard binding, attractively stamped in gold.

▽

Cosmic Mission Fulfilled

By RALPH M. LEWIS, F.R.C.

THE life of Harvey Spencer Lewis, Imperator of the Ancient, Mystical Order Rosae Crucis, is a fascinating account of the struggle of a mystic-philosopher against forces of materialism. He was charged with the responsibility of rekindling the ancient flame of wisdom in the Western world.

In the life of this great man events swung like a pendulum from triumph to tribulation. These became a progressive stimulus to achievement.

Has each man a purpose on the earth plane? Our happiness lies in understanding this and in the realization of hopes worthy of our best personal powers. The present is our *moment in Eternity*. In it we fulfill our mission.

In this book, the author combines his close and official knowledge of Dr. Lewis with the anecdotes of many other persons who knew him.

Nine full-plate illustrations are inserted into this beautifully printed and bound volume.

▽

Egypt's Ancient Heritage

By RODMAN R. CLAYSON

MUCH of what we know today began in Egypt! Out of that ancient civilization, which lasted three thousand years, came the first concepts of the origin of the universe, clothed in a symbology that showed a marvelous insight into natural law. Truth, righteousness, justice, and moral codes were first taught in the ancient mystery schools of Egypt as was the belief in a mind cause or thought as the creative cosmic force.

The belief in the soul, of life after death, and of immortality was held by the Egyptians thousands of years before Christ. The judgment of the soul in the next life evolved from an Egyptian concept and was dramatized by their rites and ceremonies.

This book tells of the amazing similarity of Egyptian thought to modern religious, mystical, and philosophical doctrines, and how many of our customs and beliefs of today were influenced by these ancient people. It is truly an amazing revelation!

Written in a straightforward easily read style, *Egypt's Ancient Heritage* is hardbound.

▽

The Sanctuary of Self

By RALPH M. LEWIS, F.R.C.

WHAT could be more essential than the discovery and analysis of *self*, the composite of that consciousness which constitutes one's whole being? This book of sound logic presents revealingly and in entirety the four phases of human living: The Mysteries, The Technique, The Pitfalls, and Attainment.

Do you not, at times, entertain the question as to whether you are living your life to your best advantage? You may find an answer in some of the 23 chapters, presented under headings such as: Causality and Karma, The Lost Word, Death—

The Law of Change, Love and Desire, Nature of Dreams, Prediction, Mastership and Perfection. Consider "Love and Desire." In much of ancient and modern literature, as well as in the many and various preachments of the present-day world, LOVE is proclaimed as the solution to all human conflict. Do you understand truly the meaning of *absolute love?* Do you know that there are various *loves* and that some of the so-called loves are dangerous drives?

Written authoritatively by Ralph M. Lewis, Imperator of the Rosicrucian Order (AMORC), this volume of over 350 pages, carefully indexed, is of particular value as a text for teachers and students of metaphysics, including philosophy and psychology.

▽

Yesterday Has Much to Tell

By Ralph M. Lewis, F.R.C.

Man's conquest of nature and his conflict with self, as written in the ruins of ancient civilizations, found in the sacred writings of temples and sanctuaries, and as portrayed in age-old tribal rites, are related to you by the author from his extensive travels and intimate experiences. This is not a mere travel book. It constitutes a personal witnessing and account of primitive ceremonies, conversations with mystical teachers and austere high priests of the Near and Far East. It takes you into the interior of Africa to see the performance of a witch doctor and to temples in Peru, India, Egypt, and other exotic lands. The author was privileged because of his Rosicrucian affiliation to see and to learn that which is not ordinarily revealed. A hardbound book of 435 pages, including sixteen pages of photographs.

The Technique Of The Master

THE WAY OF COSMIC PREPARATION

by RAYMUND ANDREA, F.R.C.

A guide to inner unfoldment! The newest and simplest explanation for attaining the state of Cosmic Consciousness. To those who have felt the throb of a vital power within, and whose inner vision has at times glimpsed infinite peace and happiness, this book is offered. It converts the intangible whispers of self into forceful actions that bring real joys and accomplishments in life. It is a masterful work on psychic unfoldment.

ORDER BOOKS FROM

ROSICRUCIAN SUPPLY BUREAU

ROSICRUCIAN PARK, SAN JOSE, CALIFORNIA 95191, U.S.A.

For a complete, illustrated catalogue and price list of the books listed herein, please write to the Rosicrucian Supply Bureau.